The Lady of Red River Valley

GABRIELLE MEYER

BELLE MAY PRESS

Dedication

To my godson, Gage, and his beautiful wife, Kendra.
A Minnesota boy who found his bride in Winnipeg.

Foreword

The story set before you is a fictional tale inspired by the real history of Winnipeg, Canada, known at the time as the Selkirk Colony, the Red River Colony, or, to those who lived there, Assiniboia. I had often heard of the Selkirk Colony growing up, because one of its members, James Green, came to central Minnesota in 1848 to build a dam and sawmill on the banks of the Mississippi River at a place called Little Falls, my hometown. When I ran across an account of Lord Selkirk's Colony, I was stunned at its fascinating history and knew it deserved a story.

Like most history, much of it is difficult to comprehend with 21st century understanding. The Red River Valley, where Lord Selkirk put his colony, was comprised of many different First Nations people, as well as English, Scottish, French, and mixed-race citizens known as *Métis* before the colonists arrived. It was controlled by the Hudson's Bay Company through a Royal Charter issued in 1670 by King Charles II, but by 1815, the North West Company, another fur trading company, had gained significant control. You can about imagine the drama that was unfolding.

As I researched the events that took place in 1815, I had to choose which point of view to tell. I could have chosen any of them and written a compelling book, because no one is the villain in their own story. Ultimately, I chose to make my hero and heroine Red River Colonists, because they were the people at the heart of the conflict, but that does not mean I condone or support every action the colonists took. There are many different points of view surrounding the history of Winnipeg, and all should be taken into consideration, respected and remembered. I do not have enough space within this fictional story to explore all of them, so I hope you will forgive me for anything that might be left out or misunderstood on my part. Since writing this story about five years ago, I have continued to study and research this history, and its complexity never ceases to amaze me.

It is my hope that *The Lady of Red River Valley* will inspire you to do your own research of this fascinating and sometimes difficult part of our shared history. Please see the Author's Note at the end for more information and resources.

Gabrielle

Chapter One

LORD SELKIRK'S COLONY
JUNE 25, 1815

Smoke rose from the barrel of the rusted cannon as Arran MacLean, deputy governor of Assiniboia, stared in utter disbelief at the burning cabins in Colony Gardens. The settlers' homes and property were being destroyed and looted by employees of the North West Company and by members of the *Bois-Brûlés*, mixed-race men filled with anger and righteous indignation. The destruction of three years of hard work was being committed right before Arran's eyes, and there was nothing he could do to stop them.

Sweat dripped from his brow and gunpowder stained his scarred hands. His muscles were weak with exhaustion and his head pounded from the hours of cannon fire. After months of fighting, the last of the two hundred colonists were rushing downriver in canoes toward Lake Winnipeg, while Arran and three other employees from the Hudson's Bay Company defended Fort Douglas from their enemies. The only weapon they could find was a forgotten cannon, and the only ammunition they had were the bits and pieces of broken chains from the carts left in the smithy.

"Aim the cannon toward the gardens," Archie Currie yelled out to his comrades manning the weapon.

"No." Arran's voice was hoarse as he tore his gaze from the gardens and took several deep breaths, trying to focus his thoughts. "They're too far away now. We canna waste our ammunition on our anger." There were dozens of men marauding the settlement to the north of Fort Douglas. When they were done destroying the gristmill and burning all the cabins and barns, they'd turn their sights on the last men standing at the fort. They would need all the ammunition they could spare. "We'll keep it to defend the fort. That's all we can hope to save now."

"How long do you think we can last?" James McIntosh, the chief factor in charge of the Hudson's Bay Company post at Fort Douglas, breathed heavily. His brown hair and beard were interwoven with gray strands, and the lines around his eyes gave testament to the hard life he'd lived, but it was the fire in his eyes that showed he was not yet defeated.

"We'll have to last as long as possible," Arran said. "It could be weeks before reinforcements arrive."

After Governor Macdonell had surrendered to the Nor'westers eleven days ago, and been taken away to Montreal for trial, Arran had been put in charge of the colony. He had sent word to the Hudson's Bay Company men at Jack River House, some three hundred miles away. They would send voyageurs to help hold the fort, but it would be a long while before they arrived.

Old John McLeod, the third employee of the Hudson's Bay Company who had remained behind to defend Fort Douglas, stared toward the river where the colonists had just disappeared. "Reinforcements willna get to us in time." His thick Scottish brogue was tight with emotion. "'Tis done. The colony is dead."

Arran refused to give in to despair. He couldn't. He had worked too long and too hard to give up now. "We're still here." He put his hand on Old John's shoulder and forced the man to look him in the eyes. "I willna leave this colony of my own free will. I will fight until I dinna have a breath left in my body. As long as one man remains, Assiniboia is still alive. You have my word."

"And mine," Archie said from his place near the cannon.

"Aye." James put his hand on Old John's other shoulder. "And mine."

They were only four men against at least fifty others, but they would not let the North West Company win.

Dusk settled over the vast prairie as smoke rose from the burning buildings in Colony Gardens. Shouting could be heard over the roar of the fires and the cries of the animals being chased from barns and corrals. Dogs barked and cows mooed in a haunting lament.

Arran's stomach turned at the sight before him. Three years of toil going up in smoke. Since arriving in Assiniboia, the seat of the Red River Colony at the base of Lake Winnipeg, the settlers had faced nothing but hardship. Thomas Douglas, the 5th Earl of Selkirk, had first envisioned the colony in the heart of the Northwestern Wilderness as a home for his destitute Scottish kinsmen. In 1811, he'd managed to purchase almost 120,000 acres from the Hudson's Bay Company in what was known as Rupert's Land. From the start, the North West Company had seen the settlers as a hindrance to their trade and done everything in their power to annihilate the colony.

The first group of one hundred and twenty colonists, led by Arran and a few other seasoned fur traders, had arrived in Assiniboia in 1812. But hunger, disease, and the North West Company chased the settlers away. Every year, Selkirk sent more desperate colonists, each hoping to make a fresh start in a new land, but none had lasted.

Arran was the only colonist who had remained steadfast and faithful to Lord Selkirk and his vision. He'd been promised a thousand acres of land, and a sizeable sum of money, if he could keep the colony alive for five years. And though he'd told himself it had nothing to do with Eleanor, he wanted to prove to himself that he was worthy of being a gentleman landowner. No matter what it took, he would not abandon the colony. He only wished he could have found a way to prevent the others from leaving. The departure of the colonists felt like a heavy weight upon his shoulders. His respect and admiration for Lord Selkirk, his vision for Assiniboia, and his desire to be a landowner, drove the passion Arran had for this colony. He had cast his lot with them and there was no turning back.

"At least Fort Douglas is standing," Archie said, his bright red hair dulled by the dust and grime of fighting. "For that we can praise God."

"Aye." Arran ran his sleeve over his forehead. "And she'll stay standing. James and I will keep watch in the western tower and you and Old John can watch from the eastern tower. If anyone approaches, we'll send a volley of warning."

The fort was large, housing several commodious buildings, but its position on Point Douglas, a high peninsula jutting into the Red River, gave it a perfect view of the surrounding area. It would be impossible to approach the fort without being seen.

Old John, as he'd been called for at least a decade, stood from the log he'd been sitting on, his gaze returning to the river where the colonists had departed. His worn clothes were stained, and his whiskered face hadn't been shaved in days, but it was his eyes, which were clouded with regret, that made him appear ancient. His sweetheart was one of the widows who had been forced to abandon the colony. He had spoken to Arran about proposing to her weeks ago, but he'd never found the courage. And now, he might never get the chance.

"I curse Governor Macdonell," Old John said as he spat on the ground. "'Tis all his fault."

The men inside Fort Douglas didn't deny the charges, though there was nothing they could do to change the outcome. Governor Macdonell, seeing the need for food for the colony, had posted an edict the previous year declaring that anyone who dealt in furs could not remove flesh, fish, grain, or vegetables from the district. For fur traders and mixed-race people who considered themselves above the English law, and made their living by exporting those very things, the proclamation had meant war.

Before, the colony had been a hindrance. After the Pemmican Proclamation, as it had become known, it had turned into a liability. Now, the Nor'westers and Bois-Brûlés were doing everything in their power to remove the settlers and destroy the colony.

As the evening wore on and the sun fell behind the horizon, Arran climbed into the western tower and could do nothing but watch the fires blaze into embers in the settlement. The Bois-Brûlés had tried to approach the fort one last time, but the cannon had kept them away. Eventually, they had ridden toward their home in Qu'Appelle, several hundred miles to the west, hollering their victory calls, leaving nothing but destruction in their wake.

The land was quiet now. Even Fort Gibraltar, the North West Company's fur post positioned upriver at The Forks where the Assiniboine River emptied into the Red, was eerily silent.

But Arran and the others would not sleep tonight. The calm did not mean the battle had ended.

Neither James nor Arran spoke as the stars filled the vast sky, and the sounds of the night danced in the cool air. Crickets chirped their evening song and wind whispered through the oak, elm, poplar, and maple trees on the riverbank. Out on the prairie, all was dark and still. The world went on as if nothing had happened.

But inside the fort, Arran's heart still pounded from the aftermath of the battle. Anger and frustration burned in his chest and blurred his vision.

His gaze slipped toward the heavens and the questions he'd wrestled with for years began to churn inside his spirit. He'd been certain he had heard God's call when he agreed to Lord Selkirk's invitation to lead the settlers into Assiniboia. It was a good calling. A noble purpose, with an honorable reward. They were making a new home for displaced Highlanders still reeling from the effects of the battle at Culloden, and others suffering from the Napoleon Wars. They were not trying to become rich or famous, but to make a difference while they could, and to give their fellow kinsmen a new start. With Selkirk's backing, and Arran's leadership, they had been sure of success.

So why wasn't God answering his prayers? Why was each step a fight for survival? If this was a worthy cause, then why was He not allowing it to thrive?

"Is it Eleanor you've got on your mind tonight, lad?" James leaned against one of the posts in the lookout tower. "You've mentioned her less and less, but I still see that look in your eyes every once in a while."

At the mention of Eleanor's name, Arran dropped his gaze. A breeze drifted from the river, lifting the hair from his forehead, reminding him of Eleanor's cool touch so many long summers ago. "'Tis days like today that I thank God she dinna marry me when I asked." He never thought he'd utter those words, but he couldn't hide the truth from James. The man had become like a father to him. "I dinna ken what I was thinking when I asked her to share this life with me. I was young and foolish."

"You were in love." There was a smile in James's voice. "There's no harm in that."

"Love." Arran tried not to let the word sound as bitter as it tasted. "That's what you get for love." He pointed to the burning houses in Colony Gardens. "Each of those houses was built by couples who thought love would overcome any obstacle life had to throw at them. And did it?" He shook his head. "If Eleanor had come, where might she be now? Trapped in this defenseless fort with me? Buried beneath the prairie sod? Or on a boat, racing downriver toward Jack River House, trying to preserve her life?" The words felt choked even as he imagined such a thing. "Nay. I'm happy she dinna come. I couldna watch her suffer."

Just thinking of Lady Eleanor Brooke, so beautiful and refined, toiling under the hot prairie sun or freezing in the bitter cold winter, starving, hungry, and afraid, made his gut ache.

Yes, he had loved Eleanor and had been foolish enough to ask her to marry him. He had thought he was on the verge of conquering life, of building a legacy in a new land, and he had envisioned her by his side each step of the way. But when she had refused him, he'd treated her poorly. His pride had been hurt and his heart broken. Thankfully, it hadn't taken him long to realize that Eleanor had been much wiser than he. She had been scared and uncertain about colonizing a new land, and why not? She had known nothing but a sheltered life on a country estate in Northumberland. She had recognized her limitations, even if he hadn't at the time.

At least, that's why he told himself she'd refused him.

He couldn't stomach the idea that the real reason was because she hadn't loved him.

"'Tis better that Eleanor remained in England." Arran flexed his hands, the tight scars from a lifetime ago reminding him of his many failures. The old wounds laced up both his hands, almost to his elbows. "Nothing good would have come from marrying her and bringing her to the Northwestern Wilderness."

"Aye," James said, his gaze on the dark land. "I suppose you're right."

Arran *was* right. It was the only thing he was certain of anymore.

Prince of Wales

Hudson Straight

June 25, 1815

Lady Eleanor Brooke stared down at the helpless infant in her shaking hands, blinking back the tears stinging her eyes. The rolling of the ship beneath her feet was second nature to her after six weeks at sea, but the shock and disbelief of losing the baby's mother was only minutes old.

When the door to the cabin opened, Eleanor faced the baby's father, but he was not looking at Eleanor. His gaze slipped to the still form of his wife, lying under a blanket pulled over her face.

"I'm sorry," Eleanor whispered. Pain and disbelief threatened to drown her in her sorrow.

Reverend West gripped the doorknob, his blue eyes blinking several times, as if his mind was trying to catch up to the reality of what lay before him. "Anne?" he whispered. "My wife?"

"She did not survive the birth." The words felt weak, as if they were coming from someone else, even as the weight of the new life in her hands grounded Eleanor to reality. Anne had been a dear friend and now she was gone. Forever. "The baby came early. Something was wrong. Dr. Pritchard tried to save her, but—" She swallowed. "Anne slipped away."

"But why?" Reverend West asked, his voice tight. "Why my Anne? Why here, in this God-forsaken place?" He ran his hands along the side of his face, panic filling his eyes.

Eleanor moved aside as he passed her in the tight cabin and went to the bed. He knelt beside it and clasped his hands before he pressed them to his forehead. "God, is this a punishment for taking Anne away from her family?"

The baby fussed, her cries growing louder by the moment. The reverend was so bereft, he did not seem to notice, nor care. It would be up to Eleanor to see to the baby's needs.

Since the ship had left Gravesend, England, at the beginning of May, there had been several births onboard the *Prince of Wales*. Eleanor didn't bother to ask Mr. West if she should find a wet nurse as the doctor had suggested. What choice did they have?

Slipping out of the cabin, Eleanor closed the door and stood in the dark hall for a moment, cradling the defenseless life in her arms, fighting more tears. The poor child would never know her kind and beautiful mother. The injustice of it made anger mingle with grief inside Eleanor's chest.

The tears finally came. They dripped down her cheeks and fell onto the downy head of the fussing babe. She could not begin to understand what Reverend West must be feeling, nor did she ever want to.

The baby's cries grew more desperate. It would not do to make the child suffer because Eleanor could not pull herself together. She must find a wet nurse, and the sooner the better.

Eleanor had not spent much time with the other colonists. They were mostly Highlanders from Kildonan, as well as a few Irishmen. Some ninety or more men, women, and children who had answered Lord Selkirk's call for more settlers. They had avoided her, often dropping their gazes when she was near. She had tried to be sociable, but as much as Eleanor longed to make friends among them, as an earl's daughter, there was an invisible barrier she could not cross.

Instead, she and Anne West had kept to their cabin in the past six weeks, coming on deck for the weekly Sabbath services Reverend West had officiated. They had dined with the captain on several occasions, but had been content to read, sew, or write in the cabin they had shared while they crossed the stormy Atlantic Sea.

Until now.

Now, Eleanor would be alone.

As the baby cried, Eleanor walked to the end of the hall, wiping at her tears. She took the ladder leading to the hold, where most of the colonists shared a communal space. The sounds here were much different than they were in Eleanor's cabin. Laughter, conversation, children's voices, and more filled the small space. The sky was dark, but the evening was still young. Most sat around with dried biscuits and ale in hand, eating while they visited in Gaelic, a tongue Eleanor struggled to understand.

Her presence was hardly noticed.

At first, it was a child who saw her descend the ladder. The little one tugged on her mother's skirt and the woman looked up at Eleanor in surprise.

"Ach, now, lass, what have we here?" She was a large woman with a wide, kind face. Two small children held on to her skirts while a baby was nestled in the crook of her arm. The woman moved as if the children were an extension of herself. "What brings you down to us?"

"This child." Eleanor held the baby close, her voice small. "Her mother has died." She could hardly acknowledge the truth.

Several others took notice of Eleanor, and a hush fell over the group. Reverend West was a well-respected man, and his wife even more so.

"What a pity it is." The woman clicked her tongue. "Mrs. West was a kindly soul."

Eleanor had been raised in a beautiful manor house, tucked deep into the woods in Northumberland. She had not known a day of want or care until her father's scandal, three years ago. But since then, she'd been forced to fight for what she needed—and right now, she needed a wet nurse.

"Is there someone who could help?" Eleanor drew closer to the woman and lowered her voice, not wanting the others to hear her speak about such a delicate subject. "Is there a wet nurse available?"

The woman looked around her at the ladies who had kept their distance. None would even acknowledge Lady Eleanor. If they didn't help, who would?

"I do not have much to offer," Eleanor said, "but what I have, I will freely give. This child needs nourishment—"

"I'll help," the woman said, lifting her chin. "It would be an honor to help the good minister in his time of need."

Eleanor briefly closed her eyes in relief. "Thank you. I'm certain we can compensate you—"

"Ach, and why should you? I'm happy to help." The lady laid her sleeping child on a narrow berth nearby and turned back to Eleanor. "My name is Fiona Ferguson. My husband is Angus." She nodded at a burly fellow in the center of one of the groups of men. He doffed his cap, revealing a shock of blond hair.

"I'm very grateful," Eleanor said as she nodded at Mr. Ferguson and then his wife.

Fiona extended her hands and took the small baby from Eleanor. "What a wee bairn. So small."

"I'm afraid she came early." Eleanor's arms felt empty after she handed over the baby.

"And her name?"

Eleanor shook her head. "She doesn't have one yet."

"It matters little at this point." Mrs. Ferguson held the baby as naturally as she'd held her own child, swaying gently in a time-worn manner. "I'll return her to you when she's had something to eat."

"Thank you." Eleanor spoke to Mrs. Ferguson, but her gratefulness went heavenward, as well.

"Go on now and help the minister," Mrs. Ferguson said to Eleanor. "I'm sure he'll need your assistance preparing the body."

Dread rippled over Eleanor as the full weight of the situation fell upon her. She nodded mutely as she lifted the hem of her skirt and climbed the ladder to the hall above, her arms and heart weak with grief. For several minutes, she just stood in the inky darkness and forced herself to breathe.

Mr. and Mrs. West were not only her friends, but also her chaperones on this journey—and it was not yet half done. The only reason Lord and Lady Selkirk had agreed to let Eleanor join the colonists in Red River was because she would be traveling with the minister and his wife. Eleanor had shared a cabin with Anne while Mr. West had bunked with the bachelors in another room. With Anne gone, what would happen now?

The air in the hall felt suffocating and unyielding. Without giving it a second thought, Eleanor walked to the opposite end and climbed the steps. She pushed open the door and stepped onto the deck.

Immediately, the cold air sliced through her, filling her lungs with life. She took a deep breath—and then her lips parted in surprise and the air came out in a gasp.

To her right, in all their magnificent splendor, blazed the aurora borealis. The green and purple lights were bright and glorious against the crisp night sky.

The *Prince of Wales* glided silently through Hudson Strait as Eleanor stepped away from the door and crossed the deck. On either side of the ship, tall bluffs reached toward the sky in stark grandeur as the aurora borealis danced and shifted behind one of the bluffs. She'd heard of this celebrated wonder but had not expected something so breathtaking.

How could life be so beautiful and so heartbreaking at the same moment?

Eleanor had been warned not to walk about the ship unescorted, especially here on the deck where the sailors roamed freely, but the lights were so mesmerizing, she could not withdraw.

She stood for several minutes in the silence, her mind shifting between the harsh realities of life and the stunningly beautiful display of God's creation. There were only a few sailors near the ship's wheel, but they were too enchanted by the phenomena to pay her any attention.

A crashing noise pulled her eyes from the lights, and she watched in horrified fascination as an iceberg floated nearby, some two hundred feet high. There was enough light for her to see the dips and valleys of the massive mountain of ice. A large piece broke off the berg and fell against itself, sounding like distant thunder. The captain had said these came from off the tip of Greenland and as they floated south, they began to melt as this one was doing.

Shivering, Eleanor stared for a long time at the sights around her, marveling that she'd had the courage to finally travel to this remote and desolate place to start a school. What other wonders existed in the world? All she'd ever known was England and Scotland. The only things she knew about the world beyond Great Britain were from the stories Arran had told her.

Just thinking of Arran made her close her eyes, and wrap her arms around herself, recalling the last night she had seen him. They had been at St. Mary's Isle Priory, walking in the park-like gardens of her cousin's home. He spoke about things such as the aurora borealis and the buffalo and Indians on the North American prairies with such fascination, she had been enthralled by his words. He had told her about his plans to help colonize Lord Selkirk's land and the need for ministers, doctors, and teachers. Her heart had bonded with his as she imagined a school for the colony children, even as she knew her dream to join him was impossible.

He had been impossibly tall, and his shoulders were broad and built strong from hard work. When she stood beside him, his height and breadth did not intimidate her, like it did others. On the contrary, it had made her feel safe and protected. His eyes, which were so brown they were almost black, had watched her gently in the moonlight, as if taking great pleasure in what he saw. He made her feel beautiful and enchanting, though she knew herself to be simple and sensible. Arran was a handsome man, but more than that, he was kind and good and full of passion to make his mark on the world.

When he had proposed marriage and asked her to go with him to colonize the Red River Valley, she had wanted to say yes—with all her heart—but the fortress of lies her father had created forced her to say no. Father's debts were so overwhelming, he needed Eleanor to marry a wealthy suitor. It was the only thing that could save them. She was embarrassed by her father's lack of self-control and could not tell Arran the real reason, so she had told him she was too frightened to go with him.

The pain in his eyes and voice had broken her heart and intensified her own sorrow. Rejecting his proposal had been the hardest thing she'd ever done. As she watched him walk away, she knew she was making a mistake, but obligation, and fear for her father's future, had kept her from chasing after him. She had resigned herself to marrying a man she did not love to save her father from ruin.

Eleanor opened her eyes and stared at the shifting aurora borealis, wondering how Arran would receive her when she arrived in Assiniboia. Would he be happy to see her, or would he be angry and bitter? Had he fallen in love and married another?

After Father's scandal, she'd been shunned by her peers and her marriage proposals had vanished. There was no other choice but to flee to Scotland, to the home of her cousin, Lady Selkirk. It took three long years, but Eleanor had finally convinced Lord Selkirk to let her go to the colony and start a school. She needed to prove to herself that she was valuable beyond being a pawn in her father's marriage schemes. That she could pursue a dream, the same as all the other colonists, even if she had no concept of the harsh reality of life on the North American plains.

It wasn't just bravery or courage that had compelled her to come—though it had taken a great deal of both. It wasn't simply adventure or excitement, or even to be a part of history. She was also going to the colony to tell Arran MacLean she had been wrong to turn down his marriage proposal. She should have had the courage to stand up to her father and follow her dreams three years ago.

She only hoped it wasn't too late.

Chapter Two

AUGUST 6, 1815

The stifling August sunshine beat against Arran's back as he lowered another log into the groove that had been notched in the corner post. Holding the opposite end of the log, James McIntosh watched to make sure it was placed correctly. The method, called pièce sur pièce, had allowed them to rebuild half a dozen settlement houses without nails in the six weeks since Colony Gardens had been burned.

"I expect the colonists to return from Jack River House any day," James said as he stepped back to admire his work after the log was in place. This was the last portion of the wall to finish before they could start on the roof. The cabins were not large, but they would act as protection for the settlers when they returned.

"Aye." Arran lifted his canteen and took a long swig. The tepid water did not refresh him, but it did ease his thirst. He took the opportunity to scan the prairie, always alert for the threat of attack. They'd had relative peace since June, but he could never let down his guard. No doubt the Bois-Brûlés were regrouping and waiting for Duncan Cameron, the bourgeois of the North West Company fur post at Fort Gibraltar, to return from Montreal. He'd gone there to take Governor Macdonell to trial, as well as guide the hundred and fifty settlers he had convinced to abandon Assiniboia for good. "I wish we could have all the houses ready when they return."

With the aid of the thirty voyageurs who had come from Jack River House in response to Arran's call for help, and the dozen or more mixed-race men they'd employed from a village upriver, they had managed to rebuild some of the cabins, erect several fences, and maintain the crops that had been planted earlier that spring. They had also cut and stacked the mature hay and repaired some of the buildings that had not been completely destroyed. The first bumper crop of wheat was turning golden in the fields along the banks of the Red River, and if all went well, they would have a decent yield of corn to add to the storehouse.

"Everyone will be pleased to see that not all was lost." James bent to lift the next log they would slip into place. "The colony continues."

Arran picked up the opposite end and lifted it high over his head to put it into the groove. His shirt was wet with perspiration and the scars on his hands were sore from chopping and preparing the logs. As soon as the log was in place, he flexed his hands and rubbed the deepest scar between his right thumb and forefinger.

A greeting call came from the riverbank and a gun fired from Fort Douglas in response.

"It looks like we willna have to wait much longer." James grinned and set the log in place, shaking it to make sure it was secure.

Arran lifted his canteen and picked up the few tools he'd brought with him from the fort. He also grabbed his musket, which was his constant companion, and set it over his shoulder. Their horses were tethered just behind the cabin, munching on the tall prairie grass. After putting their tools into their saddlebags, and their muskets into holders, they mounted their horses and rode for Fort Douglas.

A line of clouds marred the western horizon as Arran pushed Tiberius across the expanse between the gardens and the fort, skirting the back edge of the river. From where he sat in his saddle, he could see the canoes gliding to a stop at the foot of Point Douglas. Six canoes in all, each carrying eight or nine colonists and more Hudson's Bay Company voyageurs.

They would have news from Jack River House and would be full of questions about the situation at Assiniboia. Arran himself had questions he could not answer, though he'd done his best to oversee the work of the colony. He'd sent runners with letters addressed to Lord Selkirk. One letter he'd sent north, toward Hudson Bay, and the other he'd sent east, toward Montreal. If one of them was intercepted by the Nor'westers, then hopefully the other would get to the colony's founder. Even though Lord Selkirk was in Scotland, he must be made aware of the grave danger the settlers faced. If something wasn't done soon, Arran was concerned all would be lost.

Old John had been left at the fort while the others had been working. The seasoned fur trader now opened the stockade gates wide to allow Arran and James to enter.

The fort was large, housing several buildings, including the governor's two-story home, the barn, the blacksmith, the main hall, and the Hudson's Bay Company row house and store. At two corners, opposite each other, were lookout towers, and around the whole was a tall stockade.

"Is it Colin Robertson and the settlers from Jack River House?" Arran asked as he slid off his horse to the ground, certain it could be no other.

"Aye." Old John's eyes glowed and Arran didn't wonder why. No doubt Widow MacDougal would be among the settlers. "I hope they've not had any trouble coming up the Red."

There had been so little to smile about lately, it did Arran good to slap his friend on the back and smile now. "I hope the same. It will be good to see some of our friends again."

Old John grinned. "I'm happy they're home."

Home.

The word made Arran pause as he led Tiberius into the barn. Was Assiniboia home? He'd come to the Red River district from Nova Scotia as a fifteen-year-old clerk for the North West Company. For eight years, he'd labored along the banks of the Red River, working tirelessly to gain respect and admiration from the senior partners, hoping to become a wintering partner himself. But Duncan Cameron had other plans. Within two years of entering the Red River district, he'd ruined Arran's good name and reputation by accusing him of stealing.

Instead of advancing to a wintering partner, Arran had left the North West Company in disgrace, and traveled to Scotland, where he'd started to work as Lord Selkirk's agent. He'd been hired because of his familiarity with the Red River Valley and his desire to see it colonized. Lord Selkirk's promise of land and money, if he kept the colony alive for five years, was a bonus. It helped that he'd been born in Inverness and still had relations in the area. He'd spent a year trying to recruit settlers for the colony, and in between his trips to the Highlands, he'd been a guest in Lord Selkirk's home at St. Mary's Isle on the southwestern coast of Scotland. It had been there, in the fairytale-like gardens and moonlit evenings, that Arran had met and fallen in love with Lady Selkirk's cousin, Lady Eleanor Brooke.

Arran had thought that the Red River was his home until he'd met Eleanor. But when he'd returned to the district three years ago, without her by his side, he had felt adrift on the open prairie. Not a day went by that he didn't think about the lass he'd left behind, or the single letter she'd sent to him. Her words had been full of regret and longing, yet he'd realized they were just words and meant nothing to him anymore.

His wounds had still been too fresh to respond with any sort of decorum. Instead, he'd written her the harsh truth. He'd made a mistake. He should have never proposed. She wasn't strong enough for this life of conflict and degradation. He'd ended the letter by telling her to forget about him and to leave his proposal in the past, where it belonged.

He had severed all ties with Lady Eleanor Brooke and tried to forget about her. His home was here in Assiniboia now.

So why was she always at the forefront of his thoughts?

"Do you think Old John will finally propose to the Widow MacDougal?" James led his horse into the stall in the fort's barn and then lifted a currycomb from a hook.

Arran shrugged. "Who will perform the ceremony, if he does?" There hadn't been a minister in the colony since the first year. No ministers or teachers. There had been two physicians, but they had been pushed out with the colonists who were hopefully returning from Jack River House now.

"Mayhap they'll marry in *à la façon du pays.*" James gave each of the horses a scoop of precious grain, a mischievous grin on his face.

Marriage in à la façon du pays, or in the custom of the country, was a common arrangement between European fur traders and their Indian or mixed-race wives. It wasn't a legal contract and was not done with vows, but in the consensual agreement of both parties. It could also be abandoned by either partner, at any time, without warning.

"I dinna think Mrs. MacDougal would approve." Arran hung the harnesses and then left the barn with James by his side. "She might desire something a wee bit more legal."

The storm in the west was fast approaching, blotting out the last rays of sunshine and bringing darkness to the edges of the prairie. The wind picked up, pushing against Arran's back. He did not like the look of it and wished to get the settlers into the fort. The storms in Assiniboia could be relentless and destructive.

Old John was already at the bottom of the point, helping Mrs. MacDougal from the canoe she occupied. She took his hand in hers and looked up at him as if she'd never seen anything so wonderful in all her life.

The familiar faces of the settlers were like a balm to Arran's weary soul, and when they saw all that had been done to perpetuate the colony's success in their absence, there were tears of joy.

Colin Robertson, an employee of the Hudson's Bay Company personally assigned to Lord Selkirk's service, led the tired settlers, totaling forty-five men, women, and children, up the banks of the Red River to the fort's eastern gate. The dark-haired Robertson was not tall or braw, but he was fearless and ruthless in the face of his enemies, making him a priceless ally to the Red River Colony.

While the others hauled their meager belongings into the fort, and began to set up their tents, Robertson sought out Arran.

"I have news." Robertson was a man of few words, and he didn't waste time on platitudes or meaningless conversation. "Shall we speak?"

"Aye." Arran motioned to James to follow them into the governor's house.

The two-story building sat in the eastern corner of the fort, overlooking the Red River. It was the finest residence in Assiniboia, commissioned by the previous governor. For now, it was Arran's home, though he didn't know how long it would be until Selkirk sent a replacement for Macdonell.

Opening the front door, the three men entered the common living space. Long, wide planks covered the floor and small windows on either end of the room let in the last vestiges of daylight. A table, a large fireplace, and a cupboard graced one wall and on the opposite wall were two doors. One led into the governor's bedroom and the other into his office. A set of stairs in the far corner led up to several more bedrooms.

It wasn't a fancy home, but it was well-built and spacious. It had been the place of many gatherings and strategic meetings for the colony.

Arran lit a match and set it to the wick of a lantern on a nearby table. He led the men into his office and indicated the chairs across from his. The large desk, which Governor Macdonell had built to his specifications, sat between them.

"What news have you to share?" Arran asked as he took his seat and set his musket against the desk.

Robertson wore a sword at his side. It clanked against the floor as he sat and faced Arran. "I've been told that another group of colonists has arrived at York Factory in Hudson Bay. You are to prepare for their arrival before winter."

Arran met James's gaze, and he knew what the older man was thinking without even asking. They needed settlers to make the colony successful, but more settlers meant more mouths to feed and bodies to protect. Until Lord Selkirk could guarantee their safety, new and unseasoned colonists would be a liability.

October 1, 1815

A cool breeze nipped at Eleanor's nose. She bent her head against the wind and repositioned her arms to better protect Miriam's small body. The baby was snug in the sling Fiona Ferguson had outfitted for her to carry the three-month-old child. Eleanor had transported her in the sling through their days at York Factory on the shores of Hudson Bay, through their weeks traversing the Nelson River to Jack River House, while they sliced through the massive waves of Lake Winnipeg, and now as they made the last leg of their journey up the mouth of the Red River. They would reach the settlement by day's end, and their four-and-a-half-month journey would finally be over. Soon, Eleanor would begin her work as the settlement's teacher, and see that every child in Red River Colony was educated.

More importantly, Eleanor would face Arran MacLean once again. What would he say when she stepped out of the canoe at Assiniboia? Would he be happy to see her? Would he pull her into his arms and whisper the words her heart had longed to hear these many years?

She had told herself she was coming to teach, but her heart whispered the truth. She wanted to rekindle the love that she and Arran had shared on St. Mary's Isle. Yet, her head warned her heart that he might reiterate the painful things he'd written to her in response to her letter of regret.

So many questions and uncertainties plagued her as they drew closer to their destination, the greatest of which was whether Arran would be married to someone else. It was almost all she could think about.

"She's happiest in your arms," Reverend West said as he sat beside Eleanor. He lifted the collar of his coat to ward off the chill as he let his gaze rest on Eleanor and Miriam.

Eleanor couldn't deny his words. The baby was happiest in her arms. Every few hours, as soon as Fiona completed Miriam's feedings, Eleanor took the baby back and saw to all her other needs. They were rarely apart, and she had grown to love the child as if she were her own.

She rubbed the baby's back and looked out at the riverbanks. They had steadily risen higher the closer they came to the colony, and she could no longer see above them to the prairies beyond.

"Anne would be so thankful for your loving care." William, as Mr. West had asked her to call him, spoke in a soft, almost reverent voice. The grief in his eyes was still so powerful, Eleanor struggled to look at him in moments like this. He was far too young and handsome to carry such a heavy burden through life. Eleanor often prayed he would find joy again. Even his daughter was not enough to bring a smile to his face. He hadn't held her once since her birth, though Eleanor had offered her to him many times. She was all too aware of what it felt like to be rejected by a parent. It was the last thing she wished for Miriam. But still he refrained.

The child reminded him of all he'd lost. Even the name he'd chosen for her meant "sea of bitterness."

"It's an honor to care for your daughter." Eleanor smiled at the sleeping baby. Her heart-shaped mouth and delicate little nose were so like Anne's, it was difficult not to think about her friend when she looked upon the babe.

"I hope it's not too great a burden." It was William's constant concern. "I can make other arrangements if you'd—"

"She's not a burden." On the contrary, the baby had filled Eleanor with purpose as she waited to start her school and brought a sense of joy amid her grief. Taking care of Miriam had become second nature to her. "I cannot think of anything I enjoy more."

The lines in William's face eased and he nodded. "Thank you, Lady Eleanor."

She smiled at the minister. "Please. Just call me Eleanor."

Here, in this wild and desolate place, there were no distinctions between nobility and commoners. Eleanor had known what she was giving up when she left England's shores, and she had no regrets. The peerage had brought nothing but heartache and pain to Eleanor and her family for as long as she could remember. It had destroyed her mother, broken up her parents' marriage, and shunned Eleanor the moment her father had succumbed to its pressures.

"You may be the first English lady in the entire Northwestern Wilderness." William gazed upon the wooded riverbanks and rubbed his hands together, blowing into them for warmth. He spoke, more to himself than her, "I'm beginning to think that bringing you and Anne here was the biggest mistake of my life. If something happens to you, I don't think I'd be able to forgive myself."

Eleanor's lips parted at the bold statement, and it sent a shiver up her spine. Rumors and reports had trickled to them along their journey. At both York Factory and Jack River House, they'd heard about the attack by the North West Company men and Bois-Brûlés. They'd learned that over a hundred and fifty settlers had left with a man named Duncan Cameron and gone to Montreal. That would only leave about fifty settlers at Assiniboia. With the addition of the immigrants from Kildonan, they would reach one hundred and forty. A small number, to be sure. But not without hope. Surely, the Bois-Brûlés would recognize that it was useless to keep fighting. Each time they drove a group of settlers away, another would come, this time stronger.

Even now, the new governor of the Hudson's Bay Company, Robert Semple, sat in the lead canoe. He had been hired in answer to the ever-increasing troubles between the Hudson's Bay Company and the North West Company. Semple was a loud, boisterous man with more fervor than Eleanor had ever witnessed in any one human being. He was impatient and bold, a frightening combination, as she'd already witnessed. They had made the journey in less time than any of the settlers before them, to the detriment of the colonists. Five people, including Anne, had lost their lives on the journey and he had rarely taken the time to stop and bury them properly.

"Do you have great dreams and aspirations for the colony?" William asked Eleanor, thankfully changing the subject.

Over the last few months, he had kept a respectful distance while still overseeing Eleanor's welfare. When Anne had been alive, the three of them had enjoyed companionable hours crossing the Atlantic, but after her death, he'd pulled away, rarely speaking to her for more than a moment or two. Eleanor had wondered at his distance, questioning if it was because of the baby, his grief, or because he was now a single man and she an unmarried woman. Whatever the reason, she had respected his space and kept to herself and Miriam. Her relationship with Fiona had naturally grown and she had been thankful for a new friend in this foreign land, but she was happy to converse with a fellow English compatriot again.

"I hope to be of help," Eleanor responded to William. "To teach and care for the children whenever I'm able. Though, I confess"—she had not admitted this to anyone else—"I worry that I will not be as useful as I had first hoped."

He frowned. "Why not?"

They were surrounded by colonists on all sides, and she did not wish to alienate herself more than she already had by simply being a member of the aristocracy, but she couldn't deny her concerns. She spoke quietly.

"This land is far more uncivilized than I had first hoped. I fear I have taken the place of someone more useful, such as a farmer or a tradesman. Perhaps I was too hasty in believing the colony was ready for a teacher." Other than Fiona, the settlers had kept her at a distance. When she tried to offer her help, even in the simplest ways, they refused to let her be of service. She no longer used her title, but that didn't mean the others would forget that she was a lady. Would they allow her to teach their children, or would they refuse her that honor, as well? "I wonder if a school is a frivolous luxury in such a young colony."

"Education is never frivolous. It is the bedrock of society. Or, at least, it should be." He studied her, the sounds of the voyageurs' paddles slicing through the water and the hum of conversation mixing with the calls of the birds in the nearby trees. "What prompted you to come all this way? Could you not teach in England?"

She did not anticipate his question. William knew she was Lady Selkirk's cousin, but that was almost all he knew about her past. She had not shared anything about her father's scandal or her relationship with Arran MacLean. He didn't know that she was all but ostracized from her homeland. "I was ready to set my own course. When Lord Selkirk agreed to let me come, I knew I must seize the opportunity. It isn't often that one is able to make history."

"Do you not have a family in England who is worried about you?"

Eleanor looked ahead to a bend in the river, wondering how many more curves they would travel before the settlement came into view. "There is no one."

"What of your parents?"

She met his gaze with a steady look, hoping he would realize his questions were too personal. But he watched her openly, his curiosity apparently piqued. In a way, it gave her hope that he had started to look beyond his own pain and grief to think of others—even if it meant prying into her affairs.

"Are they deceased?" he asked, pressing for more. "Surely, if they were alive, they would have protested your journey as much as Anne's did."

Eleanor had left England behind to forget about the past and to start afresh, without scandal to mock her every move. If she told William the truth about her parents now, the weight of her past would follow her to this far-off land.

"Were Anne's parents very upset?" Eleanor asked, hoping to divert his attention away from her.

It had the effect she hoped it would. He turned his gaze away and stared off into the distance, as if seeing another place and time. "They made her choose between me and them. When she chose me, they said she was dead to them and they would not wait to hear about her death, but chose to mourn their loss right there, before her eyes."

Eleanor touched William's sleeve, horrified at what he'd just said. "I'm sorry."

"And they were right. I was wrong to bring her." He nodded at his daughter. "Now you know why I cannot send the baby back to England. There is no one who would take her."

"Assiniboia ahead!" one of the voyageurs called in his thick French accent.

All around, cries of excitement filled the cold October air.

Eleanor's heart suddenly beat faster, and she sat up straight, trying desperately to look calm and relaxed, while inside every nerve hummed with unease. She'd had years to think about this moment, and months to plan what she might say. But now, with her and Arran's reunion only moments away, every muscle in her body tensed and she had the sudden and irrational urge to jump out of the canoe and flee in the direction she'd just come.

Chapter Three

A northwesterly wind blew against Arran's face as he stood in the lookout tower on the corner of the stockade and watched the dozen canoes approach Fort Douglas. Guards were on duty around the clock and one of them had alerted Arran about the approaching colonists. He had left his office, where he'd been writing yet another letter to Lord Selkirk, and now waited for the advancing brigade.

Overhead, the sky was gray and thick with the threat of snow. The temperature had dropped in the past few hours, portending an early season snowstorm. Arran had not wanted to move to their winter quarters until the new batch of settlers had arrived, but now that they were in Assiniboia, they could make plans to head south to Pembina. The seventy-mile journey would not be met with excitement from the new colonists who had been traveling for the past four months, but it could not be helped. The buffalo wintered on the plains near Pembina, providing much-needed meat for the long, cold months.

"Semple will be with these people," James said as he entered the lookout tower and stood beside Arran. "Do you ken the man?"

"Only by reputation." Arran had heard enough about Robert Semple to know the man was brash, overconfident, and impatient. He was an American who had served as an army captain for the British during the American war for independence. Now retired, he was known for his upright character and bulldog courage. He would not only be the governor of Assiniboia but would be in charge of all sixty posts in the Hudson's Bay Company. His authority, unlike Macdonell's, would not come into question. Rupert's Land, which was the whole of the Hudson Bay drainage basin, had been granted to the Hudson's Bay Company by a Royal Charter from King Charles II in 1670. The North West Company men, based out of Montreal with headquarters on the northern end of Lake Superior, were, in every sense of the word, trespassing on land belonging to the Hudson's Bay Company. But they disregarded the 140-year-old Royal Charter and treated the land as their own. This had led to constant battles and bloodshed. The recent conflict within the Red River Colony had brought years of trouble to a festering head.

"Come." Arran set his musket on his shoulder and climbed down the ladder to the fort yard. "Let's welcome our new governor and neighbors properly."

James followed Arran out of the east gate and down the path to the riverbank. Several settlers had come from their homes in Colony Gardens to meet the canoes, while mixed-race children and visiting Saulteaux Indians had gathered on the opposite side of the river to watch in quiet curiosity. No doubt news of their impending arrival had already made its way to Duncan Cameron's cohorts in Qu'Appelle. No doubt they were hopeful that the settlement was dead. More colonists meant it was gaining strength again.

The voyageurs jumped from the light-weight canoes and into the water before the boats could touch the shore and ruin the thin birchbark that covered the outside. Inside the vessels, the colonists sat on the supplies and personal items that had been brought with them across the ocean, rivers and lakes. For many of them, everything they owned and held dear was in the boat with them.

"Welcome to Assiniboia," Arran called to the colonists, his gaze roaming over the weary-looking group. Robert Semple was an easy man to identify, sitting proud and confident in the lead canoe.

The others were dressed in their Highland plaids, worn and soiled from the long trip. One exhausted face after the other turned to look in Arran's and James's direction. Arran tried to meet each gaze with a welcoming nod, but his attention snagged on a woman who stood out among the peasants from Kildonan.

She sat straight and proper, her brown dress made of high-quality material. The spencer jacket she wore looked completely impractical and out of place, though it was no match for the frivolous bonnet on her dark brown curls.

But it was the face under the bonnet, with the beautiful brown eyes and familiar curvature of the mouth, that caused his heart to gallop out of control.

Every shred of self-composure and authority Arran MacLean had felt walking toward the riverbank fled at the sight of Lady Eleanor Brooke.

He stared at her, fearing he may have lost his mind. Was it truly her? But how? Why?

Almost as an afterthought, his mind took notice of the baby she wore in a sling on her front—and the self-possessed Englishman sitting close by her side—and then his shock turned from confusion to unreasonable anger and envy.

"Arran?" James asked, watching him closely. "Are you well?"

Even under battle, Arran had not felt this unsure of himself. What was Eleanor doing in Assiniboia? Had she come with a husband and baby? How could she be so thoughtless or foolish?

"Mr. MacLean?" Robert Semple stepped out of the canoe and onto a large, solid rock, much like the first pilgrim had at Plymouth Rock nearly two hundred years before. "I'm Governor Semple."

It took every bit of strength Arran could muster to turn his gaze—and thoughts—to the new governor. He stretched out his hand to Semple and sized him up in one glance. The man was tall and commanding, his red hair turning gray with age. He shook Arran's hand with a firm grip.

"I've heard good things about your leadership of the colony," Semple said. "I'm eager to see the place for myself and get settled into my quarters."

"Aye." It was all Arran could manage to say as Eleanor was assisted from her canoe by the gentleman who had been seated beside her. Arran felt like a simpleton as he stared, dumbstruck, at her approach.

"I think you'll be pleased to hear we've brought a minister and a teacher with us," the governor continued, as if nothing was out of the ordinary. "Perhaps the colony will be civilized now that the British have arrived." He laughed at his own joke, though no one joined him.

Eleanor's gaze was hooded as she walked slowly over the uneven ground, one hand on the baby's back and the other wrapped around the minister's elbow. She did not look at Arran again until she came to stop beside Governor Semple. When she did, Arran feared his heart would stop at the sight of her warm, steady gaze. He'd never thought to see her beautiful eyes again, though his dreams had been haunted by them for years.

"Mr. MacLean, may I present the Reverend William West," Semple said.

Eleanor had married a minister? He'd been certain she'd marry an earl or viscount. How had she ended up with a minister—especially one coming to Assiniboia—the land she had claimed to be too frightened to settle with Arran? Was her love for this man worth the risks inherent in colonizing a new land? Something she had been unwilling to do for Arran?

The very thought made Arran's muscles tense as he lifted his chin.

"How do you do?" Reverend West asked as he extended his hand to Arran.

Whatever shred of decency Arran had left, he used to shake West's hand, though he could not find the wherewithal to welcome him to Assiniboia.

Reverend West put his hand under Eleanor's elbow. "And may I present Lady Eleanor Brooke, our new teacher."

Eleanor's mouth parted momentarily, as if she wanted to speak, but she closed her lips again and simply looked at Arran, a thousand emotions passing through her expressive eyes.

"The lady and I have a previous acquaintance," Arran said in a thick, rough voice, hoping not to betray his true feelings.

James looked sharply at Arran, but Arran could not muster the strength to introduce Eleanor to his friend and mentor.

"How nice," Semple said while West frowned, apparently surprised at the news.

"And the babe?" Arran asked, finding it hard to make sense of what was happening.

"My child," West said in a tight voice. "My wife, Anne, was taken from us on our voyage here."

"I-I'm caring for Miriam," Eleanor finally said. "Anne was a dear friend of mine."

He'd forgotten how melodic her voice sounded to his ears. A torrent of memories and emotions rushed back to his mind and heart, almost knocking him over with the force of them. He had spent hours listening to her in the gardens at St. Mary's Isle—would have spent the rest of his life listening to her if she had agreed.

So, she wasn't married to the minister—and the babe was not her own.

But there were so many other questions warring within him. Why was she here? What had she been thinking—what had Selkirk or Semple been thinking to allow her to come? They should know, better than most, that this was no place for a woman of noble birth, coddled and protected from life's hardships. She lacked the experience and fortitude of the Scottish Highlanders standing all around her.

"I'm sorry for your loss," Arran managed to say to the minister.

Grief hung heavily around Mr. West as he looked beyond the small group toward Fort Douglas. Though Arran had not lost a wife to death, he understood the pain West felt at losing the woman he loved.

But now here she stood, alive and lovelier than his aching heart had remembered. It was almost more than he could bear.

"If you'll show us to our quarters," Semple said, "I think we're all ready to find our beds."

"Aye." Arran was the deputy-governor. He had a responsibility to all these new arrivals—even if his world had just been turned on its side. "We have room within the stockade for the settlers to pitch their tents." He absently motioned toward the fort.

"I would like the Reverend and Lady Eleanor to sleep in a house, if possible," Semple said. "I've heard the governor's house is quite large."

"Aye."

"Perhaps it's large enough for all of us?" Semple asked hopefully.

Arran only nodded. He led them up the riverbank, and after seeing that James was helping the colonists organize their tents, he showed the governor, minister, and teacher to their quarters.

"Is there a woman who could be employed to keep house?" Governor Semple asked Arran as they stood inside the main room and he inspected his new home. "And to act as a chaperone for Lady Eleanor?"

"Please," Eleanor said, the baby still in the sling on her front. She bounced gently as the child began to stir. "Miss Brooke will do."

The three men turned to look at her.

Her cheeks were pink as she dropped her gaze. "I do not wish to carry my title here, if you please."

"As you wish," Semple said with his no-nonsense attitude. "It's probably for the best."

"There is a woman in the settlement who might agree to be a housekeeper," Arran said to Semple. "She was married to a settler who recently passed away. I will send for her immediately."

"And perhaps Miss Brooke will take the room on the main level," Semple added. "While we men bunk upstairs. There are four rooms up there, correct?"

"Aye."

"Then you shall have one," Semple said to Arran. "West will have the other, and I can occupy the third, with an extra for guests." He grinned with self-satisfaction, as if he had just solved a troubling puzzle.

Arran wasn't sure he wanted to sleep in the same house as Eleanor. The last time they'd been in residence together, at St. Mary's Isle Priory, he'd become a besotted fool.

Thankfully, there was no threat of that happening again. He had dedicated his life to Assiniboia. He had no time for a wife—especially an English lady who would be a liability to the colony.

Eleanor nodded at the proposed arrangement, her gaze wandering over the spacious room. Did she find the accommodations lacking? They were nothing compared to the priory, nor to her manor in Northumberland, he was certain.

This was no place for an unmarried lady, in a home with three single gentlemen, without parents or guardians to see after her. Not to mention the hardships she was about to face. Unlike the other settlers, Eleanor had led a life of luxury and comfort. Colonizing was dangerous and grueling for the most hardened fur trader. How much more difficult would it be for a pampered lady?

The shock of seeing her had begun to wear off, and now the reality of the situation turned his confusion to anger. She had no business being here and he would not hesitate to tell her so. There was no doubt in his mind that she would be on a ship returning to England when the spring thaw allowed travel back to York Factory. If she did not choose to go on her own, as he was certain she would, he'd appeal to Semple's better sense.

But, first, he must keep her alive through the long winter ahead—a more daunting task he'd never undertaken. How would he make a level-headed decision if the fort came under attack, knowing she was inside?

The ship heading to England could not leave soon enough.

Darkness had fallen over Assiniboia as Eleanor left her bedroom and stepped into the common room, closing the door gently, hoping Miriam would remain asleep.

In a room above her head, loud snores rumbled through the cold house. Eleanor surmised they belonged to Governor Semple, since

William had gone upstairs only moments ago and she had not seen Arran since eating the simple meal the new housekeeper, Nicolette, had prepared for them. He had left the governor's house, mentioning the need to address some issues concerning the new arrivals, but had not returned.

Nicolette was a middle-aged, mixed-race woman who was quiet and industrious. Her father had been a French fur trader and her mother an Ojibwe Indian, and she'd been raised in various fur posts. She had silently made the evening meal as if she had lived in the house all her life. After serving the meal, she'd cleaned all the dishes and then made a pallet for herself in the corner of Eleanor's bedroom. The only time she'd spoken, or shown any hint of personality, was when she noticed Miriam. She had fussed over the baby like an aunt or a grandmother, speaking English in bits and pieces with her gentle smile, telling Eleanor about her family.

Eleanor suspected she and Nicolette would get along well.

Despite the hours of travel, Eleanor was too overcome with the events of the day to sleep. Not wanting to keep Nicolette or Miriam awake, she brought her traveling desk and journal into the common room and took a seat at the table where the lantern still burned low.

There was a chill in the air, but the fire Nicolette had used to make supper had dwindled to embers. She had banked the fire before going to bed and Eleanor did not want to disturb it now.

Instead, she tightened the thick shawl over her shoulders and opened her traveling desk. She took out the red-cloth-covered journal and held it for a moment.

Her journal was her constant companion. She had kept one since she was a child, loving the way her mind worked out its problems while she put words to paper. All those journals were at the Selkirks' home in Scotland with her other things.

The journal in her hands had been fresh upon her departure from Gravesend, but it was already filled with both the exciting and the mundane events that had shaped her journey thus far. It wasn't an impersonal account, but one full of her thoughts and feelings, as well as her experiences. For a child who had grown up without the love and companionship of a mother, her journal had become like a best friend. It was a place to share confidences, explore her thoughts and feelings, as well as record events.

But as she cracked open the book and laid it flat against the table, she couldn't find the words to write tonight. What could she say about seeing Arran again? It was hardly the reunion she'd hoped for. His shock at seeing her was understandable, but she had hoped that as the surprise wore off, he would have shown her some sort of excitement. Instead, he had seemed to grow angrier as the evening progressed. He'd left the house without looking back.

And now he stayed away.

The main room was quiet, except for the snores still rumbling upstairs. Beyond the house, the night was dark and the prairie silent. A few snow flurries brushed against the windowpanes, with no wind to push them about.

The front door creaked open, and Eleanor stood, clasping her hands as her heart began to pound.

Arran appeared at the door, his musket at his shoulder. He paused when he saw her, his dark brown eyes filled with emotions, none of them warm or welcoming.

Without a word, he closed the door and set the crossbar into place, locking the world out.

For a heartbeat, he faced the closed door before turning to look at her.

Eleanor swallowed the rush of nerves that fluttered up her throat. She didn't know what to say, or how to begin the conversation, but they needed to speak.

He started to move across the room toward the stairs, as if he meant to ignore her.

She couldn't let him go to sleep without telling him why she'd come. She took a step forward. "Arran." She said his name on the breath of a desperate whisper.

He paused but did not turn to her. He was tall and well-built, his shoulders wide and powerful. She had always admired him dressed in his finest clothes at St. Mary's Isle, but here, in his element, dressed in a white linen shirt with a wool vest and jacket, a cotton cravat around his neck and a pair of dark buckskin breeches covering his muscular thighs, he was masculine and devastatingly handsome. His curls were almost black, and he wore them clubbed in a queue, tied in place with a strap of leather. She was breathless at the sight of him.

"I dinna ken what to say to you." His Scottish brogue was thick, and his chest rose and fell, as if he was struggling to find his breath. "I was hoping you'd be asleep by now." He gripped the chair closest to him and finally turned, anger and disapproval deep in his clouded gaze.

She recoiled at the look.

"Why have you come?" he asked, his voice harsh.

She opened her mouth to answer, but the words seemed to fail her. She'd come for him—didn't he realize that?

"Why did Selkirk allow such a thing?" he continued. "He understands the danger. You dinna belong here, and you're so fresh and untried, you dinna even realize how out of place you are."

His words were like a slap in her face. Did he mean she didn't belong here, or she didn't belong with him? "I-I came to teach, as Governor

Semple told you. To start a school." It sounded weak even to her own ears. The colony didn't need a teacher, not when survival was more important than book learning. But how could she tell him she had come for him when he'd spoken to her so severely?

"We dinna need a teacher. We need strong, brawny lads and lassies to turn the soil and populate the colony." He looked her up and down, making Eleanor feel exposed and vulnerable. He'd passed judgment and found her lacking, just as all the other colonists had. "We need people with skills. We dinna need someone like you."

Tears stung the backs of Eleanor's eyes as she stared at him. He had no way of knowing what she'd endured the past three and a half years since he'd left. She'd borne ridicule and shame, but it had been at the hands of people she did not know or care about. Hearing him heap disapproval and criticism on her shoulders felt like an arrow hitting the very center of her tender heart.

Despite her best efforts, Eleanor's chin began to quiver, and she looked down at the journal on the table.

Just like all the other times she'd been falsely judged, she had to dig deep within and find the courage to lift her face. She did it now as she swallowed the tears that threatened to spill. She would never admit to this man that she'd come for him. Not now.

Even if the colony didn't need someone like her, she'd prove them all wrong and become invaluable to them. She would ensure that every child attended her school and learned how to read and write. She would create wonder and excitement among the children; despite the hardships they endured.

"I have come to teach," she said, her voice stronger than she felt, "and I intend to do my job to the best of my ability."

"But why?" He took a step closer to the table, his brows coming together in confusion. "You told me you dinna want to come to Assiniboia. You were too frightened." He paused, his voice growing tight. "Unless that wasna true."

"It was true—partially. It wasn't that I was afraid of coming—it was that I was afraid of leaving my father." She moved closer to him. No matter what he thought of her, she wanted him to understand. "I had no choice. Papa needed me to marry someone with wealth to pay off his enormous debts. We were going to lose everything." How could Arran grasp the pressure she'd been under? Father had gambled away everything. There had been nothing left, except Edgewood Manor. She was not a man who could find work to support them. All she had was her hand to offer in marriage.

He was quiet as he studied her, his brows low over his dark eyes. "Did you?"

"Lose everything?" She couldn't meet his gaze. They had lost everything, but not because of her. "Yes. Everything is gone. I have nothing in the world, except this job."

He shook his head. "You refused my proposal and lost everything anyway."

Eleanor pulled her shawl closer around her shoulders but could not respond.

"What became of your faither?"

She had no wish to talk about her father, but she felt obligated to offer some sort of explanation. "He's in prison."

"Debtors' prison?"

"Newgate." The word stuck in her throat, dry and unyielding.

"Newgate?" His voice was incredulous as he moved around the table and came to stand beside her.

She played with the edge of her journal, allowing the pages to brush against her fingertips, shame and embarrassment coloring her words. "It happened shortly after you left, during a game of cards. He accused the Duke of Huntington of cheating. My father was drinking heavily and had just wagered the last thing he had left, Edgewood Manor." She had never told anyone this story. Everyone in England had heard about it without her telling the sordid tale. "When Huntington laid down a royal flush, my father lost his mind. He pulled a pistol from his boot and shot Huntington in the heart."

Arran did not speak but stood next to her, silent and steady.

"Everything was gone. I had nothing left and no one to turn to." She finally looked at Arran to see how he had taken the news. "The only person who would take me in was my cousin, Lady Selkirk. I moved to St. Mary's Isle and have been living there ever since. But I could not rely upon her charity forever. I had to find a way to support myself."

"And you couldna find something less dangerous or more appropriate than moving halfway around the world to the back side of nowhere?"

She studied him, wondering if he suspected why she'd really come. She had too much self-respect to ask. "You praised Rupert's Land for months when we first met."

"I was young and foolish. I dinna ken what I was speaking of."

"But you lived in the district for eight years before you came to Scotland to recruit settlers."

"Trading furs in the Red River Valley is far different than colonizing it." He shook his head and ran his hand over the back of his neck. "We have enemies at every turn, and we dinna have enough supplies to feed hundreds of hungry mouths. This is the first year in three we've had a decent crop, and 'tis still not enough."

There was no warmth or tenderness in his words or his gaze. Gone was the fondness he'd held for her in Scotland, leaving her feeling empty.

"This is no place for a woman of your upbringing, Eleanor, or the wee bairn you've been toting about." He took several steps away from her. "'Tis too late to send you back to England this year, but I will insist you return in the spring. If you're still alive."

He left her standing in the cold room, his words echoing a warning in her heart.

Chapter Four

It had been two days since Eleanor had arrived with the colonists from Kildonan, and Arran had not yet become used to seeing her around the fort. He had tried to avoid her whenever possible, and it hadn't been difficult. He'd told everyone to begin preparing for their winter trek to Pembina and there was much to be done.

"The governor would like to see you." A young boy named Ben found Arran in the barn currying Tiberius after returning from Colony Gardens.

"I'll be along shortly."

"I can do that for you," Ben said, stepping up to Arran's side. "The governor says 'tis important. Mr. Robertson is with him."

Arran was not accustomed to letting someone else handle his stallion, but the lad was often around the barn, and he'd shown an aptitude for animals.

Tossing the currycomb to Ben, Arran left the barn and crossed the fort yard.

Wisps of snow fell from the sky and gathered in small piles along the stockade walls and at the base of the buildings. His breath puffed out of his mouth as he glanced at the heavy clouds. The sight of them made him uneasy, but there was little to do about the oncoming weather. He didn't want to make the seventy-mile trip to Pembina during a storm, or after the river froze. There were dozens of dogs in the settlement used for pulling carioles during the winter months, but there weren't enough sleds or dogs to transport a hundred and forty people at once. And they needed to remain together for their own protection. They would need to go by canoe, and soon.

Arran pushed open the door to the governor's house and stepped into the common room. Nicolette stood near the fireplace, stirring a pot, while Eleanor sat at the table with the baby in her arms. Eleanor's head was bent as she spoke softly to the bairn.

She looked up when Arran entered, and their gazes met.

The sight of her made his pulse tick faster, as it had every time he'd laid eyes upon her these past two days. She wore a blue gown, the waist cinched just under her bosom. The sleeves were long and the neckline high, but it contoured to her feminine form and was very pleasing to look upon. Her dark brown curls were piled high on her head with tendrils framing her pretty face. Seeing the baby in her arms only made her more attractive. She was so gentle and loving toward the child, he couldn't help but picture Eleanor as a mother with her own wee ones.

He steeled his reaction to her and barely acknowledged her presence as he crossed the room and knocked on the governor's door. It was the only way he knew how to protect his heart.

"Come in," Governor Semple called through the door.

Arran removed his hat and entered the governor's office. "You sent for me?"

Semple motioned to the chair next to Colin Robertson. "Have a seat. I've just been told some alarming news from Mr. Robertson."

A heightened sense of awareness came over Arran as he sat, his hand holding his musket against the floor, his back rigid. "What have you heard?"

Governor Semple was a tall man with a thick chest. His military bearing was evident in the way he moved and conducted himself. He faced Arran now with a steady gaze. "Duncan Cameron has just returned to Fort Gibraltar."

Arran's muscles tensed at the announcement. Every time Duncan Cameron was in residence at Fort Gibraltar, it meant trouble for the colony.

"He came from the yearly rendezvous at Fort William," Robertson supplied. "I saw him with my own eyes just an hour ago."

"I've been told the Nor'westers stole our six fieldpieces when they raided the colony in June," Semple said to Arran. "And that they have not been recovered."

"Aye." Arran nodded. Duncan Cameron had ordered the removal of the small cannons, leaving the fort defenseless until Archie had remembered the rusted cannon in an old shed near the river. "They took our fieldpieces, as well as our ammunition," Arran explained. "Duncan said it was payment for the two hundred bags of pemmican Governor Macdonell confiscated from them the year before when he signed the proclamation." Pemmican was a staple food for everyone in Rupert's Land. The mixed-race people were especially adept at making the concoction. After drying buffalo meat, they pulverized it to a fine powder and then combined it with animal fat and dried berries before packing it into ninety-pound bags. It could be eaten cold, but it was best when stewed with root vegetables and a flour paste. The dish was called rubbaboo.

"As the new governor of Assiniboia," Semple spoke with authority, "I'm ordering the arrest of Duncan Cameron for the theft and destruction of Red River Colony property."

Robertson exchanged a glance with Arran. Both would be happy to see Duncan punished for his actions at long last.

"I want the two of you to take a dozen armed men and go there immediately," the governor continued. "He won't anticipate seeing you this soon. Bring him back to me when you have him in your custody."

"Aye." Arran stood, eager to have the deed done but not excited to face the difficulties that waited for him. "Will that be all?"

"For now. See that the men are armed. I do not want anyone hurt."

Every male colonist in Assiniboia was always armed. It had been their way since the beginning.

Arran and Robertson left the governor's office, but Arran paused in the common room as Robertson walked outside.

Eleanor rose from her place at the table. She set the baby to her shoulder and patted her gently on the back. "Is all well?"

Things were not well, but once Duncan was in custody, things would get much better. He didn't want to concern her with his problems. The less she knew about the difficulties around her, the better.

"Aye." He put his hat on and walked toward the door.

"Arran," she called, making him pause.

He turned to look at her, his name a bittersweet sound on her lips.

Her eyes were so large and troubled. If they had been at St. Mary's Isle, he would have gathered her in his arms to ease her worries. But they were no longer in Scotland, and he no longer had the privilege of comforting her.

"Could we talk?" she asked.

One simple request, yet it held far too much weight. Wasn't it her flowery words that had made him lose his heart—and his head—to begin with? He couldn't risk such a thing again. "I have business to attend to for the governor." With that, he slipped out the door and met Robertson, who was speaking to some men in the yard.

"I will rouse James," Arran said to Robertson. "If you'll gather the other men."

Robertson nodded and turned to the task.

Arran strode to the row house, bending his head against the cold wind.

As the chief factor of the Hudson's Bay Company post at Fort Douglas, James was in charge of overseeing the work of the voyageurs. He ran the company store and traded with the Indians who brought in their furs throughout the winter. In the spring, the voyageurs would take all the furs to York Factory and bring back the trade good items used to purchase the pelts from the Indians.

With the change in the weather, James had turned his focus from the settlement to the store and Arran knew he would find his friend there now.

Arran walked into the store at the end of the row house. James stood behind the counter with the trade good items, a ledger spread open before him. He was alone in the store, but a pile of furs at his left hand indicated a recent visit from neighboring Indians.

"What can I do for you?" James asked as he looked up from the ledger.

"Semple just ordered the arrest of Duncan Cameron."

James nodded. "Long overdue."

"I need to gather a group of men, and I want you and Archie to be among them."

"Aye. I'll do what I can."

"Let's be ready to go in a quarter hour."

James didn't say another word but closed his ledger and took up his gun.

Arran left the row house and found Robertson. In no time, they were ready to leave Fort Douglas with their small army.

The North West Company's Fort Gibraltar sat less than a mile to the south. As soon as Arran and his men left Fort Douglas, they would be seen by the Nor'westers, but it wouldn't matter. Duncan would have only a handful of voyageurs in the fort with him. They, like the Hudson's Bay Company men, would trade with the Indians throughout the winter. Any fighting they planned would not happen until spring or summer, as it had in the past, when the trading was at a minimum. They would assume Arran and his men planned to do the same.

It didn't take long to reach the fort. The gates were open for trade, so Arran and his men walked in without announcing themselves. Fort Gibraltar was a handsome fort with a large store and a clean yard. A porch stretched the length of the front of the main building and was painted a jaunty red.

Duncan came to the door of his trading post. He stood without a jacket, his arms crossed, as he watched them approach. He was at least fifteen years older than Arran and had treated him like a child from the moment they'd met. But Arran was now a man of thirty. He was no longer a child to be used as Duncan's pawn. In fifteen years, he had learned a great deal about men like Duncan. They liked to use their authority to push others around. They were cunning and charming, but when it came to fighting, they rarely dirtied their hands. Duncan would rather use his words and intelligence to win a battle.

Today, Arran and Robertson would take him by force, and he doubted Duncan would put up a fight. They would have done it long ago, if they'd had the authority.

Duncan did not look worried. Instead, he wore a mixture of curiosity and boredom. "What brings you to my post?" he asked as he leaned against the doorframe.

Arran stood at the front of his men, conscious that he was not only representing Assiniboia, but the entire Hudson's Bay Company—one of the wealthiest and most powerful companies in the world. "We've come in the name of Governor Robert Semple to arrest you for the crimes committed against the Red River Colony and the Hudson's Bay Company post at Fort Douglas."

Duncan lifted a blond eyebrow. "Is that so?"

"We'll take you by force," Robertson warned, "if you try to resist us."

Several seconds passed as Duncan worked his jaw muscles. "I'll come with you."

"I also want you to tell our men where you've put the fieldpieces belonging to the colony."

"They're in the barn." Duncan nodded to a building in the corner. "You'll find the ammunition there, as well."

Arran indicated that the men should retrieve the weapons and then he and Robertson followed Duncan into his store.

Duncan didn't speak as he took his jacket and hat off a nearby hook. He slipped them on, watching Arran and Robertson with unveiled arrogance.

"You think this will be the end of it?" Duncan asked as he approached his captors. His lips curled in a half-smile. "'Tis just the beginning. The North West Company will not let this colony survive, and well you ken it."

Arran would not allow the man to intimidate him. "The governor and the crown will have something to say about your threats."

"The crown?" Duncan scoffed. "The Royal Charter is so old it doesn't bear acknowledging. You ken as well as I that the Hudson's Bay Company no longer has a monopoly on the fur trade. The North West Company far surpasses the HBC's profits each year. We're stronger and more powerful. We will take this land and keep it for our use, and the HBC will be unable to stop us."

What Duncan said was true. The North West Company had quickly grown and was now a real threat to the Hudson's Bay Company—but the Hudson's Bay Company was not dead, nor was it as weak as the man suggested. It had been in business for a hundred years before the North West Company was created and would still be standing long after the North West Company folded.

Arran had no wish to parlay with Duncan, so he simply turned and left the store, indicating that Duncan should follow him.

They left Fort Gibraltar without a fight, for which Arran was thankful. The handful of voyageurs who were there seemed as compliant as Duncan, which was a little alarming. But Arran had seen enough warfare and bloodshed to last him a lifetime. Duncan came alone, leaving his post in the hands of his men.

Half an hour later, as Arran's men reinstalled their fieldpieces in Fort Douglas, Arran and Robertson walked Duncan into the governor's house.

Eleanor was sitting near the fireplace, a sewing project in hand. Nicolette and the baby were nowhere to be seen. Eleanor stood when they entered and set the fabric on the chair she had vacated.

Duncan stopped at the sight of her. He seemed speechless, which was something Arran had never witnessed.

The older man turned to Arran. "Are you going to introduce me?"

Everything about Eleanor bespoke a lady, from the elegant gown she wore, to the way she carried herself, to the words she spoke. There was not another woman like her in the whole Northwestern Wilderness. No doubt Duncan was just as mesmerized as all the other fur traders upon seeing her.

Arran remembered that Eleanor did not wish to use her title, so he simply said, "This is Miss Eleanor Brooke. The new school teacher of Assiniboia." He nodded at Eleanor. "Miss Brooke, this is Duncan Cameron, the bourgeois of Fort Gibraltar."

"Mr. Cameron?" Eleanor's lips parted as she stared at the man. No doubt she'd heard stories about his ruthless treatment of the colony. Mayhap Arran should have warned her that the man would be coming.

Duncan bowed deeply—almost theatrically. "You sound like a real lady, Miss Brooke." He approached her and reached for her hand.

She did not give it freely, but did not pull away when he captured it and lifted it to his lips.

"'Tis an honor to meet you," he said. "I've never seen a bonnier creature in all my life."

Eleanor met Arran's gaze over Duncan, a question in her eyes.

Arran shook his head, giving her a silent warning. Duncan could be charming—he had convinced over a hundred and fifty settlers to leave the colony, after all—but he was never to be trusted.

"It's a pleasure to meet you," Eleanor said as she pulled her hand back to her side.

"How did Selkirk convince such a fine lass as yourself to come across the world to teach his settlers?" Duncan smiled at Eleanor, offering his undivided attention. "If I had a teacher as fine as you, I would have been a much better student."

"It wasn't Selkirk who did the convincing," Eleanor said, her melodic and refined voice far more charming than the brute in front of her. "It was Mr. MacLean who spoke so highly of the Red River Valley. I had to come and see it for myself."

Duncan shot an incredulous look in Arran's direction. "Are you two previously *acquainted*?" He stressed the final word, lacing it with meaning.

"You're under arrest." Arran took Duncan by the arm and pulled him toward Semple's office. "You'll not be asking the questions today."

A slow smile slithered onto Duncan's face as understanding lit his eyes.

The last thing Arran needed was for his enemy to know where his armor was the weakest—and yet, he had just figured it out.

He'd met Eleanor Brooke.

It was a loud and boisterous group that gathered in Fort Douglas's main hall the night before leaving for Pembina. Eleanor sat at one of the long tables, Fiona and Angus Ferguson nearby, smiling at the antics of one of the children.

Miriam had been left at the governor's house with Nicolette, offering Eleanor a rare opportunity to relax and enjoy the company of her fellow Assiniboins.

Laughter filled the air as men and women visited and told tales of life in the Highlands. Their culture was far different from the one Eleanor had known growing up, but she thoroughly enjoyed listening to them, even when they slipped into Gaelic and she struggled to follow their stories. Though she sat with them, she was clearly an outsider. No one spoke to her or invited her to share her own stories. She simply listened, feeling more alone than she had in a long time.

A soft glow fell over the occupants of the hall as the candles and lanterns flickered with light. A fire had been lit in the large fireplace and a picture of King George III hung above it. The ladies had prepared a communal meal, which had been enjoyed and then set aside as the ale and conversation had begun to flow.

Governor Semple sat at a table in the corner of the room with Arran and other leaders of the colony. Eleanor and William had dined with them, but when the discussion had turned to business and political matters, Eleanor had excused herself to join Fiona. Her new friend was loud and animated, sharing story after story with her husband. Each tale Fiona told was bigger and better than the one Angus shared before, creating gales of laughter from their audience.

The prisoner, Duncan Cameron, had been locked in a room in the row house since his arrest. The voyageurs had kept him in shackles and Eleanor had not seen him again, for which she was thankful. Something about him had sent a shiver up her spine, and when he had reached for her hand, she had wanted to recoil from his touch. The men had spent the past three days discussing what they should do with him, but they could not come to a consensus. Arran and Mr. Robertson wanted to transport him to England to face charges against the colony and the Hudson's Bay Company, but Governor Semple was of a mind to release him, claiming that since Mr. Cameron had come without a fight and been properly warned, he would now comply.

From the stories Eleanor had heard, she doubted Mr. Cameron could behave himself.

Arran looked across the room and met Eleanor's gaze. As always, her heart beat a little faster when she saw him. They had not had a moment to speak in private since the night she had arrived, and she was beginning to think it was intentional on his part. Every time she sought him out, he pulled away, as if the very sight of her displeased him.

William rose from the table and caught Eleanor's eye. He crossed the room and stood before her. "Do you mind if I join you?"

"Of course not." She moved to the side to allow him a space to sit, and then she turned from Fiona and her husband to give her full attention to the minister. It felt good to have someone who wanted to speak to her.

"Do you have everything you need for Miriam?" he asked, just as he did every day, his kind eyes resting on her face. "For the journey and the winter at Pembina?"

"Yes. She is quite content with the new clothing I sewed from the material you acquired at the company store." He had surprised her by bringing the cloth home after visiting the row house. In addition to cotton for Miriam's gowns and nappies, he had included a thick Hudson's Bay Company coat for Eleanor. The capote, as it was called, was long and warm, reaching down her thighs, and made from the popular Hudson's Bay Company wool blanket. It was white, with colorful stripes near the bottom. It had a large hood and long sleeves, which she would appreciate during the coming winter. She had tried to refuse the generous and expensive gift, but he had insisted, saying he wanted to repay her for all her help with Miriam.

"Have you had a chance to try on the capote?" he asked.

"I have. It fits perfectly."

William smiled, his blue eyes warming with pleasure. "I wish I could offer you something more refined, but—"

"I'm quickly learning that refinement is a luxury. I would rather be comfortable than fashionable."

"Would that you could be both." He smiled at her, his keen appreciation softening his features. The deep sadness that had permeated his countenance since Anne's death had started to ease around his mouth and eyes. He had been busy marrying voyageurs to their mixed-race and Indian wives since his arrival, as well as baptizing their children. Now that there was a real minister in Assiniboia, dozens of people had come to him to legalize their unions. He had even performed a ceremony between Old John, one of the Hudson's Bay Company men, and the Widow MacDougal the day before. He was the first minister in Assiniboia, and he was in demand. The work had been good for him, and it made Eleanor's heart happy.

"Are you anxious to reach our winter quarters?" she asked, wanting to change the subject away from the gift he had given her.

"I've been told there is a large population of voyageurs and mixed-race peoples at Fort Daer in Pembina. I will be busy marrying and baptizing for some time."

"As well as preaching and teaching Sunday school," she reminded him with an encouraging smile.

"And you will start your school when we arrive?" he asked, his attention on her and her alone.

"Yes, as soon as we're settled." She was eager to get it started, though she still wondered how it would be received when most of the colonists still avoided her.

"Will it be hard for you, with the care of Miriam?" Concern lined his words. "I would not want you to overwork yourself on my account."

"I've been told Nicolette will join us in Pembina. She will help with Miriam while I teach my classes."

William nodded, seemingly pleased with the arrangement. "Very good."

Eleanor wished to ask him about his daughter and the fact that he had not held her yet. It wasn't her place to push him—but he was the baby's father, and Miriam needed the love and affection that only he could provide.

She opened her mouth to speak, but Governor Semple rose from the table at that moment and lifted his hands to quiet the room. "We will leave Fort Douglas at first light," he said to the group. "I would recommend that all of you get a good night's sleep, so we are not encumbered tomorrow. It will take us three or four days to reach our destination at Fort Daer in the land called Pembina." He nodded at them. "I bid you good night."

The group rose to their feet, several of them picking up sleepy children to take them to their homes in Colony Gardens or their tents within the fort.

William was called away by a family who wished to speak to him about baptizing their children, so Eleanor was left to say good night to Fiona and her family.

The other colonists filed out of the main hall, evading Eleanor as much as possible. She smiled at several of the children and moved out of the way for people to pass her. She tried not to let her face show the heaviness she felt in her heart at their rejection.

"May I see you back to the governor's house?" Arran asked, suddenly at her side, his voice low and deep.

Eleanor's lips parted at the unexpected request. It was the first time he'd sought her out since her arrival. She managed to nod but couldn't find her voice.

He helped her slip into her spencer, which was on a hook near the door, and waited until she placed her bonnet over her curls. He watched her silently as she tied the ribbon under her chin.

"You'll not survive the winter in that hat or coat."

"William has purchased a capote for me, with a hood. I shall wear it tomorrow when we leave the fort."

"William?" He studied her with an unreadable expression. "He's buying you gifts, then?"

"In exchange for my help," she said quickly. "For taking care of Miriam." Why she felt she needed to explain it was a mystery to her. "He also bought several things for the baby."

Arran didn't respond but held the door open for her to pass through into the frigid night.

Large snowflakes drifted slowly to the ground and rested on Eleanor's shoulders. The air was so cold, and so crisp, she could see her breath fog in front of her face. The spencer did nothing to keep her warm and she was thankful for William's forethought in purchasing her a capote. She should have worn it tonight.

"I'll see that you have mittens and moccasins before we leave in the morning," Arran said from beside her. "And I'll inquire if James has leggings for you to wear beneath your dress."

Despite the cold, Eleanor's cheeks warmed at the mention of leggings. A man didn't discuss what a woman wore under her dress. But she had to remind herself that they were no longer in England and his words meant that he was thinking of her comfort and safety—that he was thinking of her. "I appreciate your thoughtfulness."

"You're ill-prepared and I canna lose another colonist." He said it so matter-of-factly, any warmth she felt from his forthcoming gifts was cooled.

They walked slowly across the yard, in no hurry to reach the governor's house.

"What will happen to Duncan Cameron when we leave?" she asked.

Arran looked across the fort yard and shook his head, clearly irritated. "Semple has ordered that he be released in the morning. His aim was to frighten Duncan and let him know who was in control. He spoke to Duncan and the man promised he would not bring any more trouble to the colony."

"You don't believe him?"

"Nay." Arran's voice was filled with disgust. "He's charmed Semple, just as he's charmed all the others. I wouldna trust anything he says."

"But we'll be safe at Fort Daer?" She couldn't hide the concern in her voice.

"Safe enough, for the winter." Arran's voice softened. "This is no place for you, as I've said, but as the deputy governor, I'll do everything in my power to protect you, Eleanor. You have my word."

Despite his reassurance, frustration filled her chest. "I'm tired of you telling me I don't belong here."

"You don't."

"Did you belong here when you first came as a boy?"

He didn't respond.

"I might not have experience with this sort of life, but I'm strong and smart, and I'm not afraid to learn." She no longer cared how he felt about her arrival in Assiniboia. "Please do not discredit me now, before I've even had a chance to prove myself to you."

"You have nothing to prove, Eleanor." His jaw was tight as he spoke to her. "I simply want to spare you—"

"I do have something to prove, if not to you, then to myself." She was amazed at how different Assiniboia was from the life she'd always known—yet it did not intimidate her. "My life in England is dead and I've had time to mourn that loss. God has given me the opportunity to start over, here, with these people. I might not have a great deal to offer them, but what I do have, I will give with all my heart." She looked deep into his dark brown eyes, wanting him to finally hear her. "What is a life, if it's not spent well, on things that truly matter? My life in England meant little to me or anyone else outside my home. But here." A tremulous smile lifted her lips. "Here, I might be of real use. I might have a purpose and contribute to something bigger than myself." She would convince the colonists that education was necessary and see that all the children were enrolled in her school, proving to Arran that she was needed. Wanted. "If it's your dream," she said to him, "then why can't it be my dream, as well? Why am I exempt, because I am a woman?"

"'Tis not because you are a woman, but because I canna abide the idea of watching you suffer." His words came out fast and fierce. "I ken what I speak of, lass. This land doesna care who you are, or whether you are strong or weak. It destroys without discrimination. You may be bold and courageous now, but it willna matter in the end." He shook his head. "You are brave, and you want to make a difference, but I lost you once." He paused, his careful façade slipping for the first time since her arrival. "I canna lose you to death, once and for all."

Eleanor inhaled a surprised breath. Snow had gathered on his shoulders and hat and continued to fall all around him. "I'm sorry about what happened between us in St. Mary's Isle—"

"I dinna want to speak of it."

"But we must. I didn't want to hurt you."

He moved past her and walked to the governor's front door.

"Arran, I want you to understand."

"I do understand."

"No." She met him at the door. "My father was desperate to save our estate, and I was unable to tell him no. He would have never allowed us to marry."

"It doesna matter now." His face was devoid of emotion. "I shouldna asked you to marry me. I was a fool."

The fort yard was quiet as the snow fell silently. "You were not a fool. I was honored by your proposal. Knowing that you had loved me, even if for only a short time, sustained me through the hardest days of my life. For that, I'm truly grateful."

Something shifted in his gaze, and she saw a glimpse of the man she'd fallen in love with in Scotland. But just as quickly, it disappeared and in its place was the same wall of indifference.

"Those days are gone now," he said. "I'm not the man I once was."

Eleanor nodded. "You're right. You're an even better version of that man now. I see it in the way you care for the people of this settlement. They look to you with deep and abiding respect, just as I do."

He let out a rush of air. "What do you want from me, lass? Why did you truly come?"

She blinked several times, afraid and embarrassed to admit that she had come to tell him she still loved him, especially now that she knew it would be impossible to have a future together. He had put her out of his heart for good. So, she said the only thing that made sense. The only thing she could request. "I want to be friends again."

He lowered his chin and looked at their feet for a moment.

She held her breath, hoping and praying he would not reject her once again.

Slowly, he lifted his gaze to her and nodded. "Aye. We can be friends."

Warmth filled Eleanor's chest. She'd missed him terribly and longed for more, but being friends was better than nothing at all.

"But I will insist you're on a boat back to England in the spring," he said. "I will personally see that 'tis done."

The warmth she'd felt began to cool.

She had no intention of returning to England. She'd cast her lot with the colonists and their education. She would stay—whether Arran MacLean wanted her or not.

Chapter Five

A sharp, northwesterly wind blew against Arran's back as he rode Tiberius along the shores of the Red River south toward Pembina. The snow had spit at them on and off during the past four days of travel, but it had started to fall in earnest for the past two hours, collecting quickly on the dips and swells of the prairie. It was unrelenting as it blew across the open plains and bent the trees along the riverbanks. The colonists were miserable as they huddled in their canoes, the voyageurs paddling to the pace of fifty strokes per minute. The adults held their children close to shield them from the bitter wind and freezing snow, but several children cried incessantly, tearing at Arran's heart.

One of the canoes, near the back of the brigade, had drawn Arran's attention all day. Eleanor sat in the middle of the canoe with William West at her side. She wore the coat the minister had given her, as well as the mittens and moccasins Arran had procured for her from James. He'd also gifted her wool leggings to wear beneath her dress, but Arran could only assume that she wore those now. They would offer another layer of warmth and protection from the cold. He wished he could ease her current suffering, but he admired her for her fortitude and positive attitude each time they had stopped. She was good with the children, bringing a rare smile to their faces with a story or a simple game.

But it was the adult colonists who she struggled to connect with, though it wasn't for lack of trying. She was kind and courteous, offering a smile or a helping hand, or even a word of encouragement. They were not cruel to her, but they moved around her as if she wasn't there. Though she chose not to use her title, everyone knew exactly who she was, and it was clear she did not belong with them. Not only was she British, but she was an unmarried woman, and an earl's daughter. Her position in the young colony was unnecessary, and everyone knew it.

And he was beginning to think that Eleanor realized it now, too.

She glanced up and met his gaze. He did not lower his eyes or turn away from her. Their conversation the night before they left Fort Douglas had stayed close to his heart, warming him now as much as it had done then, though he tried to fight the feeling. She wanted to be friends. It was less than he had wanted at the start, but more than he had dreamed of at the end. Though he knew it wasn't wise to long for her companionship, they had many long months ahead of them before she would return to England and the thought of enjoying her friendship filled him with more pleasure than it should.

Despite the difficult conditions, Eleanor offered him a gentle smile from the canoe. His heart beat faster, and he smiled back, wanting to reassure her that his words to her were still true. He would be her friend, come what may.

"Fort Daer ahead!" one of the voyageurs called out from the head of the brigade. All the voyageurs lifted their colorful paddles in a celebratory cheer.

Governor Semple was hunched over in the lead canoe, but at the call of arrival, he straightened and looked toward the banks of the river. The large fort sat on the plains with the Hudson's Bay Company flag flying proud in the wind. It had been built three years earlier when the first settlers had arrived in Red River Valley. Each winter, the colonists had made improvements on the dozens of buildings within. They would spend about six months in the fort, if the spring came as expected in April, though it could arrive as early as March or as late as May. There was no way of knowing.

Thirty minutes later, the cold and weary travelers stepped out of their canoes and trudged up the banks of the river one last time, met by the voyageurs who inhabited the fort throughout the winter. For many of them, it meant settling into a home for the first time in almost five months.

Fort Daer was similar to Fort Douglas in that it had a commodious governor's house, a large main hall, a trading post, and a barn. But there were other small cabins within and without the stockade, built for the settlers. There would be two or three families to each home. If the weather was mild, they might build a few more from trees cut along the riverbanks.

While Arran saw to everyone's living arrangements, Governor Semple, Reverend West, and Eleanor entered the governor's house with Nicolette and Miriam in tow.

Eleanor had carried the baby in her sling, under her coat, all throughout the journey to Fort Daer, only handing her over to Nicolette when she had stepped from the canoe. How Eleanor fed the child, or saw to her other needs, Arran wasn't sure. He couldn't imagine how much more difficult the journey would be with a bairn in tow. He admired her dedication to the small child, though there were few women who would have stepped forward as Eleanor had to care for a baby who was not a relation. It was yet another reason he admired her, though he saw the exhaustion it had caused her in the lines around her mouth and the dark circles under her eyes.

He hoped she was not becoming sick.

"MacLean," Semple called out to Arran before walking into his house. "We'll expect you to bunk with us again. Be sure to join us for supper."

Arran nodded, then returned to the task at hand. Several exhausted Kildonians looked from Arran to each other, their eyebrows raised with accusation. They did not have to speak for him to know what they were thinking. He was not one of them—one of the British high-and-mighty who had come to save the colony. He hadn't considered it at first, but over the past week, he had witnessed enough, and overheard enough, to know what they thought of the governor, minister, and teacher. Not only were they the first British people to attempt colonizing the Red River Valley, but they lived apart from the Scotsmen in a house four times the size of the cabins ten or twelve people would be forced to share.

Governor Semple and Reverend West served purposes that were necessary to the colonists. Eleanor did not.

The last thing this colony needed was to be divided from within. Arran could have quartered with his fellow Scotsmen, but it would only encourage the division. Besides, he was the deputy-governor, and it was his right and responsibility to bridge the gap. He needed to be near the governor to help oversee the colony, especially since Semple was just as new to the Red River Valley as the others. But with each passing day, the divide and prejudice would only grow stronger if Arran didn't address it soon.

It was several hours before he was able to join Eleanor and the others in the governor's house. When he did, he brought with him Sean Campbell, the chief factor of the Hudson's Bay Company post at Fort

Daer. Sean oversaw the voyageurs who wintered in the fort, as well as the trading with the local Indians.

"Ah, Mr. MacLean." Governor Semple was just about to take a seat at the dinner table. "We were hoping you would join us."

Arran stepped forward with Sean beside him. The man was about Arran's age and had grown up in the fur trade. His father had been a chief factor and his mother an Indian country wife. When Sean was old enough, his father had sent him to Montreal to be educated and Sean had returned to the interior to become a clerk, quickly working his way up to managing his own post. "I'd like you to meet Sean Campbell, chief factor here at Fort Daer."

Sean's Indian ancestry was evident in his high cheekbones and dark coloring. He was a quiet, stoic man who kept to himself. Arran often struggled to read the man, and though they'd spent countless hours in each other's company over the past few winters, he did not know where Sean stood on political, religious, or social matters. But when he spoke, he said exactly what was on his mind, a trait Arran both appreciated and abhorred.

"Welcome to my table, Mr. Campbell," Governor Semple said. "It's an honor to meet you." Semple would eventually need to travel to most of the posts under his authority. He had already spoken to Arran about several trips he planned to take over the winter months. "And may I present our minister and our teacher, Reverend William West and Miss Eleanor Brooke," Semple said to Sean.

Sean shook West's hand and then he bowed before Eleanor. His gaze lingered on her. "Your beauty precedes you, Miss Brooke. I had heard about you even before you arrived. I dinna believe the reports, but I see I was wrong."

Eleanor's cheeks colored and she offered a gracious smile. "Thank you, Mr. Campbell."

"Shall we eat?" Arran asked rather abruptly.

"Yes, of course," Semple said. "Please have a seat."

There was rubbaboo, fresh biscuits, and ale. It wasn't a grand meal, but it was warm and filling, especially after a long day of travel. Arran nodded his thanks to Nicolette, who hid her shy smile behind her hand. The baby was in a wicker basket near Nicolette, cooing and babbling as she played with a dried gourd that rattled as she shook it.

The governor's house at Fort Daer was half the size of the one at Fort Douglas, though still sizable. The main room had a fireplace, a cupboard, and a table with six chairs. There were two bedrooms on the first level and a large, open room under the eaves in the attic. Arran assumed the governor would take one bedroom and use it as his office, while Eleanor, Nicolette, and Miriam would take the other, smaller bedroom. Arran and West would share the room under the eaves. It wouldn't be ideal, but it would be more comfortable than the smaller, tighter cabins the colonists would share.

"How has trading been at Fort Daer?" Semple asked Sean as they began to eat.

"'Tis still early," Sean said, scooping a spoonful of rubbaboo out of his bowl. "The furs are thicker than usual, suggesting a long, cold winter." Though he spoke to Semple, his gaze remained on Eleanor.

She was so unlike any other woman in these parts, Arran didn't blame Sean for the interest. Her fashionable gown was tailormade for her slender body, and her dark hair, which appeared to be refreshed after their journey, was in perfect order, with gentle tendrils framing her face. She looked as if she was prepared for an evening meal at St. Mary's Isle Priory with Lord and Lady Selkirk, and not a humble meal in a far-off fur post.

The fact that she had traveled so far, under such difficult conditions, and still maintained her composure, impressed Arran more than it should.

Though she was out of place, she didn't show any discomfort. And it made Arran think about his own time at St. Mary's Isle, when she had been in her element, and he had been the one out of place. He was not a nobleman, or even a man of any wealth or status in the world. Yet, not once had Eleanor made him feel like an outsider. From the start, he had been welcomed into her world with utmost respect and admiration.

Yet, he had done nothing to ease her transition into his world. On the contrary, he'd made her feel like an unwelcome outsider. Guilt burned in his gut and he swallowed the shame he felt at the revelation. Her words from the night before they left Fort Douglas returned with startling clarity. "Please do not discredit me now, before I've even had a chance to prove myself to you."

As Sean and Semple discussed business matters, Eleanor met Arran's gaze across the table. The undivided attention she gave him made every muscle in his body tighten with awareness.

William glanced between Eleanor and Arran, his thoughts and feelings inscrutable. Arran had noticed William's increasing attention toward Eleanor and watched as he leaned a little closer to her now, as if staking an unspoken claim.

"Miss Brooke," Sean said as he turned his focus to the lady at the table. "What would make you give up civilization to come to a place like this?"

His blunt question hung in the air as everyone turned to Eleanor for an answer.

But instead of responding, her gaze slipped to Arran again, and he saw the truth in her eyes.

Realization hit him like a gale-force wind, and he suddenly felt like a fool.

It should have been obvious to him from the first day. Eleanor could have gone anywhere and done anything with her life.

But she hadn't. She'd convinced Lord Selkirk to let her traverse an ocean and endured unspeakable hardships to get to the Red River Valley. To Arran.

William's jaw tightened as Eleanor licked her lips and tried to smile as she faced Sean.

"I wanted to make a difference," she said. "To have a goal that gave me a purpose. I heard of the difficulties in this colony and knew that a school would give it permanence and stability. It is the one thing I can offer."

She had told Arran something similar, but it wasn't that simple. Eleanor had risked everything to come to the Northwestern Wilderness to be near him. Perhaps he hadn't wanted to admit it to himself before, but the look in her eyes every time she glanced at him told him all he needed to know.

Yet, he had done nothing to make her feel welcomed or wanted—even if she wasn't staying.

He would need to do something to remedy that. If he didn't, it would be a long winter for her.

Eleanor had no wish to go to sleep that evening after the others had gone to bed. Her journal had not been tended to since her arrival in the Red River Valley and she knew if she wasn't careful, she would start to neglect her writing. It was a habit she did not want to fall into, knowing how important it was to her well-being to share her thoughts on paper.

After she left Miriam and Nicolette sleeping in the room, she went to the fireplace and shifted the coals to spark them back to life. It was a luxury to use the wood for her late-night writing session, but she didn't know how long she might be awake, and the room was bitterly cold, even with the leggings she still wore beneath her dress.

Outside, the wind had picked up, blowing around the eaves with vengeance. A storm had settled over the territory, unlike anything she'd ever seen in England. It was fascinating to watch the snow pile up in the fort yard, and though she suspected she might grow weary of it in time, for now it was a beautiful and awe-inspiring sight to behold. She was just thankful she was tucked inside the snug log home, and not sleeping in a tent on the prairie as they had done the past few nights.

She lit a candle and set it on the table before pulling out her journal. The last time she'd made an entry was while camped near Lake Winnipeg, several days before their arrival in the colony.

Her words flowed freely for several minutes, capturing the sights and sounds of Assiniboia and of Arran. She closed her eyes and thought about the moment they'd been reunited, and the after-effects of her arrival. She cautiously wrote about their discussion before leaving Fort Douglas, and her hope that they could forge a friendship. At supper, he had been more aware of her than usual, and she had desperately wanted to know what he'd been thinking. But there had been no time to discuss personal matters. Mr. Campbell had stayed late, and then everyone had gone to bed when he left.

Eleanor nibbled on her bottom lip as she continued to write. She described Fort Daer and her plans to start the school. She recorded Miriam's developments and wrote about Nicolette and how much she appreciated having another woman's help with the baby. On and on she wrote, until her hand began to cramp and her eyes grew tired.

A movement at the ladder leading up to the attic made her glance in that direction. Her heart hammered against her breastbone as Arran appeared. She wasn't sure if her reaction was a response at being caught up past her bedtime, or if it was the sight of Arran in his loose shirt and trousers, without a vest or jacket, and nothing upon his bare feet.

"Eleanor." He seemed just as surprised at seeing her sitting at the table.

He wiped his hands across his sleepy face as he moved toward her. His hair was loose around his face, coming down to the edges of his chin, and his shirt was open at the top, revealing a patch of dark hair on his chest. It was the most relaxed she'd ever seen him and it did something funny to her insides, making her feel a bit breathless.

She tried to focus on something other than his bare feet and chest, and her gaze landed on his hands. The scars there were deep and wide, and not for the first time, she wondered how he'd acquired them. She'd asked him once, at St. Mary's Isle, but he had shrugged off her question and she instinctively knew not to bring it up again. It was part of a past he didn't speak of often, and if he wanted to tell her, he would. Whatever had caused them would have been extraordinarily painful. A few scars extended past his hands to his wrists, and she wondered if they went any further.

But that led her to thinking about his bare skin again, which made her hands tremble. She busied herself with closing her journal and slipped it into her traveling desk before he reached the table.

"What are you doing up so late?" His eyes wandered over the desk and her ink-stained fingers. "I thought you went to bed hours ago."

"I've been writing in my journal."

"This long?"

"I had a lot to say." She stood and pulled her shawl closer around her shoulders. "It's been almost two weeks since I wrote in it last."

He watched her movements, his gaze gently following the course of her hands before coming to rest on her face once again. "I dinna ken you were a writer."

The storm blew ferociously outside, but the look in his eyes warmed her to the core.

"I wouldn't call myself a writer." She held both ends of her shawl and crossed her arms. "I simply record my thoughts and feelings and experiences in my journal. I've done it all my life."

A slow smile lifted the corners of his mouth, and her knees grew weak at the sight of it. She'd loved his smile in the moonlit gardens at St. Mary's Isle, especially when it touched his eyes as it did now.

"Aye." He crossed his muscular arms, much like she had, and continued to smile at her. "You're a writer. Even your letters were full of poetic charm."

Her cheeks warmed at the memory of the letters she'd written to him when he'd been in Inverness, recruiting settlers for Lord Selkirk. "Poetic charm?" She shook her head, trying desperately not to succumb to the appeal of his smile, or the recollection of those letters. "I simply write what's on my heart and how I see the world."

"We would all be better off if we saw the world the way you do, lass."

She grew warm under his admiration and wished to change the subject. Her writing was personal and important to her. She liked his praise, but knew his criticism, if he offered it, would be just as powerful—and detrimental.

"Why are you awake?" she asked, longing to change the subject.

"I thought I heard something, so I came to check." His smile slowly faded, but his eyes remained warm. "I told you I sleep light."

"Light enough that you could hear the frantic scribbling of my pen?"

"Aye." He nodded toward the traveling desk. "What are you writing about?"

She held the ends of her shawl together in one hand and laid the other on the desk in a self-conscious effort to protect her words. "Just things about my daily life."

"Have you mentioned me in your journal?" His voice danced with something akin to teasing, and she was second-guessing her desire to rekindle their friendship. It was safer for him to keep a wall between them, because when it came down, it was far too easy to be drawn to him again.

A light perspiration gathered on Eleanor's palms, but she tried hard not to reveal the truth. She would be mortified if he knew how much she had written about him in her journals over the years.

"You have written about me." The teasing left his voice, and it deepened, almost imperceptibly.

"Well, of course I have." She wanted to sound matter-of-fact. "I write about everyone I meet."

"Did you write about Sean Campbell, then?"

Eleanor opened her mouth to respond in the affirmative but realized she had not written about Sean.

"And what of James McIntosh?" he asked, his voice a little lower, his brogue a little deeper. "Did you mention him?"

She swallowed and shook her head.

"And what of Colin Robertson or Angus Ferguson?" He continued to watch her closely, and she knew he was trying to sound as if he teased her—but the answer meant more to him than it should.

"I don't write about everyone I meet." She pulled her traveling desk closer to her. "Just those people in my life who are rather—rather important."

"Am I important in your life?"

"Of course you are."

"Because we're friends?"

"Yes. And because—" She'd almost said because she'd been in love with him, but she stopped herself. "Because I've known you for a long time."

The firelight danced in his eyes as he studied her. "So you only write about people once you've known them for a long time?"

"Yes."

"When did you start writing about me?"

The night she'd met Arran, she could not wait to return to the quiet of her room at St. Mary's Isle. She'd filled several pages about Arran MacLean. There was not an entry from that day on that did not mention him in some way or another—until he'd left Scotland.

But she would never tell him so. Her journal was a sacred place to confide. Sharing it with him would be like baring her heart, which would not be wise.

"It was so long ago," she said, trying to evade the question.

He was quiet for a moment, though his eyes continued to search hers. He was so handsome and strong, her pulse picked up speed and she licked her lips, which had suddenly gone quite dry. Something had shifted in him.

"What of West?" he asked quietly. "Do you write about him in your journal?"

"William?" She lifted her eyebrows in surprise.

"Aye. William." He overaccentuated the name. "Is he important in your life?"

She considered his question for a heartbeat. "Yes, of course. He's Miriam's father and my friend."

"Just as I'm your friend?"

Eleanor frowned, uncertain of the course of his questions. "He's been a good friend since I met him and Anne in England."

"Nothing more?"

"Of course nothing more, though I do not see how it's your concern." Frustration built in her chest as she sat straighter at the table. "William is the only person who truly cares that I'm here. He's the only one who has treated me like an important member of this community. He—he makes me feel needed and wanted. Perhaps it's only because I care for Miriam, but he was just as kind and thoughtful before she was born."

Her words seemed to affect him, and he offered her the courtesy of looking down at his hands in contrition. "I'm sorry I dinna welcome you like I should have. I know now that it was wrong, and I want to make it right." He lifted his gaze again. "Truth be told, I was shocked and confused."

"And angry."

"Aye." He nodded. "And angry."

A gust of wind rattled the windows and the soft snores of Semple were interrupted by a fit of coughing before he went back to sleep.

Eleanor studied Arran. There were a few more lines around his eyes and his skin was darkened by the sun. She spoke quietly, not wanting to disturb anyone else in the house as she asked, "Are you still angry?"

He regarded her for a moment. "Aye, there is still part of me that is angry, though 'tis not your fault, but mine." He lowered his arms to his sides and openly admired her. "I ken this life well, Eleanor, and by the time the ground thaws, you will be begging to return to England. 'Tis not because you're weak, or because you're a woman. I've watched dozens of strong men and women rush to leave this colony every year. If I had not promised Lord Selkirk that I would see this colony survive and thrive, I would tell all the others to leave, as well. Until things improve with the Nor'westers and the Bois-Brûlés, this place is too dangerous for a lady who is accustomed to the finer things in life. They will do everything to destroy our homes, our food, and our lives. If there is nothing to hold you here, you will leave, I promise you."

He was wrong. There were things in the Red River Valley that would hold her. Running a school and ensuring that the children in the colony could read and write had become her primary aim. But just as important was a man named Arran MacLean—as foolish as that might be.

"Good night, Lady Eleanor." For the first time since that long-ago evening in St. Mary's Isle, when he had asked her to marry him, Arran reached out and put his hand on her arm.

The touch was feather-soft, and lasted only a moment, but the feeling lingered long after he dropped his hand.

"I'm sorry I dinna welcome you properly when you came. I mean to right that wrong. This place might not be easy or safe for you, but you are needed and wanted. And I long to be friends, because I care about you. I always have and I always will."

Butterflies took flight in her stomach as she held her breath to hear what he would say next.

"But that doesna mean you should stay, lass."

She let out the breath and tasted the bitterness of his words.

"Good night," he said again. "Try to sleep."

And with those parting words, Arran left Eleanor alone once again.

Chapter Six

It took a few days to settle into a routine at Fort Daer. When the storm subsided, and the temperatures rose again, Arran led a group of men to the riverbanks to fell the trees they'd use for firewood and for building more cabins. It was hard work, but it gave the men something to do, and it kept Arran's mind busy. Or, at least, that's what he told himself.

Having Eleanor within the stockade was both a blessing and a curse. She brought gentleness and grace to the governor's house that he'd never known in all the winters he'd been in the Red River Valley. Her lyrical voice filled the rooms with laughter and joy, and she added a unique perspective to the conversations around mealtimes. He loved seeing the land and climate through her unbiased eyes, and he enjoyed the touches of elegance she added, just by her presence. She was intelligent and wise, and when they spoke of political or religious matters, she never shied away from voicing her opinions. She and West engaged in theological debates almost nightly, though neither one was ever unkind to the other. Arran contemplated their points of view and even added his own from time to time, though it was the simple act of listening that he enjoyed the most.

But having her in the fort also meant that he was constantly reminded of her. It was almost maddening how often his mind drifted to Eleanor. It distracted him from important conversations, it hindered his decision-making, and it made him forgetful. But worst of all, there were times when he was so consumed with thoughts of her that he wanted nothing more than to drop his work and seek her out, just to see her smile.

Four days after arriving at Fort Daer, Arran had one of those moments.

The temperature had risen so drastically, the snow had begun to melt, causing large puddles of mud to fill the fort yard. Sunshine warmed his back and face as he walked toward the main hall, his musket over his shoulder. The men were still felling logs near the riverbanks, but he had left them on the pretense of attending a meeting with Governor Semple. It wasn't a complete falsehood, since he planned to talk to the governor about Semple's upcoming trip, though the meeting could have waited until after supper.

Eleanor had officially opened the school that morning and he'd spent the entire day wondering how things were going for her. She had spent hours preparing her lessons and he was eager to see if she was pleased with the results.

The windows of the main hall were open to allow in the fresh air and warmer weather. A long, low porch covered the front of the building and Arran took the steps up to the porch now. He stood just outside one of the windows where he could hear a child reciting his numbers. When he missed one, Eleanor did not scold him but gently corrected his mistake and then patiently listened as he began again.

A smile lifted the corner of his mouth. She was born to teach. Her patience and gentleness were a gift from God, he was certain. He would never have the grace to spend an entire day in a room full of children and teach them their sums.

After a few moments, the child finished his recitation, and Eleanor told him to return to his seat.

"That will be all for today, children," she said with a smile in her voice. He could not see her from where he stood, but he imagined her standing in her blue dress, her hair piled on top of her head in a mass of curls. "Class dismissed."

He stepped aside as the door opened a moment later.

Two children, both with bright blond hair, walked out the door and headed across the muddy fort toward a cabin close to the governor's house. It was the cabin the Fergusons were living in so Mrs. Ferguson could be close at hand to feed Miriam.

Arran waited for more children to leave, but there was no one else. Surprised, he opened the door wider and found Eleanor organizing a stack of books on one of the tables. She looked up and he immediately saw what she had been hiding from her voice.

Disappointment.

"It was just Fiona's two children," she said as she bit the inside of her mouth, as if she was trying to remain composed. "No one else came."

Frustration built in his chest for her. She had put so much effort into her preparations. "I'm sorry, lass."

"There are twenty-three children in the colony," she said. "And all but six of them are appropriate ages for school. I should have had seventeen children here today." She lifted her hands. "Where are they? It's winter, the perfect time to devote to their studies. What else could they possibly be doing?"

He suspected she already knew the answer to her question.

"It will take time for you to gain their trust." He stepped into the building and set his musket against a table.

"They've known me for many months now but will not even speak to me."

"How did you gain Fiona's friendship and trust?"

"I asked her for help."

"Mayhap the others see you as self-sufficient. They want to be needed. Every day, they rely upon one another for their very lives. It bonds them together in a way nothing else can. In their minds, you are above such things. Removed."

Her eyes filled with sadness. "I'm not above such things. I have many needs. At the moment, I'm in great need of friends and students."

"Then let them know that."

"How?"

Arran walked between the tables and looked down at a stack of books. There were not many in the colony, though she had brought some of her own. "Visit with them. Go to their homes. Ask they what they need."

"They need a school."

"What they need is food, water, and shelter. A school is a privilege and a luxury."

"But it's right here, ready and waiting for them."

"Most of them have never had the privilege of an education and they've gotten along just fine. They probably don't think their children need one, either. In their minds, all their children need to know is how to survive. Change their mind. Explain what education can do for them."

She was quiet for a moment as she nodded silently. "I've had a very privileged life. It's hard for me to understand their needs. I will visit them and ask Fiona for ways I can help, beyond the school."

And he would find a way to encourage the colonists to trust Eleanor. They just needed to get to know her to realize she truly wanted what was best for them.

"I must meet with Semple," he said, though he hated to pull himself away from her. He had hoped that simply seeing her for a moment would ease the longing in his chest, but it didn't.

"I am going to straighten things up a bit more and then go to Miriam." Her words were tinted with a bit of sadness. "This is the longest I've spent away from her since she was born."

"You've grown to love her, haven't you?"

She nodded, though it wasn't joy he saw in her eyes, but concern. "More than I think I should. I've become quite attached to her, I'm afraid."

"Is that bad?"

"I'm uncertain what William intends to do with her. Whenever I ask him, he doesn't want to discuss it. At first, I understood his hesitancy, because he was in mourning. But Miriam is over four months old. He will need to make permanent plans soon."

"What are his options? Is there someone in England to raise her?"

Eleanor shook her head. "He says there is no one."

"Then mayhap he'll marry again." Even as the words slipped out of his mouth, Arran wanted to recall them. Who might the minister choose to marry among the women in his current acquaintance? Eleanor would be the obvious choice—and the preferable one. Not only was she a fellow Brit, but she was also beautiful, accomplished, and faithful. Besides all those things, she already loved West's child as her own. It was only a matter of time before West realized it himself, if he hadn't already. Would Eleanor consider such a thing?

"He was very much in love with his wife," Eleanor offered as an explanation. "I doubt he'll marry again."

Arran would not disagree with her, though he wanted to. Marriage wasn't a privilege in a colony such as theirs. It was a necessity. Love had little to do with such things. But the sooner he stopped discussing West and his marriage options, the better. "I must go," Arran said instead. "Semple is expecting me."

Eleanor smiled in farewell and Arran took his musket in hand as he left the main hall.

He should be thinking about the Bois-Brûlés who were probably gathering in Qu'Appelle, or the fact that there had been no buffalo spotted on the plains yet, or even planning for Semple's departure. But instead, his mind was preoccupied with Eleanor's need for students, and both her and West's apparent blindness at the answer to their problems. William West would need a wife, and Eleanor would need a future—something tangible she could cling to when things became difficult. He didn't foresee either West or Eleanor surviving in the colony long. Both would soon tire of the hardships and long for their lives in England. He'd seen it countless times before.

And when that day came, they'd be together. He felt it in his bones.

By the time Arran reached the door of the governor's house, his good mood had soured, and he was scowling, though he told himself he was being a fool. He had accepted long ago that he couldn't marry Eleanor and that some other man would get that privilege.

He just didn't realize how much he would dislike knowing who that man might be.

Fiona Ferguson stepped out of the governor's house and met Arran's scowl with a smile. Arran had discovered she came to the house several times a day to feed Miriam. They were cordial to one another, but they'd never had a reason to speak.

Until today.

"Mrs. Ferguson," Arran said, forcing himself to return her smile.

"Mr. MacLean."

"Could I speak with you?"

Her surprise was evident in her raised brows, but she was kind and she nodded. "Aye. What can I do for you?"

The sun was bright, and he was forced to squint. "I just saw Miss Brooke and she told me that your children were her only students today."

Mrs. Ferguson was a tall woman, with wide shoulders and a thick waist. Her blond hair was worn in a crown of braids around her head and her clothes were clean, but practical. She didn't appear to be someone who was easily intimidated, but she fidgeted now. "Aye. Angus and I agreed we should take advantage of the school while we can."

"What about the others? Will they not use the school?"

"They're a wee bit uncertain about Miss Brooke. They see the school as charity."

"Charity?" Arran frowned. "How so?"

Mrs. Ferguson glanced over Arran's shoulder and nodded at a passer-by. When the other lady had gone, Mrs. Ferguson leaned in. "There's a rumor she came all this way out of pity for our children, and she's not taking an income for her time. They say her father is an earl and he sent her here with all the money she needs."

"None of that is true. Have you not asked her yourself?"

Mrs. Ferguson put up her hands. "I dinna say I agreed with the rumors. I like Miss Brooke just fine, and even if she did come out of charity, we agreed to swallow our pride and take it, for the sake of our children."

"She's not teaching out of charity—and her father left her destitute. She's just as dependent on this colony as everyone else."

"The poor lamb." Mrs. Ferguson clucked her tongue. "I will try to correct the others, but it will be hard to convince them. We're a proud lot and dinna take kindly to charity. Everything we have, we have earned. If the others know that Eleanor is earning her keep, as well, mayhap they'll take advantage of the school."

"Mayhap we need a little entertainment to bring people together."

"Entertainment?"

"A dance." He remembered that Lord and Lady Selkirk had hosted a dance when Arran visited them to introduce him to their friends and neighbors at St. Mary's Isle. Eleanor had been a magnificent dancer and had enjoyed herself quite a bit.

"It couldna hurt," Mrs. Ferguson said.

The more Arran thought about the idea, the more he liked it.

He hoped it would help Eleanor interact with the other families.

But more than that, he liked the idea of dancing with her again.

The soft sound of dripping water fell from the eaves of the house as Eleanor sat near the fireplace, sewing a small dress for Miriam. In the seat opposite her, William sat with his Bible, reading silently as he held it up to the firelight. Governor Semple had left that morning with his secretary, Mr. Pritchard, for his trip to Brandon House, and Nicolette had gone into the room she shared with Eleanor to put Miriam down to sleep.

The only person missing was Arran. He had left directly after supper to help move the long tables in the main hall, where there was to be a dance.

A log popped in the fireplace, sending a cascade of embers up the chimney. The faint scent of woodsmoke filled the room and mingled with the aroma of fresh-baked biscuits, which Nicolette had made for their Sunday morning breakfast the following day.

William set his Bible on his lap and quietly stared into the flames.

Eleanor glanced up at his movements and admired the profile of his face. He was a handsome man, in a sort of scholarly way. He wasn't very tall, but his presence was large, especially when he preached. He wore his light brown hair short and combed back, and when he read, he set a pair of spectacles on the bridge of his nose. In almost every way, he was Arran MacLean's opposite, though Eleanor had no reason to compare the two men. They were as different as night and day, each serving with their own God-given purpose.

"Will you attend the dance?" he asked, shifting his gaze from the fire to her face, catching her watching him.

She set her sewing on her lap, almost certain that she would be ignored again, but determined to win over the colonists. "I believe I will."

"Do you like to dance?"

A small smile tilted the edges of her mouth. "I enjoy almost nothing more."

He watched her, a bit intently. "Do you think they will want you there?"

It was no secret that the colonists were uncertain of her. She had held school for five days in a row and the only children who had attended were the Fergusons. When she had gone to the colonists' homes, and asked if their children planned to come, they had given one excuse after the other.

Not only had it been disappointing, but she'd also been humiliated. She didn't want more of the same at the dance, but she wouldn't give up now.

"I don't know if they will talk to me, but I can't miss an opportunity to try. Will you attend?"

"No." He smiled and shook his head. "I do not believe I shall. I find my presence at such gatherings puts a damper on everyone's fun. They think they must behave a certain way, or I will pass judgment on them."

"Do you mind missing it?"

Again, he shook his head. "I am not a good dancer, so I do not miss such things."

Her thoughts slipped to Arran, who was a good dancer. Her cheeks warmed thinking about their dances together at St. Mary's Isle. He had left her breathless with delight each time he held her in his arms.

She caught William watching her, so she said, "Surely, you can dance."

He slowly removed the spectacles from his nose and set them on a nearby table. "I'm sorry, Eleanor. I used to be more exciting. There was a time when I would not have hesitated to ask a pretty lady to a dance. Before I became a minister, and before—" He swallowed and looked down at his clasped hands. "Before Anne," he said quieter.

Compassion tightened Eleanor's chest. She reached over and gently placed her hand on top of his. "I know."

He looked at her hand for a heartbeat, then laid one of his own over it. "Thank you. I long to ask you—"

The front door opened, and Arran strode in. His eyes took in the scene in an instant.

Eleanor pulled back her hand, while a rush of heat crept up her neck. She had done nothing wrong but felt guilty all the same.

Slowly, Arran closed the door.

William rose from his seat and held the back of his chair as he faced Arran. "Is everything set for the dance?"

"Aye." Arran looked from William to Eleanor. "Are you ready to go?"

She glanced at William and then back at Arran. "Yes, though I'm afraid no one will want me there."

"I want you there." His gaze was steady and very serious. "I planned the dance for you."

William stiffened, watching them intently.

"This dance is in my honor?" She lifted her eyebrows. "Truly?"

Arran did not move from his place near the door. "When I was new to St. Mary's Isle, Lord and Lady Selkirk held a dance in my honor to meet their friends and neighbors. 'Tis the least I could do for you."

"What if no one comes?"

He smiled and his brown eyes sparkled. "They've already started to fill up the hall, lass." He extended his hand. "Will you come, then?"

Eleanor stood, turning her attention to William. "Are you certain you won't join us?"

He shook his head, as he regarded her. "You go and have fun."

She nodded at him and then said to Arran, "I will need to change before I go."

"You look bonnie in what you're wearing." He smiled. "I wouldna change a thing."

"I can't go to a dance in this." She lifted the hem of her brown dress. "It isn't meant for a party."

The light in Arran's eyes dimmed and he shook his head. "Your second-best dress is better than anything the other ladies wear, lass. If you walk into the hall in a party dress, you'll only distance yourself more."

Remorse and embarrassment at her thoughtlessness filled her throat and she had to swallow it down. "You're right, of course."

She had brought several gowns with her, including a stunning ball gown, not knowing when she might have the chance to acquire another. But now that she'd come to the Red River Valley, she realized how frivolous it had been to waste the space in her trunk.

Arran motioned to the door, taking her shawl and bonnet off the hooks. "Shall we go?"

He helped her to put them on, and with a farewell to William, the two of them slipped out of the house.

Lights shone from the windows of the main hall and music spilled out into the muddy yard. Overhead, the stars sparkled in all their brilliance without a moon to dull their shine. Though it was October, the air had cooled, but it was still much warmer than it had been when they traveled to Pembina.

Arran was strong and steady as he walked beside her, causing her heart to beat an irregular rhythm. Would he always elicit these feelings inside her? He had made it clear he didn't want her to stay, but she could not convince her traitorous heart to stop responding to him.

Chapter Seven

The room was warm and bright as the Highlanders filled the space with laughter and music. One of the company men had brought his bagpipes, while another had produced a flute. A fiddle was added by one of the colonists and the trio played together as if they'd been doing it their whole life.

A fire crackled in the large hearth and the tables had been pushed back against the walls to leave the middle of the room open for dancing.

"A bonnie night for a dance," one of the men called out to Arran as he led Eleanor into the hall.

The crowd was in the middle of a lively Scottish country dance, one Arran hadn't heard since he was a boy. About three dozen people stood in four long lines, their partners standing across from them. Two by two, they danced down the lines until they came to the end, laughing and jigging the whole way. Then they began to weave in and out, bouncing on their toes in a Highland step. Several of the men wore their kilts while others were dressed in deerskin trousers.

Eleanor stood close to Arran's side, her warm hand nestled firmly in the crook of his elbow. He set his musket against the wall where all the others had been laid, and he stood for a minute watching the dancers move.

"Do you ken this dance?" he asked Eleanor.

She shook her head, her face already glowing, though she hadn't yet danced.

"I remember my maither and faither dancing to this tune when I was a wee lad." Just thinking about his mother made him flex his hands. The scars were tight from the dry winter air. He looked down at them, recalling the day his life had changed forever.

"Do you think you could teach me?" she asked—and then noticed he was studying his hands. She looked down at his scars for a moment before lifting her questioning eyes to his.

She had asked him once, many years ago, how he'd gotten his scars. He hadn't answered her then, and he wasn't sure he could answer her if she asked him now. They were a constant reminder of his weakness and inability, and they were the last thing he wanted to share with anyone. Especially Eleanor.

Instead of asking him, she lifted her free hand and set it on top of his, covering his scars with her soft, gentle touch. The look in her eyes told him she understood his pain, even if she didn't know how it had happened.

A deep and abiding affection filled Arran's chest. It was more powerful than attraction or desire and gave him a longing he'd never known before.

"Eleanor." Mrs. Ferguson approached with a hearty smile. She'd been to their home just after supper, when she'd fed Miriam. "I wondered if you'd come tonight."

Arran was both relieved and disappointed at the interruption.

The country dance ended, and the couples clapped their hearty approval. Many of them spoke in Gaelic tonight, their love of the old country flowing freely.

"I wouldn't miss it." Eleanor smiled up at Arran, her brown eyes filled with appreciation.

His heart made a funny leap, and he knew, if he wasn't careful, his well-guarded feelings would start to grow again under the light of her attention.

"Do you like to dance?" Mrs. Ferguson asked Eleanor.

"Very much."

"Good." Mrs. Ferguson turned and caught her husband's eye. She motioned him over.

Angus Ferguson was a giant of a man, but he was jolly and always had a smile on his face. He approached with laughter in his eyes.

"Angus, my love." Mrs. Ferguson wrapped her arm around her husband's elbow. "Ask Miss Eleanor to dance, will you?"

The next song, a Scottish reel, began to play.

"Of course I will." Angus grinned and extended a meaty hand to Eleanor. "Will you dance a reel with me, lass?"

With shining eyes, Eleanor let Arran go and took Mr. Ferguson's hand. "I would be honored."

"Good!" Angus said and led her onto the dance floor.

Though Arran was pleased that Eleanor had been taken away by one of the Highlanders, he couldn't ignore his disappointment that she was in another man's arms. He turned to Mrs. Ferguson, wanting to distract himself. "Will you dance with me?"

"Aye. But only if you're a good dancer." Her eyes twinkled with mirth.

"You'll have to wait and see." He led her to the middle of the room, and they joined Eleanor and Mr. Ferguson in a reel-of-four. They would stay in the same group of four throughout the dance, weaving around one another, crossing partners, and dancing in time to the music.

As the bagpipes played, they began to dance. Arran bowed to Mrs. Ferguson, while she curtsied. Behind Arran, Eleanor stood facing Mr. Ferguson and they bowed and curtsied, as well. Arran noticed the others watching Eleanor dance with Mr. Ferguson. He hoped their respect for the gregarious Highlander would sway their opinion of her.

Eleanor's eyes sparkled and her mouth curved up in a smile as they danced the reel. Though she didn't know the dance, she did her best to keep up with Angus. When she made a mistake, she laughed and tried again. It was hard to take his eyes off her, so Arran didn't even try. Most of the single men in the room were having the same problem.

When the reel was over, Sean Campbell approached and asked Eleanor for the next dance. She willingly obliged, and soon, she was whisked away. Smiling an apology at Arran as she went.

He could only admire her from a distance as she was passed from one dance partner to the other, smiling and breathless as she moved around the hall.

Finally, an hour later, he found himself beside her once again.

Her eyes glowed and her cheeks were filled with color.

She'd never looked more beautiful.

The musicians began a waltz, and Arran was afraid if he didn't act soon, he'd miss the chance to dance with her.

"May I have this dance?" he asked her above the noise of the bagpipes.

"I thought you'd never ask." She grinned and took the hand he offered.

He led her onto the dance floor, his heart pounding a little faster at the idea of holding her in his arms again. Slowly, he slipped his right hand around her tiny waist, drawing her close as he captured her right hand in his left. It was just as much an honor to dance with Eleanor tonight as it had been at St. Mary's Isle. And just like before, every nerve in his body thrummed with awareness of her. For a heartbeat, he could do nothing but look into her eyes.

In moments like this, he almost felt as if he was dreaming. All those years of yearning for her across the ocean. It didn't feel real that she was with him in the wilds of North America, in his arms again.

Eleanor gazed up at him, her features soft and tender in the flickering candlelight. She looked at him as if it was just the two of them.

With a mind of their own, his feet began to move, and his body followed, carrying her along. They circled the room, stepping in perfect rhythm together.

"I was beginning to think you lied to me," she said quietly.

His eyebrows tilted together. "What do you mean?"

"I was afraid you wouldn't ask me to dance like you promised."

He smiled. "You havena sat in the corner once," he said, a bit triumphantly.

The room was growing increasingly warmer as he held her close. His gaze lowered to her lips, and he was suddenly transported to a moonlit night when he'd walked with her in the garden. He'd wanted to kiss her then, but was afraid it was too soon and he'd scare her away. Instead of kissing her, he'd captured her hand in his and she hadn't pulled away. He didn't want to rush anything with Eleanor. She wasn't a silly maiden to use and discard. If he kissed her, he wanted to be certain it would be the first kiss of countless others, spanning the length of his life.

But now, as he danced with her on the plains of the Red River Valley, over three years and thousands of miles apart, he wished he would have kissed her then. It had been one of his deepest regrets, because even if he couldn't spend the rest of his life with Eleanor in his arms, at least he would have had the memory of her kiss to keep him warm on the long winter nights.

"What are you thinking about?" she asked with a curious smile.

Heat snaked up his neck and he wondered what she would think if he told her the truth. *I'm thinking about kissing you, lass.*

Instead, he said, "Our dances at St. Mary's Isle. You're bonnier than you've ever been."

She dipped her head and looked away, an embarrassed smile on her lips. "And you are more charming."

Arran pulled her closer, wishing he could wrap her fully in his embrace.

But even as he longed to draw her near, every shred of experience he'd had in the Red River Valley told him to keep her at a distance. After the first year in the settlement, he had promised himself not to get close to anyone. They either left or died. There were no other options. Why would Eleanor be any different? What would he gain from losing his heart to her all over again, if she was taken from him? Would it be worth the few short months of pleasure?

And then there was William West. When Arran had entered the house and found Eleanor and William holding hands, his first response had been anger, quickly followed by jealousy. But the rational part of his mind told him that Eleanor would be better off with William—in England—as far away from Assiniboia as possible. William was a good man, and he brought out the best in Eleanor. Instead of coming between them, he should be encouraging Eleanor to pursue a life with the minister. She would have comfort and security back in England, perhaps a cozy parsonage with a lovely garden where she could have her tea and spend pleasant afternoons with Miriam.

He liked to imagine Eleanor in that place, because when he thought of her toiling for her food and fighting for her life in Assiniboia, he felt helpless, as if he had failed her in some way.

William could offer Eleanor the life Arran couldn't.

As the bagpipes continued to play, and the dancers waltzed around the hall, Arran forced himself to stop thinking about Eleanor. The only way he could do his job and keep her safe was if he guarded his heart. He would cherish each moment with her, but when the time came, he would see that she was safely delivered back to England. Even if it meant she went with William.

The air had grown decidedly colder when Eleanor and Arran stepped out of the main hall in the wee hours of the morning. The last of the revelers were entering their cabin, and one of the men turned to Eleanor and waved good night.

She smiled and waved back.

The music was still humming in her ears, though the night had grown silent and the prairie around the fort was asleep. Overhead, the stars sparkled in dazzling pinpricks of light and before her lips, fog billowed from her mouth.

"Did you enjoy yourself?" Arran asked quietly as he closed the door and joined her on the porch.

"Very much. Thank you for planning it for me. I finally feel like I made progress tonight with the other colonists. I hope I'll see more of their children at my school."

He smiled as they began to cross the wide fort yard.

Dancing had a way of breaking down barriers like few other things.

"Do you have much entertainment in the winters?" she asked Arran. "Will I have more of the same to look forward to?"

"The first winter we enjoyed many diversions," he said slowly. "The buffalo were so plentiful that year, they came to the stockade and scratched their backs upon the posts. The weather was mild, and the snow was minimal."

"And the second and third winters?"

He took his time as he slowly walked her toward the governor's house. "The weather was bitterly cold, and the snow was so deep, the buffalo were scarce. Many settlers were ill, and we did everything we could just to stay alive. When we gathered, it was to hold funerals." He readjusted the musket on his shoulder and sighed. "Even if there was anyone to plan the activities, few people would have had the heart to participate."

The weight of his words dampened the joy Eleanor had been feeling just moments before. "Do you think this winter will be different?"

"I can only hope, though the Indians have told me the signs point to another long, cold winter."

"And the buffalo?" She'd heard several people discussing the lack of buffalo at the dance that evening.

"The Indians hunt them on the prairies and bring the meat to the fort to sell." His voice was hard as he spoke. "They haven't come yet, which is odd for this time of year, since the weather has just turned."

"And what of our other supplies?"

"You dinna need to worry. 'Tis my job to see that everyone is fed."

"Do you carry the responsibility alone?" It seemed like a large undertaking for one man.

He shook his head. "When Governor Semple is here, it will fall on both our shoulders. We have wheat and corn stored in the back of the main hall, and there are chickens, pigs, and milch cows in the barn. It might grow lean, if the buffalo do not return. I've warned you it won't be easy, but we will do everything we can to keep the colonists alive."

As they drew closer to the governor's house, Eleanor noticed a light shining from within.

"Who might be awake?" she asked with a frown. It was late and she had thought everyone would be asleep.

They walked faster and when they were a few feet away, the sound of Miriam's muffled cries could be heard.

Arran opened the door and held it for Eleanor to step into the house.

Nicolette stood with the baby near the fireplace, bouncing the crying child, while William stood farther back, near the foot of the ladder that led to the upstairs. He was in his shirtsleeves and trousers, his hair tousled from sleep.

"What's wrong?" Eleanor asked as she rushed across the room, not bothering to remove her shawl or bonnet.

"She's ill," Nicolette said in her broken English. "I cannot know why."

Eleanor took the baby and held her close, feeling her forehead. "She's burning with fever."

Miriam's pitiful cries split the air. Her cheeks were aflame with color, and she tensed her body as if in pain. Eleanor could feel a low rumble in her chest as she breathed, and when she coughed, it sounded tight.

"You poor girl," Eleanor whispered, trying desperately to keep calm and not give in to fear.

"I will send for one of the doctors," Arran said as he left the house.

Eleanor was surprised that William had not thought to do so already. One of the doctors had been an early settler and the other one had come over with the latest group of colonists. Both were well respected, and if anyone knew what to do, it would be them.

But in the meantime, Eleanor would do what she could. She turned to Nicolette. "Please set a kettle of water to warm over the fire." She would make ginger tea to help lower the fever, though it would be hard to get the baby to drink it, since she was not yet weaned.

Nicolette began to do as she was asked.

Eleanor turned her attention to William. "We'll also need cloths and cool water to bathe her skin."

William stood, almost like a statue, immobile as he stared at Miriam. "Will she die?"

"I pray to God that she will not." Eleanor put the baby up to her shoulder and lightly bounced as she patted her back, speaking over the baby's cries. "We'll do everything we can to save her." She wanted to be patient with William, but her forbearance was growing thin. "But we will need all the help we can get."

With a brittle nod, William did as she asked.

It felt like an hour before Arran returned with Dr. Stewart, though Eleanor guessed it to be twenty minutes. Dr. Stewart was the Scottish doctor who had been an early settler to the colony. He was an older gentleman with a thick, white mustache, and an equally thick brogue.

Eleanor had managed to calm Miriam and get her to drink a few teaspoonfuls of sweetened ginger tea. With great patience, she had used the cool water to bathe her forehead and arms, and the baby was now whimpering from exhaustion, though her cries were no longer tearing Eleanor's heart apart.

Gently, Dr. Stewart took Miriam out of Eleanor's arms and sat on a chair near the fireplace. "How long has she been ill?" he asked.

Eleanor looked at Nicolette, who was standing in the corner.

"She woke, four or five hours," Nicolette said.

"She was not showing signs of her illness when Nicolette put her to bed before I left for the dance," Eleanor told the doctor. "That was earlier this evening, around sundown." It had been almost seven hours ago. Why hadn't Nicolette or William called for them when it was clear the baby was sick?

Arran moved close to Eleanor's side, his steady presence giving her a bit of confidence and hope. He did not touch her, but his nearness, and his concern, were so powerful, it almost felt as if he nestled her into his embrace.

William stood on the other side of the doctor, his brow tight and his gaze locked on his daughter's face. He did not move or ask any questions.

After several minutes, the doctor stood and held the baby out, looking at William and then Eleanor.

When William did not move to take her, Eleanor went to the doctor's side and gathered the baby into her arms, snuggling her close.

"The child has croup," he said. "She is very young to be this sick. I will try to bleed her and restore her humors, and you will need to limit her food, so you dinna feed her fever."

Eleanor lifted the baby higher to kiss her warm cheek, not wanting to think about starving her, or bleeding her small body.

"Do what you must," William said, his voice devoid of emotion.

"When will you bleed her?" Eleanor asked.

"I think it best if I do it now." He went to the table where he had laid a medicine chest upon entering. When he opened it, he pulled out a fleam, which had several different sizes of blades to make the incision for bleeding.

Eleanor turned her gaze from the instrument and pressed her lips together. She couldn't stop thinking about Arran's words earlier when he told her about all the death and suffering among the colonists. Would Miriam be the first of many losses in Pembina?

Tears gathered in her eyes as she fought the panic rising in her heart.

Arran came close to her and put his hand on her shoulder. "Dinna fash. God is with her. We will do what we can and pray that God does the rest." The gentle pressure of his hand, and the soft reassurance of his tender words, made tears fall down her cheeks.

She didn't know what she would do if she lost Miriam.

Chapter Eight

Arran had quickly come to fear the silence more than the barking cough or the heart-rending cries from little Miriam. When there was no sound coming from the room the baby shared with Eleanor and Nicolette, Arran's neck and back became tense and his breathing grew shallow, trying to hear some sort of life from the wee bairn.

He and Eleanor had hardly spoken in the three days since the dance, but there was no need for words to know what she was thinking and feeling. He saw it in the lines around her mouth, in the sleepless circles under her eyes, and the rumpled appearance of her clothing. She was working night and day to keep the baby alive.

On the fourth afternoon, Arran sat at the desk in Semple's empty room, writing in the journal where Lord Selkirk had asked him to record the daily activities of the colony. The house had grown silent—too silent—and he stopped the scribbling of his pen to lift his head and listen.

The house creaked and the wind rattled against the windows, but there were no other sounds to mark the existence of life. Setting his pen in the inkwell, he stood and walked into the common room, his ears intent on the closed door of Eleanor's bedroom.

For a heartbeat, he waited, and then the door slowly opened. Eleanor appeared, just as exhausted as before. When she noticed him, she offered a small, sad smile, closing the door quietly behind her. "Miriam is finally asleep."

Arran didn't move. He appreciated these unexpected moments when he and Eleanor had a few minutes alone. West had gone to the main hall earlier that day to perform two separate marriages between company men and their Indian wives. The minister had found a reason to leave the house every day since Miriam became sick, and he stayed away until suppertime. His lack of interest in his daughter was beginning to wear on Arran's patience and goodwill. The man left the entire care and responsibility of his daughter to Eleanor, though she had no obligation to the child or to him.

Eleanor went to the fireplace and picked up the poker. She started to adjust the wood to coax the flame to life, but a spark jumped out at her. She swatted at the ember on her skirt.

"Here." He moved to her side and took the poker from her hands. "Sit," he said, indicating a chair nearby. "Dinna concern yourself over the fire."

She didn't protest but lowered herself into the seat. Her hair, which was usually in its proper place, was drooping, with tendrils hanging in her face. He'd never seen her so out of sorts, or worried.

Arran put several more logs on the fire and moved the teapot over the flames to warm its contents. "When was the last time you ate?" he asked gently.

Eleanor stared into the flames, as if she didn't hear him. "Fiona was here." Her mouth turned down at the corners. "Two of her children are also ill."

"Aye." He had heard rumors that several of the children in the settlement had taken ill. He'd just recorded it in the daily journal.

"Miriam wouldn't eat." Eleanor's words were slow and lackluster. "She's listless and does not rouse when I pick her up."

"What does Dr. Stewart advise?" The doctor had returned and bled Miriam for a second time just that morning. His mouth had been set in a grim line when he left.

Eleanor bit her bottom lip and shook her head. Her face pinched and tears began to course down her cheeks. "He says her breathing has worsened and there's nothing more we can do." She dropped her face into her hands as the sobs shook her body.

Pain tightened Arran's chest as he went to her and drew her into his embrace.

She came willingly, weeping into his shoulder. "What will I do if I lose her?"

This was the very thing he had wanted to spare Eleanor when she'd arrived in Assiniboia. Death and disappointment were so much a part of their lives, it would be impossible for her to avoid it.

He held her tight, whispering comforting words against her hair. "The battle is not lost yet," he said. "We will keep fighting until there's no fight left in us."

She sniffed and nodded, then pulled away from his embrace, wiping her cheeks with the backs of her hands.

A knock at the door tore Arran's attention off Eleanor.

"I do not wish to see anyone," she said.

He nodded, then waited until she reentered her room before he walked across the floor to answer the call.

Colin Robertson stood just outside the door. "Can I speak to you?"

Arran stepped aside to allow Colin to enter and then closed the door behind him.

"What news do you bring?" Arran asked, fearing there was more illness to report.

"A company man arrived from the post near Qu'Appelle today." Robertson's voice held a dire warning. "The Bois-Brûlés are gathering there in large numbers under the leadership of Cuthbert Grant. They are making plans to attack Assiniboia in the spring and have vowed to burn down Fort Douglas and drive off every settler, once and for all."

The news was not surprising, though it was not what Arran had hoped to hear. The Bois- Brûlés saw the colony as a threat to their way of life and were just as determined as the North West Company to see them gone. "Has Duncan been a part of the plans?"

Colin nodded. "He went to Qu'Appelle after we left Fort Douglas and might be there still. He and Grant are working together."

No doubt Duncan would return to his fort soon. His main responsibility was to gain the fur trade, with hopes of pushing the Hudson's Bay Company out of the region and would not leave his post for long.

"There is other news," Colin said.

Arran was almost afraid to ask. He crossed his arms and took a wider stance. "What have you heard?"

"There are rumors that Lord Selkirk was in New York earlier this fall, on his way to Assiniboia."

"Selkirk is in North America?" Arran could hardly believe the news. If it was true, it was the best thing he'd heard in years.

"It's only a rumor at this point. When was the last time you received word from him?"

"His last letter arrived with Governor Semple. It was dated from May of this year. He wrote from his home at St. Mary's Isle and made no mention of planning a trip to Assiniboia." Though Lord Selkirk had founded the colony, he had never been to the Red River Valley himself. The idea that he might be on his way was the first glimmer of hope Arran had felt in months. But was it only a rumor, or was it fact? And, if he was on his way, would he arrive in time to help? Moreover, what might he do to stop Duncan and Cuthbert Grant that Arran had not already tried himself?

"Selkirk holds the deed to all the land along the entire Red River Valley," Robertson said. "Though Duncan doesn't want to admit the truth, he is a squatter and poacher on Selkirk's land. If anyone can hold him accountable, it would be the earl."

"Aye. If Selkirk can survive the journey." Arran had long feared that the North West Company would find a way to assassinate Lord Selkirk and make it look like an accident. If the founder of the colony died, the settlement would die with him. "If he is in New York, he will probably wait until spring to make the journey to the colony."

And, by then, it might be too late for him to help against the plans the Bois-Brûlés and Nor'westers were making to destroy the colony for good.

"When do you expect Semple to return?" Robertson asked.

"In a week or two. When he is back, we will make our own plan."

Robertson nodded, his dark eyes squinting in thought. "We will need to remove Duncan."

"Aye. It should have been done already. Semple shouldn't have let him go when we had him."

Both Arran and Robertson had agreed about what to do with Duncan Cameron, though Governor Semple had the final say. "I wish we could apprehend Grant, as well," Robertson added. The man had made several threats but had not personally attacked the settlement. He would be harder to apprehend and bring to trial.

Duncan, on the other hand, had a long list of transgressions against the colony.

"I'll leave you," Robertson said. "If you hear anything, let me know."

Arran nodded and then showed the man out of the house. After closing the door behind him, Arran put another log on the fire and removed the steaming teakettle.

Miriam's cries punctured the air.

Relief filled Arran at the sound. If the baby had enough energy to cry, then perhaps she was gaining strength again.

He could only hope.

Eleanor had slept in fits and starts since Miriam had become ill. Every move or sound the baby made had Eleanor on her feet to check on the tiny child.

Evening had set on the eighth day and Eleanor had insisted that Nicolette get some sleep. The older woman had worked just as diligently as Eleanor to care for the baby and had spent the day washing the household laundry on top of her other chores. When Nicolette refused to sleep, Eleanor had said she would stay awake to see to Miriam's needs.

Darkness was descending much faster on the prairie as the winter grew long. Inside the governor's house, Eleanor was thankful for the crackle of the fire and the warm rubbaboo bubbling in the kettle hanging from the metal crane. Arran had not yet returned from the barn where he'd gone to care for Tiberius, and William had been absent the entire day, though she did not know where he kept himself.

She set the table for the three of them, her muscles sore and her eyes burning from lack of sleep. With one ear to her bedroom door and the other to the front door, she set a plate of fresh biscuits on the table. Nicolette had agreed to go to sleep, only if she could prepare the meal in advance. Eleanor was thankful for her forethought, since she had little experience cooking. Nicolette had taught her a few basic skills since her arrival in the colony, but Eleanor had a long way to go if she wanted to be self-sufficient.

The front door creaked open, and Eleanor's heart pounded a little harder, thinking it was Arran who would enter. But it was William who walked into the house.

He glanced up at Eleanor from under the brim of his hat, and when his eyes met hers, there was so much grief in them, she had to look away. Her own grief mingled with the resentment she'd started to feel toward him. She didn't mind caring for Miriam—quite the opposite. She could not imagine being anywhere else when the baby needed her most. But she had grown angry at his lack of interest or involvement where the child was concerned.

Too little sleep, and a great abundance of fear, boiled to overflowing at the sight of him. With a clenched jaw, she set the tin plate on the table with more force than necessary.

William flinched as he set down his Bible. Without speaking, he took off his hat and coat and set them on the hooks near the door.

Eleanor did not speak, either, afraid of what she might say. Tears threatened to spill, yet she didn't want to cry. The time had come to confront William, and she needed her wits about herself to do it with grace.

For a moment, William simply stood on the other side of the table. He opened his mouth as if he was going to speak, but then he closed it again.

Eleanor let out a long, low breath, hoping to steady her chaotic emotions. "Miriam has shown some improvement today."

"Thank God for that."

The fire popped, sending a spark of embers toward the chimney. Eleanor watched the flames for a moment, gathering her thoughts, and then looked back at William, the one question that had plagued her for months finding its way to her lips. "Why have you not held her?"

William was a strong man—a capable man. He was scholarly, but he was not frail. So, when he crumpled to the chair, dropping his face into his hands while he wept, Eleanor could do nothing but stare.

"I'm a coward. She's all I have left of Anne, and I cannot bring myself to even touch her."

All the resolve in Eleanor's spine melted and she went to William, her heart aching for his. "You are not a coward." She pulled a chair up beside him and put her hand on his arm.

He looked at her then, his blue eyes awash in tears. "After losing Anne, I thought I might also lose my mind. It was by sheer willpower and the divine grace of God that I did not."

She did not speak but simply listened.

"Each time I start to feel again, I am plagued by guilt. How can I go on living when Anne could not? How can I love and laugh and be happy again when she is not here? How can I make memories and enjoy my daughter when those things were stolen from Anne?"

Eleanor did not try to answer him.

"But that is not the worst of it." His voice broke and he shook his head. "I'm petrified to love my daughter." He pressed his fists to his mouth as he looked away from Eleanor. It couldn't be easy for this man to admit his weaknesses to her, and she admired him for doing it. "If I let myself love her, and then I lose her," he said, "or anyone else I love, I fear it will be the end of me." He searched Eleanor's face, panic emanating from his eyes. "I know this makes me a coward, but I do not know how to fight this fear. I'm the minister. I'm supposed to have all the answers, yet this thing has gripped me in chains. It's shaking the very foundation of my faith."

She took one of his hands in both of hers and pressed it gently. "I wish I could offer you reassurance, but I cannot guarantee you will never lose someone you love again." She had lost her mother and father, though neither had died, and she knew what it was to be adrift in fear and uncertainty. "What I can promise is that God understands your pain. He made your emotions and feels them with you. You are not a coward. You are human, and, perhaps, you will use this experience to relate to others." She took a deep breath. "But if you do not make the sacrifice to love Miriam now and selflessly give of your heart, regardless of the cost, it will be to her great detriment. She is a gift that God has bestowed upon you, and it is not up to you whether you accept that gift."

He nodded and wiped his cheeks. "I know what you speak is true, but when I try, the fear overwhelms me."

"She could very well live to be an old lady," Eleanor said a bit more gently. "And what greater love could she have than that of her father?"

The room was dark except for the faint light from the fireplace, and it offered a warm glow in William's eyes as he studied Eleanor's face. "She is blessed to have you." He placed his free hand over hers. "*I* am blessed to have you. I do not know what I would have done if you had not stepped in to care for Miriam."

"There would have been someone—"

"No." He shook his head. "No one like you."

His praise gave her a small measure of energy she had not experienced in days. It felt good to be recognized and appreciated. "Thank you."

William offered an embarrassed smile and removed his hands from Eleanor's grasp. "I haven't shed a tear in front of anyone else in years, let alone a lady."

"You have no need to fear," she said, rising to take the rubbaboo out of the heat. "It is good to cleanse your soul from time to time with tears. God would not have given them to us if we were not supposed to use them."

He shook his head in amazement. "You are a diamond among women, Eleanor Brooke."

She wasn't sure she was ready for more praise than was due, so she went about her work without responding to his compliments.

By the time supper was on the table, Arran had not returned, so Eleanor and William ate a quiet meal. She shared with him the doctor's report and he told her about the baptisms he'd performed that afternoon.

When they were done eating, Arran was still not home. Eleanor kept the stew on the trivet, close enough to the fire to keep it warm for him.

"If you do not need me for anything more this evening," William said to her, "I will say good night. I must prepare my sermon notes for tomorrow."

"Go ahead." He had helped her clean their scant dishes and there was nothing left to do. "I will check on Miriam again."

"You must try to sleep," he told her with concern in his voice. "We do not want you to become ill, as well."

She would rest when Miriam was breathing easily again, and not a minute sooner.

He bid her good night and then climbed the ladder into the sleeping quarters above.

Eleanor went to her room and listened to Miriam breathing for a few moments. Nicolette snored softly from her mat on the floor. Eleanor knew if she sat on her bed, she would fall asleep, so she quietly removed her writing desk from the room and went to the table near the fireplace to write instead.

Concern for Arran had started to mount while they had eaten and had only grown stronger the longer he was away. It wasn't like him to be gone for so long, and she wondered what could possibly be keeping him. She prayed it wasn't serious and forced herself to turn her thoughts to her journal.

Like always, she did not spare the truth from the blank pages. She shared her fear for Miriam's health, and her concern for the other colonists. When she was finished writing about the illness, she also shared her thoughts and feelings about the dance and how she had felt when she had been welcomed by the others. She hadn't reopened her school since that night because of Miriam's illness, but she hoped that when she did, the children would come.

Her eyes were heavy, and her head kept nodding forward, but she forced herself to continue writing.

Suddenly, her body felt warm and weightless. Eleanor could not force her eyes open, but there was no need. She was safe and protected, pressed close to the solid muscles of the one who held her in his arms. Her instinct was to snuggle close and wrap her arms around his neck. He smelled of woodsmoke and bergamot, and his heart beat steadily beneath her ear.

For a moment, time seemed to stand still as he simply held her, but then he carried her to her room and laid her on her bed. She knew she needed to wake up, to listen for Miriam, but she could not force herself to leave the comfort of her dream.

Slowly, Eleanor's eyes opened, and she stared at the wooden ceiling over her head, wondering vaguely how she had found her way to her bed. It was dark outside the window, but the wind had settled, and everything was still. For a moment, she just rested, her thoughts fuzzy, her body warm and comfortable under her quilt. Nicolette's soft snores floated on the cool air, but Miriam's labored breathing was no more.

With sudden clarity, Eleanor sat up in bed. Panic clawed at her chest as she pushed aside the heavy quilt and stumbled across the floor to look into Miriam's cradle.

The baby was gone.

Terror filled Eleanor's heart as she pulled open the bedroom door and ran into the common room.

Arran sat near the fireplace, smiling down at Miriam, who was cradled in his arms. He spoke gently to the little girl as she stared up at him with her wide, blue eyes. He was so big and strong, and she was so small and delicate.

Eleanor sagged against the doorframe, her muscles weak with relief. The terror in her heart melted away and was quickly replaced with something far sweeter. It warmed her through, bringing fresh tears.

Arran looked up at Eleanor, a light in his brown eyes. He slowly rose from his chair and walked over to her, holding the baby as if she was the most precious and fragile thing he'd ever touched. "We hoped you would keep sleeping."

"How is she?" It was hard for Eleanor to find her voice. She was still breathless from the fright she'd just endured.

Arran smiled down at the baby, who continued to stare at him. "She is doing much better, though I dinna ken much about these things." He spoke in a soothing voice, clearly for Miriam's sake.

The first hint of a smile lifted the baby's cheeks and Eleanor's heart soared. Miriam had not smiled since becoming ill.

A grin turned up Arran's lips as he looked down at the babe. "She's a bonnie wee bairn. I dinna think my heart will be the same after holding her." He met Eleanor's gaze. "Now I ken why you love her so."

Everything within her wanted to reach out and embrace them both, but she refrained and instead shared a quiet smile with Arran, loving that he understood this part of her.

"I dinna want to let her go, but I can see you're needing to hold her and see for yourself that she's safe and well." He gently placed Miriam in her arms.

The baby was soft and sweet, and her chest was no longer tight with the croup. "Thank God," Eleanor breathed as she closed her eyes and placed her cheek next to Miriam's.

Arran did not speak, and when Eleanor opened her eyes again, she found him watching her.

"Did you bring me to my bed?" she asked quietly.

He nodded.

Eleanor swallowed the rush of emotions clogging her throat. She was still properly dressed—even her shoes were still on her feet—but the thought of him holding her in his arms, and lying her in her bed, brought heat to her cheeks and a strange, yet wonderful, sensation to her stomach.

It had been a long time since someone had taken care of her.

"You need your sleep, lass. I dinna want you to become ill."

Now that Miriam was growing stronger, Eleanor would be able to sleep better. "Thank you for your help." It was all she could manage to say, though she wanted to say so much more.

Chapter Nine

FEBRUARY 25, 1816

The winter drew on in cold, dark nights, and bright, bitter days. As the calendar flipped from one month to the next, the snow fell for days at a time. It gathered and blew on the prairie, until it was packed tight against the western stockade wall. Anyone could have scaled the wall and climbed right into the fort without any trouble, though few people would hazard a trip out in the severe, unpredictable weather.

Semple had returned, and the colony had survived its first wave of illness, but the buffalo were still scarce, and the food supplies had started to dwindle, forcing them to ration. Each day, the settlers were allowed one cup each of wheat and corn, two eggs per family, and the little milk they had was given to the children.

One afternoon in late February, Arran stood at the window inside the governor's house and watched the activity in the fort yard. Behind him, near the fireplace, Nicolette worked quietly, preparing the simple meal of bread they would eat that night. There had not been any buffalo meat, and the pemmican had run out. It would still be months before they could return to Fort Douglas and plant their crops. Daily, he prayed for the buffalo to return.

Outside, the thermometer had taken a drastic dip and snow was falling, but the storm had not set in with a vengeance yet.

The door to the main hall burst open and a dozen children rushed out of the building, their small bodies bundled against the cold. They ran to their respective cabins, laughing and teasing each other along the way. Though things were dire, Arran thanked God that the colonists had begun to entrust their children to Eleanor's teaching. They had started to accept her after the dance, but it was Eleanor's devoted care to them during the illness that had won them over completely. Once Miriam was well, Eleanor had begun to visit the other sick families to administer help. They began to see her as an important part of the colony, like the governor, the minister, and the doctors. She was a liaison between the big house and the smaller cabins, asking for help from the governor and, in many cases, getting it.

A few minutes later, Eleanor appeared at the hall's door, her Hudson's Bay coat covering her body as she closed the door behind her and then turned toward the governor's house. She wore the hood over her head, and her pink skirts showed from under the bottom of her coat. As she walked, her brown moccasins peeked out from beneath the hem of her dress. The contrast between a fine European lady and a seasoned Red River colonist made him smile.

For the past three winters, boredom and monotony had been Arran's greatest enemy—but this year had been different. Each morning, when he opened his eyes, his heart pounded with the knowledge that he would see Eleanor at breakfast. Every afternoon, when he completed the tasks needed for the day, he began to turn his attention to the evening meal and the conversation he, Eleanor, Semple, and West would share around the supper table.

After supper, they played chess or cards, or Eleanor read aloud to them from the books she'd brought with her. There was never a boring or dull day with her in the house, and he was especially fond of the rare moments they had alone, though they were few and far between.

She had also planned weekly entertainments for the fort, bringing the Hudson's Bay Company voyageurs and the colonists together into one community. During the evening gatherings, the children recited their lessons, performed historical skits, or participated in spelling and trivia contests. At Christmas, they had told the story of the Christ child born in Bethlehem and served sweet treats to those who attended. Twice, she had planned a dance, and the adults had braved a storm to make it to the main hall both times.

Her very presence in the fort had brightened everyone's winter and showed Arran that entertainment and fun might not be necessary for survival—but it made survival bearable, even enjoyable. The others seemed to sense it, too, though he wondered if they felt the same quickening in their pulse when she appeared, or if the very thought of her kept them awake far into the night.

He watched Eleanor walk across the fort yard and opened the door for her even before she reached the house.

Her cheeks were glowing under the hood of her coat as she looked up at him and smiled. "Good afternoon," she said.

He thought his heart might stop at the force of affection he felt for her. "How are you?"

"Cold, but good."

Ever since the night he'd come into the house and found her fast asleep at the table, he could not forget holding her in his arms. She had weighed hardly anything, and the feel of her had awakened every one of his senses. He had wanted nothing more than to hold her all night, wrapped in his embrace, covering her with his affection. The desire had been so intense, it alarmed him. If she had awakened, and allowed him to kiss her, he was afraid he wouldn't have been able to stop himself. So, he quickly placed her in her bed, covered her in a quilt, and then retreated from her room as if his life depended on it.

He had always been attracted to her and desired to hold her in his arms, but the longing to possess her, heart, body, and soul, was new and all-consuming. In moments of weakness, such as this one, when his heart felt like it might burst with longing, he was tempted to throw all caution to the wind and declare himself to her—but when he allowed himself to let his mind wander down the road, and over the years, he always came to the final scene: Eleanor's grave. It was morbid and cynical, but he could not shake the fear that staying in Assiniboia would eventually lead to her untimely death.

And the fear of him being the cause of her death, as he'd been the cause of his mother's, left him feeling bereft of heart. He saw the same emotion mirrored in West's eyes, when the minister spoke of his late wife. Arran did not want to live with the grief the other man shouldered. Even if Eleanor could not be by his side, the knowledge that she was safe and healthy, even across the ocean, would be far better than knowing she was dead.

"I told the children not to come to school tomorrow," Eleanor said as she pulled her hood off her head and stepped into the house, wholly unaware of his wayward thoughts. Snowflakes fell from her coat, and she rubbed her hands together to restore the heat. "If this storm is anything like the others, we won't be going anywhere for a day or two."

Arran took her coat and hung it on a hook, thanking the good Lord for the snowstorms that forced them to stay inside, in each other's company.

"How is Miriam?" she asked.

"Fiona is feeding her now."

"Wonderful." She went to the fire and extended her hands to the heat. She smiled at Nicolette, who looked up from kneading her dough.

"You're in a good mood," Arran said as he took a seat at the table. His work for the day was complete and he had little else to occupy his time. Truth be told, he'd been counting down the hours until she returned from the school.

"Little Cora McCoy recited her lessons perfectly today." Eleanor's brown eyes sparkled with the news. "She has studied and worked so hard. I could not be prouder."

Arran could hardly pick Cora McCoy out of a line of all the students, but he loved how much pleasure Eleanor took from her work. Her passion and dedication were contagious.

The bedroom door opened, and Fiona stepped out with the plump eight-month-old Miriam on her hip.

Upon seeing Eleanor, Miriam squealed in delight and reached toward her.

Fiona laughed and handed the baby to her rightful mother. "Nicolette tells me Miriam has been eating hominy and milk-soaked biscuits in the evening."

Eleanor nodded. "She loves them, especially when we sweeten the milk just a bit."

"She'll be ready to wean sooner than later, if you can get her to drink some of the milk from a cup." Fiona was now visibly pregnant with her next child, and would no doubt be happy to complete her work as a wet nurse. The woman had not complained once, but Arran imagined it was a great sacrifice for her and her family.

"We'll begin working on it immediately," Eleanor promised, bouncing Miriam on her hip, her eyes shining as she held the little girl close.

Fiona nodded and then took her leave.

"Why not start practicing now?" Eleanor asked Miriam, who just grinned.

Setting a blanket upon the floor, Eleanor put Miriam on her bottom and placed a few of the baby's toys nearby. There was a favorite rag doll, which she promptly put into her mouth to chew on, a wooden rattle, and two tin plates, which she loved to bang together.

Arran never tired of watching the baby grow and discover the world around her. She sat straight and grinned at him, and then wobbled, as if she might topple over. He quickly righted her, taking a seat on the ground beside her. Miriam clapped her hands and giggled, then she put her hands on the floor and popped up on her knees to crawl to Arran. Her blond hair had begun to grow, and she had one curl on the top of her head, and a few by her neck. Her blue eyes were changing, becoming as light as the sky on a crisp winter day. Arran had never met Anne West, but Eleanor had told him often that the baby favored her mother. He could only imagine that the minister's wife had been a beautiful woman, if the baby was any indication.

While Eleanor retrieved a tin cup, Miriam used Arran's legs to pull herself to her feet. She wobbled and he placed his hand behind her, to catch her if she fell.

The front door opened and Semple appeared with West and Robertson close behind him. West had been called to a nearby settlement to perform a funeral for one of the residents and Semple had left with

Robertson earlier to see to one of the settlement horses that had become lame.

West stopped at the sight of Arran and Miriam on the floor together. Despite several attempts on Eleanor's part, the minister had not grown close to his daughter. He had held her, on occasion, but had quickly given her back when the child showed any fear or discomfort from being in his arms. Arran didn't blame the baby. She hardly knew her father.

"When you have a minute," Semple said to Arran, one brow raised, "I would like to speak to you and Mr. Robertson in my office."

Arran set Miriam on her bottom and then rose from the floor. He caught Eleanor's eye, to make sure she knew he was no longer minding the baby, then he followed Semple and Robertson into his office.

Closing the door, Arran took a seat across the desk from the governor.

There was heaviness around both Semple and Robertson, and Arran braced himself for whatever news they might deliver. Over the past few months, they had had many conversations about the growing numbers at Qu'Appelle, and what they planned to do to combat the North West Company's aggression. He was certain they wanted to discuss their plans once again.

"I have received a missive from Lord Selkirk today." Governor Semple pulled the letter from inside his coat and laid it on the desk for Arran to see. "It arrived just now from a coureur de bois."

The coureurs were voyageurs who were adept at crossing great distances, at amazing speeds. In the spring, summer, and fall, they went by canoe, and in the winter, they used cariole sleds and dog teams. Arran took the paper into his hands and began to read.

"He arrived in New York this fall and made his way to Montreal before winter set in," Semple explained, though Arran could plainly read the words Selkirk had written. "He plans to leave for Assiniboia as soon as the weather permits."

"When he wrote the letter," Robertson added, "he was in the process of making an appeal to the Governor-General of Canada, Sir Gordan Drummond. He is asking to obtain men to protect him on his journey."

"The opposition from the North West Company in Montreal has been trying his patience," Semple continued. "He is meeting with difficulty from every side, including the government, because the Nor'westers hold such power and authority in eastern Canada."

"He has heard about our troubles with Duncan Cameron," Robertson said next. "And he agrees that we must rout him out of Assiniboia as soon as possible."

Just as Arran and Robertson had wanted to do last fall, before they came to Pembina.

"Perhaps, if Cameron is gone," Semple added, "we will see the last of our trouble."

"If only it was that simple." Arran read through Selkirk's words, finding them exactly as Semple and Robertson reported.

"I have made a decision." Semple clasped his hands on his desk as he regarded Arran. "Robertson and I will take two dozen voyageurs back to Assiniboia this month. We will surprise Cameron and apprehend him."

"I will then take Cameron to York Factory in Hudson Bay," Robertson told Arran. "To await a ship to bring him to trial in England."

Arran nodded, approving of the plan. "It will not pay to bring him to trial in Montreal," he agreed. "They will never convict him of his crimes there."

"He will be forced to answer to the crown in England." Semple leaned back in his chair, a gleam of victory in his eyes. "I've also decided to dismantle Fort Gibraltar."

Alarm thrummed in Arran's veins as he stared at Semple. "Dismantle the North West Company's fort? For what purpose?"

"To show them they have no right to be in this country."

Arran glanced at Robertson. From the look on Robertson's face, it was clear he did not like the plan, either.

"It is almost impossible to remove the North West Company from Rupert's Land." Arran tried to speak as plainly as he could to the governor. "They are just as powerful as the Hudson's Bay Company—and they also have the aid of the Bois-Brûlés. In their minds, this land belongs to whomever takes possession of it. They care not for the crown or the Royal Charter."

"Then they are wrong."

"It matters not. I agree we need to remove Duncan Cameron, and if we can get Cuthbert Grant, it will weaken their resolve—but it will not stop them. Only power and force will win this battle."

"I disagree." Semple crossed his arms. "Fort Gibraltar is an affront to His Majesty the King. It must be destroyed to send a strong message to all the other North West Company posts in Rupert's Land. As soon as Cameron is apprehended, we will dismantle his fort."

Frustration knotted in Arran's chest. Semple was new to Rupert's Land, and he could not possibly understand the deep-seated beliefs in the hearts and minds of its people. He understood the monarchy and the supreme power and authority of the king. But there was no law governing the Red River Valley, because there were not enough of the king's men to enforce that law. It would take an entire army to gain control of Rupert's Land. Semple would make a grave mistake in destroying their fort, just as Governor Macdonell had made when he signed the Pemmican Proclamation.

"Sir," Arran said, coming to the edge of his seat, "I must beseech you not to destroy Fort Gibraltar. It will only incense the Nor'westers and strengthen the fury of the Bois-Brûlés."

"I disagree, MacLean." Semple rose, indicating their interview was over. "Robertson and I will make plans to leave as soon as this storm clears. When the weather permits, MacLean, you will see that the settlers return to Assiniboia to start farming. That is all."

Arran stared in disbelief. Wasn't it his job to advise the governor? He had given him wise counsel, yet Semple did not even take it into account. Arran did not respond but left the governor's office with Robertson close behind. He closed the office door, and they walked across the room. When they reached the front door, Robertson stopped and faced Arran.

"You must prevent him from destroying Fort Gibraltar," Arran said quietly. "Nothing good can come from removing the Nor'wester's post."

Robertson's countenance was heavy as he nodded. "Aye. I'll do all I can to stop him."

With those final words, Robertson took his leave.

Arran watched him cross the fort yard and enter one of the cabins, his mind on the dire consequences of dismantling Fort Gibraltar.

Somehow, before the governor left, Arran would have to convince him it was a mistake.

Late afternoon sunshine warmed Eleanor's shoulders and melted the snow all around her. Mud caked the bottom of her moccasins and made walking across the fort yard almost impossible, but there was little that could dampen her spirits on such a fine spring day. March had arrived and, with it, an early thaw.

A song played in her heart as she opened the main hall's doors and entered the large room. In under an hour, the building would be brimming with her students and their families to enjoy an evening of fun. It would begin with a great feast—because the Indians had finally brought buffalo meat to the fort—and end with a spelling bee, which the children had been preparing for the past few weeks.

Eleanor took off her bonnet and set it on a hook near the door. She also removed her spencer and set it there, as well. It had been days since she'd been forced to wear her heavy Hudson's Bay coat. The weather had changed so abruptly after the last storm, the Red River was beginning to swell at an alarming rate from the melting snow.

Before she began preparing the room for the evening, she removed her moccasins and slipped on her half-boots. Though the leather moccasins were comfortable, she felt more like herself in the boots.

A figure in the fort yard caught Eleanor's attention, making her pulse tick against her wrists and bringing a smile to her face.

Arran MacLean was hard to miss among the settlers. Taller than most, and with a commanding stance, he was easy to identify. He walked toward the school with a purposeful stride, and she found herself running a hand over her hair to make sure all the pieces were in place.

With the warmer weather, the men were busy chopping trees along the riverbanks, which took him away from the house in the morning and kept him away until supper. To see him now, unexpectedly, sent butterflies fluttering in her midsection. She hadn't thought she'd see him until the others arrived.

He opened the door and caught her gaze. He smiled and tipped his hat at her. The simple gesture warmed her through. She tried desperately to quell the feeling, but it was almost impossible.

"What brings you here so early?" she asked.

He openly admired her. "Is that a new dress?"

She had put on one of her prettier dresses, though it wasn't as fine as her pink silk ball gown. A bit self-conscious, she lifted the hem of the green empire-style frock and looked down at herself. "It's not new, but I haven't worn it here."

Heat warmed his gaze. "You're a bonnie sight to behold. It makes me think I should have worn something a little nicer."

Eleanor shook her head quickly. "You look very fine."

It wasn't the words so much but the way she'd said them that made her cheeks become hot.

Arran smiled, probably more at her discomfort than her compliment.

"I thought to come early and help you prepare," he said, clearly changing the subject to spare her embarrassment.

There weren't enough tables for everyone to sit and eat, so they would need to be pushed against the edges of the room where the meal would be served. Everyone would find a place to sit on the benches or on the floor, picnic style.

"Do you mind my help?" he asked, removing his hat.

His dark hair was so curly and untamed, her fingers tingled with the urge to run through the thick strands. She placed her hands behind her back and refused to think about his hair, or any other part of his well-formed body.

"Of course not. Thank you."

He went to the table closest to him and began to push it toward the wall. She joined him and helped. Together, they made quick work of the room, leaving them more time than she anticipated before the others would arrive.

The sun had set, and the last blush of color rimmed the sky beyond the stockade. Eleanor quietly walked around the room and lit the lanterns on the walls, very conscious of Arran's gaze following her.

"You've done well," he said softly, admiration in his voice.

"With what?"

"With the school and the colonists." He walked up to her and lifted one of the chimneys from a lantern so she could light it. The scars on his hands caught her attention, as they often did, but she did not let her thoughts linger there for long. "And with Miriam," he added.

His praise was unexpected and filled her with a wealth of pleasure.

"There's no one who could have done better than you."

He stood close to her as she lit the wick of the lantern. She took her time, her hand trembling ever so slightly.

"Thank you," she said just above a whisper. She wanted to ask him if he was happy that she had come, or if he'd changed his mind about making her return to England, but neither one of the questions would move to her lips. "I've never felt such joy and purpose as I have this past winter." It was true. For the first time in her life, she had felt like she was contributing to something bigger and better than herself. "Both with Miriam and the school."

"You've also made a difference in the daily lives of the colonists. You've gained their respect and admiration, Eleanor, and eased their burdens."

She wanted to know if she'd made a difference in his life, or if she had his respect and admiration now, but a simple glance at his face told her all she needed to know. She saw it there, as plain as if he'd said it.

"Aye." He smiled. "And mine, too."

"I didn't ask."

"You dinna need to ask. I saw the question in your bonnie eyes."

Eleanor smiled, delighted that he could read her so well. "I have you to thank." She blew out the match she'd been using to light the lanterns. "If it hadn't been for you, no one would have given me a chance."

"You have no one but yourself to thank." He set the chimney back and leaned against the wall, the muscles of his arms rippling as he crossed them.

His statement wasn't entirely true, but she wouldn't debate it with him.

Instead, she looked around the room. "What else shall we do to fill the time?"

"Enjoy each other's company."

She hesitated for only a moment before asking, "Do you enjoy my company, Arran?"

A look, so deep and so powerful, came over his face, causing his entire countenance to change in an instant. "I dinna ken anyone I've ever enjoyed more than you, Eleanor."

They still stood close to one another, and she feared he could hear the heavy thump of her heart as it beat against her breastbone.

"Are you happy I came?" she asked in a whisper.

He slowly took her hand in his, forcing her to meet his gaze. The look she saw there was bittersweet. "I am happy you came, but a part of me wishes you hadna."

"Why?"

"Because it will break my heart to say goodbye to you again."

"Arran, I don't want to leave. I've found my place here, among the colonists. This is where I belong."

"You should be back in England, with your own people, where it is safer and life is easier."

"I have no people." Her voice wobbled, but she would not cry. "My father is in prison, for life. This is now my home."

"And what of your maither?"

She had never told him about her mother, had never spoken about her to anyone. It had hurt too much.

"She lives in France."

"Can you not go to her?"

What was the harm in sharing her past? She was not in England anymore, and after her father's scandal, she couldn't ruin her reputation more than it had been. Besides, she could trust Arran with the truth. "My mother left my father for a man named Jean-Paul LeBlanc. He was the father of her second child, my half-brother, Marius. She left when I was nine and Marius was three."

Arran didn't speak, but he shook his head, as if he could deny the truth for her.

"She chose Jean-Paul and Marius over me." Even though it had been fourteen years, and she had told herself it no longer hurt, it felt as if the sting of rejection had happened only yesterday. "My father told me they were living in France, but she never wrote. Not once. After she walked away, she forgot about me, as if I had never existed. I don't even know if she's still alive."

Arran moved closer to her and took her other hand in his. "I'm sorry, lass." He ran his thumbs over the tops of her hands. The feather-soft touch grounded her in the present, pulling her from the abyss of the distant pass. But it was the look of fire in his eyes that captured her. "If I could heal the wounds inflicted by those who hurt you, I would. I'd do anything to keep you safe and protected."

She looked down at her hands, remembering all the times he'd held them in the gardens at St. Mary's Isle. His touch had a way of igniting a sense of longing that burned deep within her heart. It had been there, from the moment their hands had brushed accidentally in the gardens, until now, when she yearned to be loved by him more than anything.

The scars on his hands were so vivid, she couldn't help whispering, "If I could heal the wounds in your past, I would do so in a heartbeat." She turned her hands so their palms were facing each other. It was her turn to run her thumbs over the tops of his scars. "What about you?" she asked. "Where are your parents?"

His muscles tensed, and for a moment, she thought he might pull away, but he allowed her to continue tracing his scars with her thumbs.

Arran had never spoken of his past to anyone. He saw how people looked at his hands and had never wanted to tell anyone what had happened, for fear they would think he was just as ugly on the inside as he was on the outside.

But Eleanor was different. She had a way of seeing past the scars, the ugliness, the discomforts, and the hardships to find the best in everyone and everything. He wanted her to see past the scars, to reassure him that he was more than his past mistakes.

The soft and gentle touch of her hands was the last straw to break his resolve.

"When I was a lad," he said slowly, uncertain where to begin, "we left Inverness and moved to Nova Scotia. My grandda had been killed in the battle at Culloden and there was nothing left for us in Scotland. On Prince Edward Island, my da was a farmer, though he struggled to put food on the table. I was the oldest of my three brothers and a lot of the responsibilities were on my shoulders. My maither was often sick, lying in bed for days at a time. We couldna send for the doctor, because we had no money to pay him."

He wasn't sure if she realized it, but she had moved closer to him. She looked up at him, affection in her warm brown eyes. It was enough to undo him. If he wasn't in the middle of telling her the hardest thing he'd ever had to share, he was certain he would have pulled her into his arms and kissed her until she was breathless.

Instead, he focused on the story. "When I was fourteen, my da went to town and left me in charge, making me promise to watch after everything. We had been planting for days and I was tired. He gave me a list of chores to complete, but I went to the creek to fish instead. I must have fallen asleep, because when I woke up—" He paused, trying not to let his voice quaver with the strength of emotions he felt at the memory. "There was a great haze of smoke in the distance. By the time I made it back to the farm, the house was engulfed in flames."

Eleanor's lips parted in shock.

"My brothers were outside, but they said Ma was still in her bed." He swallowed, and for a second, he felt like a scared young man again. "I ran into the house, but the smoke was so strong, I couldna breathe or see. I remembered the promise I made to my da, but I couldna get to my maither. I ran outside and dinna ken what to do. I was so frightened and ill-prepared to deal with the magnitude of the problem. I went to the back of the house to break open her window and pull her out. There was nothing nearby—" He paused and held up his hands. The scars were deep and puckered, hurting now at the memory. "So I did the only thing I could and used my fists."

"Arran." Tears glistened in her eyes, and she reached out to place her hands on his forearms.

"I tried to get to her," he continued, a bit faster now. Finally talking about his past made him want to share it all. "The shattered glass tore at my hands and arms, but the smoke was so thick, and the rafters of the house were already falling in. It was too hard. I started to fear I would die, too—so I-I gave up." He looked away from Eleanor, the emotions so strong, he was afraid he couldn't tell her the rest. But it was the final part that he had carried with him every day of his life. "When my maither needed me most, I failed her."

"You were only a boy. You couldn't have done anything more."

She was wrong. He had made a promise to his da that he would protect her, no matter the cost. But when the cost was too high, he had failed. "I could have kept trying to get her out, but I gave up. I failed both her and my da."

Eleanor put her hand on the side of his face. It was cool and tender and filled with gentle compassion. "The fire was not your fault. It couldn't have been helped. If you had kept trying, you might have been killed, as well."

Arran placed his hand over hers. He didn't know if what she said was true, but there had been a part of him, in the early days, that had wanted to die with his ma. The guilt had been so intense, he thought he might. "Two days later, I ran away and joined the North West Company as a clerk and that's when I came to the Red River Valley." He lowered her hand away from his face, afraid that if she continued to caress his skin, he would lose all rational thought. She undid his resolve in ways nothing else could. He couldn't risk tearing down the wall he had so carefully built where she was concerned. It was easier to keep her at a safe distance.

"Does your father know where you are?" she asked.

"Aye. Three years later, I returned to face him and my brothers." He shook his head. "I thought they would be as devastated and unhappy as

I had been, but my da had already remarried and my brothers called the new woman ma." It had felt like his mother had died all over again. "I havena gone back."

"It seems you and I are both orphans, after a fashion."

"So we are."

"Now you know why I cannot return to England. There is nothing left for me, just as there is nothing left for you in Nova Scotia." She whispered her next plea. "I want to stay here . . . with you."

His heart felt as if it had been twisted in his chest. Her words were the words he had longed to hear almost four years ago, but they had come too late. Arran tilted his head, his brows coming together in pain. He wanted her to know how much he loved her—had always loved her—and how much he wished she could stay. But he was terrified that he would fail her, as he had his mother. It would destroy him to lose Eleanor the same way.

He gently entwined his fingers through hers and brought her hands up to kiss the delicate skin on the back. "Lass"—his voice was low and hoarse—"I canna let you stay, as much as I long for you."

"Arran—"

"I care for you too much to watch you suffer."

"But I've been here all winter, and the hardships have not broken me."

"You dinna ken what's coming."

"Neither do you."

"You're wrong. Last spring, I watched as everyone I cared about was forced to flee for their lives, and I thanked God you were not here, suffering with them." She had never been far from his thoughts, then or now. "I watched the homes we'd worked to build, and the crops we'd planted, burned and trampled before my very eyes." He pressed her palms to his chest, hoping she could feel the beating of his heart, to know it was pounding for her. "It will be much worse this spring. There are many more Bois-Brûlés gathering at Qu'Appelle, and this time, I fear they will not stop until they've destroyed the entire settlement. They will try to push out the colonists, using whatever means possible."

"But Lord Selkirk is on his way."

"Aye, but I dinna ken when he'll get here, nor how he'll stop the attack. If the rumors are true, we will be fighting for our lives."

"You sound as if you're giving up even before the battle has started."

Arran shook his head, wishing she understood—but how could she?

"The war began two years ago when Macdonell signed the Pemmican Proclamation, and each year, we've endured the battles that have been waged against our colony. Each time, we rally, but it takes a great toll on our people and resources. I believe we will win, but there will be a price to pay, and I don't want it to be your life. You need to leave before that happens." Not only for her sake, but for the sake of his better judgment. He could not protect the rest of the colony if he knew she was in danger. He would sacrifice everything and everyone else for her. It wouldn't be fair to the others.

Her eyes pleaded with him. "What if I wait until the trouble has died down, and then come back?"

Was she telling him she wanted to be with him, no matter the cost? He longed to ask her but knew it wouldn't change his decision. A sad smile tilted his lips, and he ran his thumb over the curve of her cheek, amazed at how smooth and silky it felt against his work-worn hands. "I wish I could tell you it will die down, but I canna. The fighting could last for years. I couldna ask you to waste the best years of your life waiting." She was young and beautiful, and she deserved to be with a man who could give her the life she deserved. Someone who could keep her safe and protected and offer her comfort and stability. "You should be living, not waiting."

She leaned into his hand. "Then come back to England with me."

For a heartbeat, he was tempted to say yes. There was nothing he wanted more than to leave all his troubles and responsibilities behind, but wasn't that the very thing that had led to his mother's death? Arran could never turn his back on Assiniboia and all the people who relied upon him, just for his own selfish desires. "England is not my home, nor is Scotland," he said, looking deep into her eyes. "This is my home, and I promised Lord Selkirk I would fight until I dinna have a breath left in me. I know this land and the people who live here, so I have a unique insight into ensuring this colony survives. I have made a promise to the colonists, no matter how much I long to be with you, I canna leave them to fend for themselves. They don't belong here anymore than you or me, and it's just as dangerous for them, but my heart is not tied up in their welfare—not like it is with you, and now Miriam. I could never respect myself if I left them defenseless, or if I encouraged you to stay and face the difficulties that lie ahead."

Something akin to anger sparked in her eyes. "You will not return to England with me—nor will you allow me to stay and fight with you." She pulled back from his touch. "What if I choose not to leave?"

Fear gripped his heart at the thought. "I canna force you to leave—but Eleanor"—his voice was desperate—"I beg you to go. I ken the horrors of warfare. Bullets and cannon fire dinna care who you are."

She closed her eyes, resignation in the lines of her mouth. "I would be a fool not to believe you or take your advice to heart." She opened her eyes again, and there was a longing there he could not deny. "I just wish there was another way."

So did he. With all his heart.

Chapter Ten

JUNE 14, 1816

The last of the snow had melted and the path to Fort Douglas was dry and solid once again. Arran sat upon Tiberius as the settlers floated in their canoes down the swollen Red River toward Assiniboia. A spring flood had kept them from returning earlier and he was anxious to get back to their homes to plant their late crops. His nerves were taut, and he was on constant alert. He scanned the prairie continually, looking for signs of the Bois-Brûlés. Bright sunshine and a warm, southwesterly breeze should have made his heart light with hope, but he knew exactly what he would face when they returned to the settlement.

More alarming news had reached Arran days before they left Pembina. Several of the company men from Fort Douglas, acting on Governor Semple's orders, had traveled three hundred miles to the Hudson's Bay Company fort at Qu'Appelle, by way of the Assiniboia River, to retrieve six hundred bags of pemmican to feed the settlers. On their way back, they were attacked by an armed force of forty-nine Nor'westers, under the leadership of Cuthbert Grant. After five days, the Hudson's Bay Company men were released and returned to Fort Douglas, without the much-needed pemmican, and with the dire news that a great number of mixed-race people had gathered at the North West Company post in Qu'Appelle, some coming from great distances.

Even worse, Brandon House, one of the Hudson's Bay Company forts, positioned between Qu'Appelle and Assiniboia, had been overtaken by Cuthbert Grant and twenty-five of his men. They had stripped the post of its provisions and taken the company men captive.

The news was a couple weeks old. Arran could only imagine what had taken place in the days and weeks since then. He hated to think what they might have to deal with when they returned to Assiniboia. They had no choice but to go back and keep fighting for their colony.

Paired with the discouraging news was the impending pain of sending Eleanor and Miriam away. He wanted to put off the inevitable and keep them here for as long as possible yet, at the same time, he wished they were gone already. They must be out of the territory before the fighting began.

Eleanor sat in one of the lead canoes, Reverend West beside her. She held Miriam, who was now ten months old and was much harder to keep occupied on the return trip to the colony. Thankfully, the journey took less than half the time since they were going downriver.

Ever since the night of the buffalo feast, Arran and Eleanor had been quiet and distant from one another. He had been cordial, but cold, knowing he had to protect his heart if he was going to survive losing her again. If he continued to find ways to be near her, or to touch her, he would drive himself mad with longing. Instead, he had turned his attention to his work and had given it every ounce of energy he possessed.

With a sigh, Arran focused on the horizon, trying to get a glimpse of Assiniboia. They would have to pass Fort Gibraltar before reaching home, but he didn't fear any trouble from there. Duncan Cameron had been apprehended in April and would not be a threat. Colin Robertson had taken Duncan to York Factory, by way of Lake Winnipeg, and would long be gone from the colony.

As they wound around one of the many bends in the river, Arran reined in Tiberius, his heart thudding at the sight before him.

Duncan's Fort Gibraltar no longer stood on the banks of the Red River. Everything from the stockade to the warehouse, to the jaunty red trim on the trading post's porch, was gone. It was as if the fort had never existed.

"No." Arran shook his head, dread mounting in his gut. He touched Tiberius's side with his heels and galloped toward the fort's site, but the closer he came, the more upset he grew. There was no telling how far the Nor'westers would go until they felt they had been repaid for the loss of Fort Gibraltar.

Arran pushed his heels into Tiberius again and pressed on to Fort Douglas, leaving the colonists under the protection of the voyageurs who were paddling. What if the Nor'westers had already overtaken Fort Douglas? It would have been an ideal time to attack while the colonists were gone.

As Point Douglas came within sight, Arran's anxiety began to fade. Not only was the fort still standing, but it had been enlarged. The stockade now extended twice as far into the prairie—and several new buildings stood within it—including one with bright red trim.

Arran clenched his hands into fists around Tiberius's reins and pushed the horse hard until they reached the gates of the fort. Guards stood at several lookouts, and they waved to Arran as he rode into the stockade.

"MacLean!" James McIntosh stepped out of the company trading post and waved, a grin on his face after months of being separated.

Pulling Tiberius to a halt, Arran jumped off the horse and took the reins, leading him toward James. He could not return his friend's smile as he walked. "What happened to Fort Gibraltar?"

Exhaustion creased the lines around James's eyes. "The moment Robertson left with Duncan, Semple ordered thirty men to dismantle Fort Gibraltar. It took them a week. They made a raft of the stockade and floated the rest of the material downriver to Fort Douglas. When it arrived here, they spent several more weeks adding on to the stockade and constructing new buildings."

"Why?" Arran shook his head. "What was Semple thinking?"

James's jaw tightened and he nodded toward the governor's house, which had a new addition protruding to the west. "He's in his new office."

Commotion in the fort told Arran the colonists had started to arrive at Point Douglas. A few dozen men went out to meet the returning citizens of Assiniboia. But Arran had other plans.

"I'll see that Tiberius is taken care of," James said, taking the horse's reins.

Arran nodded his thanks and then marched toward Semple's new office. He knocked lightly before the governor called for him to enter.

"Ah, MacLean, you've arrived." Semple smiled, as if all was well in his little world. "I hope the trip downriver was without incident."

"Why did you dismantle Fort Gibraltar? You ken the Nor'westers will bring retribution."

Semple's smile faded and he took a letter off a pile on his desk. He held it out for Arran. "Read for yourself."

Arran wasn't prepared for more bad news, but it wouldn't do to be ignorant. He took the letter and lowered himself to a chair.

"There's a report that the North West Company is sending an army of voyageurs to Assiniboia from Fort William." Governor Semple leaned back in his chair. "They intended to use Fort Gibraltar as a base to attack our colony, so I was forced to dismantle their fort."

"Do you ken how angry they'll be when they arrive? Fort Gibraltar was one of their wealthiest posts."

"Without a fort, how will they attack us, I ask?" Semple smiled, clearly pleased with himself. "It was a preemptive strike, and I have won the battle."

Arran rubbed his temples, a headache forming at an alarming speed. "What is being done to guard Fort Douglas?"

"As you can see, I have men keeping watch around the clock. Everyone is on full alert. Should our enemy approach, we have our six fieldpieces poised and ready to defend." He waved his hand as if to push the topic away. "But I do not believe it will come to that."

The man was ignorant, which gave him false courage. Arran had witnessed the same in Macdonell.

"It will come to a fight." Arran was convinced there was no way to avoid a conflict. "With men approaching from the west and the east, we will be completely outnumbered, not to mention, there will be women and children within the fort to protect." How would he get Eleanor and Miriam out of the colony now? There might not be enough time.

"This fort is the property of the Hudson's Bay Company, which is protected under the Royal Charter of 1670. I am the governor in charge of all their holdings. They will not dare to attack His Majesty's loyal servants, nor come against my authority."

"They will do anything and everything they can. They do not consider themselves under any law."

"Then we will show them differently."

"How?"

"We are all men, are we not? Rational discourse will be my tactic, if necessary."

Arran stared in disbelief. It was clear he would not convince Semple. The man would have to meet his enemy before he fully understood. And then it would be too late.

"The colonists are arriving." Arran stood. "Several had planned to return to their homes in Colony Gardens, but it will not be safe to leave the fort. I will try to convince them to settle within the stockade."

"I don't think that will be necessary." Semple took the letter Arran had been reading, as if the whole matter were settled. "By the way, I plan to take leave of the fort within the next four or five days and you will be in charge once again."

Arran stared at the governor. "You're leaving?"

"I have business at York Factory in Hudson Bay. I will try to return by winter."

Shock was not a strong enough word for how Arran felt at hearing the news. "You plan to leave the colony now?"

"Not now, but soon. I would like to be gone by mid-June." He rearranged several papers on his desk, seemingly unaware of how preposterous his plans were. He looked up at Arran, expectation on his face. "Was there something else you needed, Mr. MacLean?"

Arran could only shake his head. How could the governor leave now, when they needed him more than ever before?

James stood outside the governor's office waiting for Arran.

"It isna good?" James asked as soon as Arran stepped out.

"No." Arran shook his head. "Cuthbert Grant is approaching with an unknown number of men from the west and there's an army of at least a hundred approaching from Fort William in the east."

James lifted his eyebrows.

"And the governor plans to leave the fort and travel to Hudson Bay this week, and doesn't plan to return until just before winter."

"What?" James stared in disbelief. "You've got to be jesting with me."

"I wish I was. Either he doesna ken the seriousness of the situation, or he's running away because he does." Though Arran suspected the former to be true. With Semple gone, the responsibility of the colony would fall on Arran's shoulders. It was a duty he would undertake with pride, but he would not have the same authority or power as Semple. It would put everyone in the colony at more risk. And with all that Semple had done to anger the North West Company, it meant war.

The eastern gates were opened, and the colonists began to enter. With the voyageurs, company men, and settlers, there were now over two hundred men, women, and children at Fort Douglas. A meager number compared to the hundreds who would be descending upon them soon.

Eleanor walked up the steep banks of the river to the fort, Miriam in her arms. The baby had been weaned and was growing fast. Her bright blue eyes took in the unfamiliar fort, but when she caught a glance of Arran, she squealed and clapped her hands, causing Eleanor to turn his way.

James remained by Arran's side as Eleanor walked toward them. West was close behind her, taking in the changes at Fort Douglas.

"Good day, Mr. McIntosh," Eleanor said to James.

"Good day, Miss Brooke. 'Tis good to have you back at Fort Douglas."

Eleanor smiled politely at James, but then looked at Arran, concern in her eyes. "Is it as bad as I fear?"

He did not want her to worry, but it was inevitable that she would hear the reports. "Aye. And worse."

She held Miriam close as she surveyed their surroundings.

More than anything, Arran wanted to see Eleanor and Miriam safely removed from Assiniboia. Maybe now, with Semple's departure, they could travel with him.

Hope filled his heart, but he knew he would need to convince Eleanor first. He would have to speak to her, and the sooner the better.

"Mr. MacLean." Archie Currie, one of the company men who had held Fort Douglas with Arran a year ago, appeared at Arran's elbow. "Governor Semple has asked that you oversee the armaments."

"Aye." Arran answered Archie and then turned back to Eleanor. "I need to speak with you, but it will have to wait."

Eleanor nodded, her face as serious as he'd ever seen it.

There was no telling how much time they had until the battle would begin. He only hoped it would not start until after Eleanor and Miriam were gone.

Arran stood in the southwestern lookout tower, scanning the vast prairie one last time before he would take his leave. A brilliant full moon sat low in the night sky, casting elongated shadows across the land, making everything look larger than life. In the distance, cows and horses grazed, their movements drawing Arran's wary eye.

"If you have no more need of me," Arran said to James, who stood beside him in the tower, "I will try to get some sleep." There was no telling what the morning would bring, and he would need all the rest he could get.

He also wanted to speak to Eleanor and hoped she had not gone to bed already.

"I thought you would return from Pembina a happier man." James's words made Arran pause on his way to the ladder.

"Happier?" Arran couldn't hide the derision from his voice.

James lifted his eyebrows and nodded down to the governor's house at the far end of the stockade. "I thought you might utilize the minister and be married to the lass by now."

Arran wasn't in the mood to talk about Eleanor.

"What went wrong?" James continued to press.

A movement caught his eye, and Arran crossed the small space again to stand on the opposite side. It was simply an owl, flying low, his wings spread wide. The creature was majestic in flight, but the wonder of seeing the bird was nothing compared to the pain in Arran's heart. He was not prone to share his feelings easily, but James was a good friend, and he'd been holding them in for a long time. "She shouldna come." Frustration tinted Arran's words. "This is no place for her. I'm going to suggest she leave with Semple." If it wasn't too late. "I want her to be as far away from Assiniboia as possible when the fighting begins."

"Does she want to leave?"

Arran couldn't meet his friend's gaze. "Nay." But it didn't matter.

"Do you want her to leave?"

"Are you daft? I just told you I did."

James shook his head. "You told me she should not have come, and that this is no place for her. You dinna tell me if you want her to leave."

A gentle breeze blew across the plains and swirled around the lookout tower. The scent of spring was in the air, of fresh starts and new beginnings. But for Arran, it was a reminder that his time with Eleanor had to come to an end.

"Of course I want her to stay." There. He had finally admitted the truth, but it didn't change the reality of the situation.

"Do you love her?"

Arran ached with longing for Eleanor. He couldn't stop thinking about her. When she was near, he wanted nothing more than to hold her. When she was away, he counted the minutes until he could be with her again. His first thoughts every morning, and his last thoughts every night, were about Eleanor. His love for her was stronger and more powerful than it had ever been.

"Aye. I love her." It was all Arran could say, though it didn't begin to capture how he felt.

The rushing of the river and the who-who of the owl were the only sounds to fill the silence between them.

"Then why would you let her go, lad?" James finally asked.

"Because I love her too much to see her suffer."

"We all suffer."

"Aye. But I canna abide the idea that she would suffer because I canna protect her or save her." When his mother needed him most, he had failed. His inability to pull her from the fire had almost destroyed him. If Eleanor stayed, and her survival depended on Arran, he was afraid he would fail her, too. He could never live with himself if he lost Eleanor because of his own weakness.

"So you'd rather force her to leave and face the world alone?"

"I will send her with Semple."

"Aye, only as far as Hudson Bay. What about the rest of the way? A sea voyage is no place for a single lady."

It was true. The ships coming from England were often full of passengers, both male and female, who could be of aid and protection to Eleanor. But ships traveling from Hudson Bay to England were filled with hardened sailors who possessed little to no morality.

"And what of the bairn?" James asked. "Who will care for the wee one when Eleanor is gone?"

"This fort is no place for the bairn, either." Arran was not Miriam's father, but if it was up to him, the baby would return to England with Eleanor. He'd long carried the weight of the suffering women and children in the colony, knowing it was no place for them, either, but they had husbands and fathers to care for them. And he didn't have a personal connection to them. His love for Eleanor and Miriam made him even more mindful of the dangers that would befall the colony when the battle started.

James sighed and put his hand on Arran's shoulder. "I dinna envy you. I can see that you love her, and that she loves you."

Arran met his friend's gaze. "Do you think so?"

A slow smile tilted the weathered face of James McIntosh. "I dinna ken much, but I ken the look of a woman in love. She only has eyes for you, Arran MacLean. If you hadna noticed that she loves you, you're the daft one."

James's words stayed with Arran while he climbed down the ladder and walked across the fort yard to the governor's house. A light burned in the upstairs window, telling Arran that West was still awake. He often studied late into the night, when the house had quieted. The habit had not bothered Arran while they had shared the attic at Fort Daer. A little light didn't bother him while he tried to sleep, especially if it meant the fort's minister was preparing his sermon.

Arran pushed open the door and stepped into the dark common room.

A part of him was disappointed that Eleanor had gone to bed, but after speaking to James, a new idea had taken root, and it would be best to talk to her in the morning. He needed to speak to someone else first.

After lowering the crossbar in place, he went to the stairs in the corner and walked quietly up the steps. The governor's house in Assiniboia was much larger than the one in Pembina, offering Arran his own room. Semple was already snoring in his room at the end of the hall, and a light shone from the crack under West's door.

Arran stood for a long time at the top of the stairs, questioning his plan. He had prayed, every day, for wisdom where Eleanor was concerned. But it wasn't until tonight that he knew what must be done.

The truth of it had been staring him in the face for months.

Lifting his hand, and saying another prayer for guidance and strength, Arran knocked lightly on West's door. His heart pounded like mad, and he had to force himself to stand firm.

There was a bit of paper shuffling, the sound of a chair's legs scraping the floor, and then footsteps across the room. West finally opened the door, pulling his coat over his shirtsleeves, a frown on his face.

"Is everything all right?" he asked Arran. "Is the fort under attack?"

"Nay." The fort was not under attack and things were not all right. "May I speak to you?"

"Of course." West opened his door wider and allowed Arran to step into his room.

The space was much like Arran's, with a single bed, a desk, and a chair. Hooks on the wall held West's change of clothing.

"Would you like to take a seat?" West asked.

Arran shook his head. He needed to stand for this conversation. "Within weeks, the fort will be under attack." He didn't know how else to start. "An army of North West Company men is on their way from Fort William and a band of Bois-Brûlés are on their way from Qu'Appelle. I dinna ken when they will arrive, but it will be soon."

West slowly removed the spectacles from his nose and set them down slowly onto his desk. "How bad do you think it will be?"

The truth settled deep in Arran's gut. "There will be bloodshed, I'm certain." The mounting tension coupled with Duncan Cameron's arrest and the destruction of Fort Gibraltar almost guaranteed it. "No one will be safe inside Fort Douglas."

"And what of reinforcements?"

"We await Lord Selkirk's arrival, though I dinna ken what kind of support we can expect from him. The additional voyageurs in the fort are the only ones Semple could muster."

West paced to the window and looked out into the dark fort yard, his countenance heavy. "What hope do we have?"

"I have lived through two attacks on Fort Douglas." Arran spoke with a heavy voice. "And each time, the settlers were driven away by force. The violence has only increased, and I fear the Nor'westers and Bois-Brûlés will not be as lenient as they have been in the past. The only hope we have is to send those away from the fort who are most vulnerable, while we still can."

West turned back to look at Arran. "Miriam?"

"And Eleanor. This will be no place for either of them when the fighting begins."

"What do you propose?"

Sweat began to gather under Arran's coat. His heart beat so hard, he had to take a moment to breathe and remind himself this was the best choice. "I would like you to take Eleanor and Miriam away from the colony."

"To where?"

"England."

West stared at Arran. "My work is here."

"If Eleanor and Miriam do not leave soon, I fear they will not be able to leave at all. Governor Semple is traveling to Hudson Bay in four or five days. He will take several voyageurs with him on the journey. It will be the best time for you to leave. A ship will return to England in August. You should be on it."

A gust of wind rattled the windows as West slowly lowered himself to his seat. "Losing Anne was the hardest thing I've ever experienced. Since her death, I've struggled with whether I should keep Miriam here. The settlement lacks so many of the things I had hoped to give her as she grows."

"You'll take them to England, then?" Arran held his breath, hoping West was a man of common sense.

"It was proper for Eleanor to travel to North America with my wife and me. It would not be proper for us to travel back alone. Her reputation would be ruined, as well as my good name as a minister."

Arran was well-aware of what could happen if they returned to England alone—and what they would need to do to return home without ruining their reputation. It was the part of his plan that hurt the most. Eleanor and West would need to marry.

He hated to be the one to put the idea in West's head, though he would be surprised if West hadn't thought about it already. Arran had watched the minister over the past few months. His eyes had often strayed to Eleanor, though he hid his interest well. Arran wasn't sure if West's attention was purely for Miriam's sake, or if the man was attracted to Eleanor. No doubt, the loss of his wife had stayed heavy on his mind, and he would be fighting guilt if he had been drawn to Lady Brooke.

"There is a way to avoid ruin," Arran said, choking on the words. "You could marry her."

William West snapped his head up and stared intently at Arran. "I was under the impression that you and her . . . that the two of you had an understanding."

It was Arran's turn to stare at West. "What gave you that idea?"

"I have eyes. I've seen you together. I—" He swallowed and looked down at his hands. "I have kept my distance, because I thought you and Eleanor were in love."

Arran briefly closed his eyes. So, this was why West had not declared himself to her.

"Do you love her?" West asked.

It was the second time Arran had been asked that question this evening—yet William West was not his friend or confidant. He was the man who could do what Arran could not. He could marry Eleanor and take her away from Assiniboia. Arran did not feel obligated to tell him the whole truth.

"I care for Eleanor and Miriam and do not want to see them suffer." It was true, if only partly so. "But Eleanor and I dinna have an understanding between us."

"She's free?" The hope in West's voice turned Arran's stomach sour.

Arran had to force himself to answer. "Aye. She is free to marry anyone she chooses."

"I could not ask for a better mother for Miriam," West said, almost to himself. "Or a better helpmeet to serve the Lord."

Arran didn't want to hear any more. He needed an answer so he could leave. "You'll ask her?"

West nodded, slowly at first, and then with more confidence. "I believe I will."

The air left Arran's lungs as he watched West's countenance lighten. His eyes took on a shine and he sat up straighter in his chair.

"Good night," Arran said without a backward glance, needing to escape.

"Good night. And thank you."

Arran closed West's door and stood in the hall to catch his breath. His heart ached and for the first time in his adult life, tears stung the backs of his eyes. He pressed his hands to his eyelids, taking several deep breaths, and felt the scars lacing his fists.

He would have done anything to protect his mother, no matter how much it hurt, or what he had to sacrifice. It was a gift from God that He had allowed Arran the time to offer Eleanor the protection she needed.

But why did doing the right thing have to hurt so much?

Chapter Eleven

It was a strange experience to sit in the sunshine at Fort Douglas, on a wooden bench, while guards stood in the lookout towers and patrolled the stockade. William preached with passion and conviction, but even his stirring words could not prevent Eleanor from thinking about the advancing trouble. She took a deep breath, filling her lungs with the fragrance of warm earth and budding plants, in hopes of quelling the anxiety.

William had requested the Sunday service be held out of doors after the long and tiring winter. Eleanor was thankful for the opportunity to bask in the sunlight, though it was a struggle to get Miriam to keep her bonnet over her fair curls. The baby was spirited and full of curiosity, and it took all of Eleanor's patience and energy to keep her safe. She pulled herself up to standing on a regular basis and Eleanor was quite sure she would be walking before her first birthday.

"Just as Christ was buried for three days, and then rose again to new life," William said, "so too do we rise to new life when we confess our sins and ask for forgiveness. The Bible is filled with stories of rebirth and new beginnings. We are constantly reminded to die to our old selves and pick up our cross to follow Christ."

Arran stood on the edge of the group, his musket on his shoulder, his eyes roaming the stockade, while coming back to rest on William from time to time. Eleanor had an unhindered view of Arran and could look upon him without turning her head or drawing attention.

She marveled at how much he had changed—but then chided herself, realizing he hadn't changed at all. She had simply come to know him better, altering some of her preconceived notions and opinions. In doing so, he had grown more attractive in her eyes. He had stolen her heart at St. Mary's Isle, but it was in the Red River Valley where she had given it to him freely. He held it now, no matter how much he tried to push her away. She knew he was doing it because he loved her, too, and it only made her long for him more.

Arran's gaze landed on hers and she did not feel embarrassed or shy away from the intensity in his eyes.

"Let us bow our heads in prayer," William said, drawing Eleanor's attention back to the minister.

She bowed her head, but her mind wandered as William prayed. Miriam squirmed in her arms, pulling the bonnet on her head. Eleanor patiently removed her chubby little hands from the strings and bounced the child on her legs to keep her occupied for a few moments longer.

"Amen," William said when he was done.

The congregation, numbering over a hundred, rose from their benches, filling the air with murmured conversations. Nicolette did not speak to anyone but quietly walked toward the governor's house, where she would prepare lunch. Eleanor should join her, but she hated to leave the sunshine, and she wanted Miriam to use as much energy outdoors before taking her back into the confines of the house.

Setting the baby on her feet, Miriam held herself up using the bench and walked along it, making her soft baby sounds in preparation for words.

"She will be walking soon." William approached, his Bible clasped in his hands. He wore his long, black robe and white cravat. He made a handsome minister, with his kind blue eyes and confident shoulders.

Eleanor smiled and nodded, turning her gaze back to Miriam. "She favors Anne more and more."

William took a seat on the bench in front of Eleanor, though he faced her and his daughter. The others had begun to disperse, returning to their tents within the large stockade, or, if they had ignored Arran's wishes, to their homes in Colony Gardens.

For a moment, Arran remained where he was standing, his gaze on Eleanor and William. The expression on his face was unreadable as he caught Eleanor's eye. But then he turned and walked to the opposite end of the fort and disappeared around the main hall.

"It pleases me that she looks like Anne," William said. "I had thought the reminder of her would be too difficult to bear, but I'm beginning to think it will offer me comfort as she ages."

Warmth filled Eleanor's chest at his words. "That makes me very happy."

"Does it?" William studied Eleanor. "I like making you happy."

She wasn't sure how to respond, so she simply smiled.

They continued to watch Miriam waddle around the bench, smacking the top as she went.

"I've come to a decision." William's voice was tentative, as if he was taking his time with his words. "I believe it will be best for Miriam to return to England."

Eleanor stared at William, her heart pumping wildly. "You're going to send her away?"

How would she live without Miriam? The baby had been with her every day of her life. Eleanor could not have loved her more if she had been her own flesh and blood. She had not even allowed herself to think about being separated.

William watched Eleanor carefully, concern and compassion in his gaze. "I have prayed about my decision and have decided to take her there myself when Governor Semple leaves in the coming days. I never had intentions of staying in Assiniboia permanently. When I felt God calling me away, I planned to go. And now the time has come."

Tears began to form in Eleanor's eyes and she could not stop them from falling. Embarrassed, she turned from William and wiped them away with her gloved fingers.

William reached inside his robes and removed a white handkerchief, which he gently extended to Eleanor. His voice was soft as he spoke. "I'm sorry to share this so unexpectedly. I didn't know how to tell you."

She tried to pull her emotions together as she nodded. "Where will you go in England?"

"There are many villages in need of a vicar. I am hoping for a quiet little hamlet where I can raise Miriam in safety."

Eleanor used the handkerchief to dab at the tears on her cheeks. She could almost see Miriam in a little country village, growing more and more beautiful through the years. If her emerging personality was any indication, she would be a strong, vibrant, and passionate young woman. The thought of not seeing her ever again was too much for Eleanor to bear and the tears began to fall again.

"Eleanor." William moved from the bench he was on and came to sit beside her. He did not sit too close, but he did turn to face her. His eyes were as blue as the sky overhead, and full of emotions she couldn't begin to identify. "I do not wish to return to England alone, or to raise Miriam on my own. She needs a mother and—" He swallowed. "I desire a wife."

The fort began to fade around her as she comprehended his intentions and her stomach filled with nerves.

"I have grown to care for you very much," he said, a smile in his eyes. "And I know Miriam loves you as if you were her mother. You would honor both of us if you would become my wife and return to England by our sides. I know I do not deserve you, and I cannot pretend that you care for me the way I care for you, but I would hope that in time we might grow to love one another very much."

Eleanor didn't know what to say or how to respond. His declaration was such a surprise, she hadn't prepared herself to answer him. "I—"

Miriam took a giant step away from the bench and tumbled to the dirt. Her cries filled the air around them and Eleanor leapt to her feet to pull the little girl into her arms. Dirt smudged Miriam's chin, and a small scratch produced a spot of blood.

William also rose and came to Eleanor's side. He gently took the handkerchief from Eleanor's hand and used it to carefully remove the dirt and blood from Miriam's chin.

The baby cried and nuzzled her face into Eleanor's shoulder. Eleanor bounced her in her arms and patted her back, whispering soothing words.

Eventually, Miriam stopped crying, but she kept her cheek on Eleanor's shoulder, her eyes drooping with fatigue.

"She'll need to have her lunch and then go down for her afternoon nap," Eleanor told William.

"Perhaps we can speak later?" he asked her. "I had the luxury of time to think and pray before I spoke to you. I know you will need the same."

She nodded.

"Governor Semple will be leaving soon," William warned. "I do not wish to rush you, but I will need an answer within a day or two. If you agree to marry me, it will have to be done at York Factory, where there is another minister."

There were so many emotions swirling in Eleanor's heart, she didn't know where to set her thoughts. All she could do was offer William a wobbly smile.

They started back toward the governor's house, but she couldn't stop herself from glancing at the lookout tower where Arran had been spending most of his time. He was there now, facing the prairie, his back straight and his chin high.

If he truly thought it was best for her to leave the colony, she would have no other recourse than to marry William. The minister was offering her a good life, and more importantly, she could raise Miriam as her own.

If it had not been for Arran, she would have said yes to William already. Being his wife would not be an unpleasant existence.

But it would not be the marriage her heart longed for, nor the life she wanted to live.

A flash of lightning, followed by the distant sound of thunder, reverberated through the governor's house and into Eleanor's aching chest. She wrapped her shawl around her shoulders and stared at the empty page of her journal, the tears dripping silently down her face. There were no words to write that could convey the depth of her anguish over the idea of losing Miriam. The baby had become her daughter. In every way that mattered, Eleanor had become her mother. She could not fathom the grief she would endure if Miriam was taken from her.

Yet, how could she leave Arran? Her love for him was different, but equally as powerful. He had told her he wanted her to leave, but she was willing to stay and face the dangers, whatever may come, if it meant being at his side. She had made great progress with the school and longed to restart classes in the fall, building on the things she'd taught the children. Their curiosity and thirst for knowledge had given her a sense of purpose as she tried to meet their enthusiasm. But there was so much she still wanted to accomplish. She dreamed of one day building a school and opening it to all the children in Assiniboia who wanted to come.

Another streak of lightning filled the house with a flash of blue light. Eleanor wiped the tears and looked toward the window, hoping Arran would arrive soon. He had not been home all day. The last she had seen of him was directly after the church service when he had gone to the lookout tower.

Nicolette and Miriam had gone to sleep in the room they shared, while the governor was already snoring in his room upstairs. William had quietly said good night, but Eleanor knew he would be up studying for hours, as was his habit.

It was nights like tonight when Eleanor usually filled the pages of her journal with the events laying heavy upon her heart. But she could not bring herself to record the possibility of William taking Miriam from her—or the choice that would lead Eleanor away from Arran for good. They had not spoken in private since the long-ago feast, yet there were so many things she wanted to tell him—and so many things she wanted to hear.

She would need to give William an answer concerning his proposal by tomorrow. Governor Semple had spoken to them that evening about his plans to leave in just two days. Eleanor would need to make a decision by the morning so she would have time to prepare for the journey—if she decided to go. But what other choices did she have? If Arran did not want her, then she would need to leave.

There were so many unanswered questions stirring in her heart. She finally set her pen down and placed everything back into her writing desk. She would not know what to write until she'd spoken to Arran. But what if she didn't see Arran before morning? How could she give William a final answer without giving Arran one more chance to open his heart to her again?

Eleanor stood and went to the window. The sky was dark and overcast, with flashes of lightning jumping between the clouds. The wind had picked up and was blowing the tops of the trees near the riverbank. The only place Arran might be at this hour was in the southwest watchtower. Would it be wise to go to him? Would he be alone and able to speak?

Without giving it another thought, Eleanor lifted the shawl over her head and slipped out the front door, closing it softly behind her. She had to take the risk.

The wind pushed at her gown, whipping the hem around her feet. She had to walk carefully so she did not trip over the uneven ground. No one was in the fort yard this late at night, offering her some privacy as she rushed across the hard-packed dirt. If anyone saw her moving about in the darkness, her reputation would be in question—but with only one night to make the most important decision of her life, she cared little about what other people thought. She had lived through two scandals in her lifetime—a third would be of minor consequence.

Up ahead, the watchtower loomed under the swirling storm. Eleanor reached the ladder and climbed it on stiff legs. Her heart was pounding so hard, she feared she might become lightheaded and tumble to the bottom. But there was no other choice. She could not leave Assiniboia without speaking to Arran one last time.

She just hoped he was there, alone.

The watchtower was not large. A man could not lie down in it, and not more than two or three could stand comfortably in the space. When Eleanor finally reached the top, Arran stood in the opposite corner, leaning against a post, staring out at the dark prairie.

He was alone, thankfully, and there was not another person around to see them together.

She finished climbing the ladder, but before she could pull herself fully into the tower, he turned, his entire body alert as he lifted his musket into his arms and swung it in her direction—stopping a split-second before aiming it at her.

"Eleanor!" He quickly leaned the musket against the half-wall and came to her.

It was not easy to climb a ladder in a gown, and even less so to pull herself into the tower.

He offered her his hand. "What are you doing here?" He did not sound pleased to see her. On the contrary, there was accusation and anger in his voice.

"I need to speak to you." She finally stood on her feet and smoothed out the skirt of her gown. "I waited all day, but you did not return home."

It was difficult to see in the darkness, but the occasional flicker of lightning allowed her to get glimpses of the hard lines in his face. He returned to where he'd been standing in the corner of the lookout tower and turned his back to her. "I have a job to do."

"There are over a hundred other voyageurs and company men in the fort. Could one of them take a turn in the lookout tower?"

"James is in the northeastern tower."

Eleanor had not considered that someone might have seen her from the other tower, but would James tell anyone?

"You shouldna be here," Arran said, his voice devoid of emotion. "You should return to the house."

The tower was open on all four sides, with a half-wall coming up to Arran's waist and a roof overhead. Wind pushed through the openings and cooled Eleanor's skin. She pulled her shawl closer to her body. "I will not leave until you speak to me."

"We have nothing to say to one another."

Frustration warred with the pain in her heart. She crossed the small space and stood beside Arran, though she did not look out at the prairie. Instead, she looked up at him. She stood so close, he could not ignore her.

"What do you want from me?" he asked.

"I want to speak to you. That is all."

He clenched his jaw and crossed his arms. "Then speak and be quick. You should be back at the governor's house. If someone found us together—"

"Why are you ignoring me? You've avoided being alone with me since the buffalo feast."

The first smattering of rain hit the roof of the tower as Arran finally looked at Eleanor.

"You ken why I've ignored you."

She shook her head. "I know you want me to leave, but does that mean you must treat me as if I'm already gone?"

He closed his eyes for a moment and then looked back at the prairie. "I thought it would be easier."

"Has it been?"

Arran's muscles were tense and unyielding. He stood like an immovable statue beside her. She longed for him to wrap his arms around her and tell her everything would be all right.

But he did not.

Eleanor put some space between them and rested her hands on the top of the half-wall. "William asked me to marry him and return with him and Miriam to England."

Arran did not move or react to her statement. Did he truly not care that another man had proposed to her? That she might leave for good? A wave of sorrow washed over her as the rain began to pour in earnest, making it impossible to see past the lookout tower.

A fine mist wet her skin, causing her to shiver. "Do you not care?" she asked just above a whisper, hoping he would hear her over the sound of the storm.

Arran finally turned to look at Eleanor. Her eyes had adjusted, so she could see him more clearly in the dark. Pain and longing were written upon his face.

"Aye, I care. More than I should."

A spark of hope lit in her heart. "I have not given him my answer."

He studied her for a moment. "Why not?" His voice was strained, as if it was difficult for him to speak. "He is a good man, and he could offer you a good life."

"I do not love him."

He shook his head, his eyebrows coming together. "What good is love?"

What good was love? She stared at him. "It is the very thing our hearts long for. It is the thing for which marriage was made."

"It does not serve a purpose in places like this, or in marriages like the one West has proposed. He is offering protection, stability, and comfort." His voice almost sounded angry. "You would be foolish not to accept."

"You do not seem surprised that he has asked me."

He did not meet her eyes. "I suspected he was attracted to you, but he thought you and I had something between us." He swallowed and finally returned his gaze to hers. "I set him straight and he said he would take you away from Assiniboia if you'd go."

A flash of lightning filled the space. "But we do have something between us." The storm and the impending departure of William and Miriam made her bold. Tears stung the backs of her eyes, but she did not let her gaze waver. "I'm in love with you."

Thunder shook the tower as Arran drew her into his arms, intensity thrumming through his muscles. He held her tight, as if he was afraid to let her go.

She clung to him, wrapping her arms around his neck as her tears fell.

"You love me?" he asked, his lips pressed close to her ear.

"Yes," she whispered.

He kissed her then, with all the passion and pent-up longing he had held for the past four years. Liquid warmth filled her stomach, pouring into her limbs, making them weak with desire. The kiss was both gentle and tender, and at the same time powerful and all-consuming. Eleanor could not get enough of Arran. His lips explored her mouth, her cheeks, her neck, making her entire body tremble. She entwined her fingers through his hair, holding him close, never wanting him to stop. This kiss was the kiss she had dreamt about for years, and it was as wonderful as she'd always expected.

"Eleanor," he whispered as he clung to her. "I'm sorry."

"Don't be sorry." She hugged him close, allowing her fingers to explore the curls at the nape of his neck. "I've wanted you to kiss me since we walked in the gardens at St. Mary's Isle."

He was no longer kissing her, but he still held her, his face buried in her neck. "I have no respect for a man who takes advantage of another man's fiancée."

"I am not William's fiancée. I have made no promises to him." She needed Arran to understand. "How could I, when my heart belongs to you?"

"You shouldna say such things."

"Why not?" Pain filled her voice. "Do you not love me, Arran?"

Chapter Twelve

The storm continued to blow, and the thunder and lightning were now simultaneously crashing and sparking overhead. Arran embraced Eleanor as if she were the very anchor that held him to the present. Everything else that had come before, and everything yet to come, meant nothing. All that mattered was this moment. His heart pounded like mad, and all his senses were sharpened. "Aye," he whispered, unable to hide the truth any longer. "I love you more than life itself."

A sound of pleasure slipped off her lips, then she pulled him toward her again, kissing him this time.

He responded to the kiss, just as fervently as before. His hands slipped down to rest on the small of her back and he pulled her closer, pressing her body to his. His muscles responded to every dip and valley of her body, tightening with longing.

When he pulled away, they were both breathless again, and he wondered what it might feel like to hold her for the rest of his life. His heart longed to be at her side every day, for better or worse.

Yet there was a very real possibility that if she stayed at Fort Douglas, they would only have a few days together on this earth. He was not ignorant of the violence descending upon them. He could not take the risk of losing her, or of her seeing him perish. If she did not leave with William now, who would take her back to England if something happened to him? And what if they survived to fight another battle? What if they married, only to face this same trouble again in a few weeks or months? What if they eventually had a child, how could he see both of them suffer?

Arran wrapped her in a tight embrace, needing to feel her, to reassure himself that in this moment, she was still alive and vibrant. Yet he knew it could not last. This stolen moment was simply a gift that he would cherish and carry in his heart, long after she was safely away.

"What am I doing?" he whispered. "I shouldna be holding you like this, Eleanor. I ken if I ever kissed you, it would be almost impossible to let you go."

"You don't have to let me go. I want to stay here, with you."

He held her closer. "I ken that you do, and I want it, too, more than you might imagine."

She was silent for a moment. "Then why do you sound as if you are unhappy?"

With a tortured sigh, he pulled back and met her gaze. "Nothing has changed, lass. If anything, it has only become worse. I vowed to Lord Selkirk that I would not abandon this fort, despite the fight that is coming." He filled his lungs and then let out the air. "I am trying to think reasonably and rationally where you are concerned, but my head and my heart are telling me two different things. Selfishly, I want you to stay. But, I ken it would be best for you to leave, while you still can. I'd send everyone away, if I could, but the colonists have nowhere else to go. And many of them are just as determined to see this colony stand as I am."

"I want to take the risk with you." She removed her hands from behind his neck and let them lie on the sides of his face.

Her touch was everything he thought it might be, and far more. He'd never known such pleasure as he did in this moment. He choked as he said the words he needed to say. "I am not willing that you would take that risk. It would destroy me, if you came to harm because of me."

"It would not be because of—"

"Eleanor." He put his hands over hers and lowered them. He could not think straight while she caressed his face. "I am trying to be rational and wise. I dinna want to make a decision based on my feelings, but on common sense. The facts are plain, and we would be foolish not to heed them. You have a way to escape. I want you to take it."

She lowered her chin and shook her head. "What if something miraculous happens and the colony becomes safe? I will be married to another, for the rest of my life."

"I dinna ken if I believe in miracles anymore." He let go of her hands, needing even more space from her. "The North West Company and the Hudson's Bay Company have been in battle for almost forty years, why would that suddenly end now?" He needed her to understand, to see what was best for her. "West is a good, God-fearing man. He will be kind and loving." He stopped and gathered his emotions before continuing. "He will give you all the things I canna. And, in time, you will learn to love him."

"I could never love him the way I love you."

"Mayhap not, but you will love him." He knew it as well as he knew the storm would pass and a new day would dawn. "And you will have Miriam to comfort you." In time, she would probably have other children to fill her home, though the thought of Eleanor sharing intimacies with West was almost more than he could bear. "You can be happy, lass, and that is what I want for you."

"How can you say I will be happy, when I will not be with you?" Tears fell from her eyes.

At the sight of them, Arran's willpower almost eroded. He hated knowing he was the cause of her unhappiness—but it was easier knowing he was breaking her heart than to know he would be the cause of her death. He had lived with the guilt and shame of his mother's death and knew it was an infinitely greater burden to bear.

The storm continued to unleash its fury against the prairie, but in this small tower, Arran and Eleanor were safe. Rain blew in, moistening their skin and clothing, though they were spared the brunt of the onslaught.

"I dinna want to cause you pain," he said to her. "In time, you will be happy again." Though he doubted it to be true for himself. He wanted to reassure her and to send her away with nothing but hope for the future. "You will have a full life, and when you are old, you will look back at these memories through the kind lens of time. You will recall me with fondness, but all the other memories of your life will overshadow these few short months in Assiniboia, and you will see that leaving was the right thing for you. I have no doubt."

She pressed the back of her fist to her lips as a sob escaped her mouth. For several moments, she did not speak as the tears fell.

It took all his resolve to keep his distance, afraid if he tried to comfort her again, he would lose all ability to think and behave rationally. He loved her too much to send her to West stained or sullied.

The rain began to taper, and the rumble of thunder grew less and less powerful.

Finally, Eleanor wiped her tears, though her voice still shook with emotion. "I have always trusted and respected you, but in the past ten months, my admiration for you has only grown." She paused and took a steadying breath. "It would be foolish of me not to listen to you now."

Her words brought him immeasurable relief, yet they tore at his very soul. He wanted to ask her if it meant she would marry West, but he couldn't force the question out of his mouth.

"I should get back before anyone notices I'm gone." She wiped her cheeks again, her voice resolute. "I will need my rest if I'm to prepare to leave the day after tomorrow."

He did not respond. What could he say?

She stood for a moment, watching him, as if waiting for him to stop her.

Arran forced his feet to stay planted, recalling how weak he'd felt when he could not save his mother. This time was different. He was using his strength and willpower to protect Eleanor the only way he knew how.

By sending her away.

She didn't speak as she walked slowly to the ladder and then started her descent.

The rain was barely falling now, offering him a view of the prairie and the fort yard once again.

Right before she disappeared down the ladder, she looked at him one last time.

He swallowed, resolved to remain steadfast.

Her eyes were filled with the deepest sorrow he'd ever seen. Without a word, she left his sight.

A few moments later, he saw her walking across the muddy yard to the governor's house.

She did not look back to see if he watched her.

Chapter Thirteen

The first hint of dawn drifted over the prairie in subtle shades of dark pink and purple. Not a single gust of wind pushed against the tall grass or rustled the leaves of the sparse bushes that dotted the terrain. Arran watched as the sun slowly lifted itself from its eastern slumber, casting shadows over the dips and rises. He couldn't help but wonder what the day would bring. All was peaceful and quiet—for now. Would it end as it began?

Life started to stir in the fort yard, and soon, one of the voyageurs came to replace Arran in the lookout tower. He could have been replaced hours ago, soon after Eleanor came to speak to him, but he knew he wouldn't sleep anyway, so he had sent the other man to bed and stayed at his post.

But he could not avoid his other responsibilities forever.

He climbed down the ladder and entered the yard. The earth was still muddy, with puddles in the low spots. He would need to report to Governor Semple before he began his work. Despite the oncoming danger, the voyageurs and company men had planted the crops and gardens before the colonists had returned to Assiniboia, and now they must be weeded and maintained. Arran would oversee the protection of the colonists as they went into the fields to work.

His eyes were gritty and his head pounded, but he would face the day regardless.

He paused outside the governor's house and took a deep, steadying breath. The last thing he wanted to do was face Eleanor, especially feeling the way he did, but it could not be helped. He had made his decision and would have to live with it, come what may. It was for the best.

He pushed open the door and stepped into the common room.

Eleanor sat at the table, a bowl of steaming hominy before her. She was feeding Miriam, who sat on her lap. William was across from them, watching, as he also ate. There was a light in his countenance—that dimmed when he met Arran's gaze.

"You're just in time to join us for breakfast," Governor Semple said as Nicolette placed a bowl of hominy in front of him at the head of the table. "Sit. You look like you could use something to eat about now."

Arran was in no mood to be polite or conversational. His lack of sleep, coupled with his encounter with Eleanor, had left him especially out of sorts. But he couldn't be rude, so he took a seat across from Semple, with Eleanor to his left and West to his right.

Miriam grinned and clapped her hands when she saw Arran. Her blue eyes sparkled and her four front teeth gleamed when she grinned at him.

Arran's heart warmed at the enthusiasm of the baby. He smiled back at her, thankful to know that he still could. And then he met Eleanor's gaze and his smile disappeared.

Her eyelids were swollen and she looked as if she hadn't slept, either.

Not for the first time, Arran's resolve threatened to crumble at the look on her face. His love for her was so overpowering, he felt as if he was standing on shifting ground and could be swept away at any moment.

To know she was just as miserable only heightened his pain. Yet, how much more so would she be if she had to witness Arran's death? He kept reminding himself that this was for the best.

"Mr. West and Miss Brooke have shared exciting news with me this morning," Semple said as he scooped a spoonful of hominy from his bowl. He looked at West and then said, "Do you mind if I have the honor of telling Mr. MacLean?"

Dread filled Arran, even though he knew this moment was coming. He wanted to get up and escape from hearing the news but knew it wouldn't make it less true.

"By all means," West said to Semple.

"William and Eleanor are to be married at York Factory." Semple grinned. "Isn't that marvelous news? Though I am sad to see them go, in time, I hope we have more ministers and teachers than we know what to do with."

The tempest won the battle and Arran felt as if he was being swept out to sea, with no hope of ever returning to solid ground.

But wasn't this what he had wanted? What he had set into motion? He forced himself to meet West's gaze. "Congratulations."

West nodded. "Thank you."

It was even harder to face Eleanor, though he knew he must. "I hope you'll be happy," he said to her, his voice sounding hoarse and unnatural to his ears. All he could think about was the kiss they had shared the night before. It was the only thing he'd thought about in the watchtower. He could still feel the sweetness of her embrace.

"Thank you," she said just above a whisper, distracting herself with feeding Miriam.

"I think this is cause for a celebration," Semple said. "Nicolette, do we have any ingredients to make a special dessert for supper? A pie or cake, perhaps?"

Nicolette was rarely addressed, and she paused now, surprise on her aging face. She shook her head.

"Perhaps I'll stop by the fur post to see if McIntosh has any food supplies he could part with. Some flour and sugar would do just fine." Semple dipped his spoon back into his hominy, blissfully unaware of the tension ricocheting off the other three tablemates.

Semple continued to blather as Nicolette placed a bowl of hominy in front of Arran. He had eaten the meal a thousand times since coming to the Red River, but it had never tasted as bland and pasty as it did today. He had to force himself to eat it, only because he knew he would need the strength. But the moment it sat heavy in his gut, he stood. "I will await you in your office," he said to Semple.

Semple looked up in surprise but nodded. "I will be there shortly."

Arran left the room without a backward glance. He felt as if his body was moving slower than usual, and his mind was working extra hard to keep up with the events transpiring around him. How would he be of any use to the settlers in the fields today?

With a weary sigh, he took a seat in Semple's office. As he waited, his eyes grew heavy, and the next thing he knew, Semple was entering.

He must have fallen asleep.

"You look tired," the older man said to Arran. "Perhaps you should get some sleep before you see to your other responsibilities."

Arran sat up straighter and wiped his eyes. He shook his head. "I'll be fine." He'd gone without sleep before. "I wanted to check in with you before I head to the fields."

A knock sounded at the door leading outside. Semple had not yet sat, so he went to the door and opened it. James stood on the other side, two Cree Indians behind him.

"May we have a word with you?" James's face and voice were heavy with unspoken news.

"Of course. Come in." Semple opened the door wider.

Arran stood, alarm making the hair on the back of his neck rise. He recognized these men. They had come and gone from the fort many times in the past four years to trade furs. Both were considered friends to the Hudson's Bay Company and were honest in their dealings.

There were not enough chairs in the room, so they stood in a circle.

"What do you have to tell us?" Semple asked.

James shared a look with the two Cree men. All three wore serious expressions.

"We have come to warn the post." One of the Cree men, known simply as Bill, crossed his arms as he spoke. He had been educated by missionaries and spoke almost flawless English. Both men were dressed in clothes similar to those worn by Arran and James, though their Indian heritage was also visible in their long black braids, and the earrings and other jewelry they wore. "Bois-Brûlés and Nor'westers have made camp at Portage a la Prairie," Bill said, "and plan to attack in two days' time. All are armed and mounted."

In two days? Arran's heartrate began to accelerate. It would be just enough time for Eleanor and Miriam to leave. Portage a la Prairie was only fifty miles to the west, but Eleanor would be heading due north.

"How many?" Semple asked.

"One hundred, maybe more."

It was as they had feared. "And is Cuthbert Grant among them?" Arran asked.

Bill nodded. "He leads the men. He vows he will clean out settlement and leave no one."

"Are you certain?" Semple asked.

Bill nodded, his face grim. "You are friends," he said, looking from one man to the next. "I warn you to be ready."

"Thank you." Arran wished he could say more, but what else was there?

"We go." Bill motioned for his friend to follow.

James opened the door, but he did not leave with them. Instead, he came back inside.

"What will we do?" he asked Arran and Semple.

All Arran could think about was Eleanor and Miriam. They must leave today, if possible. "You must not wait to go," Arran said to Semple. "You must leave for York Factory today."

Semple frowned. "Leave? Now? I cannot leave the fort when I know there is imminent danger."

Panic seized Arran. "There has always been imminent danger."

"Until now, it was only rumors. You heard the man. Cuthbert Grant is only fifty miles to our west, with over a hundred armed and mounted men with him. I could not leave my post now, no matter how pressing my business in York Factory."

"But what of Eleanor's and West's plans to leave?"

"They will have to stay and help protect the fort."

It was impossible. Arran could not allow it. "They are innocent."

"As are we all." Semple took a seat behind his desk. "None of the settlers deserve this treatment. We will put a stop to it once and for all time."

He was right, none of them deserved it, but the only two truly defenseless people were Eleanor and Miriam. All the other women and children had husbands and fathers to offer protection. Arran had to do what he could for the woman and child he loved. There had to be some way to get them out of Assiniboia. "I will gather a group of voyageurs to oversee their journey."

"No." Semple took out a piece of parchment paper and his pen. "We need all the men we can muster. I will not allow anyone to leave the fort until this trial has passed—including you."

Sweat began to gather on Arran's brow. Eleanor was stuck in Assiniboia. He should have found a way to send her to York Factory sooner.

"I have letters to dispatch, gentlemen," Governor Semple said. "Please send a few runners in to me. I want to get these sent out to Jack River House and toward Montreal as soon as possible. We will need all the help we can get."

Arran's brain continued to work at a sluggish pace. He couldn't think. There had to be a way to send Eleanor to safety—but how?

"Come," James said to Arran. "Let us fetch runners."

Arran followed James out of the office and into the blazing sunshine. It made his head pound even harder than before.

"I canna let Eleanor and Miriam stay in the fort."

"You dinna have a choice." James's voice was weary and troubled. "All you can do now is pray they stay safe."

Arran hated to feel powerless. He had felt it when his mother had died and each time the settlement had come under attack.

But this time, it was infinitely worse.

Two days had gone by in a flash of preparations, and yet they had dragged on as no two days ever had. Just after the sun set on the second day,

Eleanor stood at the window of the governor's house, watching and praying. Nicolette had taken Miriam to their room to put the baby to sleep, but the men were nowhere to be seen.

Moments after Governor Semple had told them the news about the impending attack the day before, William had gone to offer his assistance, and that was the last time she had seen him all day. He had been up and out of the house before Eleanor had risen from her bed this morning. Arran had not returned after breakfast yesterday, and the governor had been in and out of his office from the moment the Cree Indians had visited.

While the men prepared the fort, Eleanor, Nicolette, Fiona, and the other women had prepared as best as they could with food, extra water, and bandages. There was no way of knowing what might happen, or if they would need the supplies, but it had given them something to occupy their time.

Now, as the last rays of sun fell behind the western horizon, Eleanor could not help but wonder what the morning would bring. Governor Semple had said that it was too late to leave Fort Douglas, and even if they had wanted to go, there would be no guides to see them to Jack River House and then on to York Factory.

For all intents and purposes, they were prisoners of Fort Douglas.

A familiar figure appeared in the dim fort yard and Eleanor's pulse sped at the sight of him.

Arran walked slowly toward the governor's house. The invisible load he carried was almost palpable. As his steps brought him closer and closer to her, Eleanor's breathing became more and more labored. They had not spoken since their encounter in the watchtower, or since he had learned about her engagement to William. What would she say to him? What might he say to her?

She stepped away from the window and went to the fireplace a moment before the door opened. Though she knew it was him, she turned at the sound and caught her breath at the look in his weary, sad eyes.

More than anything, she wanted to run into his embrace. But that was no longer an option. She was now promised to another man. No matter how much she longed for Arran, she had made her choice and would have to live with it.

"I was hoping you'd be alone." Arran closed the door behind him and set his musket against the wall.

He had hoped she'd be alone? For what purpose? Her heart beat even harder at his words.

Standing near the door, he studied her as if trying to memorize her appearance. Fatigue lined his mouth, and his eyes were bloodshot from lack of sleep. It had been three days since he'd slept in the governor's house. He must be exhausted.

"Sit," she said, walking over to a chair and pulling it away from the table.

His movements were unhurried and deliberate, as if it was a great burden to perform such a simple task as walking across the room.

"You should be abed," she told him. "You haven't slept in days."

"There has been much to do." He took the seat she held for him.

She crossed her arms and walked around the chair to stand before him. "You'll be no good to the fort if you do not sleep."

"The others are meeting in the main hall. I came back early to get a few hours of sleep while I still can." He watched her closely, the look in his eyes deep and hard to read. "I need to speak to you before I retire."

She hugged herself but could not take a seat at the table with him. Her legs were too restless.

"I'm sorry, lass." He shook his head, pain pulling his eyebrows together. "I shouldna let you stay in the fort as long as you have. You should be on your way downriver to Lake Winnipeg by now."

"There was nothing you could have done—"

"I could have sent you with a guide."

"With Semple's plans to leave, there was no reason to send us with a guide." She wanted to reassure him but didn't know how. "This is God's will, Arran."

He shook his head again. "I canna accept that. God gives us choices."

"Yes, but the events that have transpired are not of your making. You made the right choices, at the right times. None of this is your fault."

He clasped his hands on his lap and bent his head. His dark hair was curly and wild, and so tempting. She could still feel the strands between her fingers from the night they had kissed.

"I was foolish enough to think God had given me a second chance," he said, quietly, almost to himself.

"A second chance at what?"

"At saving someone I love."

She closed her eyes briefly, the pain of hearing him declare his love a bittersweet reminder of what had brought them to this moment in time. "You did everything you could. We must leave the rest up to God. We do not know what He plans."

"I've not always been keen on His plans."

Eleanor could no longer stand on her shaking legs. She took the seat beside him. "Please," she begged. "Don't add this burden to all your others. I need you to be clear-headed and rested when the real battle begins."

He finally lifted his head. "How will I be clear-headed when I ken you and Miriam are at risk? It is the thing I've feared from the moment of your arrival."

"Perhaps it will make you fight all the harder."

"Aye." He attempted a smile for her. "Mayhap it will. But, whatever happens, I want you to promise me that you and Miriam will return to England with West the moment it's safe to do so."

Eleanor nodded, finding it hard to voice her thoughts.

"Even if you dinna have time to say goodbye to me."

"It's the reason I agreed to marry him."

Arran swallowed hard and looked away from her. "Aye. And 'tis glad I am that you have. It makes the most sense."

"Does it?" Nothing made sense to Eleanor anymore.

Neither one spoke for several moments. Finally, Arran stood. "I should get some rest. I dinna ken what tomorrow will bring."

This could very well be the last opportunity Eleanor had to speak to Arran alone—yet there was nothing she could tell him that would change the course of events unfolding around them.

"Good night, Arran." Eleanor also stood and found herself very close to him. "I will pray for you."

He looked down at her, his dark eyes full of longing and tenderness. "Good night, Lady Brooke." He lifted his hand as if he was going to caress her face, but then he lowered it again, and let out a sigh. "My prayers will be with you, as well."

With those final words, he left her side and disappeared up the stairs.

Eleanor wanted to weep, but she had cried enough the night before.

The door opened again, and this time William and Governor Semple entered.

William caught Eleanor's gaze, concern in the tilt of his brows. His eyes wandered up the stairs, where Arran had just gone.

"I have a few things I need to address in my office," Semple said, blustering a bit. "If you'll excuse me."

He left the common area and disappeared behind his closed door.

It was just Eleanor and William, alone. Since he had proposed, they had endured a bit of awkwardness around each other. In time, Eleanor knew it would ease, but for now, it was still uncomfortable.

She hadn't allowed herself to even comprehend what it might be like once they were married and she was expected to share the intimacies of marriage with him. The very thought made her palms sweat and her forehead feel clammy.

One day at a time.

"Is all in order?" she finally asked.

"I believe so." He walked over to the fireplace, where he picked up the poker to readjust the logs. "Though there is no way to know how or when they will attack. It makes things more difficult to prepare."

"You'll not fight, will you?"

He set the poker back on its hook and turned to look at her. "I will do what is required to protect the colonists."

She was struck, again, by how blue his eyes were. They shone with intelligence and compassion. He was a learned man, not a soldier. "Do you know how to fight?"

A slow smile tilted his mouth. "I'm not completely inept."

Warmth infused her cheeks. "I didn't mean to imply—"

"Do not fret, Eleanor." He lifted his hands to quiet her defense. "I have shot a gun before, though, I confess, I am not as skilled as I would like to be. I hope it does not come to warfare."

Her hands were restless as she clasped them together. "If it becomes dangerous, I pray you do not put yourself into harm's way."

He watched her with a curious, almost hopeful, look in his eyes. Slowly, he walked to her.

She held her breath as he drew close, uncertain what he might say or do. Would he try to kiss her? Or would he wait until they were married? Should she offer him some sort of affection, on the eve of battle?

William stopped a couple feet in front of her, a gentle smile on his lips. "I would like to think you care about me, even a little."

Her response was quick. "Of course, I—"

He put his hand up and rested his fingers on her lips.

The gesture was so unexpected, she stared at him. It was the first time he'd ever touched her in such a personal way. It was not unpleasant, but it did not stir her passion like Arran's touch.

"I have no illusions of your true feelings," he said, coming closer to her as he lowered his fingers. "But it does my heart good to think you care about my welfare."

"Your welfare is very important to me," she said just above a whisper. "Why would it not be?"

William's gaze lowered to her lips and her chest began to rise and fall in an unsteady rhythm. As her fiancé, he had every right to a kiss—yet her heart would not be in it. At least, not now, not with Arran so close and the memory of their embrace the day before still so fresh in her mind. She did not want to spend the rest of her life comparing the two men, because she feared William would never measure up and that would not be fair to him.

Her shoulders stiffened and she pulled back, only slightly. It was enough for William to return his gaze to hers. She could only imagine that he and Anne had felt passionate about each other, and that he would desire the same ardor in his second marriage. Guilt washed over her, knowing she could not offer him what he wanted.

"Will you make me a promise?" he asked.

She nodded, unable to find her voice.

"If something does happen to me, will you keep Miriam and raise her as your own?"

"Do not say such things." Panic filled her chest. "Nothing can happen to you." She couldn't even imagine the great loss his death would create. Not only was he zealous about sharing his faith, but he was more knowledgeable than anyone she'd ever met.

"I will do everything in my power to come back to you and Miriam." He smiled again. "I am very eager to make you my wife and start fresh in England."

She wished she could share his sentiments, but it would not be honest. Instead, she returned his smile. She might not be eager to return to England and begin a life with a man she did not share romantic feelings for, but she was very grateful for the opportunity and for becoming Miriam's mother, in every sense of the word.

"Good night, Eleanor," he said. "I will pray God's protection on all of us."

He began to move past her, but then he stopped. Very gently, he leaned over and placed a kiss on her cheek.

She closed her eyes briefly, overcome by his tenderness.

"Good night," she whispered.

He left her then, her heart beating an unknown tune—foreign yet hopeful.

Chapter Fourteen

It was almost suppertime as Arran paced, waiting for the blacksmith, Michael Heden, to replace Tiberius's shoe. Earlier that day, Arran had ridden his horse to Colony Gardens to tell the settlers who had chosen to return to their homes to come to the fort, and a nail had come through Tiberius's hoof. Some of the settlers had listened to Arran's warning, but others had been stubborn and refused to leave.

The entire fort had been on high alert all day. At any moment, Arran expected the call to come from the watchtower. He just hoped Tiberius would be ready.

"Mayhap the Cree were wrong," James said to Arran as he leaned against the wall of the blacksmith shop, chewing on a piece of straw.

"They could have been sent as a false warning," Archie Currie added, spitting out a toothpick he'd been gnawing on. "Fear is a powerful weapon. Mayhap they thought the settlers would be easier to control if they had a couple days of fear to wear on them."

"They're coming," Arran said, certain the Cree were not wrong. "But anything could have happened to put them off by a day or more."

"I hope they all drowned." Archie crossed his arms. "Serve them right."

"I would feel better if the settlers would come into the fort tonight." Arran had tried several times to convince them it was foolish to stay in Colony Gardens, but they were a stubborn lot.

Inside the smithy, the sound of a hammer beat a steady tune. Overhead, the sky was bright blue, with nary a cloud in sight. The air was warm but not stifling. It would be a perfect evening to sleep under the stars, if they had not been in danger.

With little else to do but wait, West and Semple had spent most of the day inside the governor's house. Arran had no desire to spend more time with Eleanor than necessary, so he had stayed outside. He wasn't sure if he would join them for supper, not only because he had no appetite, but because it was torture to see Eleanor and West together.

The hammering in the smithy subsided and a couple moments later, Heden led Tiberius out by his reins.

"Thank you," Arran said to Heden. "He looks—"

"Riders approaching!" A shout came from the southwestern watchtower. Ben, the boy who often helped in the barns, had volunteered to watch the prairie during the day shift. He pointed there now. "Riders approaching!"

Arran's heartrate escalated. "Archie, tell Semple to join us immediately."

"Aye."

After quickly securing Tiberius's reins to a post, Arran rushed up the ladder into the watchtower, James on his heels.

"Here." Ben handed Arran a spyglass the moment he stood at the top of the tower. He pointed to a distant location, which was hard to see with the naked eye. "They're approaching from the west and headed a bit north."

Arran frowned. "Why would they be heading north?"

Ben shrugged while Arran placed the spyglass to his eye. They were a blip on the prairie, but with the glass he could make out at least fifty riders. From where Arran stood, it appeared to be a band of Indians—but were they friend or foe?

It didn't make any sense. They were expecting Cuthbert Grant and the Bois-Brûlés—why would Indians be on the move?

"Aye." Arran nodded and handed the spyglass to James. "They're heading north of here."

Semple appeared outside his house, West close behind. They ran across the fort yard toward the tower.

"Let's meet Semple below," Arran said to James. "We should be able to see the riders from the fort gate, just as easily as up here."

Arran and James made their way to the ground as Semple and West, along with about two dozen other men, gathered near the fort gate. Archie Currie and Angus Ferguson were among the familiar faces.

"What's happening?" Semple asked Arran.

"It appears to be a band of Indians, from what I can tell," Arran said.

James handed the spyglass over to the governor. "They're heading to the north and east."

Archie and another company man, John Burke, opened the western gate. Everyone followed Semple, who lifted the spyglass to his eye, his mouth hanging open slightly as he studied the riders. When he took the glass away, he frowned. "I cannot begin to guess why Indians would be riding so close to the fort, and at such a speed."

"Perhaps they are chasing buffalo?" West offered helpfully.

"Not the right season," Arran said, "or so close to the fort."

"It doesn't look like they intend to attack, at any rate." Semple closed the spyglass. "But I think we had better take a group of men and meet up with them to see what they are about."

"They're making to the settlers!" Ben called down to them from where he remained in the lookout tower. "And the settlers are running this way!"

Semple fumbled to put the spyglass up to his eye again. "The boy's right. It looks like they've shifted course just a bit."

"Do you think the Bois-Brûlés have incited the Indians against us?" Angus Ferguson asked.

"We will not know until we speak to them." Semple nodded decisively. "We need to make all haste to intercept them and see what they want."

Did Semple expect to reason with them? If they had been hired by the Bois-Brûlés to make war against the settlement, there would be no talking to them.

Semple addressed the men standing near. "I would like about two dozen men who are willing to go, the rest must stay to defend the fort. Who will go with me?"

At least twenty men raised their hands—including West.

"Let's be on our way, then." Semple started toward the barn, where the horses were waiting.

West began to follow, but Arran put his hand on the minister's shoulder. "I dinna think you should ride along with us."

William West turned to face Arran, a frown wedged between his eyebrows. "Do you not think I'm capable?"

"It's not a matter of your ability." Arran nodded toward the governor's house. "You should stay behind to help protect the women and children."

"Governor Semple wishes to speak with these men," West said calmly. "I may not be a man of war, but I do have a way with words. If anyone should help the governor reason with these brigands, then it should be me."

"I think you'd be better suited here, with Eleanor and Miriam. We dinna ken if this is a ploy to get the best men out of the fort, so Cuthbert Grant can attack from a different direction. We will need able-bodied men to stay and defend the fort."

"Then perhaps you should stay." West was not a bold man, neither was he loud or brash, but steel filled his countenance now, and he would not be persuaded. "I know where I am best suited. Semple will need my help for negotiations, if it comes to that."

Arran's jaw tightened and the muscles in his cheeks twitched. "I'd rather you stayed for Eleanor and Miriam's sake. If something happens to both of us, where will that leave them?"

A hint of uncertainty flitted through West's gaze, but then he shook his head. "I was sent to be the feet and hands and mouthpiece of Jesus. Right now, Semple needs me by his side. I must do my duty."

Frustration pulsed in Arran's chest, but who was he to argue with a clergyman's sense of his divine purpose?

"I hope you dinna regret your decision." Arran had no time left to debate with West. Instead, he noticed Old John standing near the main hall with his wife, the former Widow MacDougal. They stood, arm in arm, watching all the commotion around them. Old John had aged a great deal over the long winter months and would probably not saddle a horse to ride with the younger men. He was slower than usual, though a fire still burned in his gaze and Arran could see the desire in his face to be useful.

"Old John," Arran called to him as he approached, "I have a job for you."

The old fur trader lifted his shoulders with a sense of importance. "Aye? How can I help?"

"I need you to guard Eleanor and Miriam, see that they're safe. Could you do that for me?"

"Aye. With my very life." Old John would do anything for anyone. It was just his way.

"Thank you, friend." It was a relief to know that they would be looked after.

Arran did not have time for any other instructions—or to say goodbye to Eleanor and Miriam. He untied Tiberius and mounted the horse. Semple was already at the head of the group who had quickly assembled.

"Are we ready?" Semple called out to the men.

A rousing cheer rose above the chaos in the fort. Arran did not join in the call but made his way to the front near Semple.

Voyageurs, clerks, doctors, farmers, a clergyman, a governor, and Arran. They were Scottish, Irish, French-Canadian, English, and half-bloods. All coming together to save and protect Assiniboia.

"Let us be gone." Semple tapped his horse with his heels and started out, heading north toward Colony Gardens.

The prairie was wide and barren as they made their way. It was near five o'clock and there were still hours of sunshine to be had in the day. Arran was thankful for the light as he turned his gaze toward the group of riders still making their way toward the settlement. Dust billowed out behind their company as they rode. They had not yet noticed the men coming from Fort Douglas, or if they had, they were ignoring them.

Semple and his men were only half a mile away from the fort when the oncoming colonists crossed their paths. The settlers were wild with fear, and their high-pitched voices were hard to hear until Semple ordered everyone to stop.

"Half-bloods!" several people yelled, pointing to the settlement. "Riding fast toward the river."

"Not Indians?" Semple asked.

"No!" they cried as they continued to run, not stopping to say more.

Many of them shouted in Gaelic, confusing the riders who did not speak the Highlanders' native tongue.

"Bois-Brûlés," said an older gentleman who finally stopped long enough to speak to Semple. He breathed heavily and carried several random items from his home. "Hideously disguised as Indians. Their faces are painted and they're armed with bows and arrows, knives, guns, and spears."

"Is Cuthbert Grant among them?" Arran asked, his horse sidestepping beneath him.

"I dinna ken." The man looked back toward Colony Gardens. "I canna stop. I must get to the fort."

"It's as we first suspected," Arran said to Semple. "This is not a band of Indians, but Bois-Brûlés sent by the North West Company. But why are they headed north, and not toward the fort? You would think they'd be following the settlers."

Semple sat for a moment, his eyes squinting as he stared toward the north. "These men have a plan and we must be ready for them." He turned his horse to the first man in his eyesight. "Mr. Burke, return to the fort and bring back all the men you can muster. Bring along with you a fieldpiece, as well. We will wait for you here."

The horses pranced restlessly as the group of men waited and watched.

Burke nodded and then started to gallop full speed back to the fort.

"We should all return to the fort," Arran said to the governor. "We will have a better chance to defend the fort with the cannons there. Out here, we are sitting targets."

"They have not noticed us yet," Semple said. "We will have the benefit of surprise when we approach them."

"Surely this is their plan." Arran needed the governor to see reason. "They have drawn a significant number out from the fort, weakening what little defense we have left. Now that we know who they are, we need to return and keep watch."

Semple let out a long, low breath, his gaze on the distant group heading north and to the east, toward the Red River. "I would prefer to speak to them. Perhaps we can avoid a conflict altogether."

"We have heard for months what these men are planning," Arran said, barely containing his frustration. "They have come to destroy the settlement and fort. They will not be willing to speak."

"You do not know for certain." Semple's own irritation was mounting, and it was evident in the red riding high up his neck. "I could not live with myself if I didn't at least try to avoid a war." He motioned to the group. "Let us continue. Mr. Burke and the others can catch up to us later."

The governor's orders did not settle well in Arran's gut. He exchanged a look with James, who nodded once that he understood Arran's frustration—but what could they do? Semple was their governor, for better or worse.

They were soon upon Colony Gardens. There were twenty-six settlers' houses standing on plots of land edging the river, long and narrow. Up ahead, the Bois-Brûlés had come to a stop. They must have noticed the fort men, because they had turned and started to gallop toward them.

Sweat trickled down Arran's temples and dust filled his nose. There was no going back this time. They did not have the fort for protection, but only the muskets they had carried along.

"Spread out onto the plains," Semple yelled and motioned toward the west.

Arran repeated his orders, and the men did as they were told. They were outnumbered by the Bois-Brûlés at least two to one, but there was nothing they could do about that now.

They were about to face the most ruthless men in Rupert's Land. Arran's mind should have been on the confrontation, but all he could think about was Eleanor and Miriam back at the defenseless fort.

Semple and his men had gone only as far as the place known as Seven Oaks, in the middle of Colony Gardens, when the oncoming riders were close enough for Arran to see that they were, in fact, half-blood men and employees of the North West Company. Though they were disguised as Indians, several were recognizable and known to Arran, having worked with them years ago. Cuthbert Grant was also there, though he rode his horse toward the back of the group.

The Bois-Brûlés broke into two groups, fanning out to surround Arran and the others in a half-circle. The Frenchman named Francois Boucher, a clerk who had worked at Fort Gibraltar with Duncan Cameron, rode out from among them.

His face was painted and contorted into a fierce snarl. "What do you want?" he asked Semple in broken English.

Governor Semple frowned and shook his head, clearly confused. "What do *you* want?"

Boucher looked around the group of fort men, his eyes narrowed. "What do you want?" he asked again.

Semple met Arran's gaze, uncertainty in his eyes, and then he looked back at Boucher. "What do *you* want?"

Annoyed, Boucher turned his horse back toward the group of Bois-Brûlés and motioned for them to head toward the north again. Clumps of dirt flew into the air behind their retreating horses.

Arran frowned and looked among the fort men. The Bois-Brûlés were not behaving as he had thought they would. It didn't appear that they had come to fight, though they were clearly on a mission of one kind or another.

"Do they not want to fight?" one of the fort men asked, lifting his musket into the air. "Because I am ready to fight!"

Several other men shouted in agreement, mocking the Bois-Brûlés.

Semple turned to Arran, a look of perplexity on his face. "What do you think they are doing here?"

Arran had no idea. He shook his head. "I dinna ken."

"Should we follow them?" West asked Semple, moving his horse closer to Arran's.

It took a few moments of indecision before Semple nodded. "Let's keep going. It's clear they have no intention to fight us. We need to speak to them and find out what they want."

"Mayhap we should return to the fort," Arran said. "Watch and wait to see what they have in mind. We will be better protected there and able to defend ourselves. I dinna like how they are behaving. There is something wrong."

Semple seemed to weigh his options, but then he nodded toward the north. "Let's continue. I'd like to see this thing done."

Arran had no choice but to obey his commanding officer yet again, though everything within him demanded a different course.

They started, but no sooner had they returned to a gallop than the Bois-Brûlés turned back once again. This time, they were spread out even more, their group separating into two parties and forming a half-circle around Semple and his men for the second time.

Dread filled Arran as his mind tried to understand what the Bois-Brûlés were doing. Something was wrong—he just didn't know what it might be or how to stop it from happening.

"What do you want?" Boucher left the ranks of the Bois-Brûlés and circled around Semple and his horse, asking again in broken English, "What do you want?"

Semple ground his teeth together and lowered his chin. "What do *you* want?"

"We want our fort," Boucher finally said.

"Go to your fort." Semple motioned toward the south and the location where Fort Gibraltar used to stand.

"Why did you destroy our fort, you rascal?" Boucher held his musket against his shoulder. He pranced his horse close to Semple and swung his gun out to point in the governor's direction.

Semple grabbed the barrel of the gun.

Alarm pounded in Arran's head and his instincts immediately kicked in. All the men, in both groups, sprang to readiness. Backs were tight, muscles clenched, and weapons poised for attack. Arran kept his gaze locked on their enemies, watching for the slightest twitch or movement.

Boucher jumped from his horse and at the same moment, a shot rang out. Arran did not know from whom it sounded, but Lieutenant Holt, a clerk in the colony's service, fell from his horse and struggled upon the ground.

Arran and the other fort men stared at Lieutenant Holt in shock. In seconds, his writhing body went still and his eyes stared sightlessly toward the blue sky.

"He's dead," Angus Ferguson said at Arran's left. "They've killed him."

Boucher ripped his musket from Semple's hand and ran toward the Bois-Brûlés while another shot rang out from their company.

It hit Semple in the thigh. Semple stared in disbelief as the wound began to bleed, soaking his tan trousers in crimson red. His horse's eyes rolled back and he started to buck.

Arran pushed Tiberius to Semple's side, his jaw tight with panic and anger. He grabbed the reins of Semple's horse to keep him from bolting.

Semple grasped his leg and yelled at his men, "Do what you can to take care of yourselves!"

On instinct, the fort men drew close to Semple and Holt, some coming off their horses to attend to their fallen comrade.

In quick succession, the Bois-Brûlés brought the two ends of their column together and surrounded the fort men. They lifted their guns and began to fire.

Bullets zinged past Arran as he let go of the governor's horse and aimed his musket, expecting to be shot at any moment. He did not even think. Everything was done by instinct. He pulled the trigger on his musket, even as a volley rang out from the enemy, accompanied by yells and shouts of warfare. Smoke filled the air as a dozen or more fort men fell, almost at once. Arran grabbed Semple and pulled him from his horse, hoping to use the beast as a shield, but the Bois-Brûlés had circled them and there was nowhere to hide.

"Leave me," Semple said to Arran. "And fight these devils."

Arran pressed his hand against the wound in Semple's leg while the Bois-Brûlés continued to fire upon the fort men. Profanity filled the air, mingled with the cries of those injured and dying. Musket balls zinged to Arran's right and left, dimpling the ground, kicking up chunks of earth. Arran's heart pounded and his pulse surged.

All around Arran, men he had known for years lay on the ground. Angus Ferguson jumped from his horse and went to a fellow settler who was gasping for air. One of the Bois-Brûlés took aim and sent a musket ball straight through Angus's heart. He fell over his friend and did not move again.

Shock and disbelief ravaged Arran's mind, but he was defenseless as he tried to stem the flow of blood from Semple's wound—it was like watching his mother burn to death, all over again. Arran's musket needed to be reloaded to shoot again, but he couldn't do that and help Semple at the same time. He had no way to protect or shield his men, or himself. If they could not stop the Bois-Brûlés now, with some of their strongest and bravest men, how would they protect the fort? What would become of Eleanor and Miriam—or Fiona and her children? Rage spotted Arran's eyesight and he started to rise, a rush of energy convincing him he could take on fifty Bois-Brûlés on his own.

At that moment, Captain Rogers, another of the company men, ran toward the line of Bois-Brûlés, his hands raised over his head. "I surrender," he called out in desperation. "Spare my life!"

One of the men with Cuthbert Grant lowered his gun and aimed it right at Rogers. He didn't even hesitate, but shot him in the head and then jumped from his horse and stabbed him.

Arran yelled in anger at the savagery. Smoke from the muskets burnt his nose while Semple's blood wet his hands. From where he sat on the ground, he could see Cuthbert Grant sitting quietly on his horse, watching the scene unfold with little emotion. Beside him, a man Arran had known as a young North West Company clerk, Augustin Lavigne, also watched, though he didn't appear to be unaffected. His eyes were large, and his face was pale.

West was one of the last men on a horse. Arran yelled for him to get down and try to save himself, but West did not appear to hear him over the melee.

Instead, he put up his hands, his face wild with shock. "We have not come for bloodshed. We only wish to be heard."

"West!" Arran yelled at him again and tried to rise and stop him. "Dinna—"

A shot rang out and West's eyes opened wide. It was as if time stood still. He looked down at the growing patch of red on his chest and slowly lifted his hand to touch the bullet hole. A moment later, he slumped over in his saddle.

"No." Arran fell back onto the prairie, panic and disbelief pounding through his body. He felt disconnected and removed from the scene. There were only a few men still alive, but for how long? Hatred and murder burned from the eyes of the Bois-Brûlés as they reloaded their weapons and continued to fight.

Only Lavigne appeared to be shaken. Suddenly, Arran knew what he must do.

"Please, Lavigne." Arran stood, his legs weak. He put his hands up, knowing full well that Cuthbert had no intention of leaving any of them alive. He had come for revenge, and he had just taken it. There was no telling what he might do to the fort and those inside once all Semple's men were dead. Arran could think of nothing else but Eleanor and Miriam. He needed to stay alive so he could protect them. It was the only thing that mattered now, and he would do whatever it would take.

But he couldn't stay where he was. "Lavigne!" Arran walked toward the man, wondering if each breath was his last. "We are friends," he said to the Frenchman. "You ken me well. Dinna let me die today."

Lavigne focused his bewildered gaze on Arran, almost as if he was in a daze.

One of the other men Arran had worked with, a Mr. McKay, pointed his gun at Arran. "What are you doing here, *un petit crapaud*?" he asked, calling Arran a little toad in French. "You deserted the North West Company and turned against us. You do not deserve to live."

"I give myself up," Arran said to Lavigne, not acknowledging McKay, or caring if he appeared to be a coward. He would do anything to save Eleanor and Miriam. "I am your prisoner."

Lavigne dismounted, his face white as he surveyed the dead men all around them.

James was somehow still alive, though he held his forearm, blood covering his hands and clothing. Archie was also alive and was on the ground, pressing a stomach wound of one of their fallen men. Miraculously, they had survived the onslaught of the guns, while others lay moaning in anguish. West did not move on his horse.

Arran was sick with grief. How had it come to this? Miriam was now an orphan, in every sense of the word. And Eleanor? How would she return to England now?

Lavigne approached Arran, and Arran knew his former friend was his only hope.

"Kill the toad," McKay shouted. He leapt from his horse and ran toward Arran, a knife extended.

Lavigne pushed Arran out of the way and knelt in front of McKay. It caused the other man to stumble and fly toward the hard prairie ground. His face hit the dirt and he rolled to a stop on his back.

"No," Lavigne shouted while he rose, rubbing his shoulder where McKay had hit. "There has been enough bloodshed for one day. These men have surrendered."

McKay started to rise again, anger and loathing in his eyes. He wiped his mouth and spit out dirt and blood.

"Grant," Lavigne said to the leader. "These men are our prisoners now. We cannot kill them."

"I can help." Arran was desperate as he addressed Cuthbert. He was willing to do anything to spare Eleanor and Miriam, and see to Fiona and all the other widows and orphans. A year ago, he would have died in this place, defending the fort at all costs. But now? Now, there were far more important things than the colony and his promise to Lord Selkirk. "I can help you negotiate with the fort to surrender," he said quickly, keeping one eye on McKay. "I will personally see that all the colonists are removed to Jack River House."

"Arran." James stepped forward to deny his promise. "Dinna—"

"No." Arran turned and silenced James with a raise of his hand. He could not watch another friend be cut down today. "We will give them what they want. We must."

James stared hard at Arran, clenching his jaw tight.

"I will do whatever you ask," Arran said to Cuthbert. "But, please, spare the rest of these men and those at the fort. There will be no resistance, I promise you."

Semple groaned from where Arran had left him behind his horse.

Cuthbert sat quietly, his eyes calculating as he looked from Arran, to Semple, and to the fort. "Take MacLean into custody," he said to Lavigne. "We will bring him to our camp until I decide what to do."

"And our men?" Arran asked. "May we bury them?"

"Leave them." Cuthbert prodded his horse over the fallen men and went to Semple.

"I am not mortally wounded," Semple said through gasps of pain. "If you could get me conveyed to the fort, I think I should live."

Cuthbert stared at Semple in open abhorrence, but he nodded at one of his men. "See that he's brought to the fort."

"Thank you," Semple said, tears on his cheeks. "Thank you."

Arran's chest rose and fell on short breaths. He started to move toward West, but Lavigne stopped him.

One of the Bois-Brûlés pulled at West's arm. The man fell hard and shapeless on the ground, a sickening lump of a man. The Bois-Brûlé leapt onto his horse and took off to the north.

"Please," Arran said to Lavigne. "He's my—my friend. I want to see if he's still alive." He prayed to God that he was, even as the truth stung his gut.

Lavigne had already done much for Arran, but he allowed him to go to West.

Arran knelt on the ground and put his finger on West's neck to feel for a pulse.

There was none.

Rage burned deep in Arran's chest, and it took all his willpower not to turn and unleash his fury on those who had just killed this man of God.

"Come." Lavigne motioned toward the retreating backs of the Bois-Brûlés. "We have a camp not far from here. Grant will want to speak to you."

James, Archie, and the man who had worked as Semple's secretary, Mr. Pritchard, were also brought into custody. Their hands were tied behind their backs, and they were forced to walk away from their friends.

They had not gone far when another shot rang out. Arran flinched, then turned and saw a man above Semple, his pistol still smoking.

Semple lay dead on the ground.

Grant had led Semple to believe he would live.

What hope did Arran have that he, James, Archie, and Pritchard would survive to help those at the fort?

Chapter Fifteen

Eleanor stood near the window in the governor's house and held Miriam while the baby cried. She had begun to fuss moments before Governor Semple and William had been called away with news of riders approaching, and her fever had started soon after. There was nothing Eleanor or Nicolette could do to soothe the little girl, and there were no other signs or symptoms to help them diagnose her ailment.

Miriam's incessant cries only added to the fear and tension permeating the house. Eleanor had not stopped praying since she had watched the riders leave the fort gates. Old John and his wife, Isla, had come, but even they could not distract Eleanor from her worries, or Miriam from her tears.

"There, there," Isla said as she came up to Eleanor. "I've set a kettle to boil and we'll have some tea in short order. Hand me the wee bairn and I'll take a turn at comforting her."

Though the baby's cries had worn on Eleanor's patience, and given her a headache, she knew Miriam would be even more upset with someone else.

Eleanor tried to smile at Isla, but it was a weak attempt. "I'll try to lay her down again," she said. "Perhaps she's exhausted herself enough to sleep."

There was an irritated gleam in Isla's eyes, but Eleanor could not bring herself to care whether she had insulted the lady by refusing her offer.

With one last look toward the closed fort gate, Eleanor walked Miriam back to the bedroom and laid down on the bed with her.

Miriam's cheeks were red and her eyes were glossy. There was a stench to her breath that Eleanor did not like, nor recognize. She would have sent for the fort doctors, but they were two of the men who had gone out with Governor Semple. Even if they had stayed, Old John had forbidden any of them from leaving the governor's house until the men returned.

Earlier, Mr. Burke had returned to the fort, in search of a fieldpiece and all the men the fort could spare. Old John had gone out to speak with him, then came back to the house to report that they would only spare one more man to head to the plains. They needed as many as possible to stay and defend the fort.

Panic had threatened Eleanor all day. It hid at the fringes of her conscious mind, ready to attack at a moment of weakness. The only way Eleanor had known to keep it at bay was to pray and recite Scripture she'd memorized as a child at the hands of the family cook. Mrs. O'Leary had been a kind, Christ-like woman who had taken Eleanor under her wing. If not for the love of the staff, Eleanor would have had no one.

The child continued to cry, twisting and turning on the bed in a fit of frustration and pain.

"Oh, love," Eleanor whispered as she smoothed Miriam's blond curls against her sweating brow. "I wish I knew what ailed you and what would make you better."

Slowly, Miriam began to calm, though her tears continued. Her eyelids closed, and whimpers came from her lips, but her exhaustion finally won over.

The room grew quiet and Eleanor let out a long, weary breath. She whispered a prayer of thanksgiving and then lay in the silence.

But the quiet was almost worse than the cries, because in the silence, her fears grew louder. She had no way of knowing what Arran and William were facing on the plains. No way of knowing if they were safe or injured.

No way of knowing if they would return to her.

Panic seized her. It raced up her legs like a demon unleashed, rushing toward her chest. Her heart pounded and dread filled every part of her being.

She could not lie still. She had to move, to fight or to run. But she could not stay here.

Her breathing was labored as she stood from the bed and left the room.

Moving helped, as did seeing the familiar faces of those waiting with her.

"Is the bairn finally asleep?" Old John asked.

Eleanor nodded, taking one deep breath after another. Her heartrate began to slow and her legs didn't feel as weak or wobbly. She walked to the window and looked out again.

There were several people in the yard, voyageurs and company men who were speaking in small groups, and the settlers who had flooded into the fort from Colony Gardens at the first sign of attack. Their reports of half-blood men, armed and dangerously disguised, were filled with dread and fear, but they did not have any other news to share.

A distant sound made Eleanor's head come up as she listened. It sounded like corn popping over an open fire.

"Gunfire." Old John rose from his chair and went to the door. He opened it and the sound grew louder, carrying on the breeze. "Aye."

"Gunfire?" Eleanor put a hand up to her throat, the panic threatening to return. "Who is shooting?"

Old John shook his head. "I dinna ken."

About a dozen men gathered in the yard and after a few harried moments of arguing, several of them left the fort, their muskets clutched in their hands.

"Why is there so much gunfire?" Eleanor asked, joining Old John at the open door.

Slowly, Old John closed the door, his eyes heavy with sorrow. He did not answer Eleanor but went to the musket he had brought with him and lifted it to his shoulder. He walked to the window and stared outside.

The sounds continued, though more sporadic. Each popping noise made her flinch, forcing her to consider where the bullets landed. Had any of those taken down Arran or William? She couldn't even comprehend what might happen if it took down both of them—or any of the other men from the fort. Was Angus with them? What might Fiona be feeling?

"I must go to Fiona," Eleanor said. "Nicolette, please come for me if Miriam awakens."

"Nay." Old John shook his head. "I canna let ye leave. Arran said to watch over ye."

"I must go to my friend." Eleanor reached for her bonnet on the hook near the door. "She must be afraid."

"I canna allow it." Old John's wrinkled face was set like stone. "If those bullets took down our men, the enemy will be upon us shortly. I canna risk ye leaving now. I will defend ye with my life, as I promised Arran."

The Bois-Brûlés might be upon them soon? A different kind of fear filled Eleanor—this time for Miriam. She could not leave Miriam now.

She nodded at Old John and then set her bonnet back on its hook.

An hour passed, and no one said a word. Miriam continued to sleep while the others sat in the common room. Isla stitched, and Nicolette ground wheat, but all Eleanor could do was stare out the window with Old John. Finally, she went to her room to check on Miriam and then brought her journal back with her. For another hour, she sat at the table and wrote.

Still, no one left the fort, and no one returned.

It was cathartic to spill her heart onto the page, and she had this overwhelming need to record everything that had happened, if—God forbid—she should perish today. Perhaps someone would come across her words and know the names of the people who meant the most to her. In some small way, she felt that if her journal remained intact, the lives of those who mattered would live on.

A commotion started in the yard. Eleanor looked up from the book, her heart pumping hard again.

"The gate's being opened," Old John said. He held his musket in tight hands, his knuckles turning white.

Eleanor gripped her pen, her fingers stiff from writing for so long.

Old John watched for several moments, then he moved toward the door. "It looks like two of our men. I'm going to see what they have to say."

He left and closed the door. Eleanor stood, her journal forgotten, and went to the window.

Several dozen men had already congregated in a group as Old John joined them.

Though only a few minutes had passed, it felt like another hour before the group broke apart and Old John made his way back to the governor's house.

Eleanor met him at the door and pulled it open wide. "What is the news?" She almost didn't want to know—but she couldn't wait another moment. "Is it good? Bad?"

Old John's countenance was heavy. "It isna good."

Eleanor briefly closed her eyes and pressed her mouth together, refusing to give in to her tears. She had to stay strong, if for no other reason than to care for Miriam.

"Mr. Burke and the ten others who left when the gunfire started were too late. Twenty-three men were already dead near Seven Oaks when they arrived. Mr. Burke was shot and another man from the second group was killed. The dead men were being robbed by the Bois-Brûlés who remained. It's thought that some men got away and are still hiding, while others were taken prisoners of Cuthbert Grant."

"What of Reverend West—or Arran?" Eleanor asked.

Old John shook his head, his brow tilted as he met Eleanor's gaze. "The runners who just returned were sent back before they could identify the slain, though they did see Semple's body."

"The governor is dead?" Isla asked in horror.

"Aye."

Eleanor clung to Old John's sleeve. "But they did not see Arran or William's bodies?"

"I dinna ken, lass." Old John put his gnarled hand over Eleanor's, compassion in his eyes. "But ye must prepare for the worst."

Grief and shock washed over Eleanor and she stumbled as she tried to find a chair.

"Dinna fash," Old John said in a gentle, soothing voice. "We dinna ken the whole of it. Mayhap they're alive."

Pain unlike anything Eleanor had ever experienced, or even imagined, pierced her soul. She turned her desperate gaze to Old John, trying to hold on to reality, though she could only find a delicate thread to grasp.

"Please," she begged Old John, though she didn't know what to ask. "Please." It was all she could think to say.

The Bois-Brûlés made a camp not far from Seven Oaks, at the northern end of the settlement, at a place called Frog Plains. Dusk had settled over the prairie as Arran sat beside James, Archie, and Pritchard, the tall prairie grass jabbing at his back and bound hands. Close by, the half-blood men pitched their tents and watered their horses, laughing and joking as if nothing horrendous had just transpired.

Fire and sorrow burned deep in Arran's heart as he thought about the fallen men lying dead on the plains. Men such as Semple and West, who had been full of life just hours before. The loss was incomprehensible and senseless.

But the battle was not yet lost. If Arran had breath in his lungs, he would fight for everyone inside the fort. He couldn't even imagine the grief and agony filling the hearts of the widows and orphans—and for what purpose? What did the deaths of those men accomplish?

Arran was not about to let them die in vain.

"Grant wants to see you," Lavigne said to Arran, motioning toward one of the tents along the banks of the Red River. "Come."

His wrists were already sore from the rope as he followed Lavigne, twisting his hands this way and that to see if he could escape the bonds. Lavigne pushed open the flap and Arran entered, ducking his head.

"MacLean." Grant sat on a folding chair with a traveling desk in front of him. At the sight of Arran, he set his pen down and then blew the ink on the missive he'd just composed. Taking his time, he folded it and then handed it to Lavigne, a self-satisfied smile on his face. "Send this letter to Alexander Macdonell at Portage a la Prairie. He and the others will want to be apprised of our success today."

Success? It took every ounce of self-control, and the constant reminder of Eleanor and Miriam, to stop Arran from taking vengeance on this man. His anger felt like a wild animal, caged and demanding release. It screamed and beat against his chest—but Arran had to keep it in hand, for fear of the repercussions it would have on those in the fort.

Lavigne left, casting Arran a weary glance as he went.

Grant folded his arms and stared at Arran, hatred brimming in his eyes. "If you had remained with the North West Company, instead of changing allegiances to the HBC and Lord Selkirk, you would be on the winning side today."

Arran did not respond. He only wanted to return to the fort and see to Eleanor's safety. Whatever he needed to do—or to give up—to get there, he would, no matter how much he wanted to lash out at Grant. "I am here to negotiate the terms of surrender. I will return to the fort and convince the others to hand it over to you and your men. But I must be released first."

"What does it benefit me to let your fort surrender?" Grant asked. "I can easily overtake it, just as I did your men at Seven Oaks."

Panic swelled in Arran's chest, but he refused to show his fear. "You are only fifty strong and the fort has four times that number in men."

It was a falsehood, but he could not tell Grant that there were only a hundred and fifty within the fort, and a third of those were women and children.

"We did not intend to meet you on the plains today." Grant rose and came to stand in front of Arran, impatience and irritation in his voice. "We were to camp north of here and await the men coming from Fort William within the week. When we had enough men to outnumber those at the fort, we were going to take it by night, and leave no man, woman, or child alive." He stood very close to Arran. His breath was foul and he smelled of sweat. "I am still tempted to hold fast to the original plan. I can have you executed and then wait for the Fort William men to arrive to finish off the rest. What good are the settlers to us, anyway?"

Arran breathed heavily through his nose, his chest rising and falling rapidly. He could not allow Grant and his men to kill one more soul. "They are your father's people," he said, trying desperately to appeal to any shred of decency the man might possess. "You canna kill your own people. I will personally see that they leave Fort Douglas and dinna bother you again. We will not leave one man, woman, or child behind. We can be gone as early as tomorrow."

"I do not simply want them gone." Grant crossed his arms and narrowed his eyes. "If I let them go, they will leave everything behind—including their weapons. It will all become property of the North West Company."

All their property? The settlers had next to nothing—if they were forced to leave all their earthly belongings, they would be completely destitute. And how would they defend themselves on the trek to Jack River House or hunt for wild game to feed their families, if they left their weapons?

"Either complete surrender," Grant said, "or we will destroy the fort."

It would be almost impossible to convince the men at Fort Douglas to surrender, but even more so if he had to tell them to leave all their things behind.

But what good were things if they lost their lives, or the lives of those they loved? Arran would give up anything to ensure Eleanor and Miriam's safety—and he was sure any woman in the fort who lost a husband would give up everything to have him back.

The hardest to convince would be the voyageurs and company men, who had little to lose but their self-respect. They would live and die for Fort Douglas, as Arran had these past few years. He understood their mentality. But now that he had more at stake to lose, he couldn't risk putting up a fight. He didn't doubt that Grant would cut down every inhabitant at Fort Douglas if they did not comply. He had watched how ruthlessly they had killed Semple, West, and all the other men who still lay on the plains.

"Allow me to return to the fort," Arran said, trying to sound confident and not desperate. "And I will convey your terms of surrender."

Grant studied Arran for several moments. "I could kill you now and overtake the fort within days. You do realize that, don't you?"

Arran knew he was the only thing stopping Grant from destroying all that Arran held dear in the world. If he could not convince Grant to spare them, then everything would be over.

"Aye," Arran said. "I ken you are in a position of control. But the settlers are innocent. There are women and children in the fort who have nothing to do with the animosity between the North West Company and the Hudson's Bay Company. Please do not cut their lives short. Allow me to escort them out of Assiniboia and you may have the fort and everything within."

Wind picked up outside, pushing the sides of the tent as it blew toward the river. Grant finally answered, "I will give you until tomorrow morning to convince the others to surrender, and then another day to compile an inventory of all the property being handed over to the North West Company. I want a list at first light the day after tomorrow. You and I will both sign it and it will show that you surrendered of your own free will. The settlers may keep their clothing and personal items, but everything else must be forfeited."

Arran ground his teeth together, hating that after everything he had sacrificed, it would all be lost. "Aye. I will see that it is done."

"Go, then. And do not tarry." Grant took a knife from the sheath at his side and slit the ropes binding Arran's hands together.

Arran rubbed his sore wrists. "May I take my men? I will need assistance in compiling the list."

Grant nodded. "But you only have until sunrise to return and tell me if the fort is surrendered."

Arran did not wait another moment. He lifted the flap and was about to step out when Grant called to him. "And do not try anything foolish. We will have our eyes on the fort throughout the night. If anyone tries to escape, we will open fire and leave no one alive."

It was a daunting task that lay ahead of Arran, but he would do anything to get everyone out of Fort Douglas alive.

Chapter Sixteen

A storm had gathered over the prairie as Arran, James, Archie, and Pritchard walked back to Fort Douglas. It had taken almost two hours in the mud and darkness, but they had finally passed through the main gate. Arran wanted to go to Eleanor immediately, but his men needed to know what had happened. He was now the acting governor, once again, and he had to be the strength for the colony.

As he passed the governor's house, his heart beat with longing for Eleanor, but he forced himself to continue to the great hall where all the men would be gathered.

Archie opened the door, and the men entered. Those inside had tapped a keg of ale and were sitting at the tables, growing louder and angrier by the minute. A fire crackled in the hearth, making the room warmer than necessary.

"The governor's back!" someone called from the front of the room.

A round of cheers passed over the space, though Arran wondered if they would applaud him when they heard what he intended to do.

"Quiet," Old John said, going to the keg to get a cup for himself. "Let MacLean speak."

The room simmered to a low hum and Arran took a deep breath. He had been their governor before, though he didn't crave the job. It was not an easy position to fill. Victory or defeat would lie upon his shoulders.

"Today, we have lost more lives than in any other day during the history of Rupert's Land." Those who had come upon the massacre had counted twenty-three dead. They had wanted to bury them, but the Bois-Brûlés guarding the fallen men had forced them to return to the fort. The bodies remained exposed on the prairie. God only knew what would happen to them.

Sorrow and remorse weighed heavy upon everyone's countenance, relieved only by the anger.

"I have spoken to Cuthbert Grant," Arran continued, "and he told me it was not their intention to attack us today—"

"'Tis a lie!" someone shouted from the back.

"We canna trust anything Grant says," came another.

Arran held up his hands. "He told me there is a regiment coming from Fort William within the week. It was their intention to join forces and attack the fort in the dead of night. They were not planning to leave any survivors."

The hum grew louder in the room as the men discussed this revelation among themselves.

"Even now, they are watching the fort," Arran continued. "Grant says they will fire upon anyone who tries to leave."

"They canna lay siege to Fort Douglas," one of the older settlers said.

"They can." Arran nodded. "And they have."

"What will we do?" Old John asked. "I canna let my wife suffer one more day than she already has."

Arran took another steady breath and then laid down the news. "Grant has agreed to accept a full surrender."

A great uproar was unleashed in the room. From every corner, the men protested. "We canna allow it!"

Holding up his hands again, Arran was able to get the men to quiet once more. "We have no choice. Soon, they will outnumber us. I dinna want to see another man die a senseless death. It isna worth the sacrifice."

"How can ye even speak such vile things?" One of the men stood and stared at Arran. "Ye have poured yer blood and sweat upon this land longer than the rest of us. And ye'll just give up?"

Arran was tired and weary. He'd never known such exhaustion in his life. All he wanted was for it to end. "I willna ever forget watching my friends and neighbors be slaughtered in front of my eyes at Seven Oaks." He swallowed the emotions clogging his throat. He could not give in to them, especially here, in front of these men. "As governor of Assiniboia, I canna allow anyone else to die for this settlement. We will surrender to Grant in the morning and remove to Jack River House. From there, each man and woman will have the liberty to go where they please."

"Where will we go?" asked an Orkney man. "I have no homeland to return to."

"There are some who have gone southeast into America," Arran said. "Others have gone to lower Canada."

"Lord Selkirk promised us land," said another. "I will not leave Rupert's Land until I hear from Selkirk."

Several sounded their agreement.

Arran nodded. "Then you may wait at Jack River House until Lord Selkirk makes his wishes known."

"We will be back," said a Highlander who put his arm around his teenage son. "This is our home now. We may remove to Jack River House, but we'll be back."

There were nods all around. Arran admired their dedication—had felt it himself time after time—but today had changed everything. Eleanor and Miriam were now his priority.

"In the morning, I will return to Frog Plain and surrender the fort to Cuthbert Grant."

There were still those in disagreement, but they were fewer and less intense.

Arran hated what he would have to say next, because he knew it would break the spirit of many of them. "Grant's other stipulation is that we leave with only the clothing on our backs, and whatever personal items we can carry."

"We must forfeit our animals?" the Orkney man asked.

"And our weapons?" said the Irishman.

"Aye." Arran's voice was grave. "Everything must stay."

Another outcry filled the room, this one louder and more passionate than before. For several minutes, Arran let them scream and yell at him, but he could do nothing. It was Grant's stipulation—not his own.

"If we want to leave with our lives, and the lives of our wives and children, we have no choice," Arran said. "I ken you're angry—I'm angry, too—but nothing is as important as the lives of those we love. I canna watch anyone else die." His friends' deaths would haunt his dreams for the rest of his life. He had been unable to save them—he couldn't let that happen again.

The men railed against him.

James finally stood, lifting his hands to quiet the room.

"Finally, a voice of reason," one of the voyageurs said.

Arran's back tightened and he prepared himself from an onslaught by his friend. He had watched James's response to Arran's surrender in front of Grant. James would be ashamed of Arran's fear and willingness to give up the fort.

"I have been at Fort Douglas longer than Arran or the rest of you." James crossed his arms, his graying beard resting on his sleeves. "MacLean may be the governor of Assiniboia, with authority over the settlement, but I'm the chief factor for the Hudson's Bay Company post, and I have authority over this fort."

A hush fell over the room and Arran clenched his jaw. In all these years, he had never thought that he and his friend would come down on two different sides. They had always been a team—of the same mind. Losing James's friendship would be just as detrimental as losing everyone else.

James turned and met Arran's hard gaze. "I have always respected you, Arran. I stood by your side time after time, defending this fort with my very life. But today—" James stopped and worked his jaw back and forth for a second before he continued. "I saw what it truly meant to defend this place with a life—twenty-three to be exact—and I can say I never want to see it again."

Arran's pulse picked up speed as James walked to his side and then turned to face the others.

"I will surrender this fort," James said, "and everything within, if it means we all live."

No one said a word as they stared at Arran and James, disgust and betrayal in some of their eyes.

"What do we need to do?" Old John asked.

"We must each make an inventory of our belongings," Arran said, relief coursing through him. He gave James a brief nod of thanks and then continued addressing the others. "Grant will come to the fort tomorrow, but he has given us until the day after to finish our inventories. Both he and I—and James—will sign the terms of surrender. Then we will leave for Jack River House." He hoped to get away before the men arrived from Fort William. They were coming with plans to annihilate the fort. Who knew if they would let the settlers leave as easily as Grant?

"That could take us days," said the Irishman.

"We only have one day," Arran said. "Those of us who can read and write will need to help those who canna."

More grumbling followed, but Arran didn't have the time or patience to listen. More than anything, he wanted to go to Eleanor. At sunrise, he would have to ride out to surrender to Grant, but before that, he needed to tell her he was sorry. For everything.

"Everyone should rest," he said to them. "Tomorrow will be another trying day and we must keep our strength."

He turned away from the group and they began to talk among themselves.

"Go home to Eleanor," James said. "She needs you."

"Thank you." Arran put his hand on James's shoulder. "You are a true friend."

The night would hasten to morning and Arran would have to face his enemy again, but for now, he wanted to be with Eleanor.

Darkness had fallen, and with it, a fierce storm. It blew in with a cold wind from the northwest, arriving with a powerful vengeance upon the prairie. Rain slashed against the windows of the governor's house and pounded on the roof. Eleanor sat near the fireplace, a blanket wrapped around her shoulders. Though she sipped the hot tea Nicolette had made for her, and the fire was burning bright, she could not shake the chills that had come over her soon after Old John had returned to the house with news of the massacre.

The storm matched the oppressive mood hovering over the fort. Grief, so intense and overwhelming, had taken root in the hearts of those within the stockade walls. Eleanor had stayed at the house on Old John's orders, and to attend to Miriam's needs. The baby was still running a fever and had cried for most of the evening until Eleanor could get her to sleep again.

Though Eleanor could not leave, she had sent Nicolette out to see what might be done. When the woman had returned, she said that some of the slain men had been identified.

And William was one of them.

Tears ran down Eleanor's cheeks as she stared into the flickering flames, disbelief hovering on the edges of her thoughts. Her tea was growing cold in the mug she held, but she did not take another sip.

She and Miriam had not had time to say goodbye to William. He had left with Semple while Eleanor was changing Miriam's nappy in the other room. When she had come out, William and Semple were gone. She thought she'd see him again.

It was hard to describe the feelings swirling in her mind and heart concerning William. Grief—yes, but there was an emptiness, also. She had agreed to marry him, and though she did not love him, she did care for him. There had been a part of her that had started to envision what her life might look like as his wife—it was the only way she could cope with the turn of events that had led her to become his fiancée. But that life was now gone. Vanishing in an instant, without warning or permission. It made her future unknown, causing the emptiness.

Even more disheartening was the uncertainty about Arran's fate. Where was he? Was he among the dead? But wouldn't he have been easily recognizable to the others, if he was? Had he somehow escaped and was making his way back to her even now? Or was he captured? If so, what might happen to him at the hands of his enemy?

Fear and grief had made her heart numb, and all she could do was sit and stare into the flames.

The house was quiet. Deathly quiet. Semple's customary snoring would be no more. His life was another loss that left Eleanor numb with grief.

Nicolette slept in the room with Miriam, while Old John and Isla took one of the rooms upstairs. There were watchmen on guard all throughout the fort, and Eleanor almost expected a cry of alarm at any moment.

The handle on the front door wiggled, but Old John had put the crossbar in place before he had gone to bed, so whoever stood outside could not get in.

Alarm filled Eleanor and she stood, clutching the blanket to her chest. "Who is it?"

"Eleanor?" a voice called from outside, though it was muffled and competed with the tempest in the sky. "'Tis Arran."

"Arran?" Eleanor whispered his name in disbelief.

"Eleanor?" he tried again, pounding on the door. "Eleanor?"

"Arran?" She ran to the door, the blanket falling from her shoulders as she crossed the space. She struggled with the crossbar. Her arms were weak and she was trembling uncontrollably.

He continued to pound on the door, saying her name over and over.

"Arran!" she called back, working to dislodge the bar.

Finally, it came loose and fell to the floor. She yanked the door open. A gust of wind and rain blew into the house, sending the firelight flickering and wetting the front of her gown.

Arran stood, drenched and dearly alive.

Eleanor flew into his arms, her tears flowing freely.

He embraced her, his arms tight around her shivering body. "Eleanor," he whispered against her hair. "Thank God."

She wept, clinging to him, unable to find the words to express her feelings.

He pulled back and placed his cold hands on the sides of her face. Fear, relief, and anguish warred within his brown eyes, but it was the love she saw there that undid her.

He loved her. Had always loved her. And she loved him, more now than ever before. The thought of losing him was the most dreadful thing she'd ever endured.

She rose on her toes and kissed him, wrapping her arms around his neck and savoring every blessed moment of this sweet reunion. It was a miracle to be with him again—one she would never take for granted.

He returned the kiss, drawing her closer as they stepped into the room and he used his foot to close the door. The front of her gown became wet, pressed up against his rain-soaked clothing, but she didn't care. The heat from his kiss warmed her through, banishing the chills that had plagued her all day. Arran was home, alive, and kissing her as she'd never been kissed before.

He pulled back, breathless. "I'm getting you wet."

"I don't mind." She didn't want to move away from his embrace, but wanted to stay there forever.

Arran looked down at her, moving aside a tendril of hair that had fallen across her forehead. "You're the bonniest sight I've ever beheld."

He frowned and put his hand on her forehead. "You're burning with fever, lass. How long have you been ill?"

"I haven't felt well for most of the day, but I thought it was from the fear and worry." A thought suddenly made her gaze focus. "Miriam has been running a fever and crying for most of the day."

"And you dinna ken what ails her?"

Eleanor shook her head. "The fort doctors went with you."

And had been killed.

"Come warm yourself by the fire," he said as he took her hand and led her away from the door, stopping to pick up the blanket off the floor.

He pulled the chair closer to the heat, and after she took a seat, he gently placed the blanket around her shoulders. She wiped at her tear-stained cheeks, the ache of grief dimming in light of Arran's arrival, but not diminishing completely. They had lost so much today, she wondered if she'd ever be truly happy again.

He squatted before her, rubbing her cold hands. "The only thing that kept me going today was the hope that I could return to you," he said. "Your touch, your voice, your eyes, the curve of your lips—it's all I could think about." He swallowed and shook his head. "I was a fool, Eleanor. A prideful, idiotic fool. I placed this colony and my promise to Lord Selkirk above all else, and today, I realized how wrong I have been. As I watched Angus and West die, and I thought about the women and children they had waiting for them back at the fort, I ken in that moment that they had far more to live for than I did. It isna fair that they were taken and I remain." He stopped and lowered his head as a sob wracked his body.

Eleanor placed her hands on his face, her own tears beginning again at hearing this strong, stubborn man brought to tears at the atrocities he witnessed. "But you do have something to live for," she said. "You have me and Miriam."

He looked up at her, tears in his brown eyes. "If it hadna been for you and her, I would have died on that prairie today. I would have foolishly run into battle, even if it meant my life. I would have died for the colony." He shook his head in disgust. "Nothing on earth is more important than you and Miriam." He stopped again, this time searching her eyes. "I ken I've been a fool, Eleanor. I pushed you away and I'm sorry. If you dinna want me anymore, I—I understand."

"Don't want you?" she whispered. "I've never stopped wanting you."

"I dinna deserve a third chance," he said. "Especially now, with all we've lost—and all we have yet to face."

"Shh." She put her trembling finger over his lips. "We do not know what tomorrow may bring. Let's thank God for this moment, while we still have it, and not speak about what we've lost."

Arran wiped one of the tears from her cheek. "You're right. We don't know what tomorrow will bring. The others have agreed to hand the fort over to Grant, and I will be riding out in the morning to sign the terms of surrender."

"Arran." She shook her head, her heart breaking for a new reason.

"After today, I dinna think I can ever look at this place the same," he said quietly. "I thought I would live and die for Assiniboia, but I was wrong. I saw what it looked like to die for her and 'tis not worth it." He met Eleanor's gaze. "I'm ready to leave here for good, and I'd like to take you and Miriam with me. And when we're free of this place, I'd like to make you my wife, Eleanor."

She had always thought that grief and joy were opposing emotions, but in that moment, they came together to fill her heart with hope. It was the very thing that brought meaning to life and gave her the strength and energy to keep going. She would mourn William's loss for years, especially for Miriam's sake, but if it was God's will, she and Arran would raise Miriam as their own.

"Will you marry me?" he asked her.

She had no reservations. “Yes.”

He smiled, and for a moment, all the horrors of the day were dismissed from his heavy countenance.

If only they would stay that way.

Chapter Seventeen

A cold, steady drizzle fell against the colonists as they made their way in eight canoes down the Red River toward Lake Winnipeg. Assiniboia had disappeared from sight hours ago, yet not one of the evacuees had looked back.

Eleanor sat in the lead canoe with Arran, shivering. Her head pounded and her teeth chattered. For two days, she had battled whatever ailment had befallen her and Miriam, trying desperately to help where possible. When she learned that everyone must inventory their property, she had spent hours going from one tent to another, writing endless lists.

"Only a few more hours," Arran said to Eleanor, "and we'll make camp. Mayhap the rain will stop and I will build you a fire to take away your chill."

Eleanor tried to smile for him, but she could not find enough energy for such a small task.

Miriam lay in her arms, listless and dull. Her fever still raged, but there was nothing they could do. Cuthbert Grant had come into the fort the day after the massacre and overtaken Semple's house. Eleanor, Miriam,

Nicolette, and Arran had removed to the main hall, where they had slept on the hard floor for two nights before all was ready for their departure.

"Let me hold Miriam." Arran reached for the baby, concern tightening his voice. "You should rest upon my shoulder."

If they had been back in England, it would not be possible for Eleanor to lie upon a man's shoulder in public—but here, where they were fighting for their lives and freedom, no one would look at her twice.

Miriam didn't protest as Arran took her into his arms, holding her in a way to shelter her from the rain under his jacket. She looked up at him with her glossed-over blue eyes.

"Here," he said to the baby, "try to drink some water." Arran took a canteen and put it up to her lips. She fussed and turned her head. "You must drink, Miriam, my love." He tried again. Water dribbled from her lips, down her cheeks.

Eleanor had no more tears in her. All she could do was watch helplessly as Miriam suffered. Her head pounded and her throat felt as if she'd swallowed fire. It was so raw and sore, she could not swallow. If Miriam felt the same, no wonder she didn't want to drink the water.

Arran set down the canteen and put his free arm around Eleanor, drawing her into his warmth. "I feel so helpless," he said, pressing a kiss to her head. "What can I do to make you feel better?"

"There is nothing."

Voyageurs paddled the canoes, while the miserable settlers sat huddled together. Tears fell down the cheeks of several. Fiona sat in one of the canoes with her four children around her, including her newest arrival, who was not yet three months old. Her grief was so intense, Eleanor struggled to know what to say to her friend. Though Eleanor had experienced loss, she could not fathom being alone in the world with four children depending upon her.

Eleanor must have fallen asleep, because when next she opened her eyes, the rain had stopped and the humidity had risen. The air was thick and sticky, and the mosquitoes began to swarm. Arran worked to keep them off Miriam, who was sleeping in his arms.

"You're awake." He placed his hand on her forehead, his eyebrows coming together. "You're still burning."

All Eleanor could think about was a cool bath and a soft bed. Never had she missed Edgewood Manor and her previous life as much as she did in this moment. As a child, there had been an endless number of servants to see to her needs when she was ill. She had been treated by a country doctor with a gentle touch and a kind smile. Her bed had been plush and her baths had been drawn whenever she so wished.

She struggled to keep her eyes open and the constant push-pull of the canoes as the oars moved them forward made her dizzy and sick to her stomach.

"Eleanor?" Arran's voice seemed to be calling to her through a fog. It was thick and hard to push through.

The next thing she knew, she was in a tent, on a hard cot. It was dark outside, but a single candle flickered nearby. Nicolette was there, on her own cot, with Miriam nestled in the crook of her arm. Both were sleeping.

The only sound was the call of a loon somewhere beyond the camp—and Arran, moving about as he bled her.

She came to awareness with a start and he held her down with a gentle pressure on her shoulder. "Dinna fash," he said tenderly, his words just above a whisper. "I'm bleeding you again."

"Again?" Her voice was weak and all she had the energy to do was turn her head.

"Aye. I bled you when we made camp this afternoon."

"Afternoon?" She felt stupid as she kept repeating his words.

"You were unconscious. I told the others we needed to make camp so I could tend to you. Nicolette has been helping." He nodded at her and Miriam. "I bled Miriam earlier."

"How is she?" Eleanor whispered, afraid of what he might say.

He didn't answer immediately but finished bleeding her and put a tincture of friar's balsam on a piece of lint, which he pressed against her inner arm. "She isna doing much better than you."

Eleanor allowed her head to loll back against the cot. "Please," she begged. "Don't let her die."

Arran put the fleam and lint into the medicine chest, all while applying pressure to her cut. The chest was one of the items Arran had insisted on taking from the governor's house, and since there were several others in the fort, Grant had allowed it.

"We are doing everything we can to make sure you both live." He sat on the floor beside her cot and took one of her hands into his. He brought it to his lips. "We've lost so much already, my love. I canna lose you, too."

She tried to smile, but a tear slipped past her eyelid instead.

"Dinna cry, lass." He wiped the tear away. "You'll be well again. Here." He took the canteen and helped her sit up enough to take a sip.

Her throat felt as if she was swallowing broken glass, but she forced herself to drink the water. She had to push the canteen away when it became too painful.

"You should rest." He put the canteen down and then checked the lint on her arm. "I will wake you again to take another sip of water in a couple hours."

"When will it be morning?" she asked, conscious of each word and how much it cost her to speak.

"In a few hours."

"And will we . . . break . . . camp?"

"We will stay here until you and Miriam are better."

She shook her head, frowning. "But the Fort . . . William men."

"We will take our chances. I canna let you travel until you are better."

"They'll over—take us."

"Shh." He caressed her cheek. "Dinna worry about the Fort William men, or anything else. Just get better."

Her eyelids grew heavy again and she began to drift off into sleep. But all she could think about was the danger she was placing everyone in. She was the one who was supposed to be helpful when there was a need. And, right now, the need was great.

Eleanor blinked. Bright sunshine blinded her, forcing her to turn her face away from the light. Her eyesight was blurry, but it soon cleared and she was able to survey her surroundings.

The canvas tent was musty and warm. Nicolette and Miriam were no longer on the next cot, and Arran was nowhere to be seen. The medicine chest was still between the cots, but there was no other sign of anyone.

Outside the tent, the sounds of the camp came to her awareness. Fires popped and sizzled, people spoke in low tones, children ran and played, happily oblivious to their current situation.

Eleanor was covered in sweat, but she no longer shivered. Placing a hand to her forehead, she was relieved to feel it was much cooler than it had been. Hopefully her fever had broken.

Slowly, she sat up, but the world spun and she had to take her time. She couldn't ever remember being this weak before. Her head still hurt, but the pounding was now a dull ache. And her throat didn't hurt nearly as much.

"Thank God," she breathed. They could continue with their journey to Jack River House. She would insist upon it.

"You're awake." Arran appeared at the open flap, a steaming tin bowl in one hand and a cup in the other. "I was hoping you could sit up and eat something."

"Where is Miriam?" It was the only thing she needed to know.

"She's with Nicolette. Her fever broke and she's finally eating and drinking again."

Eleanor briefly closed her eyes, tears stinging the backs. But she wouldn't cry. She couldn't. She needed to be strong. There had been enough tears. It was time to focus on recovering.

"I brought you hominy and tea." He entered the tent and took a seat on the opposite cot. The space was small and he sat close.

She was suddenly self-conscious of her appearance. She must look—and smell—

dreadful. Her hair was stiff from dried sweat, her mouth tasted awful and felt like she'd been chewing on wool, and she was wearing the same gown she'd been wearing since the day of the massacre. It was covered in mud, sweat, and tears.

Eleanor ran a hand over her disheveled hair. "I look awful."

"Nay." His eyes shone. "I've never seen a bonnier sight than you, sitting up on your own."

Embarrassment warmed her cheeks and she took the bowl he offered.

He was more handsome than ever, his dark brown hair curly and wild, though he tried to contain it in a queue. He hadn't shaved in several days and his facial hair only made him look more masculine and powerful.

"Thank you," she said after she swallowed her first bit of hominy. "For taking care of us."

A smile softened his lips. "'Tis my pleasure. I thank God He gave me the chance."

She was as weak as a newborn kitten, but she would rally so they could move on. "When will we break camp?"

"Are you ready?" he asked, searching her face.

She nodded. "After I clean up a bit." She had brought one trunk of her personal items, and one of her books.

"There is a creek which empties into the river nearby. You may bathe there with little trouble."

She desired a bath more than she did food, but she ate every bite and drank the tea he had brought for her. The warmth of it felt good as it flowed down her throat.

Arran sent Nicolette in to help her prepare for her bath, and then Eleanor and Nicolette took Miriam to the creek. Arran promised to stand guard at the mouth of the creek, near the camp, to make sure no one intruded upon their privacy. He told her to take her time, but she did not want to make the others wait. Though she had gained their respect over the last several months, she did not want to lose it now by being selfish.

Miriam laughed as Eleanor held her in the water. The baby splashed and giggled as Eleanor washed her hair with the soft soap she had brought from England. When Miriam was done, Eleanor handed the baby to Nicolette, who dried her in a towel and then began to dress her in a clean gown made from the fabric of one of Eleanor's old dresses. She put a white bonnet on Miriam's blond curls, then entertained the baby while Eleanor finished her own bath.

The water was cool and refreshing. Eleanor washed her hair and every inch of her skin, allowing the gentle pressure of the flowing water to lift her off her feet to float for a few moments, unencumbered by the pull of the earth.

All too soon, she was finished. With a quick glance to see if she, Nicolette, and Miriam were still alone, she hastened out of the water and onto dry ground.

The air was still thick and humid, but the sun was shining bright, and she was soon dry and properly clothed again. She tried to press the water from her long, dark curls, but her hair was still damp as she turned it up and placed several pins to keep it off her back. The coil of hair was heavy as she and Nicolette made their way back to camp.

Arran stood right where they had left him. When he saw her coming, he smiled and took in the full length of her, from the tips of her half-boots to the top of her wet head. From the look of pleasure on his face, she could tell he liked what he saw.

Butterflies filled her stomach and for the first time since the massacre, a flood of hope filled her chest. Now that she was feeling better, she could turn her thoughts to their wedding at Jack River House. They had all lost so much, she was eager for a little joy amid the pain.

It would be a long two-week journey across Lake Winnipeg, but on the other side of the trip, she would become Mrs. Arran MacLean.

"I told everyone to break camp while you were bathing," Arran said as he took Miriam in his arms and held the baby as naturally as if he'd been a father for years. "We are ready to go, if you are."

She nodded and followed him back to their camp.

Just as he'd said, the tents were down and the canoes were packed and ready for departure.

While Arran helped Nicolette into the lead canoe, Eleanor looked up the riverbank at the settlers who were ready to leave. Fiona sat in her canoe, her children tucked close to her side. Her gaze was fixed on a point far removed from the banks of the Red River.

Now that Eleanor was better, she would see to her friend's needs, just as Fiona had met Miriam's needs after Anne had died.

Soon, the brigade was off again, and this time, Eleanor was awake and alert. She was still fatigued, but the bath and meal had done wonders for her outlook.

Arran sat beside her, his calm, steady presence a balm to her weary soul. From time to time, he would squeeze her hand. He did not talk about anything beyond Jack River House, and she did not wonder why. There were still so many unanswered questions.

They had not been on the water for more than an hour when the lead *avant*, the voyageur at the front of the canoe, spotted a brigade approaching from around a bend downriver.

Eleanor's muscles tensed as she counted nine canoes and one bateau. All were laden with men—men who spotted them at the same moment and lifted their muskets, preparing to fire.

"Halt!" a voice cried out from the canoe directly in front of Arran's.

The hair on the back of Arran's neck stood on end as he found the owner of the voice. Archibald Norman McLeod, the Justice of the Peace for the Western Territories—who also happened to be a partner in the North West Company.

"Who are ye?" McLeod asked as he searched the canoes for a familiar face. "I demand an accounting of yer party."

"Aye." Arran lifted his hand to gain McLeod's attention. "And you'll have it."

"Arran MacLean." McLeod shook his head, his lips turning up in a sneer. "We meet again, though I am not surprised to see ye are the head of this band of ruffians."

The group with Arran could no more be called ruffians than a litter of puppies. They were hungry, destitute, and afraid. Without weapons, mourning the untimely death of loved ones, and forcibly removed from their homes, they posed no risk to anyone—let alone the Justice of the Peace and his hundred or more armed men.

McLeod had been the officer responsible for discharging Arran of his duties as a North West Company clerk when Duncan Cameron had falsely accused him of stealing from the company. No doubt, he would assume the worst of Arran and his men.

"I can only surmise that ye are the last of the settlers from Assiniboia?" McLeod asked. He smiled and a gleam filled his beady eyes. "Did ye have trouble?"

"Aye." Arran had nothing but his wits and intelligence to defend himself and these hundred and fifty men, women, and children with him. "We have come from Assiniboia and have had a great deal of trouble."

McLeod looked over the group and then nodded toward the shore. "I want everyone to disembark for a thorough investigation. I expect a full account of the events leading up to yer departure from the colony."

Arran had hoped and prayed they could avoid McLeod. The man was known to be ruthless and single-minded. There was no telling what he might decide to do with the settlers. They had been so close—just a half-day more of travel and they would have been to Lake Winnipeg. They could have easily taken a different course along the lake to avoid McLeod if possible.

But none of that mattered now. "Disembark!" Arran called to his men. "Post-haste."

A great commotion of humanity unfurled as almost three hundred people from both groups found their way to the riverbanks. Here, the land was full of marshes as they drew closer to Lake Winnipeg. Mosquitoes swarmed and crickets hummed as the settlers tried to find enough solid ground to unload their belongings. Each time a canoe was brought onto land, it had to be emptied of all its weight or the thin bark lining the hull could easily be punctured.

Eleanor was quiet as she stepped out of their canoe. Arran helped her, Nicolette, and Miriam onto dry ground.

"Dinna be afraid," he said quietly to Eleanor. "We'll be on our way soon."

McLeod's men had also disembarked, and dozens of them circled the colonists with their muskets at the ready.

"What will happen?" Eleanor asked Arran as she eyed the Nor'westers.

"I will meet with McLeod and tell him exactly what happened at Seven Oaks. There are several witnesses to corroborate my tale. I will bring them forward."

"He is a Justice of the Peace?" she asked. "He will see that justice is served?"

Arran did not have the heart to tell her that justice was the last thing McLeod would have in mind. He had come to help remove the settlers from Assiniboia, and he would not care how it was done. The most Arran could hope was that McLeod would allow them to proceed as planned. "Just sit here and rest. You've had a hard few days of illness."

"If we had not stopped early last night for Miriam and me, and had left at daybreak today, could we have avoided these men?" She searched his face.

He would not tell her the truth. There was no point in heaping guilt upon her shoulders. "There is no way to know." He tried to smile. "Please rest, for me."

Her brown eyes filled with apprehension, but she nodded and offered him an encouraging smile. "I will pray."

His heart was filled with such love and affection for her. She constantly amazed him with her fortitude and faith in his abilities. It warmed his chest and gave him the courage he would need to face McLeod.

James, Archie, Pritchard, John Burke, and another man, the blacksmith, Michael Heden, who had gone out to the plains with the second group of men, waited for Arran. They walked toward McLeod, who had set up a makeshift office, complete with a folding chair and traveling desk. Several pieces of paper and a feather pen were before him on the desk. At least a dozen of his men stood by, watching and waiting.

"Are these the only men who have an account to give?" McLeod asked Arran.

"Nay." Arran crossed his arms and lifted his chin. "Every man, woman, and child in this party could give you an account of the horrors we have just endured."

McLeod's jaw tightened and he breathed through his nostrils. "I willna tolerate lies or innuendoes, MacLean. I simply want the truth."

"Have you not heard?" Arran asked. "About the massacre at Seven Oaks?"

"Massacre?" McLeod's eyes narrowed and he studied Arran. "What massacre?"

Arran, James, Archie, Heden, Burke, and Pritchard did not spare any details about the events leading up to, and comprising, the battle with the Bois-Brûlés. Pritchard even wrote down the account for McLeod. But the entire time the men recounted the affair, he did not ask any questions. He just listened, his face devoid of emotion.

Finally, when they had exhausted their story, McLeod stood, his face red. "I have never heard such rubbish in all my life. I dinna believe a word of it for a second."

Arran pounded his finger on the paper Pritchard had written. "Every word of it is true."

"I should have ye all arrested for libel against agents and clerks of the North West Company." McLeod snapped his fingers and called two men over to his side. "I want a thorough search of everyone's property. Bring me any books or papers ye find, so that I may use it in the court of law when I bring these people to justice."

"Bring *us* to justice?" James asked, holding his arm. Eleanor had tried to clean the wound and bandage it, but there had been no doctors to attend to the injury. "We're innocent in this matter."

"Are ye innocent in the removal and destruction of Fort Gibraltar?" McLeod asked.

"Aye!" James said emphatically. "Governor Semple, who was brutally murdered by your men, was responsible for Fort Gibraltar."

"And are ye not the chief factor representing the Hudson's Bay Company?" McLeod asked.

"Aye."

"Then ye are guilty by association."

"Guilty?" Arran could not sit back and let his friend be prosecuted for Semple's mistakes.

"Dinna let me get started on ye, MacLean. Ye have been at the heart of Lord Selkirk's colony for four years now. Every atrocity committed by the settlement is upon yer shoulders."

"We've only been defending what is ours by right of the Royal Charter." Arran's fists clenched. "You have no right to accuse us and search the property of these defenseless settlers. They have nothing to do with these charges you've brought."

"They have everything to do with them." McLeod nodded to his men to begin. "Do ye have Semple's things? Or did ye leave them at Fort Douglas?" he asked Arran.

Arran had no weapon or authority to stop McLeod. He would be forced to stand by and watch as McLeod's men tore apart what few belongings the settlers had left. What did it matter if he kept Semple's things a secret? The man would find them eventually.

"Aye. We have his belongings." They had West's trunk with his few personal possessions, as well.

"Bring it to me."

Semple's things were near Arran and Eleanor's trunks, so he went that way, watching as McLeod's men heartlessly ripped clothing, personal items, and utensils from bags, boxes, and trunks. There were only a few who possessed any sort of papers or books—all except Eleanor. She had one small trunk dedicated just to her books. They were dear and precious to her. She had read from them to the men in the governor's house at Pembina over the long, cold winters, and on more than one occasion, Arran had witnessed her writing in her journal. She also used them to teach the children. Would they now become the property of Archibald McLeod?

Arran hastened his steps, needing to warn Eleanor to somehow protect and hide her journal. He did not know what it might contain, but if there was anything in there about the activities of the settlement, it would be confiscated by McLeod.

One of McLeod's men trailed close on Arran's heels.

"Eleanor." Arran spoke her name on an urgent whisper. He busied himself with Semple's trunk while speaking to her. "McLeod is looking through everyone's things for papers and books that he might use against the settlement. He will take anything he finds."

She did nothing more than nod, her gaze straying to McLeod's man, who stood a little way off. Though she didn't speak, he could see in her eyes that she clearly understood his meaning.

"I will take Semple's things to McLeod," he said loud enough for the man to hear, but then he dropped his voice, "but you must hide your journal if you—"

"You, there," McLeod's man said to Arran. "What are you saying to that woman?"

Arran lifted Semple's trunk in his arms—which was not an easy feat—and turned to face the man who had addressed him. "I'm taking Governor Semple's trunk to McLeod."

"What were you saying to that woman?" The man was tall, with deep-set eyes. "Were you telling her to destroy something important?"

"Nay. I was explaining to her what McLeod plans—"

He pushed past Arran and stood in front of Eleanor. "What do you have?"

Eleanor sat on her trunk and stared at the Nor'wester. "Nothing."

"Dinna bother her," Arran told the man, venom in his voice. "She doesna have anything of importance."

"I'll let McLeod be the judge of that." He took Eleanor by the arm and hauled her off her trunk.

Arran dropped Semple's large trunk and pushed the Nor'wester aside. "Dinna touch her," he said with a hiss. "Or you'll have to deal with me."

The Nor'wester lifted his chin and fisted his hands.

"What's the meaning of this?" McLeod asked, walking toward Arran.

"Mr. MacLean is warning this woman to destroy something of importance," the Nor'wester said.

"Is this true?" McLeod asked Eleanor.

Arran had never known Eleanor to lie before, but she stared at McLeod now and said, "I do not have anything you will find important."

McLeod studied Eleanor for a moment and then he said, "Who are ye?"

"Miss Eleanor Brooke."

His eyebrows rose in surprise. "Lady Eleanor Brooke, the daughter of Lord Brooke, Earl of Rathmore?"

Eleanor did not voice her answer, but simply nodded.

Several of McLeod's men took notice of Eleanor then, eyeing her with more than a passing interest. Arran's entire body became rigid, and suddenly the host of McLeod's men became enemies for an entirely different reason.

"I had heard Selkirk was sending a lady into the colony to bring some refinement, but I dinna believe the rumors." McLeod looked between Eleanor and Arran, his eyes calculating. Then he nodded toward her trunk. "Show me yer things, Lady Eleanor."

Eleanor's hair was still damp from her bath. It drooped in the back, her pins having come loose. But she was beautiful as she stoically opened her trunk.

McLeod looked inside, but it was only her gowns and personal effects. "And that one?" He pointed to her smaller trunk, the one with the books.

"The books I brought with me from my father's home at Edgewood Manor." If ever Eleanor had used her status and breeding, it was now. She lifted her chin and looked down at McLeod, reminding Arran that she was, at her heart, a member of the aristocracy. "You will not find anything of interest in there."

McLeod nodded toward the Nor'wester with the deep-set eyes. He opened the trunk and showed him her books.

"Take them to the bateau," McLeod ordered.

"You cannot take my books." Eleanor's voice rose high as color filled her cheeks. "I use them to teach the children."

"I can do what I please, Lady Eleanor. I am the Justice of the Peace and everything within yer possession is evidence." His gaze landed on the traveling desk placed close to the smaller trunk. "And what is this?" He walked over to the desk and lifted the lid.

Eleanor's journal sat within.

She stiffened and Arran stepped forward, but McLeod held up his hand to stop Arran.

Arran stared hard at McLeod as the man leafed through Eleanor's personal writings. He read a few lines and then his gaze lifted and he looked from Eleanor to Arran, comprehension in his gaze. "Are ye lovers?"

Heat rose up Arran's neck as he ground out, "Dinna insult the lady with such vulgarity. She is my fiancée." But what had he read within the pages of Eleanor's journal that would lead him to believe they were lovers?

"Ye're affianced to a lady? Well done, MacLean."

"That is my journal," Eleanor said, her lips tight. "You have no right to read it."

"I have already told ye my rights—and responsibilities." McLeod motioned to one of his men to take the writing desk, as well. "I will keep all of this as evidence."

Eleanor stepped forward to grab the journal at the same moment Arran did—but both were apprehended by McLeod's men.

"Take MacLean and the other five liars into custody," McLeod said to the Nor'westers. "The rest may continue on to Jack River House, as planned."

"Custody?" Arran asked, his heart pounding. He tried to pull away from his captor. "Why are you arresting us?"

"Ye will be charged with crimes against the North West Company and subpoenaed to appear in court in Montreal no later than September the first." McLeod's self-satisfied smile made Arran's anger boil. "I will also see that ye are charged with the murder of one of Cuthbert Grant's men."

"That's a lie!"

"Ye told me yerself that one of them fell in the battle instigated by yer men. Ye'll hang for the offense."

"It wasna instigated by us!"

"Ye approached Grant's men. They were not approaching ye."

"They fired first!"

"I'd like to see ye prove that." McLeod motioned for his men to take Arran away.

"No." Arran fought to get free. "You willna get away with this."

McLeod ignored him and returned his attention to Eleanor's journal, one eyebrow raised, as if he was reading something sordid.

"Please," Eleanor begged, trying to free herself from the grasp of another Nor'wester. Her fatigue was evident as she weakened in his hold. "Do not take him."

"Unhand her," Arran yelled at the Nor'wester. "She's a lady!"

"Dinna fash, Lady Eleanor." McLeod nodded at the large man to let her go. "I will send one of my best men to make sure ye and the others arrive safely at Jack River House."

Rage pounded in Arran's chest and he tried to lash out, but another brute came to help the first two men haul Arran toward McLeod's canoes.

"Arran!" Eleanor rushed after them, alarm in her eyes. "Where will they take you?"

"I dinna ken." He shook his head, wishing he knew. "Montreal, mayhap." He stopped fighting his captors, and, at McLeod's nod, they eased up a bit. The other men were gathering the books and papers they had found among the settlers' things and returning to the river.

He didn't have much time with Eleanor.

"Where should I go?" she asked. "Shall I make my way to Montreal?"

Arran shook his head, confused. "No. It would be too dangerous. Stay at Jack River House. I will get word to you once I ken what will happen."

"Will they—" She choked on the words and put her hand to her mouth. "Hang you?"

The courts in Montreal were influenced and populated by North West Company employees. His chances of a fair trial were almost infinitesimal. He could not make any promises, but he couldn't let her fret, either. "I will do everything in my power to return to you."

It would be dangerous for Eleanor to be on her own. He didn't want to contemplate all the horrors that might await her. He tried to think, but everything had happened too fast.

"Old John," he said suddenly. He looked around the settlers, his gaze panicked.

"I'm here," Old John said to Arran, coming to his side as the Nor'westers started to force Arran to the boats.

Arran was breathless as he said, "See to Eleanor and Miriam, please."

"Aye." Old John placed his hand over his heart. "Ye have my word."

They were at the riverside and Arran was pulled into the water. "Thank you," he said, turning his gaze back to Eleanor, helpless to stop this madness. "I'm sorry."

"I love you," she said, reaching for him.

Their fingertips grazed as he was pushed into the canoe.

"I love you, too. Kiss Miriam for me."

Eleanor nodded as the other Nor'westers entered the river all around her, their arms laden with more than books and papers. They had stolen the very few precious possessions the settlers had left.

McLeod came to her side, Eleanor's journal in his hands. "I wish ye well, Lady Eleanor. It was a pleasure to meet ye." He smiled and lifted the journal. "Thank ye for this riveting account. I will thoroughly enjoy reading it. I have a feeling it will aid me in convicting your fiancé."

Eleanor's cheeks became pale as her lips began to tremble.

McLeod entered his own boat and called to his men to push off and head south toward the settlement.

The last thing Arran saw as the boats turned the bend was Eleanor standing on the banks of the Red River, sobbing.

Chapter Eighteen

As the miles spread between Eleanor and Arran, she had to force herself to take one breath after the other. Exhaustion wore on her tender emotions, but she could not weep any longer. She *would* not weep any longer. Now was not the time for hysterics or sentimentality. She had a baby to care for and a group of settlers to rally.

Yet, her heart cried out for the man she loved. Would she ever see him on this side of eternity again? Would he get a fair trial, or would he be sentenced without so much as a word of protest? Arran was a fighter, but was this battle now too big for him to win?

And worst of all, McLeod might use Eleanor's written words to convict Arran. The loss of her journal was like losing her best friend. One more thing to mourn in a long succession of defeats.

Panic threatened and dread tried to take a foothold, but she held it at bay with sheer determination. She would be strong for Arran and Miriam. She would fight just as hard as he, for just as long as it would take. She could not give up hope—not even for a moment. Because if she did, she was afraid that despair would wrap its icy grip on her heart and never let go.

The river was smooth as the voyageurs paddled in their steady rhythm. They were close to the mouth of the river and would soon enter Lake Winnipeg. Despite what Arran had said, she knew she was the cause of their calamity. If she hadn't been ill, they would have entered the lake much sooner and had the opportunity to take a different course. Guilt assailed her, and each time she met the bedraggled gazes of her fellow passengers, she couldn't help but blame herself for their lack of leadership. But it was the threat to Arran and the other five men that weighed the heaviest upon her. How long might it be before she heard from Arran again? It could be months—or years—or never.

"He's gotten himself out of worse situations before," Old John said to Eleanor as he patted her hand. "He'll be back, ye'll see."

"Truly?" Eleanor asked. "Has he been in worse situations?"

Old John's eyes were a cloudy blue and the wrinkles in his skin were deep. Several days' worth of gray stubble was on his chin and his hair was thin, but the kindness in his face made him appear precious to her. "I wish it were true—but I have faith in him and in God. Dinna give up praying for a miracle, lass. We will see him again. And, in the meantime, the missus and I will care for ye and Miriam like ye were our own."

"And I will care for you," she said, thankful for the sweet man at her side. "Arran and I are blessed to call you a friend."

Without Arran or James, the settlers now turned to Old John as their leader. He had lived in the Red River Valley for years and was well-versed in the lay of the land.

Finally, they left the marshland around the Red River and entered Lake Winnipeg just before sunset. They continued for a bit longer and found a place to make camp on a sandy beach. Several voyageurs came to assist Eleanor and Nicolette as they set up Arran's tent for their use. Old

John pitched his tent nearby and Isla helped with Miriam as Nicolette prepared their supper.

"I do not know what I would do without all of you," Eleanor said to her small makeshift family. God had blessed her, in her darkest moment, with people who cared about her. She tried to tell her grieving heart that it was enough—at least for now—but it would not listen. She continued to fight despair, wondering where Arran was at this very moment, praying, as Old John had told her, and trying to believe.

"Lord," she whispered as she gathered kindling from nearby scrub brush, "help me in my unbelief."

"Is there room for one more around yer fire?" Chait Fraser was the man McLeod had assigned to oversee the settlers until they reached Jack River House. He was a tall, broad-shouldered half-blood man, no more than thirty or thirty-one. From the little he had interacted with Eleanor, she had found him to be well-educated, with impeccable manners. His high cheekbones and dark eyes and hair were reminiscent of his mother's ancestry, but his bearing and the fine clothes he wore spoke of a bourgeois, or boss. She wondered at his past but would never presume to ask—nor did she truly want to know. He was yet another reminder of all that had been taken from her and the others.

Eleanor shared a glance with Old John. Should they welcome him to their fire? Would it be rude to send him away? He was a Nor'wester, after all, but hadn't Arran been a Nor'wester at one point? They couldn't all be bad. Old John appeared to know him.

Old John nodded at her and she, in turn, nodded at Chait. "You're welcome to join us, though we have little to offer."

"I've brought some sea biscuits with me." He opened the handkerchief he held and revealed three hard biscuits, double-baked to preserve them. They were a common food on ships and within Rupert's Land, though Eleanor had never been able to stomach them.

"Thank you." She took the biscuits and offered them to Nicolette, hoping she would find a way to make them palatable.

"Won't ye have a seat?" Old John asked.

There were large pieces of driftwood lying on the beach near the fire and Chait sat on one now. His legs were long and lean as he confidently rested in their presence. There was an easiness about him—so unlike all the other Nor'westers Eleanor had met in her short time in the wilderness. "Thank ye for welcoming me," he said. "I ken ye are angry."

"Angry doesna begin to describe how we feel." Old John's patience was thin and he watched Chait closely. "Yer men have taken everything from us and we are exiles from our homes once again."

"Aye." Chait glanced up and met Eleanor's gaze. He held it for a moment, but then looked back at Old John. "I am sorry for what has happened. If it had been up to me, we wouldna be here right now. I may be an employee of the North West Company, but I dinna approve of all their practices. I think there is enough land for our company and the Hudson's Bay Company to stay in business. And if the Nor'westers could live peacefully with the HBC men, I dinna believe we would have any trouble."

"You speak of peace," Eleanor said, crossing her arms. "How do you come by a different opinion than all your comrades?"

Chait tilted his head and nodded in recognition of her comment. "I grew up at Fort Assiniboine, near Brandon House, where my faither was the bourgeois. He was much older than my maither, and when I was very young, he retired and left his post—leaving my maither behind. He brought me to Montreal and I was raised there by his legal wife, as their only child."

Eleanor's eyebrows rose in surprise. She was unable to imagine what kind of life he must have led. Had he been wanted by his father's legal wife? Had his birth mother been given an option when he was taken? Surely he hadn't been a welcome addition to his father's community.

She had a hundred questions, yet his early life was none of her business. "How long have you been back?"

"I entered as a clerk ten years ago and was just made a partner at last year's rendezvous at Fort William." He crossed his arms in a congenial pose. "I spent time at Fort Gibraltar."

"Aye." Old John watched Chait closely, but Eleanor could not read his thoughts. Was Chait a trustworthy person—or one they should all avoid? "Arran was the senior clerk when Chait was there."

"You know Duncan Cameron, then?" It was Eleanor's turn to study Chait a bit closer.

"Aye." Chait nodded but did not give any more information.

Had Chait assisted Duncan in getting Arran removed from his post, or had he been a friend?

Eleanor caught sight of Fiona making a fire with several other settlers. Some of the widows had banded together and were cooking around a communal pot, their children gathering firewood and kindling in the surrounding brush. Fiona glanced up and met Eleanor's gaze. Sadness clung to Fiona, and Eleanor wished, with all her heart, that she could relieve her friend from all her suffering. Neither woman said a word, but Fiona nodded at Eleanor as if she understood what Eleanor was trying to communicate.

As the sky darkened, the shadows from their fires danced with eerie movements against the settlers' faces. Beyond the camp, the lake stretched out as far as the eye could see, and stars sparkled overhead.

Here, near the water, it was cooler and the humidity was less severe. The mosquitoes, also, had dissipated, offering a bit of respite.

Eleanor's eyelids were heavy and she noticed that Miriam had fallen asleep in Isla's arms.

"Would you mind terribly if I went to bed?" Eleanor asked those sitting around the fire.

"What about supper?" Isla asked.

Eleanor shook her head. "I am not hungry." She hadn't had an appetite since Arran had been taken earlier that day.

Had it only been that morning when she'd bathed and felt hopeful for the first time in days? It had been so short-lived, she almost felt like a fool for thinking it would last.

"Ye need to keep up yer energy," Old John warned her.

"I think I need sleep more than anything else right now." She tried to smile for him. "I'll take Miriam with me." She went to Isla and lifted Miriam into her arms. The baby was warm and soft. She snuggled into Eleanor's shoulder, fitting perfectly. Affection filled Eleanor and she kissed the top of Miriam's head, thankful the baby was feeling better.

Chait rose. "Good night, Lady Eleanor."

"Please." She stopped on her way to the tent. "I prefer Miss Brooke." What she actually preferred was Mrs. MacLean, but she wondered now if that was ever meant to be. Tears threatened, but she needed to be in her tent before she gave in to their demands.

Chait nodded and bowed, his hands behind his back, as if he was saying good night to her in a formal parlor at an English manor.

She said good night to the others, her curious gaze returning to Chait Fraser more than once before retiring to her tent.

As soon as she laid down, with Miriam tucked in by her side, Eleanor finally gave in to the tears and despair.

Fort William

North West Company

Northern Lake Superior

August 16, 1816

The mid-August sun bore down on Arran as he and the other five men from Assiniboia walked toward the Great Hall at Fort William. Two armed men followed them from the Bell House, where they had been kept among senior North West Company clerks since their arrival four weeks before. None of the Red River men spoke when they were under guard—which was almost constantly. They had learned early on that they were being observed, their conversations repeated to the partners. Instead, they kept their mouths shut and their eyes and ears open. In this way, they had learned several important details about the North West Company and their plans.

The Great Hall sat in the middle of Fort William, the hub of the village-sized headquarters for the North West Company since 1803. The old headquarters at Grand Portage were now part of the United States since the Louisiana Purchase, and to avoid US tariffs, the company had moved forty miles north over the border into Rupert's Land. Almost five thousand fur traders, voyageurs, and native people came through the fort during the months of May through September. There were at least forty buildings of various sizes, built specifically for the needs of the fort. Warehouses, dormitories, shops, a tinsmith, a cooper, a blacksmith, as well as boat builders, an apothecary and infirmary, not to mention the gaol, all within the walls of the fort.

Trade goods, sent from Montreal, and before that from England, were delivered in the spring by voyageurs known as pork-eaters who were strong French-Canadian men employed to haul the thousands of tons of cargo in light-weight canoes. Once the cargo arrived at Fort William, it was dispersed to the voyageurs known as north men. These were rough, seasoned French-Canadians who stayed in the interior throughout the long winter. The north men would arrive at Fort William with all the furs collected by the Indians through the long winters. Here, the pork-eaters, named for their primary food source, would take the furs and return to Montreal, where they would be put on ships bound for England. The north men would take the trade goods brought by the pork-eaters and return to the interior to use them to purchase more furs. It was an endless cycle that had begun over sixty years ago, and many men had become very powerful and rich because of the trade.

Now, in mid-August, the commotion of Fort William had dimmed as brigades of north men returned to their interior posts, and the majority of the pork-eaters had gone back to Montreal. There was still a strong contingency of employees, though, and every time the men left their room in Bell House, there were guards to keep them from escaping.

They stepped onto the long porch attached to the Great Hall and Arran opened the door leading into the dining room. Two hundred people could sit within, though only about fifty men were there now. Arran led his men to a small table in the corner, where they had taken all their meals. The Great Hall was reserved for partners, clerks, interpreters, and guides, while the voyageurs were strictly forbidden from entering. They allowed the Assiniboia men to eat there, as well, and Arran was grateful for that small favor, though he and his men were treated no better than the lowly voyageurs.

The guards left Arran and his men at their table and then went to a different one occupied by their friends.

"When do ye think they'll send us to Montreal?" Archie asked Arran quietly.

"I dinna ken." Arran was surprised that they hadn't been sent already. Their September first court date was only a few weeks off, but it would take at least six to reach Montreal.

"Mayhap they're waiting for McGillivray to take us," James said, sitting across from Arran. "I heard yesterday that he plans to stay for another week, until the rest of the pork-eaters are ready to return."

William McGillivray was the most prominent partner still residing at Fort William for the remainder of the summer. There were others, of lesser rank, men who had come in from Montreal for the annual rendezvous, in large flotillas and great fanfare. These wealthy men lived in luxury for the winter months in the east, and then made their way to Fort William for the summer to conduct business—still living in grand style at the fort. Many had been wintering partners, spending their time at posts throughout the interior, years before, and knew the land as well as those who traded with the Indians now.

"Aye." Arran nodded at James's assessment. "They'll send us back with McGillivray."

For four weeks, they had resided at Fort William, waiting to be removed to Montreal. Before that, it had taken them almost four weeks to travel to the fort from the Red River. It was an infuriating experience to sit idle, when Arran knew how hard Eleanor must be working just to survive.

The dining room was overly warm, though the windows were open to allow a breeze to blow in from the Kaministiquia River. The river ran parallel to the fort, which had been built near the mouth of the river as it emptied into the northern shores of Lake Superior. A long wharf had been built on the banks of the river for the ease of the canoes that came in and out almost daily through the warm summer months.

An Indian woman arrived at their table with steaming platters of delectable food. Fresh bread, salt pork, beef, ham, fish, peas, Indian corn, potatoes, butter, and cranberry sauce. They were also offered tea, high wine, and plenty of milk. Arran had not gone hungry since arriving at Fort William, but each time he filled his belly, all he could think about was Eleanor and Miriam, wondering if they were as fortunate.

"I ken what you're thinking when you get that look in your eyes," James said as he put a spoonful of Indian corn on his fine china. "Old John will take care of her and the bairn."

The other men glanced in Arran's direction, though no one mentioned Eleanor's name. Arran was not the only man among them who had been forced to leave the woman he loved. Heden and Burke were married with children, and Pritchard had been courting one of the settler's daughters.

"I wish there was a way we could know if they arrived at Jack River House." Arran had said the same at least a hundred times since arriving at Fort William. "What if something befell them along the way?"

Heden's face was long as he said, "My fear is that they tired of waiting for us and left, or took up with another man."

"That's a rotten thing to say." Pritchard shot Heden a stony look. "If you don't have anything nice to say, then keep your mouth shut."

"And why wouldn't they?" Heden challenged. "There are five men for every woman among the settlers. Why would they wait?"

"Mayhap they love us?" Burke asked with sarcasm dripping from his voice. "And they're committed to us."

"You all need to calm yourselves," James admonished. "We are not the enemy. They are." He pointed with his fork. "We'll have to leave our loved ones in God's hands and deal with what comes one step at a time."

Arran pushed his boiled potatoes around his plate, the injustice of the entire situation making his stomach turn to knots.

There was no way of knowing if the settlers reached Jack River House, or if they would be waiting for them on their return. He had asked Eleanor to wait for him, but what if circumstances forced her to leave Jack River House? What if she lost hope of seeing him again and accepted someone else's proposal to ensure her and Miriam's survival?

Arran couldn't think about such things. He had to do as James said and trust God.

A clerk burst through the front door of the dining hall and everyone's conversation died.

"It's Lord Selkirk!" the clerk exclaimed, rushing to McGillivray's side, a missive in hand. "He's landed at a point a mile upriver, and he's in the possession of at least a hundred or more soldiers!"

"What's this?" McGillivray rose and tossed his napkin on his plate. He ripped the missive from the clerk's hand and quickly scanned the contents.

Arran's entire body became still as he watched and waited. James and the other men did not move a muscle. Selkirk was here? It was too good to be true.

McGillivray crumpled the missive and turned his angry gaze on Arran and his men. His jaw clenched and for a moment, he looked as if he might address Arran, but then he turned and spoke to the partners and senior clerks sitting at his table. "If this report is true, Lord Selkirk is currently at a point west of here, with over a hundred retired de Meuron soldiers."

De Meuron soldiers! The regiment of Swiss mercenary soldiers was first raised over forty years before for the Dutch East India Company and named for its commander, Colonel Charles-Daniel de Meuron. Arran was familiar with their service in both the Napoleonic wars, as well as the War of 1812, when they were posted in Canada. He had heard they were disbanded, but had never dreamed Selkirk would think to hire them—if indeed he had.

"I want the Red River men returned to their quarters," McGillivray ordered, "until further notice." He stormed away from the table toward his room, which also served as his office. He spoke to the other partners as he went. "No doubt Selkirk is here for his men. If he gets them now, they'll never face charges. We must remove them from here before Selkirk demands them, and sneak them off to Montreal."

A handful of the clerks rose to remove Arran and the Red River men from the dining hall, but they did not need to be told. They left their food on their table and walked back to Bell House, on the other side of the Great Hall, with several guards following them.

"I dinna like this," Arran said the moment they entered their quarters. He still spoke quietly, knowing the guards were posted outside their door. Three bunks filled the spacious room and a table with six chairs sat in the center. The men went there now.

"I wouldna doubt that the Nor'westers are hatching a plan to assassinate Selkirk in his sleep," Archie said. "He is the only man who stands in the way of their plans."

Arran leaned forward and whispered, "If Selkirk delays in coming for us, McGillivray will remove us from the fort. Once we're in Montreal, he'll not be able to free us from prison. Our fates will be sealed." He tapped his fingers against the wooden table, unable to sit. He left his chair and walked to the window, looking out at the back side of the fort. "He needs to be told to strike immediately. And I will be the one to tell him."

"It won't work," Pritchard said, his voice low. "They'll be watching us even closer now."

"I'll find a way to escape."

"We'll all go," Heden said, his voice tight and quiet.

"Nay. It'll be harder to escape with the six of us. If I can get away tonight and warn Selkirk to strike in the morning, it'll be our best chance."

"And what if Selkirk is not ready to come in the morning? What will we tell the Nor'westers when ye dinna appear for breakfast tomorrow?"

"He'll have to be ready. We won't have any other choice."

"And what if you're captured?" James asked.

"What more could they do to me?" Arran lifted his shoulder. "I'm already a prisoner, facing trial for murder."

"It could be a lot worse, my friend."

"I will take the risk." Arran had sat around for four weeks, wishing he could do something. Now was the time to act. He had to save his friends.

Chapter Nineteen

JACK RIVER HOUSE, HBC
NORTHERN LAKE WINNIPEG
AUGUST 16, 1816

Fog rolled over Little Playgreen Lake, hovering above the waters like a soft blanket. The sun had not yet crested the horizon, but there was a pale purple hue to the sky, with ever-brightening shades of pink on the rim of the earth. Eleanor liked this quiet part of the day best of all. Few of the fort's occupants were awake, allowing her to sit for a bit on her favorite log, facing the lake, praying.

If she had her journal, she would have used this time to write about the past six weeks since arriving at Jack River House. She mourned the loss of her books almost as much as she mourned everything else that had been taken from her. The words she'd written could never be recaptured. They were a part of her heart and soul. An extension of her deepest thoughts and most precious memories. To know that strangers were reading them felt like the worst sort of intrusion, as if she had been stripped bare for all to see.

A sigh deflated her chest as she let her eyes linger on the horizon, forcing herself to find a reason to be thankful for this oncoming day. She had started the school again, to keep the children occupied and provide weekly entertainment as they had done over the winter in Pembina. Mr. Barlas lent her the use of his books and the main room of his fur post. It had given her a sense of purpose and kept her mind occupied.

For the most part.

Jack River House was a modest fort, residing on Little Playgreen Lake at the head of the Nelson River, which ran from Lake Winnipeg to Hudson Bay. They had passed this way on their journey to the colony the year before, when Miriam was only two months old. It had been difficult for the fort to take over a hundred refugees, with no supplies and few necessities among them. But the voyageurs and Indians who summered there had given what they had, and everyone had learned to make do. Thankfully, there had been a large garden planted by the half-blood women who resided at the fort year-round, and it had started to produce vegetables. Fish had been their mainstay, as well as small game. They still had their tents and blankets, and a few cooking utensils, for which Eleanor was grateful.

Her thoughts turned to Miriam and how the baby had grown, having passed her first birthday the month before. Though, she could hardly be called a baby any longer. She toddled around the fort as if she'd been walking her whole life, and made friends with several company men, including the chief factor, Dugan Barlas, who doted on the child as if he was her long-lost grandfather.

A heavy footfall sounded behind Eleanor and she turned to find Fiona Ferguson approaching.

"Mind if I join ye?" Fiona asked.

"Of course not." Eleanor moved to the side to allow her friend to sit beside her. The two women had grown closer over the past few weeks as they had endured the hardships of grief and uncertainty together. "How is Catriona feeling this morning?"

Fiona nodded. "Her fever broke in the night. She is sleeping peacefully now."

Catriona, the youngest of the Ferguson children, often had ear complaints, and would cry for hours on end. The doctor at Jack River House had given her oils to use and it had done a great deal to help the baby.

"I've come to a decision," Fiona said quietly as they both looked out at the calm lake. Indian wigwams were spread out along the shoreline and dozens of overturned canoes dotted the landscape beyond the stockade. "I will marry Mr. Kelly, in the custom of the country, until we can make it legal. He will start sharing my tent tonight."

Eleanor closed her eyes briefly and took a few breaths before she responded, her voice tight. "He is old and prone to drink."

"Not all of us have the luxury of waiting for a knight in shining armor to come and rescue us." Fiona's back went rigid. "I have four babies who need a faither, and Mr. Kelly is the only one who has offered."

Eleanor had known this conversation was coming. Mr. Kelly had been relentless in his pursuit of Fiona from the moment they had reached Jack River House. "It's only because he has not allowed anyone else the opportunity. He monopolizes your time and threatens anyone who might approach you." There were dozens of eligible bachelors among the settlers. Eleanor was well-aware. Ever since Arran had been taken away, several had made advances.

"Who would approach me?" Fiona asked. "I'm ugly and large—"

"You are beautiful." Eleanor turned to face her friend. "You are perfect the way you are."

Tears filled Fiona's eyes as she played with a stray thread on her worn skirt. They were the first Eleanor had seen her shed since Angus's death. Fiona dipped her chin and impatiently wiped at her cheeks.

"I want you to be happy, Fiona."

"How will I ever be happy again? My Angus is gone."

Eleanor gently took Fiona's work-roughened hand into her own. "Please," she begged. "Do not settle for Mr. Kelly. I know Mr. Aiken and Mr. McGlynn have both spoken about you, and I see them watch you as you go about the fort. They are strong, able-bodied men who both love God and have impeccable reputations. I will even speak to them on your behalf."

"Ach, ye couldna!" She shook her head. "I'd be mortified."

"You'd be miserable if you marry Mr. Kelly." Just the thought brought nausea to Eleanor's stomach. All three men were colonists from Assiniboia, but Mr. Aiken and Mr. McGlynn had proven their courage in the face of danger, unlike Mr. Kelly who had cowered.

"To be honest," Fiona said, "I've not cared one way or the other about who I marry. It doesna matter if it's Mr. Kelly or anyone else. If it isna Angus, then why does it matter?"

"It matters because it's a lifelong commitme—"

"Nay." Her voice was bitter. "I thought marrying Angus was for life. Marriage, like everything else, isna forever. Nothing lasts."

Eleanor could not debate her friend after what they had endured, but she could encourage her. "You may be right. We don't know how much time we have. But you might have another fifty years to live. Wouldn't you rather spend those years with a man who is kind and good, rather than one who is controlling and manipulative?"

Fiona crossed her arms and studied Eleanor closely. "Do ye really think Mr. Aiken or Mr. McGlynn might be willing to marry an ugly old widow?"

"You are neither ugly nor old. You've not yet had your thirtieth year."

"I feel old."

"You are a wonderful woman and any man in this fort would be blessed to have you." She grew very serious. "Promise me you'll turn Mr. Kelly down. I could not watch you and your babies suffer even more than you already have."

Fiona sighed. "Mayhap ye're right, though I dinna think he will be happy. I've already told him yes."

"Then tell him you changed your mind, and if he gives you trouble, I will speak to him."

"Ach." Fiona laughed. "Ye're a wee bit of a thing, Eleanor. Ye're the last person I'd send him to."

Eleanor smiled. "As long as *you* come to me, that's all that matters."

A loon called across the lake, its warble echoing on the water's surface. It sounded close, though Eleanor could not see where it was sitting in the fog.

Fiona took a tentative breath, as if she would speak again, but then paused.

"What?" Eleanor asked.

"There's talk of leaving here for America."

"Who's talking?"

"Many of the settlers."

"But what of the rumors that Lord Selkirk is on his way?"

"To what end? Will he restore us to Assiniboia?" Fiona shook her head. "I dinna think I can ever go back there, not after what happened to my Angus."

"Perhaps Lord Selkirk has a different plan. He is an honorable man. If he cannot restore us to Assiniboia, he will find a home for us somewhere else. We need only wait." Eleanor had promised Arran she would remain at Jack River House. If the others left, she would be on her own.

"Ye saw the force and authority the North West Company possesses. How will Lord Selkirk prevent them from removing us again?"

"I don't know—but I do know he is passionate about colonizing Rupert's Land. He will find a way."

"And do ye plan to return there?" Fiona asked. "What will happen to ye?"

Eleanor wrapped her arms around herself, suddenly taking a chill. "I don't know." She had not yet heard from Arran—and could not even contemplate what the future might hold if he was found guilty on all the charges McLeod had claimed. Would she ever see Arran again? If not, where would she go? She would not give up Miriam. The little girl was now hers. Would she be forced to marry a man she did not love, as Fiona planned?

"All I know is that we must keep up the faith," Eleanor said. "If not for ourselves, then for our children."

"If I dinna have my bairns, I would have given up long before now." Fiona put her hands on her knees and then pushed herself off the log. "The day awaits. I canna sit here and be idle." She had not gone more than four steps when she stopped and smiled at Eleanor. "Thank ye for yer words and understanding."

Eleanor nodded. "I do not have much, but what I have, I'm willing to share."

After a few moments, the fort began to stir and Eleanor soon returned to her tent. She would need to eat and then call the children to their classes.

Nicolette was making breakfast near the campfire outside their tent and Miriam sat close to her on a mat, gnawing on a sea biscuit, which proved to be soothing to the child's teething gums.

"Has Isla not come out yet?" Eleanor asked. Isla was usually the first one up.

"Old John not well," Nicolette told her, trouble in her eyes. "Isla see to him."

Concern wedged between Eleanor's brows, but before she could move to their tent, a familiar figure appeared near their campfire.

Chait Fraser came to a stop with a nod. "Good morning."

Nicolette lifted her nose to the man and pretended he was not there. She was not fond of the Nor'wester and was not alone in her feelings. Almost everyone at Jack River House wondered why he stayed on. The fort was held by the Hudson's Bay Company and there were no North West Company posts nearby. It had been his job to safely deliver the settlers to Jack River House and then be gone—yet he stayed for these six weeks.

He was an affable fellow and had known the chief factor, Mr. Barlas, who had served at Brandon House when Chait was a child. Chait's father and Mr. Barlas had been good friends, even though they served opposing companies. Mr. Barlas had invited Chait to remain at Jack River House for as long as he liked—though most people had thought he overstayed his welcome.

Eleanor didn't mind him. He was a refined man with a taste for the elegant. He was also well-read and intelligent. They had enjoyed many stimulating conversations about books and poetry since their arrival at Jack River House, making him a frequent visitor to their campfire.

"Good morning," Eleanor said. "Would you care to join us for breakfast?"

Chait shook his head. "No, thank you." He hesitated and glanced at Nicolette, who had her back to him, then he spoke to Eleanor. "May I have a word with ye?"

"Of course." She waited for him to speak, but he tilted his head toward the shores of the lake.

"In private," he said.

Nicolette looked at Eleanor, a question in her eyes, but went back to her work. She never spoke up unless Eleanor invited her to, and even then, she was slow to give her opinions.

"I don't have much time before I need to start school," Eleanor said, "but I can give you a few minutes."

The fort sloped down a gentle incline toward the water and there were very few trees on the shoreline. It was all wide-open spaces, with a vast sky overhead. The sun was now low on the horizon, promising another warm day.

"I am leaving Jack River House soon," Chait said as they walked slowly toward the lake.

"I was wondering when you might go."

"I have been delaying my departure." He came to a stop and faced her. He was a handsome man who wore the elegant clothes of a gentleman bourgeois. Dark trousers, black boots, a white shirt with a royal-blue suitcoat, and a white cravat. Though he was an easy conversationalist, there was reservation in his eyes—as if he was holding something back. He spoke eloquently about any number of things, but when it came to his own personal thoughts and feelings, he rarely shared them. Instead, he would wax on about philosophical ideals, and other people's opinions. In the weeks they'd spent together, she didn't truly feel as if she'd come to know Chait Fraser.

"We all thought you would leave Jack River House as soon as we arrived here."

He smiled. "I have been rather preoccupied of late, and had no wish to leave until I had settled my mind."

"Oh?" Was he hoping she could shed light on one of his problems? He seemed to enjoy her opinions. Was that what he was looking for now? "May I be of help?"

"I believe ye may."

"I would be happy to offer whatever assistance is needed. What has your mind troubled?"

"It's not troubled." He laughed, almost to himself. "Rather, it's been captured—by ye."

She frowned, uncertain what he meant.

"No one has ever captured my heart before, Miss Brooke, so it has left me a little befuddled."

Eleanor's mouth slipped open, but she was speechless. He had not once shown a romantic interest, or if he had, she had not noticed. She'd always thought herself to be a good judge of such things.

"I—I didn't expect—"

"Neither did I." He put his hands behind his back and focused all his attention on her. "I am a man who takes a long time to make up my mind, but when I do, it's rarely changed."

"I'm flattered, Mr. Fraser, but—"

"And I've made up my mind about us. I believe we would be a good fit."

"Mr. Fraser, I am—"

"My faither and stepmaither still reside in Montreal and they would be honored to have ye in their home. My stepmaither is also a lady, and she often told me to marry a member of the peerage, if the opportunity allowed."

"Mr. Fraser"—Eleanor was growing quite uncomfortable—"you must know, I am already engaged."

"I had heard."

"I could not, nor do I intend to, break my engagement to Mr. MacLean."

Chait frowned. "He's a fugitive."

"He is innocent."

"He is facing murder charges—could possibly be tried and sentenced already. I thought ye'd cast him aside after what he did in Assiniboia."

"What he did?" Eleanor swallowed the anger that swelled at his words. "He saw his own men massacred at his side."

"Yet he somehow survived."

"I do not like what you imply."

"It matters not what happened in Assiniboia." His voice was growing impatient and irritated. "I want to marry ye."

Eleanor tried to remember her manners as she said, "I'm honored by your proposal, but my answer is no."

Chait did not speak for a moment as he stared at her, his face incredulous. "We are a good match, and ye are a lady. Ye deserve to be with a man of exceptional taste and family connections. MacLean is nothing."

If he thought to convince her, he was failing miserably. "Arran MacLean is an honorable, courageous, and brilliant man. He is my fiancé, and I will not dishonor him by continuing this conversation. Good day, Mr. Fraser."

Eleanor turned to walk away, but he grabbed her arm.

Her heart thumped hard. "Unhand me!"

He immediately let her go. "Pardon me." He lifted his chin. "But I have not concluded our conversation."

"I have." She smoothed the sleeve of her gown where he'd grabbed her. "Now, please, do not seek me out again." She turned, and this time, she was able to remove herself from his presence.

Her entire body shook from the force of her emotions.

"I will not leave Jack River House until I have yer consent to marry me," Chait called out. "I never change my mind and I always get what I want."

She continued toward her tent as if she had not heard him—but his words stayed with her. Something about Chait Fraser's proposal did not sit well with her, and she had no wish to find out what it might be. She prayed, with all her heart, that Arran would send word soon.

Fort William, NWC

Northern Lake Superior

August 17, 1816

A cold, steady rain fell against Arran's shoulders as he silently pushed the light canoe away from the banks of the Kaministiquia River. Though the rain made his task more difficult and uncomfortable, it also aided in his escape. There were few men willing to venture out of their warm beds on a night such as this, and fewer still who might notice a lone figure fighting the current in the profound darkness. He had snuck out of the small window in their room, skirting the stockade wall until he reached the western gate, closing it behind him. There, he had stolen a small canoe and set out to warn Lord Selkirk.

It was near two in the morning, but Arran was not tired. His nerves were so taut and full of awareness, he couldn't have slept even if he had wanted to. His friends were in imminent danger and so was Selkirk. Not only was Selkirk a friend and employer, he was also Eleanor's relation and the founder of the colony Arran had worked tirelessly to build.

In the two months Arran had been away from Assiniboia, he had missed it more than he imagined. Though he'd been devastated in the days immediately following the massacre, he couldn't deny that the colony still held his heart. It was the dream and hope of a colony for his fellow Scotsmen that had propelled him, and the goal of one day owning his own land. Assiniboia would always be a part of him, and no matter how many times he was defeated, he would always keep fighting for it. A flicker of hope burned in his heart for what he knew it could be—even if he didn't live to see it.

That hope propelled him against the choppy waters of the Kaministiquia. Not only did he fight against the current, but also the wind, which seemed to push him back each time he moved the canoe forward.

His muscles soon grew fatigued, and his fingers became numb from the cold. But he continued to fight, focusing on first one stroke and then the next. On and on he went, blindly following the course of the river until he was able to make out the shape of tents on the high banks.

He had no concept of time, or how long it had taken, though the sky was still dark. He couldn't rest, at least not yet. He still needed to get into the camp without drawing fire from one of Selkirk's men.

Wet through, Arran landed the canoe and pulled it to shore, securing it under a bush so it wouldn't float away.

Eleanor was not far from his thoughts as he worked. It was his love for her that gave him the courage to keep going. If he failed, he and his friends would suffer much more than they already had. But if Arran could get to Selkirk, and the earl had the de Meuron soldiers, then perhaps they would all be free soon. That thought alone gave Arran a surge of energy to pull himself up the riverbank in the slippery mud.

"Who goes there?" A tall, barrel-chested man appeared from around a tent. He brandished a musket in a flash, pointing it at Arran's chest. He wore the uniform of a soldier. A red coatee, gray trousers, a black shako on top of his head, and the white leather baldric, which he wore crossed over his chest. "State your business," he said in a French accent.

Was this one of the de Meuron soldiers? Arran lifted his hands and blinked as the rain dripped over the brim of his hat. "Arran MacLean, Lord Selkirk's agent at the Red River Colony. I've come to see his lordship."

"We heard you were a prisoner at Fort William."

"Aye. I escaped to warn Lord Selkirk of a plan to assassinate him and remove myself and my men in secret."

"How do I know you are MacLean and not a clerk from Fort William, come to assassinate the earl with this story?"

"You may check me for weapons. I have none."

Another guard appeared from the opposite direction, his musket raised. The first one nodded toward Arran. "Search him for a weapon."

The morning hours were quickly approaching. Arran had little time to tarry, but he waited patiently as the guard searched his person.

"He has no weapons."

The first guard motioned for Arran to follow him. They moved around several tents and past doused campfires before coming to a large, white tent. It sat in the middle of the others, with an ornate fringe around the top.

"Lord Selkirk?" the guard asked, loud enough to wake him. "My lord?"

"Yes? What is it?" came the startled response.

"A man claiming to be Arran MacLean is here to see you."

"MacLean?" Selkirk's voice was more awake now. Within a minute, he was at the flap, squinting into the night. "Arran? Is that you?"

"Aye, my lord."

Selkirk grinned and motioned Arran into his tent. "Come out of the rain."

"Is he safe, my lord?" the guard asked.

"Yes, yes." Selkirk put his hand on Arran's shoulder and drew him into the tent. "I am surprised to see you, my boy. You are drenched." He took a quilt off his cot and draped it over Arran's back. He then went to a lantern and struck a match, lighting the wick. "How did you get away?"

"I waited until dark and made my escape. I had to come and tell you not to delay in your plans. The Nor'westers plan to remove us from the fort and get us to Montreal before you can release us. They also hope to assassinate you."

Selkirk paused as he drew bread and cheese from a box near his table. He slowly set them down and then took a glass goblet from a different box. "I am aware of the threat to my life." His face had aged a great deal since Arran had last seen him in Scotland over four years ago. As the youngest of seven sons, he never thought to inherit the earldom. Instead, he had spent his early years in educational pursuits, hoping to become a lawyer. While studying at the University of Edinburgh, he took notice of the poor Scottish Highlanders being displaced by their landlords. When he became the 5th Earl of Selkirk, after the untimely death of each of his brothers to yellow fever and lung disease, he decided to use his wealth and power to help colonize the Red River Valley for his fellow kinsmen. He was only forty-five, but he looked much older. The work with the colony had not been kind to him. "I have fought enemies every step of the way," Selkirk said. "First in England, then in Montreal, and now here."

"I am sorry, my lord."

Selkirk shook his head and lifted a hand to stop Arran's platitudes. He put chunks of bread and cheese on a plate, then poured Arran a glass of wine. "It is to be expected. The fur trade is one of the largest industries in the world."

"What do you plan to do?" Arran received the plate and goblet and set them on the table nearby. He was hungrier than he thought and soon devoured the food and drink.

"When I learned about the increasing trouble in Assiniboia, I came to Montreal and petitioned for assistance from the Canadians, but was given none. I finally was able to secure a position as Justice of the Peace and was awarded six armed guards for my protection—but that is all the help I was given to combat what is happening to my people in the Red River Valley."

"I'm surprised you were given that much, since the majority of Montreal is in the control of the North West Company."

"I am well-aware." Selkirk poured himself a glass of wine and took a seat across from Arran. He wore his long shirt untucked over a pair of breeches. "When I knew I would get no help, I hired the de Meuron soldiers."

"So, then it's true?"

Lord Selkirk nodded, a smile lifting his lips. "Yes, and they have not disappointed me. In payment for their help, I have guaranteed them land in Assiniboia, with all the necessary implements to farm. If they are not happy there, I have promised to return them to Europe at no cost to them."

Arran's stomach turned sour at the thought of Assiniboia. He set the last of the cheese on the plate, unable to finish it. "I'm afraid I couldna hold the fort."

"I heard." Selkirk took a sip of his wine, his voice heavy. "I do not blame you, MacLean. It was a massacre. I'm appalled at what happened."

"How did you learn we had been removed to Fort William?"

"I was able to free Miles Macdonell in Montreal and sent him ahead to Assiniboia with a few dozen voyageurs employed by the Hudson's Bay Company. They left several weeks before I did, and when they reached Assiniboia, they heard what happened. Knowing you had been brought to Fort William, they immediately turned back and met up with me at Sault St. Marie. I tried, in vain, to get the help of two other magistrates, one from Drummond Island and the other from Sault St. Marie, hoping to have disinterested parties act on my behalf, but neither were able to leave their posts. With little choice, I had to come on my own. I redirected my course and have just arrived."

"For which I'm grateful." Arran could not deny God's timing was perfection. Not only was Selkirk here, but he had an entire army with him. "How many soldiers are in your employ?"

"Nearly two hundred."

It was even better than Arran had hoped. "And they will all reside in Assiniboia?"

"Yes, after we've cleared the trouble here at Fort William." Selkirk set down his goblet and crossed his arms. "I thank God you came tonight. I had thought to send spies to survey the fort and make a map for us, but it would have taken days or even a week. With you by my side, it will be much easier to overtake our enemy."

"We must not wait. We will need to enter before daybreak and before they're aware that I left."

"We will be outside the stockade by first light. I give you my word."

"Thank you." There were so many things that could still go wrong, but Arran would do whatever was necessary to help.

"But first," Selkirk said, "you have not spoken of my wife's cousin. How is Lady Eleanor? My wife received a letter from her dated July of 1815, just after they arrived at York Factory. We were very sorry to hear that Mrs. West had passed away—and then later that Reverend West died in the massacre."

"Lady Eleanor is very well." Arran couldn't help but smile thinking about her. "Though, I have not seen her since my arrest two months ago. She—" He paused. "She was engaged to Reverend West at the time of his death."

"Oh, I had no idea, though I am not surprised."

"He had asked her to raise his daughter as her own, if something should happen to him."

"What a momentous responsibility for an unmarried lady."

"I pray to God she willna have to raise Miriam on her own." Lord Selkirk could not be ignorant of Arran and Eleanor's romance at St. Mary's Isle. "She has agreed to become my wife."

Selkirk smiled and nodded. "Congratulations."

A heavy weight settled in Arran's stomach. "I only pray she is well and patient as she awaits my return."

"We will both pray for such a thing. Now." Selkirk clapped his hands together and rubbed them in anticipation. "We must plan our strategy for overtaking Fort William. The hour grows late."

Arran nodded. He was ready for redemption.

Chapter Twenty

The first blush of dawn hovered over the Kaministiquia River and Fort William in anticipation of a new day. Arran stood quietly on the wharf, awaiting the signal to advance, seeing the fort for what it was: a sleeping giant. Thankfully, it was not at full occupancy. If it had been, Selkirk and his two hundred soldiers would not have a chance to overtake the headquarters of the North West Company. Even now, it would take a miracle to do what Selkirk had in mind.

With his status as Justice of the Peace, he had come with arrest warrants for McGillivray, as well as eight other partners who were still at the fort. Once they were arrested, he fully intended to occupy Fort William.

"Constables?" Selkirk called to the two men he'd appointed to carry the warrants into the fort. Behind them stood nine armed guards, along with two hundred soldiers positioned along the riverbanks and around the fort at various gates. "When ye're ready."

The constables nodded and then walked toward the main gate leading into the fort. It was closed, as it often was overnight.

Arran stood beside Selkirk and his two commanding officers, Captain D'Orsonnens and Lieutenant Fauche. The small army was well-trained and impressive in their red coats and black shakos, swords and muskets at the ready. Arran himself had become armed once again. He carried a musket and wore a sword in a scabbard at his side.

"You say Mr. McGillivray resides in the main hall?" Captain D'Orsonnens asked.

"Aye," Arran answered. "And the others you're looking for will be in the North West House to the left of the main hall." Arran had drawn a detailed map of the fort for their use. He had told them where the Nor'westers kept their guns, ammunition, and cannons. He'd also advised them where there were gates and the captain had ordered guards to watch the exits, in case anyone tried to escape.

The constables pushed on the main gate facing the river but met resistance. One of them pounded. "Allow us to enter, in the name of the Honorable Lord Thomas Douglas, 5th Earl of Selkirk."

"Nay!" came a cry from the opposite side. "Ye are not welcome in Fort William."

"We demand you allow us entrance," said the other constable. "We have arrest warrants for the partners of the North West Company."

"Ye'll not get in here."

The first constable motioned for the armed guards to push down the gate.

Four guards banded together and became like a battering ram.

Several people cried out their alarm and anger from within the fort, but the guards were able to push their way past the gate.

"Stand back!" one of the guards said to the occupants of the fort. "Or meet your fate."

"Ye have no right," they cried.

"Gentlemen?" Selkirk asked. "Shall we enter?"

Captain D'Orsonnens nodded, indicating that Arran and Selkirk should proceed them.

A whole host of voyageurs, half-bloods, and Indians stood inside the fort, shouting profanity and warnings as the soldiers entered. Up ahead, the constables went in separate directions. One walked toward the main hall, while the other went to the North West House.

"I will need to set up a space to interview the offenders," Lord Selkirk said to Arran. "Where might I be most comfortable?"

"In the main hall, my lord. There is space enough in there for your court."

"Thank you, MacLean. I will expect you to be present for the proceedings, and to give your own testimony."

"Aye." Arran would happily tell Lord Selkirk, as well as the partners of the North West Company, the atrocities he'd seen in Assiniboia. He had shared some of it with Selkirk while they were in his tent, but there had not been time enough for the whole story.

"MacLean, why don't you take some of the soldiers and bring your men to me?" Selkirk motioned to a small contingent of soldiers standing at the ready. "We shall see you in the main hall within a quarter hour."

"Yes, my lord." Arran did not waste another moment.

While Selkirk walked toward the main hall with Captain D'Orsonnens and Lieutenant Fauche, Arran led the soldiers to Bell House.

Several senior clerks were just rising when Arran entered the dormitory. Their eyes grew large at the sight of the de Meuron soldiers, but no one tried to stop them.

Arran opened the door into the room he occupied with his men. James sat at the table, while Heden and Archie were still lying in bed, and Pritchard and Burke were just finishing their morning ablutions.

"Arran!" James stood, a grin on his face. "We were afraid you'd come to a bitter end."

"I've brought reinforcements." Arran was just as happy to see his friends as they appeared to see him. "Even now, the partners are being arrested. Lord Selkirk will hold investigations in the main hall this morning. He has requested your attendance, so you may tell him your side of the story."

"Mayhap we'll finally be vindicated," Pritchard said.

"Aye." Arran had not felt this much hope in a long, long time. "The sooner we get these proceedings underway, the quicker we can return to our families at Jack River House."

Heden slowly climbed from his bed. He'd grown melancholy over the weeks and did not show the same excitement as the others at being released. Arran suspected that he and his wife had not been happy and that he was afraid she had taken up with another man in his absence. Arran did not blame Heden for being reluctant to return to Assiniboia. If Arran suspected that Eleanor had left him for another, he would not want to see them together, either. The difference between him and Heden was that he would return and fight for her.

"Let's hasten to the main hall," James said to the men. "And have our redemption." He slapped Arran on the shoulder.

The soldiers made quick work of overtaking the fort. John McDonald, one of the partners, was the only person who tried resisting arrest. He declaimed the warrant for his arrest and said Lord Selkirk had no jurisdiction over the North West Company. Surprisingly, McGillivray gave himself up without a fight.

In the dining hall, Arran sat at a table near Lord Selkirk with the other Red River men, while the partners and clerks sat at the tables behind them. Several armed soldiers stood guard inside and out, while the remainder kept watch over the stockade and yard.

For hours, Selkirk listened to Arran and his men give their testimonies. He was patient and thorough and had everything written down and recorded by a scribe. The room had grown overly warm and stuffy. They opened the windows, but black flies invaded their space. They buzzed around everyone's heads, and there was an occasional slap of a hand against a tabletop in an attempt to kill one of the annoying creatures.

McGillivray and the partners sat stoically, their grave faces giving away nothing.

"Do you deny these charges?" Selkirk finally asked McGillivray after Arran and his men had exhausted their stories.

"I do."

"Was it not you who authorized McLeod's departure from Fort William with a hundred voyageurs to aid the Bois-Brûlés in their attempt to exterminate the colony?"

"I authorized his departure." McGillivray nodded. "To ensure our holdings in the Red River Valley. McLeod remains there now."

"What holdings?" Selkirk asked. "Rupert's Land is owned by the Hudson's Bay Company and I was granted the entire basin of the Red River Valley for settlement. It is your company that invades *our* holdings."

"That is not the way of the west," McGillivray said, his face red and his jowls shaking. "The land is owned by whoever has the power to control it. That has been the way of it since the beginning of time."

Arran watched both parties closely. Tension was high and anger boiled at the surface. Selkirk had gone through years of hard work and spent a vast part of his fortune to legally claim the land of the Red River Valley. But the North West Company had spent years of hard work and a vast amount of money to control it, as well. Neither would give in to the other unless forced.

"Are we not gentlemen? Do we not live by a chivalric code that honors law and order? Selkirk shook his head in disgust. "Lawlessness and selfish gain have led to the untimely death of good people. We must agree to live by the law or bloodshed will continue."

McGillivray did not respond.

With a sigh, Selkirk said, "It has come to my attention that you have attempted to destroy evidence in advance of our arrival."

"I dinna ken what ye mean." McGillivray looked down his nose at Selkirk.

The earl held up half-burnt papers. "These were found in the mess-room kitchen. From what I can see, they are letters with directions to exterminate the settlers at Red River, using whatever means necessary. This is enough evidence to bring you to trial for the deaths of twenty-three Red River men, including the governor of the Hudson's Bay Company."

McGillivray did not speak.

"And my men have told me that large quantities of firearms and ammunition have been removed from the fort. I can only assume they are being held in reserve to make an attack on me and my men."

McGillivray only stared.

"I have issued a search-for-arms warrant," Selkirk added. "Already, my men have located eight barrels of gunpowder lying in a swampy place near the fort. It was evident where it was hidden from the newly trampled grass."

Still, McGillivray did not speak.

"I have made a decision." Selkirk stood and addressed the entire assembly, his voice resolute, if weary. "Because of the obstruction of justice and the attempt to destroy evidence, as well as the stockpiling of weaponry, I am ordering the removal of all voyageurs, half-bloods, and Indians from this fort. I am also ordering the nine partners present to be taken, under guard, to York Factory for trial. Lieutenant Fauche will be tasked with your removal."

"Ye canna do that!" Mr. McDonald rose from his seat and lifted his fist in the air. "Ye have no right."

"I am working under the authority of the office of the Justice of the Peace." Selkirk motioned for his soldiers to remove the partners. "You will be confined to your rooms until Lieutenant Fauche is ready to leave."

Mr. McDonald yelled all the way out of the main hall. Several of the other partners also voiced their displeasure, but left without incident.

When they were finally gone, Selkirk dismissed the rest of the North West Company clerks, with orders to keep them under guard, as well. Captain D'Orsonnens was tasked with the removal of the voyageurs, half-bloods, and Indians from the fort while Lieutenant Fauche made plans to leave with the partners.

"What will you do now that you have Fort William in your grasp?" Arran asked Selkirk when it was just him, his scribe, and the Red River men remaining.

Selkirk sank into his chair with a heavy sigh. "I wish I did not have to do these things. But I have no other choice." He met Arran's gaze. "I will remain here until all my business is concluded. I have dozens and dozens of letters to write and reports to send to Montreal and England. I might have weeks of work ahead of me."

"And what of the settlers at Jack River House?" Arran was ready to leave at this very moment.

"I will retain fifty de Meuron soldiers," Selkirk said. "And send the rest on with you to retrieve the settlers and overtake Fort Douglas. When I am done here, I will continue to the colony and we will rendezvous at Assiniboia. If you agree."

"Aye." Arran nodded. Though he had not slept for over a day, he was revived and energized to begin the journey immediately. "I will be ready to depart as soon as you can spare the soldiers."

"There will be work for them in the next day or two—possibly longer. We must locate the weapons and remove the inhabitants. But when I believe all threat has passed, you may leave."

Arran could not wait even another day. His feet itched to move and his muscles contracted with the need to expel the anxious energy he felt at the knowledge of his freedom. There was nothing keeping him from Eleanor now. Nothing but an earl who had need of the soldiers.

"If you are amenable, I will leave for Jack River House immediately, on my own. I can be there in half the time and collect the settlers. We will then head directly to the colony and meet your soldiers there."

"You will not go alone," James said. "I will go with you."

"And I," Archie said.

"And I," Heden, Pritchard, and Burke echoed.

Selkirk was quiet for a moment, but then he nodded. "I can spare a dozen soldiers to accompany you, in case you meet trouble."

"I insist we leave immediately," Arran said. He could not wait another moment.

A slow smile lifted Selkirk's mouth. "I understand your eagerness. Go, with my blessings. We will see each other again in Assiniboia."

The Red River men did not let another minute pass before they went to their room and gathered the few possessions they had brought to the fort.

"I hope you are ready to travel hard," James said to the men with a wide grin. "Because I dinna think Arran will let any of us rest until we reach Jack River House."

The men laughed for the first time in a long time.

September 14, 1816

"Nay," Isla said as she looked at Eleanor, sorrow in her rheumy eyes. "Not my John, too."

"I'm sorry." Eleanor sat beside the now twice-widowed woman, feeling as if she'd had to apologize far too many times for the loss of loved ones this past year. "Old John was a good, kind soul."

"Ye dinna have to tell me, lass." The widow did not cry but looked at her husband of only ten months. He lay completely still on his cot, having died of an illness no one was able to identify. He had not suffered long and had passed in his sleep. "I never thought I'd live to bury two husbands. I count myself blessed that both men were good to me. I ken some women who marry and regret their decision. I never regretted mine."

Eleanor smiled, appreciating the older woman's positive attitude.

"I wonder if I'm too old to marry a third time," she mused. "There are men enough to go around." She glanced out to the fort yard beyond the flaps of her tent. "I wonder."

Eleanor did not know if she should applaud the woman for her practicality or be appalled by her tactlessness. In the end, she did neither, just sat with the widow until she was ready to have John's body buried.

It was a simple ceremony, one that Old John would have been proud of, though Eleanor could not help but think that Arran and James should be there to say goodbye to their friend. They were fortunate to have a missionary priest visiting the fort who had said a word and a benediction for the aged fur trader. Old John had faithfully given his life to the Hudson's Bay Company, and though he'd never had the ambition to rise to a chief factor, he had been a senior clerk for several decades and had done his duty. He was well-known and well-loved.

Eleanor could not stop thinking about Arran and how much he would miss Old John as she and Nicolette walked back to their tent with Miriam toddling along between them.

When given the opportunity, Miriam would rather walk than be carried. Though it often took longer for Eleanor to complete her tasks this way, she loved the little girl's independent spirit. It would serve her well in a world that was not always kind.

Clouds hung on the horizon, covering what little sun they had left to the day. Isla had stayed behind to speak to the priest, but it was time to get supper ready. A hungry little girl did not appreciate a deviation to her schedule.

The small camp they had inhabited with Old John and Isla felt oddly deserted. No more would Old John be nearby to offer his entertaining stories or his protection. Eleanor did not anticipate any problems, but it had been good to know the fur trader was there, if the need arose.

Nicolette did not speak as she stirred the coals and coaxed them to life. She put sticks on the fire and brought it to a flame. Eleanor helped by retrieving the precious ration of corn they had tucked away in their tent from Mr. Barlas.

"I wish we had a garden of our own," Eleanor said, almost to herself. Nicolette rarely responded, though it did not stop Eleanor from talking to her. "I appreciate the squash and beans and corn from the fort garden, but I haven't had carrots or peas since leaving England."

More and more, she found herself longing for the life she once had. If not for her, then for Miriam, who knew nothing of a different sort of existence. Eleanor's childhood had been full of comforts she'd taken for granted. Warm beds, roaring fireplaces, delectable foods, leisure time for lessons, games, and riding.

The only thing that gave Eleanor a bit of reprieve from the monotony of their current predicament was the classes she offered four days a week for anyone who chose to attend. She had both children and adults now, those who had never learned to read. They did not meet for long, but the two or three hours she spent with them a day had made a huge difference in their ability to read and write.

Fiona Ferguson was one of those adults. While Nicolette and Isla had watched the children, Fiona had learned how to read, practice simple sums, and write a letter. She had rejected Mr. Kelly's proposal, to his great dismay, and had allowed other men to start to court her favor. She had yet to choose which man would be honored with her hand in marriage, but Eleanor was certain she was getting close to a decision. She had watched her and Mr. Aiken on several occasions and saw a spark of interest in her friend's eyes.

Nicolette took the last stick of wood from the pile that Old John had kept stocked.

"I'll retrieve more," Eleanor said. "Will you watch Miriam?"

She waited for Nicolette to nod, then she left them by their campfire and walked toward the fur post, where the voyageurs kept a vast supply of firewood. Those who needed it, like Eleanor and Fiona, had permission to take a certain amount each day—but those who had a man to cut and chop their own wood in the surrounding countryside, were asked to get their fuel somewhere else.

The fur post was a long, narrow rowhouse, comprised of several rooms. On the far end was the Hudson's Bay Company store. Now, in the month of September, the trade was slow. It would pick up again when the cold winter months set in. Mr. Barlas spent his days overseeing the work of his voyageurs, preparing for the long winter months.

Stopping at the woodpile behind the post, Eleanor began to fill her arms with the small sticks of wood. Splinters jabbed into her skin and the fabric of her sleeves. She stopped and looked at her work-worn hands, amazed at how different they looked in just one year.

"Would ye mind a little help?" Chait appeared around the corner of the rowhouse. He leaned against the wall in a casual pose, his arms crossed.

Eleanor's heartrate escalated at seeing him again. Though she knew he had not left the fort since their conversation weeks ago, he had not approached her again. "No, thank you." She continued to stack the pile, focusing on her work and not on the penetrating look he gave her.

Chait pushed away from the rowhouse and came to her side. He began to stack wood in his own arms. "Whether ye realize it or not, lass, ye need me, especially now that Old John is dead."

Anger made her pulse tick faster. She did not need him, nor anyone else, but Arran.

She could have held more wood, but she did not wish to stand in his presence any longer. She turned to leave, but he caught her elbow with his free hand.

The force of his grasp caused her to drop the wood. It fell down the length of her shins and pounded into her toes. Pain raced up her legs, but she did not cry out.

"Ye walked away from me once. I willna let ye walk away again." He was close at her back, speaking into her ear. His words tickled and burned her skin.

Here, on the back side of the rowhouse, close to the stockade wall, there were few—if any—people to see them. She'd been foolish for putting herself in this position.

"I want to protect ye, Eleanor," Chait said.

"From men like you?" She pulled out of his grasp and turned to face him. "I have given you my answer, Mr. Fraser."

"And I have told ye I always get what I want."

"Not this time." She started to walk away again, but he tossed down the firewood he held and took two quick steps, grasping her by the upper arms. He turned her and pressed her against his chest in the matter of a second.

Anger burned in his eyes. "I will wed ye before the priest leaves this fort, and then I will take ye to Montreal to live with my parents. It's for yer best."

She pushed against him and opened her mouth to cry out, but he pressed his hand over her lips.

"If ye dinna agree, there are ways I can force yer hand." He pressed her back against the wall of the rowhouse, his voice and movements suggestive.

Terror coursed through Eleanor's body and she tried, with all her strength, to push against Chait. He grabbed her wrists and held them against her chest.

"Now," he said, as calm as if he was sipping tea from an elegant cup. "Let's think rationally. Yer fiancé is facing murder charges in Montreal as we speak, and ye no longer have the protection of that old man to see to yer needs. Ye are at the mercy of Mr. Barlas and have no money or resources to return to England. Even if ye did, who would take ye in? Yer cousin, Lady Selkirk, is herself now residing in Montreal."

Dread and dismay warred in Eleanor's mind. All the things he said were true, but surely she had other options. Even if she did go to Montreal to be with Lady Selkirk and to be close to Arran as he stood trial, she could find a job as a governess or lady's companion—but who would take her on with a toddler in tow? And hadn't she promised Arran she would not leave Jack River House? But how would she survive the winter in a tent? Already, the weather was getting colder at night. There would only be a few more weeks before she would need to find more permanent lodgings.

"I can see in yer eyes that ye're taking my proposal seriously." Chait lifted a corner of his mouth. "If I let ye go, will ye promise not to run away again?"

She would promise him almost anything to be free. She nodded.

"Ye are a wise woman." Chait took his hand away from her mouth and moved back, so he was no longer pressed against her.

Eleanor breathed deeply, keeping her eye on him.

"I am not completely without feeling," he said. "I am a gentleman, despite what ye may think of me."

He was anything but a gentleman, but she would not say such things, afraid she'd anger him.

"I will not have my way with ye, unless 'tis necessary. I'm patient, if nothing else, and I am not a brute." He let his eyes wander the length of her body.

Despite the layers of clothing she wore, she felt exposed and vulnerable under his eyes.

"If we are to make our way to Montreal before the winter sets in," he said, "we must leave soon. And, if ye want a wedding, we'll have to have one before the priest leaves. But I ken ye have things to settle, so I will give ye a couple days to make plans."

"Settle?" What did he mean by that?

"The bairn. Ye will need to find a home for her."

Eleanor was done with this conversation. There was nothing left to discuss. She had no intention of marrying Chait, nor to give Miriam away. But if she told him, he would only grow angry again and do something she would regret for the rest of her life. She needed time—but how much time would she need? And what, exactly, was she waiting for? Word from Arran? Directions for her to follow?

"I will let ye go now," Chait said with a slight bow. "But I will speak to the priest on our behalf and ask that he stay for another day or two. In that time, I fully expect you to be rid of the bairn." He looked at her expectantly.

What could she do? If she disagreed with him, he'd ruin her.

She did the only thing she could. She nodded, slightly, and then left. She walked quickly, and then began to run. Tears threatened to fall. Where was Arran? Would she ever see him again? How would she protect herself from Chait? She could not tell Mr. Barlas what he'd said—the man was Chait's friend. He would never believe Eleanor over Chait. All the men she had known and trusted in the settlement were either gone or dead. Arran, James, Governor Semple, William, and Angus. The others she only knew by name.

"Lord," her heart cried. "Please deliver me." It was all she could pray. All her battered heart could whisper.

So many of her prayers had been unanswered this past year, she could hardly find the faith to believe this one might be heard.

Chapter Twenty-One

SEPTEMBER 16, 1816

Arran opened his eyes. Nothing had awoken him but the stirrings of his own heart. Stars sparkled overhead, while the silhouette of tall pine trees pointed to the heavens. The fire had long been extinguished, but smoke still spiraled up into the early morning hours.

It was too early to wake the others, but Arran could not force himself to return to sleep. They were just a day's journey away from Jack River House and the last thing he wanted was to waste his time sleeping. The sooner they woke and left camp, the sooner they could reach the settlers.

"I hear you," James said quietly beside Arran. He was wrapped up in a Hudson's Bay Company blanket, his head toward the campfire. All eighteen men slept this way, like spokes of a wagon wheel. "You canna sleep?"

Arran turned onto his back and stared up at the stars. "Nay."

"You've only been sleeping three or four hours a night. You canna keep on this way. You'll get sick and then what good will you be to Eleanor?"

Eleanor. Arran placed his hand over his heart as he closed his eyes. Warmth filled his chest and his stomach turned with nerves born of eagerness. Would he be by her side at this time tomorrow? He had no way of knowing if she was even still alive—though his heart told him she was. He could almost feel her in his arms, even now. Dreams of their wedding and life together had kept him going these many months since they were forced to part. For four years, he'd longed for her. Could it be that he only had to wait one more day?

"I canna sleep." Energy coursed through Arran's arms and legs. "I have a mind to go the rest of the way on my own. I wouldna have to wait—"

"'Tis safer to be in the company of others. There's still a mark on your head. If you fell into the wrong hand—"

"I dinna care about anyone's hands but Eleanor's." He lifted himself onto his side and looked at James. "I'll take the lightest canoe."

"And paddle all that way on your own?"

"I have the energy of five men coursing through me today."

James sighed and sat up. "You ken 'tis only three in the morning?"

Arran also sat and shrugged. "I dinna care."

With another sigh, James began to roll up his mat.

"What are you doing?" Arran asked.

"I'm not letting you go by yourself, that's for sure. And I ken you well enough. You've made up your mind to go. If I go back to sleep, I'll wake up in a few hours and find you've gone."

Arran smiled. His friend did know him well.

"So, let's be off." James secured the bed mat in a roll and fastened it to his knapsack with the leather straps on the bottom.

"And what of the others?"

"Most of them are surprised you dinna leave on your own already. When they wake up, they'll realize what happened."

Arran quickly packed his own things, and in less than five minutes, they were paddling a light canoe on a long, narrow lake, heading toward the northwest.

It was cool, but Arran didn't mind. The weather reinvigorated him and gave him the stamina to paddle without ceasing for over an hour. Neither man spoke as they pushed their oars into the water. When they stopped for a short break, they listened quietly to the call of the loon, and then resumed their journey.

Slowly, the sun began to rise, dimming the bright stars. The light first appeared as a fine shadow on the eastern horizon, turning from black to purple to pink. It slid up and overhead, the sun appearing behind, and soon it domed above their heads in beautiful grandeur. Everything looked different in the light of day. Shortly after daybreak, they reached a portage.

"This will be the last portage before entering Little Playgreen Lake," James said to Arran, his voice teasing. "It's not too late to turn back now."

Arran laughed. "Nothing in all of God's great creation could persuade me to go back." He lifted the canoe on his shoulders while James took their bags. Droplets of water rained all around him from the bottom of the canoe.

The portage was over a mile long. If they had been with their entire entourage, they would have had to make several trips over the portage to move all their supplies. Lord Selkirk had sent them with food, weapons, and other sundry items. There were barrels of flour, wine, and corn, as well as salt pork and sugar. They had a hundred bags of pemmican and dried peas, not to mention the bags of sea biscuits. They had carried them all the way from Fort William. Arran felt a small measure of guilt leaving the other men to haul the supplies, but in most situations, the deputy-governor of Assiniboia and the Chief Factor of the Hudson's

Bay Company at Fort Douglas would not have been required to carry supplies. Besides, they had worked tirelessly for the past four weeks to bring them this far.

They walked in silence until they came to the shores of Little Playgreen Lake. Arran was familiar with the body of water, having been through there several times on trips to and from York Factory. They entered a small bay in the lake and Arran set the canoe into the water.

"If I remember correctly," James said, putting down their bags, "we have about three miles to paddle before reaching Jack River House."

"Aye." Three miles. Less than two hours, if they paddled with all their strength.

Every nerve and muscle in Arran thrummed in anticipation. He had never longed for something or someone more than he did Eleanor. With every breath he took, and every minute that passed, it only grew more intense.

Yet, the fear that she was no longer at Jack River House consumed him. He'd asked her to wait, but had she? What if something had happened beyond her control? Or, worse, what if she had given up on him?

"Dinna fash," James said as he stepped into the water and put their packs in the center of the birchbark canoe. "She'll be waiting for you."

"How can you be sure?" Arran also stepped into the water and held the boat as James settled into the front. Arran stepped into the vessel on ginger feet, balancing his weight so they did not turn it over. He'd become adept at such things in his years in the interior.

"She loves you. I've known it from the moment I met her." James set his paddle into the water and began the long, steady strokes as Arran did the same.

"What if she was forced to leave or—"

"Dinna borrow yourself trouble, Arran." James's back moved with the rhythm of his paddling. "God has brought you both this far. Trust He'll take you the rest of the way."

Arran hoped and prayed James was right.

They paddled without ceasing until Jack River House became visible. One of the first things they saw was the Hudson's Bay Company flag flying high over the fort. Just the sight of it gave Arran a burst of energy to keep going. The lake and surrounding land were still and quiet. There was no wind and the water looked like pure glass. The only disturbance was from their canoe and paddles. With each dip and push forward, a ripple of water dispersed.

The fort sloped toward the lake and was surrounded by a large stockade. It was easy to make out the dozens of settlers' tents encamped within.

"It looks like they made it here," James said.

Arran's heart pounded harder with each stroke of his paddle. "I pray to God Eleanor and Miriam are among them."

Someone from the fort noticed their approach and soon there were several people who had gathered near the fort gates. It wouldn't be unusual for a two-manned canoe to visit. As far as the inhabitants of the fort knew, they could be two Indians, two half-bloods, two voyageurs, or even two company men visiting from another fort.

Arran strained to look at the people standing near the open gate, but it didn't look like there were any women among the men. His gaze then went up the hill toward the settlers' tents. He could see people near their tents and campfires, but it was impossible to make out individuals.

Soon, they were upon the fort and they glided to a stop.

"MacLean! McIntosh!" One of the settlers recognized them and threw his hands up to the sky in praise. "Where have ye come from?"

"Fort William," Arran said as he stepped into the water. "The others will be here later today."

"Arran couldna wait." James grinned.

Arran wanted to ask about Eleanor, but it wouldn't be seemly. Not yet.

James also stepped out of the canoe and they took their bags from the center.

"We'll take the canoe up," the settler said. "Mr. Barlas will want to see ye."

"I'm thinking there will be others anxious to see you, too," James said to Arran, slapping him on the shoulder.

They walked through the gate and into the fort yard. Fiona Ferguson stood by a cauldron set over a fire, a stick in hand as she stirred the contents. She glanced up and met Arran's gaze. Her mouth slipped open and she stared at him as if seeing an apparition.

"Good afternoon, Mrs. Ferguson," Arran said.

Instead of smiling, as Arran had assumed, her eyes grew large and she looked toward the tent community with apprehension and something akin to fear.

Something was wrong. Very wrong.

"What?" he asked her. "Is it Eleanor?"

She wiped her hands on her apron and nodded. "Aye."

It felt as if the ground tilted under his very feet. He reached out and put his hand on her shoulder. "Where is she?"

"In her tent."

"Take me to her." He didn't care if Eleanor had the black plague and she was contagious. Nothing could keep him from her side.

It had been two days since Chait had cornered Eleanor near the woodpile. She hadn't strayed far from her tent since that fateful day, keeping Miriam close. The little girl was peacefully sleeping on Nicolette's cot, even now, oblivious to Eleanor's concerns.

Eleanor sat on her own cot, her feet drawn up beneath her like she saw the Indians sitting around their campfires. Mr. Barlas had been kind enough to spare some of his paper and a charcoal pencil. It was all Eleanor had, but it was enough. Someday, when she had a new journal, she would slip these pages inside. She still mourned the loss of her other journal, and all those she'd left behind at St. Mary's Isle Priory. But for now, she would use what she had and pour out her thoughts and feelings on the paper.

As she wrote, her gaze traveled to the closed flaps of her tent. Each little sound made her look up. At any moment, she feared Chait would force his way into her camp to demand she stand before the priest and become his wife.

If she didn't, she was certain he would follow through on his threat and ruin her reputation to force her hand. The very thought sent a shiver up her back. She wouldn't put it past the man. There was something about him that made her cringe, and she wondered how she had ever enjoyed his company.

Nicolette and Isla had gone to Fiona's tent to watch after her children while Fiona washed her family's clothing at the communal cauldron near the lake. Fiona was aware of Chait's threat and had promised to keep her eye on Eleanor's campsite, in case the man forced his way into her tent.

A commotion in the fort yard made Eleanor's breath slow. She stopped scribbling on the paper and listened closely. It was hard to make out what was being said, but it sounded as if several people had been stirred into motion.

Panic seized her, and for a moment, she feared the Nor'westers were descending upon the fort to exterminate the colonists once and for all.

But no one was screaming or yelling. There had been no call of alarm. No gunfire.

The sound came closer, as if people were moving in her direction. Eleanor set down her paper and stood from the cot. Her body was sore from sitting in the same position for so long, but she hardly gave it thought as she untied one of the strings holding the flaps of her tent in place so she could peek out.

Fiona strode toward Eleanor's tent—and beside her was—

"Arran!" Eleanor cried out his name, heedless of Miriam sound asleep on the cot.

She tore at the canvas strings, trying desperately to open the flaps. Her hands trembled and her heart pounded erratically. Butterflies filled her stomach and warmth flooded her limbs. Arran had returned! It was almost too good to be true. Tears of happiness filled her eyes as she struggled with the confounded strings.

Finally, the flaps were free and Eleanor burst out of her tent.

Arran walked with purpose toward her and when she appeared, he stopped in his tracks.

She had never seen anything more beautiful or wonderful in all her born days. He was taller and broader than she remembered. His hair was longer, though he wore it tied back in a queue. Several curls escaped and teased his cheeks and forehead. His brown eyes were focused on her, and her alone. Love and relief radiated from them now and his wide mouth turned up in a smile that could have rivaled any sunrise or sunset she'd ever seen.

"Eleanor." He said her name like it was a prayer.

She ran the short distance between them and pressed herself against him, wrapping her arms around his neck. He pulled her close, lifting her feet off the ground, embracing her in a hug so powerful, it took her breath away.

"Arran." She said his name on the breath of a cry.

He kissed her then, right there, in the presence of the entire fort. His lips were searching, fervent, and hungry. She responded with all the passion and love she'd stored in her heart these many weeks. She could not get enough of him. His strength empowered her and made her feel as if anything was possible again.

And perhaps it was.

He finally pulled back, breathless and a little embarrassed. "I'm sorry, lass. I couldna help myself."

She laughed and placed her hand on his dear face. "Do not apologize. I'm just happy you're home."

He wiped a tear on her cheek, one she had not known was there, and smiled at her. "Home." He nodded. "I am home." His gaze shifted toward the tent and his smile grew even bigger. "Miriam."

The toddler had climbed out of her bed and was standing near the open flap of the tent, wiping sleep from her eyes. Her blond curls were in disarray and her face was puffy from slumber. But when she saw Arran, all trace of sleepiness disappeared and she grinned.

She had not forgotten him.

More tears fell from Eleanor's eyes as Arran left her side and went to Miriam. The little girl lifted her arms and Arran picked her up. She hugged his neck and snuggled into his embrace.

Arran turned back to Eleanor, wonder in his eyes.

She went to his side and allowed him to bring her into his embrace again.

"I have dreamed about this moment every single day since I left you," he said to Eleanor.

"I feared it might be years before you returned. I was so afraid—" She couldn't continue, too overcome with relief that she would not have to face Chait now.

Fiona had made herself scarce, as had everyone else. It was just Arran, Eleanor, and Miriam at her campsite.

"Why was Fiona so upset?" Arran asked Eleanor. "Just now, when I saw her at the cauldron, she made me believe you were in great danger. I thought I'd find you here on your deathbed."

Eleanor shook her head, not wanting to tell Arran about Chait. The whole experience had left her feeling defiled and shaken—but she could not keep it from him, either. She never wanted to keep anything from him. So, she told him about Chait's proposal and his threat.

Arran's jaw tightened and he scanned the fort, as if looking for the offender.

"No." Eleanor put her hand on his arm. "Do not concern yourself with him. Now that you're here, he's not a threat to me any longer. He'll leave. I know he will." She lifted her hand to his cheek to turn his gaze back to her. "Please don't do anything to ever put yourself at risk again. I cannot bear to be apart from you."

His features softened. "And I you. Not for one more night."

Heat filled his gaze and Eleanor's insides melted at the look in his eyes.

"There's a missionary priest visiting the post. He plans to leave soon." She dropped her gaze and toyed with a buttonhole on his vest. "If there was anything you wanted him to do before he leaves."

The corners of Arran's mouth came up. "Aye. I have something very important I'd like him to do, as soon as you're ready."

"I've never been more ready in all my life." She met his gaze, hoping he saw how very much she wanted to marry him.

"Will you marry me, lass?"

Eleanor nodded. "Yes."

He lowered his lips to hers again, his kiss full of the promise of so much more to come. "I love you," he whispered.

"I love you, too." She leaned her cheek against his chest, not wanting to part with him for even a moment.

"I'll go speak to the priest. How long do you need to get ready?"

"I'm ready now—though, if you'd rather I change into a prettier dress—"

"You're the bonniest bride I've ever seen. I dinna care what you're wearing."

Her cheeks warmed at his words. "I'll have Fiona help me change. I still have a few pretty things."

He smiled and nodded. "And I'll take Miriam with me to find the priest, so you can change without keeping an eye on the little one."

His thoughtfulness warmed her as much as his passionate kisses.

"Dinna take too long," he said. "I may not have the patience to wait."

"That makes two of us."

"We'll wait for you by the lake." He walked toward the fur post and Fiona materialized, as if she'd been waiting for Arran to leave.

"Ach, lass." Fiona's cheeks glowed and tears rimmed her eyes. "Look what the good Lord has done this day."

Tears filled Eleanor's eyes as well, but not only from her reunion with Arran. Her heart ached for her friend and all that Fiona had lost.

"Dinna let one day go by that ye dinna thank God for Arran and Miriam." Fiona's smile trembled. "Each day is a gift."

Eleanor wiped at her tears and nodded. "Will you stand up with me at my wedding?"

"I would be honored."

"I have a gown I've been saving for today." Eleanor went to the trunk in her tent and lifted out several pieces of clothing before she came to the bottom. She removed the wrinkled garment and gently shook out the folds. "It's one of my nicest dresses, though I don't know why I brought it with me."

"For yer wedding, of course." Fiona touched the fine pink silk almost reverently. "'Tis lovely."

"I have a silk ribbon that matches, for my hair."

"Mr. MacLean will be very happy to see ye in this dress."

"Do you think so?" Eleanor's heart beat hard with the desire to please him.

"Ye could wear the filthiest rags in the fort and he'd still think ye were the bonniest girl he'd ever seen. Love has a way of doing that." She nodded a bit brusquely. "Let's not keep him waiting."

An hour later, after Isla had joined them to help in the preparations, Eleanor was washed and dressed, and her hair was restyled. She stood near the closed flaps of her tent, Fiona behind her, tying the sash around her waist. Isla had left to retrieve Fiona's children and Nicolette, and would send them all to the lake for the ceremony.

"Are ye ready?" Fiona asked, finishing the bow at Eleanor's back.

Eleanor turned and took a deep breath. "Yes."

Fiona hesitated, but then she said, "And do ye ken the intimacies of the marriage bed?"

Eleanor's cheeks grew warm and she nodded quickly.

"That's good." Fiona patted her hand. "And if Arran is a good man, he'll be sweet and gentle with ye."

More heat filled Eleanor's cheeks, dipping down her neck and into her hairline. "He *is* a good man." Eleanor had no worries about Arran's kindness or his affection. If his kisses were any indication, she would love being his wife in every way.

"We've made the lad wait long enough." Fiona held the flaps open for Eleanor and she stepped out into the light of day.

The sun was high in the sky and the air was warm. Not a cloud marred the blue overhead.

It was the perfect day to become Arran MacLean's wife.

Chapter Twenty-Two

The first hint of a breeze ruffled Arran's hair as he stood by the shores of Little Playgreen Lake watching Miriam. She lifted stones off the ground and threw them into the water, clapping when they made a splash.

James stood near the little girl, keeping his eye on her, too. When he caught Arran watching them, he smiled.

Mr. Barlas had welcomed Arran and James into his fort with a hearty greeting and been quick to find the priest, who had agreed to perform the wedding ceremony. While James had kept his eye on Miriam, Arran had quickly cleaned and prepared himself to meet his bride. He had taken a quick swim in the lake and then shaved his face and put on a clean outfit of clothes. It had not taken him long, pressed as he was with excitement.

His hair was still moist when he caught a glimpse of Eleanor at the top of the fort hill, walking toward him, Fiona by her side.

Arran's breath caught in his throat.

The sunshine streamed down on her, as if causing her to glow. Her soft pink gown made her look delicate and feminine—almost too fragile, as if she might break if handled incorrectly.

Suddenly, he was overcome with uncertainty. Not about his love for her—but his right to make her his wife. Of all the men in the world, how and why had she chosen him? What could he offer her? His old fears returned, and he remembered why he had suggested to William West that he marry her and take her away from all of this. She didn't belong in the wilderness. She was made for finer things.

But then she smiled at him and every rational thought fled from his addled brain.

He couldn't have stopped himself from marrying her, even if he had been forced. He longed for her, heart, body, and soul, and despite all his misgivings—and her apparent lack of wisdom in choosing him—he loved Lady Eleanor Brooke with every fiber of his being. Whatever he was made of, it all belonged to her.

In that moment, no one and nothing else existed in all the world but Eleanor. Her brown curls were piled on her head, with soft tendrils playing in the wind at her cheeks. The dress she wore exquisitely accentuated the soft swell of her bosom, and displayed her milky white arms. She did not hold flowers, nor come to him on the arm of her father, but there was no mistaking this maiden was a bride today.

Arran moved to meet her at the gate and offered her his arm, speechless at her beauty.

Her smile was shy as he wrapped her hand around his elbow and drew her close to his side. She smelled of lavender and felt like rose petals.

The scars on his hands looked rough and unworthy next to her smooth skin. He looked down at them now, praying to God that he would never fail Eleanor again. There was so much at stake taking her as his bride, and Miriam as his daughter. The responsibility of their lives weighed heavily on his shoulders, but it was a weight he would gladly bear all the days of his life—and, if God saw fit to bless them with more bairns, then he would welcome them with all his heart.

The thought of bringing more children into the world made Arran's pulse rise and he could not help but lift Eleanor's hand to his lips.

Her cheeks blushed and she lowered her eyelashes in a way that completely beguiled Arran.

"Are you ready, lass?" he whispered.

She lifted her gaze to his again, her brown eyes shining with love and devotion. "More than ever."

The entire fort showed for the wedding—everyone except Chait Fraser. Arran had glimpsed him while in the fur post, but the man had made himself scarce. If Chait showed himself to Arran—or Eleanor for that matter—Arran would make him regret how he'd treated his bride.

"Dearly beloved," the priest said in French. "We are gathered here today in the sight of God and these witnesses to join together this man and this woman in holy matrimony."

James stood to one side of Arran and Fiona stood on the other side of Eleanor. Nicolette held Miriam and Isla minded the Ferguson children. Mr. Barlas was there, as were the other members of his fort. A part of Arran wished Archie, Heden, Pritchard, and the others were there to celebrate his union, but his impatience had won the day. Nothing could have kept him from marrying Eleanor in this moment. Not even the sad news of Old John's passing. In due time, Arran would mourn the loss of his friend, and welcome the others who would probably arrive within the day.

But, for now, all he thought or cared about was his bride.

She caressed his face with her gaze, a gentle smile on her soft lips. He wondered if she was as oblivious to what the priest was saying as he was.

He understood French, but even if it had been in his native tongue, he wouldn't have been able to focus or retain the words that the man spoke.

"Take her right hand into yours," the priest said to Arran, "and repeat after me, I, Arran, take thee Eleanor to be my wedded wife."

Arran turned to face Eleanor and took her right hand into his. She did not wear gloves and the heat from her fingers soaked into his. He repeated the words, adding in his thick Scottish brogue, "To have and to hold from this day forward, for better for worse, for richer for poorer, in sickness and in health, to love and to cherish, till death us do part, according to God's holy ordinance. And thereto I pledge thee my troth."

Eleanor watched him, love and admiration glowing in her eyes. Could he ever live up to the way she was looking at him now? As if he could do no wrong? As if he was capable of anything?

He would try, with every breath he took.

"I, Eleanor, take thee Arran to be my wedded husband," she repeated after the priest. "To have and to hold from this day forward, for better for worse, for richer for poorer, in sickness and in health, to love and to cherish, till death us do part, according to God's holy ordinance. And thereto I pledge thee my troth."

It was done. She had consented to be his wife, no matter what life brought their way. For better or worse. It was a gift—her life—and he didn't deserve it.

The priest lifted a ring off his Bible. It was the ring he'd given to the priest before the ceremony. It was Arran's mother's ring, which his faither had given to him the last time he'd been in Nova Scotia. It was a simple band of gold, but it was full of memories of her soft hands nurturing Arran in his childhood.

"Bless, O Lord, this ring," the priest said, "that he who gives it and she who wears it may abide in thy peace, and continue in thy favor, unto their life's end. Through Jesus Christ our Lord. Amen."

He handed the ring to Arran.

Arran's hands trembled slightly as he took the small band of gold, repeating what the priest had told him to say before the ceremony. He slipped it on the fourth finger of Eleanor's left hand. It fit perfectly. "With this ring I thee wed in the name of the Father, and of the Son, and of the Holy Spirit. Amen."

Eleanor looked down at the ring, a question in her eyes.

"'Twas my maither's," he whispered.

"I'm honored to wear it," she said back to him.

"O eternal God," the priest prayed, "Creator and Preserver of all mankind, Giver of all spiritual grace, the Author of everlasting life, send Thy blessing upon these Thy servants, this man and this woman, whom we bless in Thy Name, that they, living faithfully together, may surely perform and keep the vow and covenant betwixt them made and may ever remain in perfect love and peace together, and live according to Thy laws, through Jesus Christ our Lord. Amen."

"Amen," Eleanor and Arran whispered together.

"What God has put together, let no man put asunder." The priest closed his Bible and smiled at Eleanor and Arran. "I pronounce thee man and wife, in the name of the Father, and of the Son, and of the Holy Spirit. Amen."

"Amen," they repeated.

"You may kiss your bride."

Arran did not hesitate, but wrapped Eleanor in his embrace and kissed her.

She was soft and tender, receiving his affection with her own, a smile on her lips.

Those who had gathered clapped and cheered at their union. Eleanor's cheeks colored deeper than before and Arran felt himself smiling like a fool.

Eleanor was his wife, for the rest of his life. Every decision, from this day forward, would be made with her and for the benefit of his family. He no longer lived for himself alone, but for the good and prosperity of his wife and daughter. He'd always had a natural instinct to protect and shelter them, but a deeper desire to keep them safe overwhelmed him.

Miriam clapped and grinned with the rest of them, though he was fairly certain the wee bairn didn't understand why everyone was so excited. If she did, she would understand that she was no longer an orphan, but his daughter, for as long as he drew breath.

He reached for her now, taking her from Nicolette's arms. She came to him willingly, her toothy grin a little wet.

"Mama," she said to Eleanor, and reached for Eleanor next.

Eleanor took her into her arms and pointed at Arran. "Papa," she said.

Miriam studied Arran for a heartbeat before she said, "Papa!" and lunged back into his arms.

Arran held his daughter, took his wife's hand, and walked them back into the fort. A small feast would quickly be arranged by their friends, with what little they had to offer, and then Arran had arranged for Miriam and Nicolette to sleep in Isla's tent for Arran and Eleanor's wedding night.

Eleanor sat beside Arran at the long table the settlers and voyageurs had set up in front of the fur post. There had not been much by way of food, but what the settlers had produced was the very best of what they had left. Hominy and sea biscuits had never tasted as wonderful to Eleanor as they had that afternoon. Everyone apologized profusely for their lack of elegance and refinement, but Eleanor could not have imagined any other wedding meal. It was perfect.

Now, after the meal had been cleared away, a settler produced his bagpipes, and two others their flute and fiddle. People had begun to dance and laugh for the first time in months.

Arran held Eleanor's hand as they watched the settlers. He had not let her go once since they had sat down, and she was in no hurry to be separated from him.

"I haven't seen this much joy since Pembina," Eleanor said a little wistfully. "This has been good for everyone."

"Especially me." He lifted her hand to his lips and pressed a kiss there. Pleasure danced in his eyes and a shiver of excitement raced up her spine.

"Canoes!" A cry rose from the gate.

Eleanor looked over the heads of those dancing toward the lake. The sun was just setting on the horizon. Pink tinged the world as Arran stood, drawing Eleanor with him.

"'Tis my men." He grinned. "With the de Meuron soldiers."

Arran had already told Eleanor about Lord Selkirk's mighty little army in bits and pieces, between the festivities.

Everyone went to the shores of the lake once again and welcomed the new arrivals. Mr. Heden was the first to disembark and his wife, Helena, was there with tears coursing down her cheeks. She hugged and kissed him and he pulled her into his tight embrace. Their children gathered around and he took turns hugging them, as well.

"That makes me happy," Arran said to Eleanor while nodding at Michael Heden.

"And me," Eleanor agreed. From the little she had come to know Mrs. Heden, she had suspected their marriage was on shifting ground, but it was clear they were relieved to see each other again. Perhaps their separation would help to heal their wounds.

There were greetings all around, and then more dancing and festivities. Now that all the men were restored to the colonists, along with the promise of Lord Selkirk and his de Meuron soldiers, the mood had grown even lighter and more cheerful than before. Those who had lost loved ones at the Battle of Seven Oaks, as it had become known, smiled again for the first time. Even Fiona danced with Mr. Aiken, her merry laughter the greatest gift Eleanor could receive on her wedding day.

After the sun set, campfires were lit to aid in the revelry. Isla and Nicolette had long since brought Miriam back to Isla's tent to sleep. She had almost fallen asleep on Nicolette's lap, her day having been full of more excitement than the little girl was accustomed to.

"Are you happy?" Arran asked Eleanor as he watched her, the firelight flickering in his eyes.

She smiled. "Never happier in all my life."

"And this is just the first day, love." He wrapped his arm around her as they stood by one of the campfires, the music almost drowning out his words.

Her happiness seemed too good to be true.

He stepped away from her and gently took her hand in his again. He slowly led her away from the festivities toward their tent.

She wrapped her free hand around his arm as they walked, slowly, but with purpose. Her pulse thrummed and her mind twirled with all the things to come. She glanced up and he looked down at her, a smile on his lips.

They moved away from the warm fires and into the coolness of night. Neither one spoke as they climbed the hill toward their campsite. When they arrived, Arran started a small fire of their own. The shadows from the flames flickered on the canvas tents.

Eleanor simply watched Arran, savoring every move he made. His coat became tight as he bent and set the logs on the flames, his muscles rippling beneath the fabric.

When he turned and caught her admiring him, he only smiled and then motioned her to join him by the fire. "'Tis been a long and exciting day," he said. "I thought we might sit for a minute and visit before we retire."

She went willingly and sat beside him on an overturned log for that purpose, relieved for a bit of normalcy. The fire was warm, banishing the tremors she'd begun to experience at the thought of being alone with him for the first time.

He put his arm around her, pulling her close. "You dinna need to be scared of me."

"I'm not scared," she said, though it was a half-truth. She wasn't scared, but she was very nervous.

He kissed her temple, his lips smiling against her skin. She was warm and complete beside him. And slowly, as they just sat there, her nerves began to fade. This was Arran MacLean, the man she had loved for four years. The man she'd written about in her journal more times than she could count. The man she had dreamt about every single day since the day she had met him.

There was no other place she'd rather be than here, beside him, as his wife.

"What will we do now that you and the others have returned?" she asked. "Will we go back to the Red River Valley?"

"Aye. For a time. Lord Selkirk plans to meet us there. We must take back Fort Douglas and restore the colony."

"And will the de Meuron soldiers aid in this endeavor?"

"Aye." He nodded, rubbing his hand up and down her arm. "They will settle opposite Colony Gardens on the eastern side of the river."

His touch was deliriously distracting, but she was able to ask, "And will they stay in Assiniboia?"

"That is the plan."

"And when might we leave here to meet them in Assiniboia?"

"Within the week. My men will rest from our journey and then we must continue."

"A week?"

"Aye."

"And will you rest?"

He made a sound deep in his throat. "Not when you look so bonnie."

A delicious shiver raced up her spine. "And will we stay in Assiniboia? Or will we go somewhere—"

He touched her chin and turned her face toward his. "We will go wherever you want to live. But we need to aid Selkirk in restoring the colony first. Does that suit you?"

She nodded.

Arran kissed her, slowly and deliberately, making her weak with longing.

"Do you still want to talk, lass?" His voice was low and gravelly, as if it took all his willpower to speak. He slowly moved aside the shawl she wore to reveal a bit of her bare arm. The day had been warm enough for the short sleeves, but the evening had become cool. When he touched her skin, gooseflesh arose, but she did not feel cold any longer. "Because we can stay by the fire as long as you like."

Her chest rose and fell in short, breathless movements. She swallowed and shook her head.

"Neither do I."

The fire had not burned for long, but Arran stood and separated the logs with his boot. He then offered Eleanor his hand.

She took his hand, her arm tingling from his touch.

He slowly reached down and lifted her shawl back onto her shoulder, brushing her bare skin with his fingers.

When he straightened to his full height again, he met her gaze, looking deeply into her eyes. "I love you, Eleanor MacLean. I've loved you for five years, and though I tried to forget you for four of them, you never left my mind or my heart." He shook his head, his dark eyes taking her in. "I dinna ken what I did to deserve you, but I will dedicate the rest of my life to loving you and serving you."

He lifted her hand to his lips once again and she bent her head, love and affection blooming in her chest. She put her hand on his cheek. "You have had my heart since the moment you took my hand in the garden at St. Mary's Isle. Do you remember that?"

He smiled. "Aye. How could I forget?"

"You never lost my heart, Arran. It's been yours, and it will continue to be yours, for as long as I live. I will dedicate the rest of my life to loving you and serving you, as well. I could not be prouder to bear the name MacLean, or to wear your mother's ring upon my finger." She looked down at the ring now. It was shiny with age.

"And you're not sad you dinna marry a lord?"

She put her hand at the back of his head, lacing her fingers through his curls, and pulled his lips to hers. "I want no one but you." She kissed him then, as thoroughly as he'd kissed her.

And slowly, almost without her knowing, he led her to their tent and drew her into the dark and private interior.

Chapter Twenty-Three

A cold, pelting rain pummeled Arran and the hundred and fifty men at his command. Lord Selkirk had sent half his army to the shores of the Red River and they had met the colonists where the river emptied into Lake Winnipeg. For two days, they had planned their attack, familiarizing the de Meuron soldiers with the fort's dimensions, and then took three days to travel up the river to the colony.

"Dinna fash," Arran said to Eleanor as he stood in front of her, the rain dripping from the brim of his hat. He could hardly make out the form of her face in the inky darkness as she held Miriam in her arms. "Wait in the tent I've set up for you. It will take us an hour or so to reach the fort, and less time to take it back from the Nor'westers."

A flash of lightning filled the sky, followed close by a clap of thunder.

"And what if—" Eleanor paused and dropped her gaze from his face.

"I will return to you, like before." He pressed a kiss against her wet forehead.

It had been three weeks since Arran had returned to the colonists. Three weeks since he'd taken Eleanor as his bride. It had been the most glorious three weeks of his life, though he knew what they must face at Fort Douglas. Leaving her with the other women and children, even under the protection of a dozen soldiers, was the hardest thing he'd ever done.

"Pray, *leannan.*" He used the Gaelic word for sweetheart, which he'd come to call Eleanor since their wedding night. "We will be smart, but we canna let our enemies win."

"I will pray. Ceaselessly." She pressed her warm lips to his. "May God go with you."

He made sure she, Miriam, Nicolette, and Isla were safe in their tent before he left them to return to the canoes.

Captain D'Orsonnens was present, though he looked to Arran for leadership. Lord Selkirk was still on his way from Fort William, having been detained. He had sent the de Meurons ahead, knowing Arran had been anticipating them. He had retained his six guards, supplied by the Canadian government, and twenty other soldiers. The rest were now approaching Fort Douglas with Arran.

The rain filled their canoes as they continued their course. Lightning sliced across the sky and thunder reverberated in Arran's chest. The storm did not pass quickly, as in the summer months, but lingered, dumping a vast amount of water on the land. It rushed over the banks of the river and ran into the water with great, destructive rivulets cutting into the soil. The river had already begun to rise and it took several strong men to paddle against the current.

Arran recalled another such night, when it was just him against the Kaministiquia River, on his way to warn Lord Selkirk.

Then, he had been alone, but tonight, he was surrounded by dozens and dozens of trained soldiers, all of them loyal to Lord Selkirk and to Assiniboia. This would be their new home.

The men had crafted ladders in the two days they had made their plans at the mouth of the Red River. Those ladders were in the canoes even now, waiting to scale the fort walls.

No one spoke as the storm blew and the men paddled. James was in Arran's canoe, while Archie and the other prisoners from Fort William were in their own canoes. Every able-bodied man had come, including the voyageurs employed by the Hudson's Bay Company who would inhabit the fort once it was back in their control. These men worked directly for James and were following his lead, even as James followed Arran.

It felt like it took all night to finally arrive at the base of Fort Douglas. Even in the dark, Arran knew it well. It had been his home for four years. Without a word, the men pulled their canoes onto the shores, removing the ladders.

Arran, James, and Captain D'Orsonnens led the way up the banks of the river. The pitch-black night was perfect for their mission, though the mud made it difficult for them to traverse the riverbanks.

The soldiers had specific instructions and did not need anyone to tell them what to do. All at once, they surrounded the massive fort and put their ladders against the stockade walls. The walls were not terribly high, but they'd be impossible to climb without the aid of the ladders.

When all were in place, the men scaled the ladders, one after the other, and jumped into the stockade.

Arran, James, and D'Orsonnens waited near the riverside gate for one of the soldiers to open it and let them in.

Already, there were half a dozen Nor'westers in custody by the time Arran entered Fort Douglas again. Lights burned from the governor's house, which was where Arran led James and D'Orsonnens now. He held a musket to his shoulder and wiped the rain from his eyes. With over a dozen soldiers now at his back, Arran pushed open the governor's door and entered the common room.

Archibald McLeod sat close to the fireplace, a book in hand, while Chait Fraser and another man played a game of chess. A fourth man sat sewing a patch onto a pair of pants.

"What's the meaning of this?" McLeod rose to his feet, the book falling to the floor. His eyes were wide as he took in Arran and the de Meuron soldiers behind him.

"MacLean," Chait said.

"We're here to recover Fort Douglas and send you vermin to York Factory for trial." Arran nodded at several soldiers, who took the men into custody. "You'll be removed from here and placed in the main hall for the night. In the morning, you'll be transported under the guard of a dozen soldiers."

"You canna do this!" McLeod stared, his mouth open. "This is our fort now."

"Nay." Arran shook his head. "This has been, and will forever remain, Lord Selkirk's colony."

A soldier grasped McLeod by the arm.

"Wait," McLeod said. "Allow me to get my things."

"Nay," Arran said again. "We will bring them to you." He motioned for the soldiers to remove McLeod and his men from the governor's house.

Chait came to a stop in front of Arran, his face in a scowl. "Ye dinna deserve Lady Eleanor."

"Aye." Arran nodded. "But she deserves someone better than you."

Chait didn't respond as he was pushed out of the governor's house by D'Orsonnens.

In less than ten minutes, the fort was under Arran's control once again. It almost seemed too easy after all the trouble they'd endured.

"How does it feel?" James asked once they were alone in the governor's house.

Arran stood in the room where he'd spent several hours with Eleanor, West, and Semple. He could almost see Miriam pulling herself up to the table, her little legs bobbing with uncertainty. He would love to bring Eleanor and Miriam back here, though it would never be the same without West and Semple. "Good," Arran said. "Good, but different."

"Aye. Nothing stays the same." James put his hand on the back of a chair. "If it hadna been for Selkirk's army, we wouldna had the power to regain control of the post. I'll forever be in his debt."

Arran nodded. If the soldiers hadn't come, he, James, Archie, Pritchard, Heden, and Burke might be in Montreal, facing the gallows.

"Thank God we need not face the battles of life alone," James mused. "I'm grateful He places us in communities. There is strength in numbers, is there not?"

"Aye." Just like in his marriage to Eleanor. Having her as his wife had made him feel stronger and braver. "All these years, I'd thought if Eleanor had been with me, I would have been a weaker man. But the opposite is true."

"She's a strong woman." James nodded. "She's held her own, even during the darkest days of Assiniboia."

"My greatest fear was that Assiniboia would destroy her. But it hasn't."

"Nay." James smiled. "I think 'tis made her stronger."

"And she's done it with such grace and elegance."

"Mayhap God made her for this life." James smiled. "All this time, you thought to protect her from the colony, when the truth was, the colony needs her. She might very well be the key needed to solidify this colony and make it flourish and grow."

Could it be true? She had brought so much joy and life to everyone she'd met. In the darkest days of winter, and while exiled at Jack River House, she'd been light and laughter to the lives of those suffering. She'd taught school, organized entertainments, and mourned with those who mourned. Countless people had told him of her love and devotion to them since his return to the colony. She had given them hope to continue, even when there had been talk of leaving Jack River House.

Optimism sparked in Arran's heart again. He had no desire to leave Assiniboia. It was his home and his labor of love. Could he and Eleanor make a life here now that they had the added protection of the de Meuron soldiers? Would she want to, after all that had happened?

"Come," James said. "Let's return and bring the settlers up to the fort. Your family is in need of a warm house again."

"In a moment." Arran lifted the book off the floor that McLeod had dropped earlier. It was far too familiar.

"Eleanor's journal?" James asked.

"Aye." Anger slithered through Arran's chest, knowing that McLeod had read Eleanor's personal words. It was her heart on the page, he was certain, though he himself had never read what she'd written. He set the book on the shelf near the fireplace. "I will see that it's restored to its rightful owner before the night is through."

They left the governor's house and returned to their canoes. About thirty men were charged with bringing the colonists back to the fort.

Arran could not wait for Eleanor and Miriam to come home.

A flash of lightning was soon followed by another crash of thunder. Eleanor shivered as she sat in the dark tent with Miriam, Nicolette, Isla, Fiona, and the four Ferguson children. No one said a word as the rain pounded against the canvas. Miriam had fallen asleep in Eleanor's arms, for which Eleanor was thankful. It would have been difficult to keep the child occupied and entertained in the crowded tent.

"I've made my decision," Fiona whispered next to Eleanor.

"And what decision is that?" Eleanor asked.

"I've consented to marry Mr. Aiken."

Eleanor smiled. "He's a good man."

"It hasn't been an easy decision." Fiona held Catriona in her arms. The child was also sleeping. "I miss my Angus with every breath I take, but I ken he's not coming back. I need to move on and start living my life again. Mr. Aiken has promised to love my children as his own, which is what's most important to me."

"I'm so happy you've made the decision. Mr. Aiken will work hard for you and the children."

"I told him I'd marry him in the custom of the country, but he insists we wait for a priest or minister to visit Assiniboia to do the honors. He doesna want to start our marriage off without it being blessed. I told him it could be a long time before a clergyman visits, but he said he'll wait. And while we wait, he'll begin to care for us." Fiona's voice caught. "I dinna ken what I did to deserve such a man."

"You are a wonderful woman, Fiona." Eleanor reached out and squeezed her friend's hand. "Don't ever think less of yourself. You deserve the very best."

"Thank ye for yer friendship, Eleanor. I dinna ken what I'd do without ye." Fiona squeezed her hand back. "Do ye think ye'll stay on at Assiniboia?"

Eleanor and Arran had not spoken extensively about their future. So much depended upon the success or failure of recapturing Fort Douglas. Once that was done, and after Lord Selkirk's arrival, they would have a better understanding of what the colony needed.

"I would very much like to stay," Eleanor confided to Fiona. "Though I don't know how my husband feels." Ever since the massacre, Arran had seemed intent upon taking Eleanor and Miriam away from the Red River Valley.

"I hope ye stay." Fiona's face was hard to see in the pitch-black tent, but Eleanor could almost hear a smile in her voice.

It had been at least two hours since the men had left them. Eleanor had no way of knowing when Arran might come back for her. And with each passing moment, her nerves became tauter. If their enemies knew that fifty defenseless women and children were huddled in the small tents along the banks of the river, they would be like sitting prey, easy to pick off. The very thought sent a shiver up her spine.

Everything was wet and cold, and it was almost impossible to get comfortable. Eleanor's muscles ached and she prayed they would not have to remain this way until morning.

"Do ye hear that?" Fiona asked.

Eleanor strained to listen, but she could hear nothing over the sound of the rain hitting the canvas.

"It sounds like someone's approaching us."

"I pray to God it's our men and not the enemy," Eleanor said, almost to herself.

In a few minutes, Eleanor was able to hear it, too. The sound of men approaching on the river.

Could it be Arran so soon? Her heart picked up its pace and she clutched Miriam closer.

The flap of the tent suddenly opened and Arran stood there. "'Tis done."

Eleanor closed her eyes briefly, whispering a prayer of thanksgiving.

"Let's go home, lassies." Arran offered his hand to Eleanor and helped her off the cot she'd been sitting on. He took Miriam from her.

"Was it very difficult?" she asked him.

"Much easier than I had anticipated." He escorted her to the canoes, a smile in his voice. "It turns out that having an army at your disposal makes things a lot less difficult."

"I imagine so." She also smiled. "Do you think there will be any more trouble now that we have the soldiers?"

"The Nor'westers will rebuild Fort Gibraltar, and they'll continue to give us trouble, but they won't have the power to remove the settlers from the colony ever again."

His words gave her the first measure of relief she'd felt since her arrival in Assiniboia. "Do you think the colony will grow and prosper now?"

"I dinna see why not." He helped her into the canoe and handed the sleeping Miriam into her hands.

Next, he aided Nicolette and Isla into the canoe, then helped Fiona and her children inside. Soon, all the women and children were in the canoes, making their way to Fort Douglas once again.

"This is the third time I've been exiled and returned to the colony," Isla said, almost to herself. "I'm getting too old for this."

Eleanor smiled. "Hopefully it will be the last."

"It better be." Isla crossed her arms. "I need to get on with my life."

"Aye," Arran agreed, reaching through the darkness to take Eleanor's hand in his own. "'Tis time we all get on with living our lives."

It took about an hour for the little brigade to reach the base of Fort Douglas. The rain had ceased, but lightning still danced in the eastern sky. Arran helped everyone disembark from the canoes and then he carried Miriam up the riverbank to the gate.

Fiona stood for a minute at the fort gate and took a deep breath. Eleanor said a prayer for her friend that the memories of Fort Douglas would not be too painful for her to continue her healing.

"Isla," Fiona said to the older woman, "seeing that we're both widows, I thought ye might like to live with the children and me for the time being."

Isla's eyes lit up and she nodded. "I think that will be just fine."

"The soldiers have set up the tents," Arran told them. "You can sleep in one for tonight and then in the morning, I'll help you move into your home in Colony Gardens."

"Thank you," Fiona said to Arran. "For everything."

Arran nodded and he and Eleanor watched as they were directed to one of the tents.

"Now, Mrs. MacLean," Arran said to Eleanor, "'tis time to take you home."

Warmth filled Eleanor at the word *home*.

They entered the governor's house and Eleanor stood for a moment to take it all in. It was evident that it had been occupied very recently. Coals still smoldered in the fireplace, there was a pair of pants lying on the floor, and there were dirty dishes on the table.

"Nicolette," Arran said, handing Miriam to the housekeeper, "would you take Miriam upstairs to one of the rooms?"

"What of the mess?" Nicolette asked, taking the sleeping child from him.

"We'll see to it in the morning."

Nicolette nodded and then went toward the stairs without a backward glance.

"Don't you think Miriam should sleep down here with us?" Eleanor asked.

"She's old enough to be in her own room," Arran assured her. "And Nicolette will be close at hand, should she need something."

Eleanor watched Nicolette walk up the stairs, uncertainty in her heart. She'd slept with Miriam ever since the child had been born. There had always been so much unrest, she'd wanted Miriam close if there was trouble in the fort.

"She'll be fine." Arran set his musket next to the door and went to the fireplace to stir the coals to life, then he put a few logs on the fire. "She'll only be upstairs."

"To you, it's upstairs. To me, it feels like a hundred miles."

Arran smiled and walked to Eleanor. He removed her wet shawl and hung it on the hook by the door. "Come," he said, taking her hand, "warm yourself by the fireplace. Your hands are freezing."

She went to the fire with him and he took both her hands in his, rubbing them until there was heat in her fingers again.

His eyes were gentle as he watched her.

Eleanor smiled at him, amazed at how much she loved being his wife. "Thank you," she whispered.

"For what?"

"For taking such good care of all of us."

"'Tis my pleasure, *leannan*." He moved a tendril of hair off her cheek and hooked it behind her ear. "We'll have much to decide once Lord Selkirk arrives."

"Like whether or not we'll stay?" She watched him closely, wanting to know how he truly felt about remaining in Assiniboia.

He dropped his gaze to their hands. "Aye."

"Do you want to stay?"

"I want to do what's best for my family."

Eleanor put her hand on his cheek, forcing him to look at her. "As long as we are together, it matters not where we live. This is our home. These are our people. We belong here."

"But the hardships—"

"There will be hardships no matter where we live. You and I were not meant for a boring life. We cannot turn our backs on Assiniboia now."

Arran drew her hands to his lips, hope in his eyes. "Do you really want to stay?"

She nodded. "You have given your heart and soul to this colony. It's a part of who you are—a part of what I love so much about you. I cannot think of a better way to spend our lives than to do it here."

He pulled her close and wrapped her in his embrace. "I'll build you a beautiful house," he promised, "with a dozen rooms to fill with bairns."

"Half a dozen should be sufficient," she said with a laugh.

"Whatever you wish." He kissed her, slowly at first, and then with a deeper and more intense passion. She was breathless when he was finished.

"I almost forgot." He left her near the fireplace and walked to the shelf, where he removed a red book. "I found something I thought you might like."

"My journal." Her heart started to pound at the sight of her old friend.

Arran handed it to her. "I thought you would be happy to see it again."

She took it in her hands and pressed it to her chest, already thinking about all the things she would write when she had a chance. "Thank you."

He stood behind her and pressed a kiss to her neck. "We should get out of these wet clothes before we catch a cold."

She smiled and allowed him to lead her to bed. The book would have to wait for another time.

Chapter Twenty-Four

It took the better part of a week to resettle the colonists in their homes at Colony Gardens. Arran and the other men worked tirelessly to make the necessary repairs to the buildings, while the women and the de Meuron soldiers harvested the crops that had been planted earlier in the year.

"Will we need to remove to Pembina for the winter?" Eleanor asked Arran one evening when he'd come home for supper.

"I haven't decided. With the bumper crops and supplies Selkirk sent with us, we might be able to stay in Assiniboia." Arran had been debating with himself about this very issue. He knew the colonists desired to stay in their homes, but if they grew short on food, they would need the reassurance of buffalo that Pembina had offered in the past.

A knock sounded at their door. Arran rose from the table to answer. It was Archie.

"There's a company of men coming down the Red River," Archie said, excitement in his voice. "Looks to be Lord Selkirk and the other soldiers."

Arran nodded and smiled. "Thank you. I'll be at the gate in a minute."

"Lord Selkirk has finally arrived?" Eleanor asked.

"Aye. Would you like to join me in welcoming him?"

"I'm eager to hear news of my cousin," she said. "It feels like a lifetime since I've seen her or Lord Selkirk." She went to the door and took her shawl off the hook. "Having a firsthand account is far better than a letter."

Miriam stayed with Nicolette while Eleanor and Arran walked through the fort to the riverside gate. They stood there and watched the six canoes as they floated downriver. The sun was just setting, offering a spectacular pink-and-orange glow across the heavens. A golden hue covered all of Assiniboia, crowing it in magnificent splendor. It seemed as if the colony knew who was coming and was putting on a show for its founder.

Across the water, on the east side of the Red River, dozens of tents had been set up in the area designated for the de Meuron soldiers. Some had begun to build their houses in preparation for winter. Their presence had already sent a message to the Nor'westers and Bois-Brûlés. If anyone tried to bother the colony again, they would have to face nearly two hundred mercenary soldiers, as well as a hundred and fifty determined settlers.

Not one person had abandoned Assiniboia since the Battle of Seven Oaks. No one wanted the death of the twenty-three men to be in vain—including Arran and Eleanor. The decision to stay had not once been questioned by either of them.

In due time, the brigade arrived and Lord Selkirk disembarked. The canoes were laden with an abundance of supplies, which were quickly unloaded and stacked on land.

Lord Selkirk slowly walked up the riverbank and came to the gate. His weary look disappeared when he saw Eleanor.

"My dear," he said, stretching out his hands. "You look lovely."

"Lord Selkirk." Eleanor curtsied and then went into the earl's embrace for a hug. "It is good to see you again."

"And you." After he hugged her, he held her at arm's length, his bright blue gaze taking in the length of her. "You look radiant. Assiniboia has been good for you."

"If I'm radiant," she said, "it's because of my husband."

"Husband?"

Arran could not contain his smile.

"Arran and I were married at Jack River House," Eleanor said, taking his hand in hers. "Four weeks ago. We wish you could have been there to witness the happy event."

"Congratulations, MacLean," Selkirk said to Arran, offering his hand to shake. "You are a very lucky man."

"Aye," Arran said. "I dinna ken a happier man in the entire Northwestern wilderness."

Eleanor looked up at Arran with complete and utter devotion. He still couldn't believe she was his wife.

"And how is your wife?" Eleanor asked Lord Selkirk. "I'm anxious to hear word of her."

"She sends her love, though she wishes she could have come. I left her and the children in Montreal." Lord Selkirk sighed. "I thought it best, given the dire circumstances facing the colony earlier this year."

"Aye," Arran agreed. "A wise choice."

"I'm happy to see you've taken back the fort, MacLean." Selkirk glanced around, appreciation and approval in his voice. "Well done."

"Thank you, my lord. It wasn't difficult with your army at the ready."

Selkirk stood for a moment, slowly turning to take in the full scope of his colony. He shook his head, amazement and disbelief in his gaze. "I never thought I'd see Assiniboia with my own eyes. God is good, indeed."

"She's a fine colony," Arran said. "None better. And we have you to thank for that."

"You have yourself to thank." Selkirk shook his head. "If there's anyone who should get the accolades for her success, it should be you. I owe you everything, Arran."

"Many brave men and women have worked hard for Assiniboia." Arran would not take all the credit. "I have been only one person in the midst of many great people."

"Yes," Selkirk agreed. "But she's only as fine as her leaders." He smiled at Arran. "I look forward to getting a full tour in the morning, when the light is better."

"And so you shall."

After the supplies were brought up to the fort and put in one of the storehouses, the soldiers went across the river to join their comrades and Lord Selkirk followed Eleanor and Arran back to the governor's house. He would lodge with them while visiting the colony.

"How long do you intend to stay?" Arran asked.

"A few weeks, at most," Selkirk said. "I'd like to return to Montreal before winter to be with my family." He sighed. "I'm sure I will be facing endless hours of meetings, trials, and interviews regarding all that has happened."

"I'm sure your family will be eager to have you return." Eleanor pulled out a chair for the earl. "Please sit, we have much to discuss."

Nicolette brought another bowl and served the earl rubbaboo and fresh biscuits. He ate heartily, praising her for the food, though it was nothing compared to what he was used to at his ancestral home.

They spent the first part of their evening discussing all that had transpired since Arran left Fort William. Selkirk told them about a storm that had capsized one of the canoes transporting the North West Company partners to York Factory. Despite their heroic efforts, one partner, six Indians, and two de Meuron soldiers had lost their lives. The others continued on and were now at the factory, waiting for transportation to England to stand trial.

"I'm sorry to hear about the loss," Arran said.

"It's been a bad business, all around." Selkirk pushed aside his bowl and leaned back in his chair. "I fear I will be dealing with the consequences of these events for years to come. Already, I have much to answer to."

"I will aid you in whatever way possible," Arran promised.

"Thank you." He smiled, though the expression did not reach his eyes. "But my greatest hope is that you and Eleanor will stay here in Assiniboia and continue the work we've begun. I promised you a thousand acres of land, if you could make this colony survive for five years," he said to Arran. "It has only been four, but for all the hardships you have endured, and the dedication and bravery you have displayed, I want you to have the deed to the property before I leave. It's time you two start to build your lives. How does that sound?"

Arran looked to Eleanor, who smiled.

"It would be our pleasure," she said. "Our pleasure and honor."

"I must confess," Selkirk said to Eleanor. "When you asked to come here, Jean and I were concerned that the hardships would be too much for you. But we knew you were in a difficult place and needed a fresh start." He smiled. "I'm happy to see our concerns were unfounded."

"I wouldn't say they were unfounded," Eleanor said, her brown-eyed gaze resting on Arran. "It wasn't easy, but it was worth everything we endured. And I couldn't imagine being here with anyone other than Arran. Despite his modesty, he really is an excellent leader."

"I truly hope you two will continue to find happiness and joy in Assiniboia." Lord Selkirk looked from one to the other. "My greatest dream is for families to flourish and grow here for many generations to come."

"And so they shall," Arran said to the earl. "I will see it is done."

"Thank you." Selkirk pushed away from the table. "And now I will retire. It's been a long journey and I intend to wake early to see my colony."

"Good night," Eleanor said.

Selkirk bowed before her. "Good night." He walked toward the stairs and the room Eleanor had sent his luggage to when he first arrived.

Arran and Eleanor sat at the table for a minute longer, both in quiet contemplation.

"With the additional supplies Selkirk brought," Arran said to his wife, "I believe we will have all we'll need to stay here throughout the winter."

Eleanor smiled. "That makes me very happy."

"And with the additional manpower, we will break more cropland and plant earlier in the spring."

"Do you think Selkirk will send more settlers?"

"I'm certain." He rose and offered her his hand. "And once we have cattle, we will be truly self-sustaining."

"Your dream is not far off." She took his hand. "I'm so proud of you, Arran. It takes a great deal of fortitude to believe in something enough to see it through to completion even when there are hardships."

Arran was reminded of the night, over a year ago, when he, James, Archie, and Old John were the only people left at Fort Douglas. That night, like so many others, he had cried out to God, asking Him why He wasn't answering Arran's prayers. He'd been certain he had heard God's call to come to Assiniboia. It was a good calling and a noble purpose, so then why was each step a fight for survival?

Now, as he drew his wife to his side and thought about all the things that had happened in the past year, he could see God's hand in it all. Yes, there had been a great deal of suffering and hardship, but there had also been blessings and abundant joy. They still had many obstacles to overcome, and there were a lot of unanswered questions, but Arran was confident that God would continue to guide them, come what may. And though He had not answered all of Arran's prayers in the ways that Arran had hoped, God was still good and faithful to answer in the ways that were best.

It was a bright and sunny afternoon. The kind of autumn day that Eleanor wished she could somehow bottle and break open again during the long, cold months of winter. The air was warm and pleasant, smelling of rich, fertile soil. There were no bugs or other critters to hinder the gathering of colonists, nor any clouds to mar the vast sky overhead.

"I have called you here to this place," Lord Selkirk said to the colonists gathered, "to dedicate and consecrate this land to the Lord."

They were standing at a place north of Colony Gardens where Lord Selkirk had made a new division, this one for the additional colonists he expected the following year.

Eleanor could almost see William, Governor Semple, Angus, and all the others standing there with them. Even if they weren't there physically, they were there in spirit. Their contributions to the colony were just as important as those of everyone else who had lived and worked in Assiniboia.

"We shall name this parish Kildonan, in honor of your homeland," Lord Selkirk said to those who had come the previous year. "And here, you shall build your church." He pointed to a lot across a rivulet of water called Parsonage Creek. "And there, you shall build a school." He caught Eleanor's eye and smiled. "There shall be a church and a school in each parish."

The crowd cheered. Many of the colonists had become prejudiced against the earl over the past year when their expectations had not been met, but upon meeting them, he had quickly won them over. He was a good and honest man who truly cared about the people he had sent to Assiniboia.

"And I will provide provisions for you to build roads and bridges," Selkirk continued. "There shall be a road to Jack River House, and one to Pembina, so you no longer need to rely upon the lakes and rivers for travel."

Clapping and happy chatter filled the air.

"And there will be another gristmill, as well as a sawmill," Selkirk continued. "So you can be self-sufficient, at last."

He bowed his head to say a prayer.

Arran stood beside Eleanor, with Miriam in one arm. His musket had been left at home for the first time in her remembrance. With his free arm, he held Eleanor close to his side as Selkirk prayed.

"Dear Heavenly Father," Selkirk said, "today, we dedicate and consecrate this land we call Assiniboia to Your loving hands. It is through Your blessing and guidance we build our colony, and it is through Your love and grace we use it to honor You. May this land always proclaim the name of the Lord Jesus Christ. Amen."

When the prayer was complete, the group moved as a whole back to the fort for a feast and dance. Hope and optimism filled the air as Eleanor helped the ladies spread out the food.

Fiona was there, her face shining. She caught Eleanor's eye and smiled.

Near the main hall, Arran stood with James and Archie, laughing and visiting as only old friends could. Miriam played close by and Arran kept an eye on her every move. Never had Eleanor seen a more attentive father.

Isla sat on a bench with a beau at her side. She looked ten years younger and full of purpose once again. As soon as another clergyman visited Assiniboia, there would be several weddings to celebrate.

Almost four hundred individuals were packed into the fort. People from several nations, tongues, and tribes. Eleanor just stood for a moment to marvel at the scene and hold it close to her heart. It was a good day. A promising day. One she would think of with fondness for the rest of her life.

Soon there would be schools, churches, businesses, and streets. One day, the streets of Assiniboia would rival those of other cities across the world, she was certain. But like all those other places, it would take the dedication, courage, and perseverance of its citizens to grow. It would take people like Arran and Lord Selkirk, people with vision and sacrifice, to see that it was done.

Arran lifted Miriam into his arms and came to stand beside Eleanor.

"You look lonely standing over here on your own," he said.

She shook her head. "No. Quite the opposite. I'm just standing here envisioning what this colony will look like ten, twenty, or fifty years from now."

"Can you even imagine?" His voice and eyes held a bit of awe. "There were times when I thought it would be erased from the face of the earth."

"But you persevered." She took his hand. "And look what the Lord has done with your faithfulness."

"With our faithfulness, *leannan*." He smiled. "It does my heart good to see it."

Miriam laid her head against Arran's shoulder, her eyelids drooping. It was past her naptime.

"Shall we go inside and lay her down to sleep?" Arran asked.

"And miss the party?"

He laughed. "They'll be celebrating for the rest of the day."

"You won't be sad to miss out on the fun?"

"There's nothing I enjoy more than a quiet afternoon with my wife and daughter." He drew her with him toward the governor's house. "Besides, we both need to get some rest if we want to dance later this evening."

She followed, a smile on her lips.

When they went into the house, Arran laid Miriam down on their bed. The little girl closed her eyes and was immediately asleep.

They quietly left her and returned to the common room.

Despite the commotion in the fort yard, Eleanor felt completely alone with her husband. It was a rare experience, living in a house with Nicolette and Lord Selkirk.

"I think we should enjoy this little reprieve," Arran said, taking a seat on a chair near the table. He patted the chair beside him. "Would you care to join me, wife?"

She nodded but held up her hand. "A moment, please." She went to the traveling desk she kept in the corner of the common room and removed her journal.

Arran watched her but did not ask her what she had in mind. When she returned to the table, she sat and opened her journal.

"I ken this is a very special book to you," he said.

"It's like an old friend." She turned the pages until she came to the last one and then she looked at her husband. "All my life, I wrote in my journals because I didn't have anyone I could truly trust and confide in." She placed a kiss on his lips. "But now that has changed."

He looked concerned. "You'll not stop writing, will you?"

She shook her head. "No. I will always write. But now it will not be the first place I turn to pour out my heart."

"I'm happy you can trust me."

"I have never read my journal to anyone." The only person who'd ever read her words was Archibald McLeod, but he didn't matter to Eleanor. She would never have to see him again. "But I want to read something to you that I wrote just last night."

He moved aside a lock of her hair and slipped it behind her ear. The intimate gesture had become so familiar and dear to her since their wedding, she anticipated it before he even did it. "This book is important and personal to you. You dinna need to feel obligated to read it to me."

"I want to read it to you." Her cheeks grew warm, thinking about sharing her words with him for the first time. "When I write in this book, I always know when I've hit upon something especially important to me. It always brings tears to my eyes, and when that happens, it confirms for me what both my mind and heart are feeling."

His hand slipped around her waist and he drew her closer to him as she read.

Fort Douglas

Assiniboia

September 27, 1816

Tomorrow, Lord Selkirk will dedicate a new division in the colony. Everyone will attend and I anticipate a great feeling of community pride and hope will prevail. For many, this will be the confirmation they need that their home is here to stay and that it is, indeed, truly growing.

For me, it has been a long year since I arrived at the Red River colony. When I first set foot in Fort Douglas, it was with optimism and a misguided belief in my own abilities. I was foolish enough to think that I had come to teach the settlers, when in fact, they have taught me unique and valuable lessons about life, death, and love. I am amazed and honored to be counted among these people, and hope and pray that I will have many years left to see this colony prosper, as I know it will.

Arran has asked me several times if I am happy, and I always answer him the same. I am truly and completely happy. Not because of anything I have, but of what I have to give. God has blessed me with an abundance of love, and it is in giving that I find my greatest joy. Pouring that love out on him and Miriam is a privilege I will never take for granted.

As I sit here and ponder this place I now call home, and I think about all that happened to bring me here, I see God's hand in all of it. It does not hold the comforts I knew as a child, nor does it contain the society or entertainments, but what it lacks in these things, it makes up for in hope, optimism, and purpose. Those things may all come with time, but how many people can say they were the original groundbreakers of a great city? For whatever reason, God has chosen Arran and me to be the first. I truly believe that God made us for Assiniboia and He made Assiniboia for us.

For me, it's where my heart has been for years. I simply joined my heart and have now found my home.

She finished reading but did not remove her eyes from the page.

Arran reached up and gently wiped away a tear that had escaped from her eyes.

"'Tis beautiful, lass."

"It's my heart," she said, finally meeting his gaze. "You brought it with you four years ago when you left Scotland. It took me that long to find it again."

"And you had my heart," he said. "I'm so happy you brought it with you when you came."

She leaned into him for a kiss.

"I love you, Eleanor Brooke MacLean." He placed his hands on either side of her face. "And I'll love you for the rest of my life."

"I love you, too, Arran." She embraced her husband, her heart full.

She had found her home in the Northwestern Wilderness, and she'd never look back again.

Author's Note

The history of the Red River Colony (present day Winnipeg, Canada) is complex, sometimes difficult, and extremely fascinating. I heard about the colony most of my life living in central Minnesota because my hometown (about 340 miles south of Winnipeg) was founded by a Red River colonist in 1848, and because the famous Red River Ox Cart Trail passed through my hometown as it followed the Mississippi River. It was a trading route between present day Winnipeg and St. Paul, Minnesota. It was well known because the ox carts were notoriously loud and cumbersome. Early pioneers claimed you could hear the carts coming for miles.

Several years ago, I ran across a book about the Red River Ox Cart Trail, and it talked about the early years of the colony. I was blown away that I had never heard the story before. I quickly knew that I wanted to write a book about it and decided to tell it from the colonists' point of view, since they were at the heart of the drama, though there are multiple points of view that could tell a fascinating tale.

The colony was founded by Thomas Douglas, the 5th Earl of Selkirk, in 1811. Lord Selkirk was the 7th born son and never expected to inherit the earldom. Because of that, he went to the University of Edinburgh to become a lawyer, and it was there that he noticed the plight of his fellow Scotsmen who were being displaced by their landlords. After he became the earl, he started to help poor Scotsmen relocate in different parts of Canada, and by 1811, he had petitioned the British government for a large tract of land, known as Rupert's Land, to start a colony. They refused, because the Hudson's Bay Company had a monopoly of that land to trade furs. Selkirk wouldn't be deterred. He and another man bought up enough shares in the company to gain control of the land. It would become an agricultural settlement and the colonists were not allowed to participate in the fur trade. Because Selkirk now had a stake in the company, he also saw this as an opportunity to displace the North West Company, a rival fur trading company, in the Red River Valley. Unfortunately, sending the colonists only made the rivalry worse, and put hundreds of additional people in danger.

Much of what I learned about the Red River Colony came from several books I read. *The Substance of a Journal During Residence at the Red River Colony*, by John West and *Early Days at Red River Settlement*, by Ann Adams, are both written from personal accounts of the authors living there in the 1820s, after the Hudson's Bay Company and the North West Company merged. Neither person experienced the events in my story, but they would have known people who had, and, they would have been influenced by the colonists' perspectives, which placed the blame for the Battle of Seven Oaks on the North West Company and the *Bois-Brûlés*, mixed-race people who were *Métis*. The Métis were descendants of Indigenous and European ancestors, specifically French, Scottish, and English. The oral history of the Battle of Seven Oaks, told from the Métis point of view, is slightly different than the colonists' accounts. What both sides agree on is that neither group intended to fight that day. After the British government called for an inquiry into the conflict, the Métis were exonerated.

The other two books that were very helpful were *The Romantic Settlement of Lord Selkirk's Colonists: The Pioneers of Manitoba* by George Bryce and *The Red River Colony: A Chronicle of the Beginnings of Manitoba*, both written in the 1910s, around Winnipeg's centennial anniversary. Another book that influenced part of my story was *Many Tender Ties: Women in Fur Trade Society 1670-1870*, by Sylvia Van Kirk. I highly recommend all of these books to get a better understanding of life in the Red River Valley during European settlement, as well as the conflicts that took place there.

Many of the people mentioned in the story were real, with the exception of my main characters. They lived and breathed and should be remembered with respect, regardless of which side they were on in the Pemmican War, as it was known between 1812-1821. I tried, to the best of my ability, to only portray the recorded history, which was corroborated by many eyewitnesses.

It was fun to use the research I learned to add details to the story. For instance, the buffalo were so plentiful at Fort Daer in the early years that they were known to rub their backs against the stockade walls. And the snow blew with such strength and ferocity, it piled up against the fort, so that a person could easily scale the walls. Some of the unbelievable history is also true. When the colonists returned to the fort after wintering in Pembina, Governor Semple had the North West Company fort torn down—and then planned to leave the colonists to fend for themselves as he headed north to visit other fur posts! After the Battle of Seven Oaks, the colonists surrendered their fort to the Bois-Brûlés, and were almost to Lake Winnipeg, and safety, when they were overtaken on the Red River and several of their men were arrested. Lord Selkirk arrived in the nick of time to save them at Fort William, bringing about a hundred mercenary soldiers to help. Unfortunately, Selkirk spent the remainder of his life, and almost all of his wealth, in litigation over the whole affair, and died in 1820 before it was settled. The Hudson's Bay Company and North West Company merged a year later, ending the Pemmican War and the conflict in the Red River Valley.

As with every story I write, I hope that it encourages my readers to do their own research. I firmly believe that gaining knowledge and understanding about our past better helps us shape our futures.

Gabrielle

About the Author

Gabrielle Meyer is a Christy-Award winning, bestselling author of over 40 books, including her popular Timeless Series. For over a decade, she worked for the Minnesota Historical Society, where she became passionate about sharing real history through the art of storytelling. She continues to write fictional stories inspired by real people, places, and events. Gabrielle currently lives in central Minnesota on the banks of the upper Mississippi River with her husband and four children. You can learn more about Gabrielle and her books at www.gabriellemeyer.com.

Find Gabrielle on Facebook at www.Facebook.com/AuthorGabrielleMeyer, Pinterest at www.Pinterest.com/gabriellemeyer/, Twitter at www.twitter.com/MeyerGabrielle, Goodreads, and her website at www.gabriellemeyer.com

Other Books by Author

Timeless Series

American Brides Series

GabrielleMeyer.com/books

Printed in Dunstable, United Kingdom

70456883R00201